CHUCKLERS

LAUGHTER IS CONTAGIOUS

JEFF BRACKETT

SEVERED PRESS
HOBART TASMANIA

CHUCKLERS

ISBN: 978-1-925493-96-2

DEDICATION -

Edward Lorn is a horror author whose work will keep you up at night listening for the things that go bump. We first met in 2012 while using the same editing company, and for some reason, we quickly became fast friends. I suppose it was because we had both just published our first novels, and perhaps we were high on the possibilities of what might lay in the future. For whatever reason, Ed is one of only two people close enough to me that I consider him a brother in all but blood.

In February of 2013, Ed asked if I would be interested in collaborating with him on a project. He wanted to develop an idea from one of his short stories and turn it into a novel. The original short story was "He Who Laughs Last" and you can find it in his story collection "What the Dark Brings".

Our project would be an apocalyptic / horror tale, and since my first novel was post-apocalyptic, while his was horror, he thought we would make the perfect team for the book. Several conversations and chat sessions later, we had developed a basic premise and quickly realized that the story was too big and too dark to tell in a single book.

So we went back to the drawing board. We gave the characters more room to develop, encompassed a much larger setting, and gave our tale free rein to wander as we felt it should. In no time, we were nearly half way done with the first book.

That was when things started to go sideways.

My day job became shaky when the company I worked for put our division up for purchase. At the same time, my father's health was beginning to falter (he'd been battling cancer for a few years), and my writing began to suffer.

In the meantime, Ed (who was already a much faster writer than I was) began work on another project, and Chucklers was temporarily left by the wayside. We kept after it as we could, but the momentum was gone.

Ed ended up with some pretty lucrative offers on other projects, and in late 2014 told me that he needed to dedicate all of his time to the new work. He said he needed to step out of the project completely, and graciously let me know that if I wanted it, Chucklers was mine for the writing.

That was almost two years ago, at the time of this writing. I didn't feel right about using his characters, or any of the manuscript he had written, so I went back and pulled out what he had done. Once again, it was back to the drawing board. It was painful to do, because Ed wrote some pretty fantastic characters and scenes that will likely never see the light of day now. Gone now are Ross's stoner roommate, Felix, and his dysfunctional family, as is an amazing scene where Ross, Felix, and Felix's family get caught at a Walmart Black Friday Blowout sale when the outbreak begins.

There were scenes with crazed clowns, attacks in trailer parks, and a military tank training exercise that went horribly awry. And there was the television evangelist who sold "holy water" that spread the virus in pretty glass vials. All of these elements will likely never exist outside of my hard drive or Ed's.

But the deed is finally done. The idea that started with that insane and inspired evening chat session is born and you, dear reader, now hold it in your hands.

Thank you Ed, for trusting me with our demented love child. I hope it's turned out as twisted as you envisioned.

Jeff Brackett, July 19, 2016

And now for a few words from Edward Lorn…
 "What he said." – Edward Lorn, 2016

AUTHOR'S NOTES —

Much of what I would normally write into the Author's Notes actually went into the dedication for this book. But that little "What he said…" after the dedication really needs a bit of explanation.

You see, when the first draft of this story was complete, I sent it to Edward Lorn (if you've read the dedication, you already know why). He got back to me shortly after, asking if he could write an introduction for it. Well, I'm nobody's fool, so of course I took him up on the offer.

But after edits were winding down, I still hadn't received anything from him. I was going to let it go, thinking he'd gotten busy with one of his other projects, but as fate would have it, Ed called me on another matter just before I finished edits. I mentioned I was about ready to turn the manuscript back in and tentatively brought up the subject of the intro.

The conversation went something like this…

Me: Hey! You gonna do that intro or what?
Ed: Sure. But you were supposed to send me your dedication so we don't end up repeating each other.
Me: Oops. I'll send it right away.

So I did. We finished our conversation and hung up. Later, he hit me up in a chat window online. (We do a lot of "chatting".)

Me: So, are you okay with the dedication?
Ed: Yeah, but now I got nothing to add.
Wait! Actually, add this right at the end…
"What he said." —Edward Lorn, 2016

Seriously, do that. End your section with, "Now for a few words from Edward Lorn." Then add, "What he said."

I don't care who you are, that's some funny shit right there!

So there you have it. A brief insight into the deep musings and inner workings of a couple of modern day authors. How's that for disappointing? We're just like everyone else.

PROLOGUE

Synopsis of events at and around McMurdo Station on August 26
Ross Ice Shelf, Antarctica

At 2:15 PM on August 26, McMurdo station in Antarctica detected unusual seismic activity near the Ross Ice Shelf. It was speculated that the shelf was undergoing an unusual amount of shifting, and a two-man team was sent out by helicopter (flight ANTEX 101) to investigate.

The following is a transcribed excerpt from the recovered flight recorder.

ANTEX 101 — McMurdo, this is ANTEX 101. We're at the edge of the shelf and we can confirm that there has been considerable calving.

McMurdo Station — Understood. Any danger to upcoming supply shipments? We've got a fuel ship coming in next week.

ANTEX — It's possible, McMurdo. These are some of the biggest 'bergs I've ever seen. It's like... (undecipherable)

McMurdo Station — ANTEX 101, please say again?

ANTEX — I say, it's possible that Cape Bird is going to have some trouble. We're gonna take some pictures and then head back.

McMurdo — Roger that, ANTEX. Watch your time. Sunset's at fifteen-thirty. That's just a few minutes away.

ANTEX — Ah, yeah. It's already pretty dim. Gonna grab some pictures and head home. Keep the lights on for us.

McMurdo — Roger that, ANTEX.

(Three and a half minutes of silence.)

ANTEX — McMurdo, we're seeing something pretty strange up here. It looks (undecipherable).

McMurdo — Say again, ANTEX. You broke up there.

ANTEX — (undecipherable) …terfall pouring out of a huge cave in the shelf. Looks like calving has opened it up and water's coming down the side of the shelf and…

McMurdo — Lost part of that again. Did you say there's a waterfall coming out of the ice shelf?

ANTEX — Affirmative, McMurdo. And you're not gonna believe this, but the water is glowing.

(pause)

ANTEX — McMurdo, are you there?

McMurdo — Roger that, we're here. Just to confirm, did you say the waterfall is glowing?

ANTEX — Affirmative. It's getting dark up here, and you can definitely see the water glowing. As a matter of fact, as we get closer to the fall, you can see that there's a slick of the stuff on the surface of the ocean where it's pouring in.

(approximately forty seconds of silence)

ANTEX — Base? You guys still there?

McMurdo — Ah, affirmative ANTEX. Sorry. We've got a bunch of the eggheads in the control room here, and they're chomping at the bit (undecipherable) get your pictures. They're arguing over whether the seismic activity let one of the subglacial rivers break through the shelf, or if the river shifting was what caused the sudden calving of icebergs.

ANTEX — Got yourself a real chicken or egg argument, do you?

McMurdo — (chuckle) Roger that, ANTEX.

ANTEX — Makes sense. Do they want samples? It's getting pretty dark, but if they want, I think I can lower a sample container.

McMurdo — That's a go for sample acquisition, ANTEX. Be careful, but if you can get a sample safely, Dr. Hough says he'll trade you a bottle of scotch for a bottle of water.

ANTEX — Sounds like a hell of a deal to me.

(approximately ninety seconds of silence.)

McMurdo — McMurdo to ANTEX 101. What's your status?

ANTEX — Just about in position for bucket drop. It's actually kind of pre—holy shit! Dave, did you see that?

McMurdo — See what? What are you seeing, ANTEX?

ANTEX — (undecipherable raised voice)

McMurdo — Say again?

ANTEX — Sorry, McMurdo. There's a pod of orcas churning the water down there. Looks like they've got a minke whale. Poor bastard.

McMurdo — (chuckles) You had us worried for a second there.

ANTEX — Sorry about that. It's not something you see every day.

McMurdo — Roger that. Real circle of life shit.

ANTEX — Ha. Yeah, that it is.

(approximately thirty seconds of silence)

ANTEX — We're right above the falls now, McMurdo. This is amazing. It's like some crazy special movie effect.

McMurdo — Roger that, ANTEX. Get plenty of pictures. Video, too. The doc says there's another bottle for video.

ANTEX — I feel a party coming— (frantic - undecipherable) Dave! McMurdo, Dave's lost it! He's — (undecipherable shouting, followed by a mixture of laughter and screaming)

McMurdo — ANTEX 101, what is your situation?

(More laughter, followed by more screaming)

McMurdo — ANTEX 101. Please respond.

(Sound of anti-collision alert - "*Whoop, whoop*, collision alert. *Whoop, whoop*, collision alert.*")

ANTEX — (sound of two distinct voices over the collision warnings, one sobbing, one laughing)

McMurdo — ANTEX 101. Please resp—

("…ision alert. *Whoop, whoop*, collision alert. *Whoop, whoo*…")

[Sound of impact]

PRELUDE

If it bleeds, it leads. It's a common saying with regards to news and entertainment. So while the headlines were filled with the latest celebrity scandals, there was little mention made of an anomalous slick flowing through the ocean. And while there was some minor excitement among some marine biologists about the reports, the news outlets were much too busy reporting which former child star had entered rehab and whose cell phone had been hacked and their nude photos released to the public.

It's a shame really, that so few people were able to appreciate the silent beauty of that shimmering, phosphorescent ribbon that flowed serenely upon the ocean, making a leisurely escape from its Antarctic prison. Extremophiles, freed from their fourteen million year detention beneath the icecap, shone bright with a distinctive blue bioluminescence, spreading out into the Antarctic Circumpolar current. Over the course of several weeks, the glowing ribbon dispersed, breaking into a multitude of expanding patches.

One such slick flowed into the South Atlantic current where it eventually made landfall on the western coast of Africa. If anyone noticed that the beaches of the Congo Basin were unusually stunning, it was never mentioned anywhere. People in that part of the world were too busy worrying about what guerrilla warlord they had to pay fealty to from one week to the next. It was only when those warlords went on a bloody campaign of mindless genocide on a level previously unprecedented that the news agencies had anything to say, and luminescent beaches were not high on the reporters' lists of potential headlines.

Meanwhile, Nature did as she always had. Fish ate plankton. Birds ate fish. The food chain continued to deliver its beautiful bounty from the lowliest of life forms, to the topmost rungs of the evolutionary ladder. Life went on as it always had.

And the only constant in life, is change.

FRIDAY
NOVEMBER 4

CHAPTER 1

CHARLES GRIFFE
MYSTERY SONG CHALLENGE

Charlie was just about to hang up when the phone finally clicked and a voice spoke to him. "Congratulations, you're the one-hundredth caller! What's your name?"

"Charles. Charles Griffe." He smiled and gave Felicia a thumbs-up. She squealed and ran to turn up the radio. They had been trying to call in for hours and had either gotten a busy signal, or the one other time they had managed to get through, they had been the wrong caller.

"Hello, Charles, I'm Johnny Jay, and it's time to see if you can guess this week's WROK mystery song challenge. Are you ready to try?"

"I'm ready."

"Okay, first, can I get you to turn down your radio? It causes an echo effect when we're on the air."

Felicia's eyes got wide as she realized what she had done. "Sorry," she mouthed to him.

"Thank you, Charles. So have you been listening to the previous guesses?"

"Yeah, I have."

"That's awesome. Well for our listeners who might not have heard them, I'll go over the previous clues again. Clue number one — This week's mystery song was first released in 1961. Clue number two — The song has been a number one hit on US Billboard's Hot R & B singles, on the UK singles chart, the Irish singles chart, US Billboard's Hot Country Singles chart, and the US Billboard Hot Latin Tracks listings. Clue number three — There have been over four hundred recorded versions of the song released, including versions by Cassius Clay, John Lennon, and even The Muppets.

"So Charles, you got all that?"

"Yeah. Sure do." He still wasn't sure what the song was, but at least he'd had enough time to think about it and narrow it down to a handful of 1961 hits. If he got a good clue, he just might luck out and win.

"Okay then. Are you ready for the latest clue?"

"I sure am."

"Excellent. Then for a mystery prize worth more than ten thousand dollars, here is clue number four. This mystery song was also recorded for a charity event in 1998 by a famous horror author, twelve years after the release of a movie bearing the same name as the song—a movie based on a story by this same author, though the story had a completely different title."

Charlie blinked. He actually *blinked* at that clue, trying to follow the twists and turns of its varying layers. The song was released by some guy. The guy was a horror writer, and he had a song that had a movie that came out with a different title? No, he had a story that came out with a different title, but the movie had the same title? What the hell?

"Now I'm going to repeat this clue one more time…"

Thank God!

"…after which you'll have ten seconds to give us your answer."

But Charlie was already scanning his list of Billboard's Top 100 hits for 1961, looking for a song title that could conceivably have been the title of a horror movie. His finger stopped almost immediately on the number three hit "Michael" by the Highwaymen. He remembered seeing a movie back in the nineties called Michael. But he immediately rejected it. It wasn't a horror movie.

But he didn't actually say the movie was a horror movie, did he? He said it was based on a story written by a famous horror author.

As he ran his finger on down the list, the radio DJ was just finishing up his repeat of the latest clue. "So, Charles Griffe… for the grand prize, can you name our mystery song? You have ten seconds starting now."

"Ah…" He ran his finger frantically up and down the list. There was *The Fly* by Chubby Checker. That was the name of a horror movie.

Maybe *Runaway*? Or *Surrender*? Those titles sounded like they could be horror.

"Five seconds."

And suddenly he saw it. He nearly shouted into the phone, "*Stand By Me*! It was *Stand By Me*!"

There was silence on the line, and for a split second, Charlie thought they had been disconnected. That would be just my luck. Finally catch a break like this only to be cut off before I can collect on it.

But the voice of the DJ dispelled those thoughts with his sad sounding voice. "Oh Charles, I'm so sorry."

Charlie's heart dropped. *Son of a bitch! I really thought I had it.*

"I'm sorry, Charles, because you're going to have to rearrange your vacation time at work. You've just won the WROK mystery song challenge!"

"I won?" he nearly shouted. Felicia did shout. She jumped up and down, screeching loud enough that he had trouble hearing the DJ on the phone.

"You did. Congratulations, Charles. Hang on the line and we'll get your information off the air." And Johnny Jay put him on hold without another word.

The WROK operator was a young woman who sounded bored to tears with her job. She took Charlie's personal information and had then asked him which prize he wanted.

"Sorry? Which prize? I didn't know there was anything to choose."

"Yes, sir. As the winner of the grand prize, you get your choice of a year's worth of movie tickets for two with free popcorn and soft drinks, or a ten-day cruise for two on the new luxury liner, Bahama Queen."

"A year's worth of movie tickets?"

"Yes, sir. Plus refreshments."

"Or a cruise on a luxury liner?"

Once again, his ears were tested to their limits as Felicia screamed behind him.

"A cruise? Oh, pick the cruise, Charlie. We've never been on a cruise before."

"Hang on, baby." He tried to keep the irritation out of his voice. Felicia was a bit simple-minded at times. Luckily, his needs from her were equally simple. And talking was not the most talented thing she used her mouth for. Still, if he wanted to use it for one, he had to tolerate the other.

The woman on the phone was explaining the details to him. "If you choose the movie tickets, you will receive a packet of 732 individual movie passes good at any CineScan Theater that will let you and one other person see any movie and get free popcorn and soft drinks on any day of the week beginning on January first. The passes will expire on December thirty-first next year."

Charlie was beginning to get that old feeling. His dad had always warned him about watching for the strings attached to everything. It sounded to him like WROK had some sort of deal worked out with the theater chain. Those passes probably didn't really cost the radio station anything. *Cheap bastards.*

"And the cruise?"

"That prize consists of two tickets to the Thanksgiving cruise aboard the Bahama Queen. It's the newest luxury liner in the Regal Cruise Line fleet. You would have to be able to leave on the ten-day Thanksgiving cruise on November 18, and the cruise returns to port here in Fort Lauderdale the Monday after Thanksgiving."

"So how much are the tickets worth?" For a moment, Charlie thought he might be better off taking the movie tickets. Maybe scalp them for a bit of extra cash. Before he could explain that to her, Felicia leaned over his shoulder and bit his earlobe in that way he liked.

The attendant on the phone droned on. Something about not being able to divulge the exact price of the prizes. There was some reasoning she mentioned, but Charlie found himself having difficulty concentrating while Felicia went from his ear to lightly nipping at his neck.

"Please pick the cruise, Charlie," she whispered huskily into his ear. "I've always wanted to go on one."

"I don't know, baby. The movie tickets might be worth—"

"But I just know we'll enjoy it." She reached into his lap and stroked her fingernails up and down his zipper. "I can promise you."

Charlie took a deep breath and swallowed. He put the phone back up to his mouth. "I'll take the cruise."

MONDAY
NOVEMBER 7

CHAPTER 2
AUGUST GRAPPIN
CHANGES

"So you're absolutely sure?"

"I'm sure." Gus licked his lips nervously before nodding. "I've already come this far. Let's do it."

He looked in the mirror as Danielle turned the clippers on. They popped loudly, and the person in the mirror jumped. There was a second's mental disconnect as Gus realized it was him. He smiled at the shoulder-length purple hair Danielle had just dyed for him. He'd been growing it ever since Dad had left them to run off with his secretary five months ago.

His secretary! How cliché can you get, anyway?

Dad had always been a stickler for what he considered proper grooming, and his only concession to Gus had been to let him grow his hair down to his collar. Over the last few months, it had grown considerably longer. The new color was a further statement. It was his own personal "screw you" to his dad. His only concern was whether or not his mom would approve.

He watched in the mirror as Danielle brought the clippers closer. The loud buzz of the tiny motor sounded almost ominous as she brought them closer to his head. In three minutes, it was done.

***

"Y U think she likes me?"

August shook his head as he read Donny's IM-speak. No matter how common it was with his friends, he could never bring himself to use it. It just felt too juvenile. He typed his answer in the chat window, typing faster in complete sentences than his friend could using every acronym in the book. "Definitely."

"How u no?"

"Because I talked to her this afternoon."

"U didn't tell her did u?!?!?!"

"I'm not an idiot. Of course I didn't tell her. I was smooth. She probably doesn't even remember we talked about you."

"Howd u do dat?"

"She was busy cutting my hair. I made her think I was nervous, so we talked about things. You were one of those things."

"Dude! U cut ur hair?"

"Yes. Focus. We're talking about you and Danielle, remember? The hot girl that follows you around like a little puppy? You should see how she looks at you when you walk into class."

"Really? U think she'd go out wit me?"

"I think she'd lick the dirt off your kicks if you asked her to."

"LMAO. Dat wud b sum shit! Wat else u think she'd lick?" This was followed by a little devil head emoticon.

"You're such a perv! Just ask her out. She's cute, and you need someone who'll put up with your skeezy ass."

"LOL. True."

"Gus? You home?" his mom's voice drifted from downstairs.

"Upstairs, in my room," he shouted back. He furrowed his eyebrows at her tone. There was something in her voice that he hadn't heard in quite some time. She sounded… happy? He quickly typed one of the few acronyms he'd adopted. "G2G. Mom's home."

"K. L8rs."

"Laters." He closed the chat window as his mom walked in.

"Whatcha do…" Her voice drifted off as she got a look at him. "…ing?"

August had carefully arranged his room so she would see him clearly as soon as she came in. "Just chatting with Donny." But he knew the topic of conversation had taken a left turn as soon as she'd seen his hair.

She raised her eyebrows, then walked over to stand beside him. Gently, she reached out to touch his hair on the left side, the side Danielle had shaved down to where only a light purple stubble showed. The stiff hair felt strange as she laid her hand on it.

He swallowed nervously. "So what do you think?"

She remained silent as she circled around behind him, running her fingers through the shoulder-length hair in back and on the right side. When she came back around in front of him, her lips were pursed contemplatively.

"Mom?"

Finally, she smiled. "You dad's going to hate it."

Gus grinned back at her. "Isn't he, though?"

She laughed outright, and the sound instantly lightened his heart. It had been months since he'd heard his mother laugh. The two of them had been walking on eggshells for too long. Mom had obviously been moping in her feeling about Dad's infidelity. Gus had been torn between wanting to help his mom, and his own feelings of having been betrayed by his dad. He'd finally had an epiphany. His dad had been a grade-A asshole. But that didn't mean Gus had to be miserable. Hell, his dad was living it up with a young hottie who was less than ten years older than Gus himself was.

His mom laid an envelope on his desk. "Looks like we both decided it was time to make some changes."

"What do you mean?"

"I decided that if that son of a bitch can start a new life, then so can I."

What the hell? Did she find some guy to go out with? Am I going to have to start getting used to her having some stranger in the house all the time?

"I was talking to some friends at work, and they convinced me that it was time to quit wallowing in all the guilt and misery." She pushed the envelope toward him.

"What's this?"

She grinned. "You know how we always wanted to go on a Caribbean cruise? Well, we're going! A ten-day cruise on the newest luxury liner in the Gulf."

"What?"

"The divorce is final, and I think we could use the time off. So I decided to spend some of the settlement and get us away from here for a while."

Gus grinned at that, then sat back when reality set in.

His mom saw his expression change. "What's wrong?"

"School. I can't afford to miss ten days."

She laughed at his chagrin. "You won't. It's a Thanksgiving cruise. You're already out of school for that time."

He pumped his fist in the air. "Awesome! Mom, this is great! Wait'll I tell Donny and the gang. We're going on a freakin' cruise!"

TUESDAY
NOVEMBER 8

CHAPTER 3
CHRIS TALLANT
CAN I TELL THEM YOU'LL ACCEPT?

He answered his phone with a professional sounding, "Tallant here."

"Mr. Tallant? It's Rika."

He was suddenly conscious of his heart pounding in his chest, and concentrated on keeping his voice steady as he replied. "Hi, Rika. What can I do for you?" Rika was the Human Resources recruiter who had talked him into applying for the first officer's position. He thought the testing had gone well, but there was always an element of doubt with these things, and the direction of his career with Regal Cruise Lines was at stake.

"I thought you might want to know, I got a peek at your test scores."

He waited for her to continue, but the line was silent. "Rika, for God's sake, you're killing me! Did I pass or not?"

"Pass?" She giggled. "You scored top of the class, Chris."

Tallant whooped. "So I got the promotion?"

The laughter left her voice as she replied. "No. Sorry, but there aren't any first officer's positions open right now."

He sighed. He'd known that might be an issue, but he had still hoped. "So I'm still a second?"

"Yes. But here's your silver lining. You qualified for a new berth. There's a navigation slot open on the Bahama Queen, and it's yours if you want it."

The Bahama Queen was the Regal's new flagship. It had all the latest systems and technology. It would be one hell of a notch on his resume. He was about to ask for details when Rika continued.

"This is a good move, Chris. Especially since their first officer is only two years away from retirement."

That caught his attention. "Really?"

"Yes. And they specifically requested you for the open slot."

"Me? Why would they request me?"

Rika giggled again. It was a pleasant sound, and under other circumstances it would have prompted Tallant's thoughts in less professional directions. But this conversation had him focused on his career. "Don't you get it, Chris? They're grooming you to take over the first officer's position on the Queen."

He was stunned. When Rika had talked him into testing, he'd hoped for a promotion on another L-Class liner. He'd never dreamed he would do well enough to be pulled up to the top tier.

"Mr. Tallant? Are you there?"

"Yes. Sorry, Rika. I'm here. What did you say?"

"I asked if I can tell them you'll accept the position."

He chuckled. "Yes, ma'am. You certainly can."

THURSDAY
NOVEMBER 17

CHAPTER 4
ERICA CHAPMAN
SORRY FOR YOUR LOSS

"Again, I'm very sorry for your loss."

Erica just nodded. What do you really say to such platitudes? It didn't seem to be the sort of thing to which one says "thank you." Besides, she didn't owe this shark in cheap pin-stripes a thing. She didn't know him from Adam, and she was certain he'd never known Uncle Jimmy. And the news he'd brought hadn't exactly endeared him to her. But like sharks, lawyers had their place in the world, however low on the food chain that place may be.

She closed the door behind him and leaned back against it. Just over one week. That was how long she had to wind up her uncle's affairs. After that, the ranch was to be sold off to pay his medical bills and back taxes.

For what seemed like the hundredth time that day, she knuckled back the tears that threatened, knowing that if she let that first one out, the dam would break. She distracted herself for a while, straightening up the many odds and ends that marked Uncle J's life around the ranch house. The coffee pot had sat unattended so long that the half inch of sludge in the bottom of it had begun to grow something gray and fuzzy on top. The laundry room smelled of soured clothes, and his cell phone lay on the coffee table, unused for days. *Guess I'd better terminate the service on that.* Without thinking, she pulled out her own cell and slipped the ear bud in place. Pressing the side, she waited for the beep.

"Say a command," it instructed.

"Call—Ross—mobile." She enunciated each command carefully, and the headset repeated it back.

"Did you say—call—Ross—mobile?"

She hesitated. She really wanted to talk to him again. But things weren't going well with them, and she wasn't sure that he would want to hear from her just now. "No," she finally answered. "Cancel."

"Cancelling."

Looking out the window at the sun setting on the horizon, she felt a sudden need to get out of the house. The walls that been home for so many years felt more like a prison that night. Grabbing Uncle Jimmy's old leather jacket from the hall tree by the door, she wrapped it around her shoulders and stepped into the brisk November evening.

Days in south Texas were usually beautiful at this time of year, but the nights could easily drop into the thirties. Tonight wasn't quite that cold, but it was still cool enough that her nose felt the drop in temperature as soon as she stepped outside.

She let her feet take her where they would, and eventually found herself at the top of her mountain. It wasn't really hers, of course, and it certainly wasn't anywhere close to being a mountain. But it was the only raised bit of dirt on Uncle J's God-forsaken ranch, and she had claimed it as her own when she'd come to live with him.

To a little girl who had just lost her parents, imagination was all-important. So that fifteen-foot-tall hill had become her mountain, and the lone Bois d'Arc tree at the top was her forest. That tree had been the source of one of her first lessons with Uncle J. He'd taken a long branch from the tree and brought it into his workshop. She'd hovered nearby as he had worked that branch, stripping the scaly bark, and sanding the bright yellow wood beneath. "This here's a special tree, young'un. See how the wood's a bright yaller?" He slammed it down on the workbench, making her jump and the tools bounce. "Hardest wood 'round these parts, too. Ain't too many of 'em down this far south."

He had smoothed the wood to a fine polish over the next three nights, each night teaching her a little more about it. "Folks 'round these parts usually call it Osage Orange, or sometimes a horse apple tree. That's on account o' the fruit it bears in the summer. Looks sorta like a big, green orange. That's the fruit, not the color." He winked at her, and she couldn't help but smile. "But ya wouldn't want ta eat it."

"Why not?" She hadn't even realized until years later that Uncle Jimmy had worked that tree limb to draw her into the first conversation she'd had since her parents' accident. Those two words were the first she'd spoken in more than a week.

"'Cause it tastes like cow spit!"

The image had made her crinkle her nose in disgust at the time. Now though, thinking back to those nights, she smiled. Reaching out to caress the bark of the old tree, she spoke to the memories in her head. "I bet there were times you came to regret getting me to talk again, didn't you, Uncle J?"

And in her mind, she could hear his reply. *Not fer one second, youngster.*

She smiled at the thought. Life with Uncle Jimmy was always like that. He was always teaching her something, whether she realized it or not. And the lessons were often multi-layered affairs. That stick was a prime example. It eventually gained a net on the end, which triggered exactly the questions she now suspected Uncle J had expected.

He taught her the basics of lacrosse and entered her in a league at the local Y. She quickly learned that the old Bois d'Arc stick was too heavy for a lacrosse stick. It didn't move quickly enough, and her stick work was clumsy compared to many of the other girls. Eventually, through patience or pure stubbornness, she gradually gained enough proficiency to hold her own.

But she didn't excel until she got in high school. The old homemade stick wasn't allowed on the high school team, and someone put a regulation composite stick in her hands. That was when she discovered that working with that heavy old Bois d'Arc stick had been another lesson in itself. Compared to her old stick, the composite was light as a feather. She was unstoppable on the field, and did so well that she earned a college scholarship.

And that had been another hard lesson. Leaving home was never easy.

By this time, the brisk evening air had become uncomfortably cool, and the crimson sky had darkened to ebony. Erica patted the old tree once more. "Guess you had one last lesson to teach me, Uncle. Didn't you?" She headed back to the house with his voice in her head.

Home ain't really a place, Erica. Home is where your loved ones are.

She made it into the house before the dam finally broke, and through the agonizing sobs, one thought echoed in her head. *If that's true, then where is my home now?*

Uncle Jimmy didn't seem to have an answer to that one.

* * *

Sleep was an elusive thing. Her thoughts kept circling her loss, and when she did manage to drift off, her dreams were less than soothing.

"I'm sorry, Miss Chapman, but your uncle's medical bills constitute a sizeable debt."

"I understand, but he always told me that the ranch was worth more than two million dollars. Isn't that enough to cover the bills?"

The estate attorney at least had the decency to look sympathetic as he shook his head. "Well, if that were all the debt he had, then it would. Unfortunately, there are also considerable tax liabilities, and to make matters worse, I'm afraid your uncle sold you into slavery to pay off some of that debt. Now, if you would be so kind as to disrobe, I would like to make sure that you are worth the price we paid for you."

She finally gave up on sleep and turned on the flat screen. Scrolling through the selection at just after two in the morning revealed just how limited the options were. There was the almost-porn of after-hours cable, infomercials, or the news channels. Not in the mood for either of the first two, she settled on a cable news channel. Uncle J had always called the channel the Communist News Network, and the memory made her smile sadly. His politics and hers had always clashed.

The news was about the same as it had been the night before, and the night before that; the holidays were coming, the economy still sucked, politicians were still crooked, the weather was still unpredictable, and now it looked like there was another pandemic scare in Uganda. After half an hour, she found her eyelids growing heavy again. She turned the tube off and curled up for round two in her battle with insomnia.

FRIDAY
NOVEMBER 18

CHAPTER 5

CHARLES GRIFFE

THE FREE CRUISE WAS GOING TO COST HIM

WROK radio had provided the tickets, all right. But the radio station had made sure to let him know that anything beyond the cruise itself would have to come from his own pocket. In essence, the free cruise was going to cost him hundreds, if not thousands of dollars. Still, his woman had her heart set on it, and he had agreed.

So on November eighteenth, Charlie and Felicia walked into their cabin, Charlie huffing and puffing as he lugged their bags into the room. Felicia squealed with delight for what must have been the fiftieth time since they'd boarded. "Look, Charlie, a balcony!"

She ran across the cabin and threw open the sliding glass door. "It's beautiful."

Charlie tossed the bags onto the bed and joined her. He snorted as he looked out at the view. "Yeah, it's a great view all right. I can see a parking lot full of about a thousand cars, and a lifeboat right below us."

"But once we get out to sea, there will be ocean and clouds as far as the eye can see. It'll be wonderful!"

It was hard to stay upset with her when she was like this, though Charlie gave it a good try. As much as Felicia seemed enchanted by the idea of the cruise, the idea of going to sea and being cooped up on a floating tin can miles away from the closest dry land was more than a little disconcerting for him. Having never been on a ship before, he was off his game, unfamiliar with how things worked. And Charlie didn't like not being in control. He did his best to push away his feelings of unease. Maybe being at sea wouldn't be all that bad.

He had to admit, the cabin was actually pretty nice. He'd expected one of the cheapest, crappiest little rooms on some bottom deck, tucked away from anything and everyone. Instead, he was pleasantly surprised to find that they had gotten a nice, ocean side, balcony suite on Deck Seven. It wasn't bad at all. Charlie took a deep breath and decided to make the best of things.

Besides, it wasn't like he had too much choice in the matter. Felicia would never let him hear the end of it if he spent all his time bitching about everything. And as the saying went, if Mama ain't happy, ain't nobody happy. She could be a pain in the ass with her whining sometimes, and there were times when she acted dumber than a box of rocks. But that woman was a wild little minx in the bedroom, and Charlie could put up with a lot for someone with a rack like hers. He knew he was man enough to handle her the way she needed to be handled, both in the bedroom and out.

Yeah, it was going to be a good cruise. Charlie would see to it.

CHAPTER 6
AUGUST GRAPPIN
MAYBE THIS WON'T BE SO BAD

Gus tried to ignore his mother's incessant chatter about what a great time they were going to have. She meant well, but her recent constant cheeriness was just a bit much to swallow sometimes. Still, it was better than the moping, so he was determined to let it ride. Her emotional state still seemed fragile enough that he didn't want to rock the boat any more than necessary.

Rock the boat? He looked up at the massive ocean liner as they waited in line to board. *Real clever, Gus.* He shook his head at the inadvertent pun. They waited in a long line to board, but the crew really seemed to know what they were doing, and the boarding process was relatively quick. Gus estimated that less than half an hour passed from the time they left the taxi to the time they walked into their adjoining suite. He nodded approvingly at the cabin his mom had gotten for him. *Maybe this won't be so bad after all.*

The room adjoined his mother's, but at least it was separate. She could have gotten a single room with two beds, and oh, wouldn't that have been fun? Gus shuddered at the thought. He loved his mom, but the idea of the two of them sharing a cabin was just uncool. He tossed his suitcase onto the bed and opened the room's mini-fridge. It had a couple of bottles of water and a variety of sodas. Laying atop the refrigerator was a price card. According to it, each of those sodas would cost more than he would spend on a two-liter bottle in the grocery store.

He raised an eyebrow at the list of alcohol also shown on the card. Evidently, the shelves above the mini fridge were normally stocked with booze. Equally as evident was the fact that his mom must have had the ship stewards remove it before they boarded. He sighed. It wasn't like he really drank, but if by some chance he ended up getting a girl into his cabin, the cool factor would have only worked in his favor.

Another card lay on the nightstand. It listed all sorts of activities designed with his age group in mind. There were teen parties almost every night, each one with a different theme. And the upper decks were full of games, sports, water parks, and even a zip line that ran a hundred feet over the boardwalk nine decks below.

He grinned. Waterparks, eh? That meant girls. Girls in bikinis. He nodded. Yeah, this cruise thing looked like it just might be a lot of fun.

SUNDAY
NOVEMBER 20

CHAPTER 7
ERICA CHAPMAN
WHERE HIS HEART HAD FAILED HIM

At some point the night before, Erica had eventually won another battle with insomnia. Of course, she woke up the next morning so groggy that it seemed otherwise. A brisk shower in the guest bathroom helped wash the sleep from her eyes. She could have used the master shower, but in her mind, that was still Uncle Jimmy's territory, and she wasn't quite up to crossing that particular border. The reminders were still too fresh.

So she puttered around the place doing busy work that did little more than move things from one place to another. She checked the refrigerator and managed to put together a breakfast of scrambled eggs with diced tomatoes and jalapeños.

But she quickly found herself at a loss for more busywork and realized she couldn't put it off any longer. She began to clean. She was torn as to whether or not to throw out the soured load of clothes. After all, it wasn't like Uncle Jimmy was going to need them. But in the end, she just couldn't do it. She restarted the washer and kept cleaning. The hard part was that everywhere she turned, there were more reminders of her childhood. She would walk into a room with every intention of getting in, cleaning, and getting out again. But each room she entered brought a fresh wave of nostalgia, and she was drawn into memory anew.

There were dirty dishes in the sink where Uncle J taught her to gut fish and break down a chicken; and the dinner table where they laughed, and sometimes fought. When she retreated back to the room where she had slept the night before—her old bedroom—she suddenly realized that Uncle J had left the room just the same as she'd left it, and that realization brought another bout of tears. She began to wonder if she would ever be able to get the place ready within the week allotted.

The buzzing of the washing machine drew her out of her funk, and she checked the load. A quick sniff told her the clothes had been soured too long for a single wash to clean them, so she poured more detergent in and started them again. She eventually had to wash the load three times to get the smell out, then dried and folded it neatly. That brought a last problem. To put the clothes away, she would have to go into his bedroom—the room where his heart had failed him. She would finally have to cross that border.

Erica stood outside that door for what seemed like hours before finding the courage to open it. *This was where it happened.* She tried to focus on the task at hand, did her best to see only the dresser that was her destination. But her self-induced tunnel vision was disrupted by the broken glass beside the nightstand. *Did that happen when he had his heart attack? Was it broken by the panicked neighbor who found his body—two days too late?* The sight of it set off a string of imaginary scenarios in her mind from which it took considerable strength of will to break loose. Finally, she took a determined step to the dresser, placed the pile of clothes in a drawer, and closed it. There was a finality to closing that drawer that was both depressing, and comforting. It was one last thing she could do for him.

She turned then, to clean up the broken glass. She made the bed, and straightened the knick-knacks on the dresser, and before she knew it, she had cleaned the entire room. And a strange thing happened as she performed the old, familiar tasks. She found that finally, she began to feel at home again.

The rest of the day held less angst than the day before, and she managed to get quite a bit accomplished. To be sure, there were still plenty of reminders, but they became less torturous, and released their grip on her heart. At least somewhat.

Over the next few days, the memories were more bittersweet than painful, and she managed to get the house and the workshop cleaned up, all the while, maintaining the cattle and garden out back. Working the little ranch felt good, if somewhat pointless. In a matter of days, she would be forced to leave, to go back to Alabama, taking only whatever keepsakes the lawyers would allow her. She had little doubt that if it weren't for the impending holiday season, they wouldn't have given her even that last week. Even at that, she suspected that it wasn't out of concern for how painful Thanksgiving might be for her, but rather for the inconvenience they might face in working through that all important week with their families.

TUESDAY
NOVEMBER 22

CHAPTER 8
ROSS MAYFIELD
CONTROL

It was the Sunday before Thanksgiving and Ross wondered, not for the first time, what the celebration of a holiday felt like to "normal" people—people who could allow themselves to "feel." He had wondered this often enough that it was barely a conscious idea anymore, more of a conditioned thought process that followed the acknowledgment of the holiday. His mind slipped over the thought and past it as he and he moved his mind closer to his Zen state.

He concentrated on feeling his pulse as he progressed through the movements of his warmup forms. Finding the rhythm of his heart, he held onto it in his mind, focusing on the thump, thump, thump… until he knew its beat without having to think about it any longer. Moving through the next positions of his warmup, his hands and feet flowed gracefully, almost of their own accord. Once he was sure of the synchronicity of his movements and his heartbeat, he added his more personal regimen.

He flowed into the next form without pause, but in his mind, he noted the transition, and mentally added an audial focal point. It was a trick he had developed years ago to help with his personal circumstances, a conditioning and discipline that had moved him far beyond all his fellow students, and had garnered him the one-on-one training he really needed. This audio focus was the simple tone of a single piano note. He imagined the ivory key tapping in unison with his heart.

Once he was able to hold the note to the same rhythm as his heart, he mentally searched his movements. He noted a slight mental tension, the result of his concentration. He took a cleansing breath, forcing himself to relax as he moved through his form. Tension was the enemy. Calm and relaxation were his allies.

Finally feeling himself in complete control of his body and his mind, he slowed the tone in his mind. Where he had earlier imagined the piano tone mimicking the rhythm of his heart, he now imagined the two of them linked, beating as one. And as the imagined tone slowed, so too did the linked heartbeat. Moving into the next of his forms, he slowed his heart and breathing, the movements of his limbs now becoming secondary to the exercise.

It was a meditative technique he had developed on his own, a blending of self-hypnosis, relaxation, and breathing exercises he had gathered from various martial arts. He had searched for many years, struggling with his condition. This was the best he had been able to come up with. He had finally come to accept that he would never be normal. So he had determined to do his best to be *better* than normal.

And for three years, he had thought he'd done it. He excelled in his studies, was the best student his Tai Chi instructor had ever taught, grasping both the health and the combat benefits of the Yang style movements, and while many of his friends in school had moved to more violent sports and activities, Ross had sought only peace and calm. The irony was that his quest for peace had found him a home in the study of martial arts. It was an irony that wasn't lost on him.

Then he had met Erica, and her very presence had shown that she had the ability to unbalance his composure. She was bad for him, broke his calm. But he couldn't keep from thinking about her. And every time he thought about her, his self-control slipped. Even now, as he moved through his sixth form, he lost control of his heartbeat. His attempt to once more grasp the Zen of the moment caused him to hesitate slightly in the placement of his foot, and in that instant, he knew he was done.

"You started thinking again, didn't you?"

Ross nodded. "Sorry, Sifu."

"Were you thinking about the girl again?"

"Yeah."

Sifu Alex Cope shook his head. "You know she's no good for you, don't you?"

Ross walked to his gear bag and grabbed a bottle of water. He twisted the lid off and shrugged. "There are times when I wish I'd never met her." He took a swallow, relishing the feel of the cold liquid sliding down his throat, then he sighed. "And there are other times when I think she's the best thing that ever happened to me."

He tossed the water bottle back into his bag and picked up his *dao*. The Chinese broadsword was his specialty, and he took a certain amount of pride in his level of mastery over the blade. "No, I think the real problem is that *I'm* the one who's no good for *her*."

He turned and saluted his sifu as he stepped back into the center of the training area. His movements now were shorter, chopped and precise. The movements required for the dao forms were faster, more energetic as he spun the blade in mesmerizing patterns. The blade work was more physical, and for most people, would immediately drive up their respiration and heartbeat. Ross had to struggle to keep one part of his mind on the blade form while working to keep control of his cardiovascular system. He was only three movements into the form, and he knew it was going to be more difficult than usual today. *Green Dragon Comes Out of Water* was a simple sequence, but as he came out of the leap, his foot placement was off. It was a subtle thing, but it told him that his balance was shot, and while he had to concentrate on that problem, he had to relinquish some concentration on his heartbeat.

Some days were like that. And they usually came when he allowed himself to dwell on Erica. To top it off, his sifu began to speak to him, knowing that it would add another layer of complexity to Ross's struggle with mind over body.

"Why do you prefer *dao* over *jian*? The broadsword lacks the grace and subtlety that you usually show in your unarmed forms. It's not much more than a crude hacking implement. But the straight blade and balance of the *jian* would fit your unarmed style better."

Ross fought to maintain the sequence of his form, while he formed his response. It was a discussion he and Sifu Alex had had more frequently in the last few weeks. His sifu saw his lack of interest in the *jian* as a weakness in his training, and perhaps it was. But Ross had special needs, and controlling the broadsword gave him something that the double-edged straight blade of the *jian* couldn't. "It teaches me through that contrast. Controlling the harsher movement forces me to work more on my inner control. It brings me closer to mastering my inner spirit."

Alex was silent for the moment, apparently mulling that over as he watched Ross leap and spin across the floor. Evidently, he finally came to a conclusion after Ross completed another sequence. "You do realize that's complete and utter bullshit, right?"

Ross slid his foot back, raised his knee and hopped over the imagined body of a fallen opponent as he neared the end of his form. "But it's the sort of bullshit people expect from a Jedi master, right?"

His instructor chuckled at that, and Ross dropped back into a relaxed stance, completing the form. "Jedi master?" Alex's voice raised from his normal baritone to imitate the little green master. "If Jedi we are, then master *I* am. My Padawan are you."

Ross allowed himself a small smile. It was the most he ever allowed.

Sifu Alex approached him and held out his hand. "May I?"

Ross handed him his *dao* hilt first, and Alex looked it over carefully. "Holy crap, Ross. This is really nice."

"Thanks. It should be. It cost me five hundred bucks."

Alex whistled. He was ten years older than Ross, but acted younger. Whether that was because Ross acted older than he needed to, or Alex acted younger was something Ross had wondered on many occasions. Either way though, Alex's casual teaching style coupled with Ross's formality in class would have the casual observer confused as to who was the teacher, and who the instructor.

"Five bills?" Alex handed the broadsword back to Ross. "I'd be afraid to train with something that expensive."

Ross slid the blade back into its scabbard without comment. Alex already knew Ross's parents were loaded. And that they doted on their son. *Yeah, their poor, broken son.*

"Put it back with your gear and then come back to the floor."

Ross did, and when he stepped back onto the training floor, Alex held out another *dao*. This one was blunted, and Ross immediately knew what his sifu planned. Alex held a similarly blunted *jian* in his other hand. "I want to show you the difference in a more practical application."

This was another thing that Ross liked about sifu Alex's training methods. Where most instructors would show him how his foot placement, or his balance was off just so, Alex often demonstrated the *why* of the movements in combat scenarios. It gave Ross the chance to apply his techniques, both martial and meditative, and test them in a more realistic environment. With the blunted blades, neither of them would get hurt beyond a few bruises. They were both too skilled for anything more. But it was also evident that his sifu felt he had something to teach Ross today, and that sparring was the best way to do so.

Ross took the training *dao* and saluted his sifu, stepping back and resting the blade of his broadsword in the crook of his left arm. Alex nodded back and stood with his *jian* in a relaxed stance, blade tucked behind his own left arm, all but hidden from view.

"Ready?" Alex asked.

Ross nodded.

In a flash, Alex's hands came together, transferring the straight and narrow blade from left hand to right and thrusting it out toward Ross. As he did so, he flung his left hand backward, a counterbalance to his thrust.

Ross had anticipated this opening and easily warded off the strike, deflecting it to the side as he stepped inside, attempting to negate the advantage of his instructor's longer blade. But Alex leapt back, whirling his blade in a narrow circle that temporarily entangled Ross's *dao* and forced him to retreat. Ross spun away, whirling his own blade in a defensive pattern in case Alex pursued, but his instructor simply slid forward, as graceful as the water his movements represented.

Their dance continued for several minutes, neither man saying a word. Something that Ross noticed for the first time was the almost musical sound of their blades as they brushed and slid against each other. Very seldom was there a harsh clang of edge on edge. The two of them were good enough that the parries and attacks were more subtle. They consisted mostly of thrusts, light parries, and understated redirections.

But as good as Ross was with his *dao*, Alex was even better with his *jian*. He was playing with Ross, biding his time. Ross knew it was unlikely that he would actually win the match. But he was determined that he would not give the victory to his instructor through any mistake on his part. Alex would have to show some superior technique that would overcome Ross's. It was a subtle distinction, but in Ross's mind, it was important.

So he lost himself in the dance. The sound of blade on blade, feet on the wooden floor of the gymnasium, and as always, his heartbeat sounding in the back of his mind... all of these faded into insignificant background noise. After a few more minutes, there was nothing but the rhythm of the bout, and he was comfortable enough with the movements that he was able to add the piano tone in his mind once more.

Heart slowing, breath easing... he surrendered to the moment.

Several minutes later, and he wasn't sure how long that was, Ross noted something new. There was an ache in his shoulder and wrist. He realized he had been aware of it for a few minutes, but had ignored it as insignificant. Now, though, it refused to be ignored, and it intruded into his mind. Suddenly, his control was in jeopardy. His movements became strained, and his blade heavy.

And just like that, the flat of Alex's *jian* slapped him on his shoulder, then the tip poked at his chest. They both stepped back, the match over. Ross strained to maintain control of his heartbeat as Alex spoke.

"What happened?"

"You won."

"I know that. I even know why. The question is, do you?"

Ross thought about it for a second. Was it a trick question? No, that wouldn't be like Alex. So he needed to take the question seriously. "My shoulder and wrist gave out."

"I know that. I could see when it began." He stepped forward and held out his hand for Ross's *dao*. "My question is, *why* did your shoulder and wrist give out?"

Ross raised an eyebrow as he handed the practice blade over. "Because my blade weighs almost twice as much as yours."

Alex smiled and nodded. "That's a big part of it. But it's not the whole answer." He turned to place the practice blades back in their places on the wall. "The weight, and more importantly the weight distribution of the blade, forces you to work more of the larger muscle groups to keep it moving. The *dao* is designed as a slashing and hacking blade. As such, the balance is toward the end of the blade. This means you have to sling all that weight around. It gives the *dao* an advantage in cutting, but it wears you out quicker." Alex smiled at him. "I'll give you credit, though. You kept it up for a lot longer than I thought you'd be able to. You're better than anyone I know at finding your zone and keeping inside it... better even than I am, by far.

"But the *jian* is a longer, lighter blade, and when two opponents are closely matched in skill, the *jian* will usually win out. It requires more balance, but less gross motor control."

Ross nodded. "I don't argue the point, Sifu. It's just that the combat application of the blade is secondary for me. Don't get me wrong, I enjoy the hell out of that aspect of our studies, too. But my main goal is to conquer my condition, or at least control it as much as I can. My meditative techniques are my primary focus. The blade is just a means to that end."

"But couldn't you do the same with the *jian*?"

Ross shook his head. "All the reasons you listed are precisely why I *don't* want to use the *jian*. It wouldn't work me hard enough. It wouldn't force me to pay attention to my body as much."

After considering that, Alex nodded. "All right. You do realize that you'll likely never progress to full mastery of the style this way, don't you?"

Ross shrugged. "With all due respect, Sifu, mastery of the style isn't my goal. Mastery of *myself* is more important."

Alex sighed. "All right. I can respect that. But I won't stop hoping that you'll change your mind. You'd be one hell of a competitor. Even better, you'd be a great teacher if you would work more on the other aspects of the art."

"Thanks. But I think we both know better. I can't afford to get invested enough to ever be a good instructor. What would the students say when I have one of my episodes?"

Alex nodded. "Sorry. You always seem to be in control. I guess I tend to forget that you're walking that tightrope every day. Besides, I would truly love to see what you could do with the other weapons if you put your mind to them. I have to admit, there's a certain selfishness to me pushing you toward the long blade."

"I appreciate the compliment, Sifu, and the confidence you have in my abilities. But truthfully, in this day and age, when is knowledge of swordplay ever going to be important other than as a mental discipline?"

They finished with some slower unarmed forms to allow their muscles to cool down, and parted outside the gymnasium. They were the last ones out, as they usually were.

"You have plans for Thanksgiving?" Alex asked.

Ross felt his heart skip, and immediately clamped down on it. "Thought I did, but some friends told me today that Erica had to leave town. Something about a death in the family."

"Sorry to hear that. Nothing with your parents?"

"No. They're in Europe for the holidays."

Alex whistled. "Must be nice."

"Yeah. I figure I'll just hang around the dorm, play some video games... work out."

"Why don't you come over to my place? Jeanette and I can make room for one more."

Ross pretended to think about it for a second. "No thanks. I think I'll just take the down time and relax."

"Well, you have my number if you change your mind." He turned and headed toward the parking lot. He pulled his keys from his pocket and pressed. A horn beeped once and the lights flashed on one of the three cars left in the lot. "Give Erica my condolences," he called over his shoulder.

"Will do. Thanks." But the parting comment brought the tightness of anxiety back to Ross's chest. *Why did I have to hear about it from friends? Why didn't she tell me on her own?* They had fought last time they were together. Was that all it took? He hadn't had many relationships, and he knew he put a special strain on theirs. But he thought she would at least tell him if she was going to end things.

He sighed as he walked toward his dorm, concentrating on the beating of his heart, struggling with it now more than when he'd been wielding the *dao*.

CHAPTER 9
CHRIS TALLANT
THE SLICK

Chris was shadowing the first officer on the evening watch when Captain Eckles dropped in to make a quick round. He was wearing his dinner uniform, so it was obvious he wasn't planning to stay long. But in the week Chris had been in his new position, he had learned that the captain liked to show up unannounced to make sure everyone was on their toes. The Bahama Queen was a new ship, less than two years out of dry dock, and Eckles had been chosen as the best to run her. He had a reputation for running the tightest ships in the company, a reputation that from what Chris had seen so far, appeared to be well deserved.

"Good evening, gentlemen. How are things on the bridge?"

"Everything is running good, Captain." First Officer Berthold Seuss still pronounced it with a slight German accent — "goot." His English was impeccable, but the pronunciation of certain words still gave away the fact that it wasn't his primary language.

"Excellent, Doc." Chris winced inwardly at the captain's use of the nickname. The first officer tolerated it from the captain, but Chris had been warned by other members of the bridge crew that the older man would make anyone else's life a living hell if they dared use it. He could only imagine how much the man must have been teased, growing up with the name most associated with a famous children's author.

But Eckles continued without pause, either unaware or uncaring of his first officer's dislike of the name. "I assume by your presence that you're taking the night watch?"

"I am, sir," Seuss confirmed. "Mr. Tallant is my second. I thought I would check him on the new navigation systems."

The captain looked at Chris for the first time since walking into the bridge. "Are you familiar with them?"

Chris stood up a little straighter. "The software itself is the same as what I used on the L-class liners. The interface is a little different, but I'll get used to that."

Eckles smiled. "That's what I like to hear." He looked again at Seuss. "All right, Doc. I'll leave the bridge in your capable hands, then. There's a pretty young divorcee sitting at the captain's table tonight, and I'm just aching to offer her my condolences."

"Aye, Captain."

Eckles was almost to the door when Jesse Perez, the Apprentice Deck Officer, called from the observation window. "Captain? Before you leave, sir, you might want to take a look at this."

With a wry grin, the captain shook his head. "You're bound and determined to make me late for dinner tonight, aren't you, Jesse? You saw the good-looking women on this cruise, and you're just trying to keep me from getting lucky." But he walked across the bridge to where Perez was staring at the ocean through a pair of binoculars. "What have you got, son? Iceberg? UFO, sea monst..." The captain's voice trailed off. "Oh, now that *is* pretty awesome."

He turned to call the rest of the bridge crew. "You folks might want to come take a look at this. It's not something you get to see very often."

Curious, Chris walked over with the dozen or so others on the bridge. The lower ranks parted for him, deferential to the stripes on his shoulder.

"I'll be damned," Eckles said. "I don't think I've ever seen a patch so big. This thing stretches for miles!"

Chris gaped. The captain was right. The Bahama Queen had just entered a huge patch of blue glowing water. Like anyone who had spent any time at sea, he had seen patches of bioluminescent algae before. But this one was by far the largest he had ever seen. It shimmered like a glowing slick of oil before the ship, churning brighter in some places, as if it was some sort of special lighting effect straight out of Hollywood.

"Captain. Take a look ahead, about four hundred yards off the starboard bow."

Not having any binoculars handy, Chris squinted to see where Perez indicated. From where he stood, he could tell there was something churning frantically, thrashing about in the glowing water. Looking closer, it looked like it was several large fish. Tuna? Redfish? Sharks?

"Was ist das?" Chris was surprised to hear Seuss momentarily slip back into his native German. It was the first time he had heard it in the week he had been on board. It somehow made the man seem more human.

"Looks like a pod of dolphins."

"But what the hell are they doing?" Perez asked. Then he answered his own question. "It looks like they're fighting."

"Each other?" Chris asked.

Captain Eckles lowered his glasses. "It looks that way." His brow crinkled as he thought. "Mr. Tallant?"

The transition was so abrupt, Chris started. "Yes, sir?"

"Please contact the public relations office and ask them if they have a photographer on duty. Video is preferable."

Chris was moving to his station before the captain had completed his sentence.

"Give them the location and ask them to film as much of this as they can. There's something strange going on, and I want as much documentation as we can get."

"Aye, sir."

"I want footage of the dolphins for the company's biology department. Also, ask them to get some footage of the water. The bioluminescence will make great filler for advertising."

Chris started to answer but was interrupted by a voice on the line. "This is Dalton."

"Dalton, this is Second Officer Tallant on the bridge. The captain would like someone from PR to get topside with some video equipment. There's a pod of dolphins fighting off the starboard bow, and there's a huge glowing…" He hesitated. How to describe it so the layman would understand? "Just call it a slick. We need to get footage of both."

"Yes, sir. I think I have a man doing film footage for families right now. I'll call him and send him starboard."

"Thanks."

"Not a problem, sir."

Chris hung up the line after speaking with the public relations office. He waited patiently as Captain Eckles gave more orders. The man stared through his binoculars, never looking up as he spoke to no one in particular. "Reduce speed for a bit to let the video crew get some good footage. We can make up the time later."

And as people scrambled to turn his words to reality, Chris cleared his throat to get the captain's attention.

"Captain?"

"Yes, Mr. Tallant?" The man still didn't put down his binoculars, but he seemed to know who he was speaking to, nonetheless.

"I just spoke to Mr. Dalton in Public Relations. He's going to get a man up to start filming."

But Eckles didn't look up, obviously preoccupied with the view. "Very good, Mr. Tallant. Would you please call down and cancel my dinner plans?" His jaw clenched tightly at some sight in the gulf, but he continued. "And please send my regrets specifically to Miss McSherry at the Captain's table. Tell her some unexpected business on the bridge has come up and I'll have to take a rain check on our dinner."

"Aye, Captain."

CHAPTER 10
CHARLES GRIFFE
LE TRÔNE DE LA MER

It had taken four days, but Charlie had managed to book dinner reservations at the fanciest dining room on the ship. *Le Trône de la Mer* was a French-themed dining room on Deck Four, and was definitely one of the luxuries the station hadn't paid for. Charlie had thought long and hard about whether or not he should spring for it, but he'd wanted to show off a little for Felicia. Expose her to some of the fancier things in life. So he'd hesitantly made reservations for the gourmet dining experience. The dining room had been walled with huge aquariums, and Felicia squealed with delight every time a pretty fish swam past.

Looking back, Charlie would be able to point to that meal as the point at which everything had gone sideways for him.

He ordered Felicia the most exotic sounding item on the menu, but when he was about halfway through his plate, he noticed that she had barely touched her meal. "What's the matter, baby? Something wrong with your food?"

Eyes downcast, she looked as if she was afraid to say anything. She mumbled something so low he couldn't hear her over the background sounds of the dining room.

"What?"

"I don't like lobster."

"You what?" He couldn't believe she was pulling this on him. Who didn't like lobster? He and Felicia had been living together for almost a year now, and she'd never once mentioned that she didn't like lobster. He was sure of it.

"I'm sorry, Charlie."

"Then why didn't you say anything when I ordered?"

"I didn't know what you were ordering. It was in French."

And he remembered looking at the menu and simply finding the most exotic sounding dish, ordering *Homard Thermidor*, and being so proud he could afford to spend the dining room's ninety dollar per person entry fee that he hadn't paid attention to the description. Even now, that price was the thing that kept going through his head. "You do realize how much this dinner is costing me, don't you?"

"I'm so sorry, Charlie." She looked up with tears in her eyes, and Charlie struggled to rein in his temper.

He smiled past tight lips, choking back his frustration. In his peripheral vision, he saw other diners at the table watching the exchange surreptitiously. "It's okay. Don't worry about it. So what would you like to eat?" He even managed to keep his annoyance in check when she ordered a hamburger.

Whenever he began to get angry, his father's voice echoed in his ears. *Seriously? Ninety dollars a head, and she orders a fucking hamburger?*

Yeah, Charlie had always been able to count on dear old Dad for support. Like the time he'd pegged Charlie with a fastball in the forehead to teach him to keep his glove up. Charlie had been nine at the time. Nine with a concussion.

But Charlie pushed the voice back. The therapists had taught him long ago that listening to Dad's voice invariably got him into trouble. So he forced a smile and bit back his initial response. After a while, he even managed to enjoy the dinner. Complimentary glasses of wine helped, and he and Felicia spent the time between courses chatting and joking with fellow passengers. Three courses later, dessert came, and Charlie knew he was almost through what had become an ordeal of dancing on eggshells. He had ordered the two of them Grand Marnier soufflés with Crème Anglaise.

The fluffy cup of heaven smelled slightly of orange liqueur when it arrived, and when he scooped the first warm bite into his mouth, he tasted tiny flecks of orange peel on his tongue. The creamy vanilla sauce was the perfect counterpoint for the tang of the soufflé. He watched Felicia's face as she took her first tentative bite. Her smile told him all he needed to know. She had loved his order this time. Charlie smiled. *Yeah, baby. Charlie's gonna get lucky tonight.*

The last few minutes of the meal went smoothly, and his mind began to drift more toward his planned activities for later that night… after they were back in their cabin. He smiled as he imagined her in the bed. She was so enthusiastic, skin so smooth, and her mouth was exquisite. She had that one trick she did with her tongue… Charlie found himself with an uncomfortable tent in his pants when Felicia interrupted his reverie.

"Can we, Charlie? Please?"

"Ah, I'm sorry. Can we what?"

"Go dancing with the others." She pursed her lips in a coquettish little circle, drawing his attention once again to that mouth. "I really feel like dancing."

He pretended to consider it for a moment, then shook his head. "Not tonight, baby. Maybe tomorrow night."

Felicia's lips went from smile to moue. "But I really want to go tonight." She shimmied her shoulders at him and his eyes were immediately drawn to the way her ample cleavage shifted. It only reinforced his desire to get her back to their cabin. He had another kind of dancing in mind——a night of mattress mambo was in order. After all, he hadn't just dropped ninety bucks on a damned hamburger for nothing.

He turned to their tablemates. "I'm really sorry, guys. I think we're going to have to pass tonight. It's been a long day, and we're a bit tired. Maybe another night."

But Felicia pouted. "Oh, come on, Charlie. I'm not tired. Let's go! Just for a little while? It'll be fun." She was still smiling at that point, not yet realizing how badly she'd overstepped. She had contradicted him in front of strangers.

Whether or not she realized what she had done, that was the moment. After all he'd done for her… all the trouble he'd gone to so this would be a memorable experience for her… all the inconvenience he'd put up with… and she wanted to bitch about him not wanting to go dancing with a bunch of people he didn't even know? And to top it off, she was trying to embarrass him in public?

Still, he tried one last time. "Not tonight, baby. We need to get back to the cabin."

She pouted. "Pah-leeeaaase?"

It was too much. She had pushed him too far, and Charlie had finally had more than he could take. He slapped his open palm on the table. "Damn it, Felicia. I said no!"

Everyone at the table stopped what they were doing and looked at him. Looked at him like he was something they needed to scrape off the bottom of their shoes. Charlie looked around. The surrounding tables had suddenly gone silent, and as his gaze fell upon them, the other patrons of the dining room found sudden fascination with their silverware or tablecloths.

Throwing his hands in the air, Charlie snorted. "So now I'm the bad guy? Hah! If you knew how many times this stupid cow has done this to me, you wouldn't be so quick to judge."

Felicia burst into tears and fled the room.

"Well shit." He threw his napkin on the table and stood. There was a brief moment where his head took a moment to catch up with his sudden change in altitude, and he realized he was a little buzzed from all the wine. As big a man as he was, there was still a limit to what he could drink without showing the effects. He steadied himself with one hand on the table. Equilibrium restored, he smiled at the others seated at his table. "Don't guess I'll be getting lucky tonight, will I?"

He left the dining room, not looking behind, but feeling the eyes of the other patrons staring as he walked out.

Fuck 'em.

CHAPTER 11
AUGUST GRAPPIN
MIDNIGHT POOL PARTY

One of the teen activities mentioned on the brochure were the nightly pool parties. Initially, Gus had thought it was a little chilly outside for a pool party, but the pools were heated, and he was determined to meet some girls on this trip. He was at the stage of his adolescence where he pretty much had one thing on his mind. And if there was a chance that there would be girls his own age, in swimsuits no less, then he wasn't going to miss out.

And if they happened to get out of the warm pool while wet, and the outside air was cold? He smiled at the possibilities.

Ironically enough, the midnight pool parties actually began at nine o'clock. Tonight was the third one, and he was beginning to lose hope that he was going to have any luck. The last two nights there had been mostly guys at the pool, and he hadn't been interested in staying around for a sausage-fest.

But tonight looked like it was going to be different. Looking around the pool, Gus had to smile. Tonight there were several girls his age. And while Gus wasn't the smoothest guy in the world when it came to talking with the fairer sex, he was at least smart enough to know how to work to his strengths. He had long ago learned that the best way to get his foot in the door with the girls was by being honest with them.

For the most part.

He didn't bother trying to think up smarmy pickup lines, or lying to them. He treated them with respect. Sometimes it worked, and sometimes it backfired. But he figured that any girl that fell for some stupid line a jock laid on her, or who couldn't appreciate him for who he really was, wasn't really someone he wanted to hang out with anyway.

And he had been surprised at how often the girls responded favorably to that attitude.

Tonight was no exception. Her name was Cindy, and she was cute, in a "girl next door" kind of way. She had pale skin and wore a black bikini that left little to the imagination. A bikini that forced him to stay in the water most of the time, for fear that the bulge in his swimsuit would cause her to think he was only after one thing.

He wasn't. Not exactly, anyway. He was genuinely interested in her. But he was also a normal sixteen-year-old boy, and Cindy's rocking hot body had the same effect on him that it would have had on any other horny teenaged boy. He just had to make sure she didn't see that effect. She had a quick wit, a pretty laugh, and before he knew it, they were talking like they were old friends.

"So your parents are cool with your hair?"

Gus shrugged, trying to maintain an air of nonchalance. "My dad's gone. Left me and my mom about eight months ago. Mom's cool with it, since she knows it would piss him off."

Cindy's expression turned soft. "Sorry, I didn't know."

He gave her a lopsided grin, going for the pained look of a hurt young man trying to make the best of his bad situation. "No way you could have."

"But I like the way your mom thinks—liking your hair because it would piss off your dad." She grinned. "My folks would have a fit if I did something like that to my hair. Hell, I had to sneak out wearing clothes over my swimsuit so they wouldn't see the bikini."

Gus raised an eyebrow. "They don't know you're wearing that?"

She shook her head and laughed. "They think I'm wearing my one-piece from swim team."

"Wow. You're on a swim team? That's why you look so, ah…" Gus caught himself, but didn't know how to finish. He swallowed as Cindy raised an eyebrow at him.

She smirked at him. "Why I look so what?"

Gus flapped his jaw open and closed before realizing she was playing with him. When he realized she wasn't offended, he smiled back at her. "Sorry. I was going to say hot, but thought it might piss you off."

She grinned broadly, then shrugged. "Nothing wrong with a guy telling a girl she looks good. Especially since that's kinda the effect I was going for." She moved a little closer to him in the water, and Gus swallowed. Was she going to kiss him? Did she want him to kiss her? Suddenly, she was only inches away from him. "You know what I really want to do now, though?"

"N-no." He cleared his suddenly dry throat as she put her hand on his shoulder. He had trouble concentrating on her words as she moved even closer and put her lips up against his ear. His heart pounded as he felt her breasts pushing up against his chest.

"I want," her grip tightened on his shoulder, "to play tag!" And she slipped her leg behind his and shoved back on him. Gus was underwater before he realized it. He came up sputtering and laughing, looking around just in time to see her scantily clad rump roll under the surface of the water as she swam away.

Gus took off after her.

CHAPTER 12
INTERLUDE – TURSIOPS TRUNCATES

He was known in the pod by a tiny tear in his dorsal fin he had received years ago in an unfortunate shark encounter. It wasn't the first time his impetuous nature had gotten him into trouble, and it wouldn't be the last. The sound for Bite Taken out of Tip of His Dorsal was commonly shortened by members of the pod to a name more humorously, and somewhat insultingly, interpreted as Dorsey. Dorsey was more curious than most dolphins, so when he sensed the screams and laughter of another pod nearby, he sounded the call to the rest of his pod.

His call was first answered by Speckled Tail, who swam up to him, pinging the waters with his own sonar. His curiosity also piqued, he added his call to Dorsey's, and the rest of the pod joined them, swimming toward the crazed echoes of fellow dolphins thrashing about in the cool waters. There was something unusual in the calls and movements of the others—something erratic, and almost panicked.

Dorsey and Speckled Tail led the pod, their concern increasing as they neared the others. The sounds of the others were frantic, thrashing about in the glowing water of a phosphorescent sheen floating on the water. One of the giant human not-fish things floated through the water nearby, and at first, Dorsey thought it had attacked the pod, but to his dismay and amazement, he saw one of the strange pod clapping his jaws loudly to announce his attack, then ram into one of his pod mates with a force hard enough to rupture internal organs.

As Dorsey and his pod watched, several more of the other pod engaged one another in biting and ramming, clearly attempting to kill one another. Dorsey sounded his dismay, and raced forward. It wasn't the first time his impetuousness had gotten him into trouble. But this time, it would *be the last.*

CHAPTER 13

CHARLES GRIFFE

IS THERE ANY OTHER WAY?

Knowing his nighttime plans were ruined, Charlie decided he didn't want to bother going back up to the cabin. He walked slowly down the corridor, snaking the back of his hand out every few feet to brush the railing on the wall. It was a trick he had learned in his younger days to keep from weaving as he walked. It was a matter of pride for him that no one should know he had a buzz on.

A buzz, yes. But this fucked up evening calls for some serious drinking.

So he wandered the ship for a while, looking for a nice bar. *I dressed in a damned suit, after all. Might as well find a classy joint to go with it.* Most of the bars on the lower decks were crowded, noisy affairs, and didn't suit the mood in which Charlie found himself. Eventually, he found himself on Deck Seventeen, standing outside a quiet little jazz bar. On the stage, easily within sight of the entrance, a live band played. And Charlie had to admit they were pretty good; the perfect accompaniment to his mood. He walked in and took a seat at the bar.

"What can I get you, sir?"

"Something to help me unwind. Got any Jack?"

"Yes, sir. We have Gentleman Jack, Tennessee Honey, Old Number Seven, and Single Barrel Select."

Charlie was momentarily overwhelmed. He'd always thought Jack was Jack, but he'd be damned if he was going to admit that in front of some penguin-suited bartender. "Gentleman Jack."

"Excellent choice, sir. Rocks or neat?"

"On the rocks. Is there any other way?" Charlie cocked an eyebrow as if the bartender had asked a stupid question.

The bartender scooped a few ice cubes in a glass and poured two fingers of the amber liquid. Over the course of the next two hours, Charlie became extraordinarily well acquainted with his newfound friend and gentleman, Mr. Jack Daniels. So much that the bartender had cut him off, gently suggesting that he have a cup of coffee instead. Charlie started to argue with the man, but was interrupted by the lurching in his stomach as his body betrayed him. He staggered off the barstool, and barely made it to a bathroom stall before spewing the contents of his ninety dollar lobster, as well as a considerable volume of Gentleman Jack down the toilet.

Too exhausted and depressed to get back to his feet, Charlie laid his head on his arms and began to sob quietly.

CHAPTER 14
CHRIS TALLANT
FLIPPER'S FLIPPED

There was a small observation deck outside the bridge, and the crew had all been stepping outside to watch the glowing sheen as their duties permitted. Chris had managed to sneak a few minutes in, but being the newest of the bridge officers, he felt compelled to show more of his conscientious side. After all, the first officer's position next year was his to lose.

So he monitored the navigation systems, trying to show the captain what an asset he was to the ship, while everyone else milled back and forth at the windows and outside deck. Even Captain Eckles seemed more intent on the biological anomaly than the operation of the ship. He had spent the better part of an hour watching through the windows.

The young apprentice who had originally brought the glowing abnormality to their attention walked inside from the outer deck, pointing ahead. "More dolphins, sir!"

Eckles trained his binoculars where Perez indicated. "They're fighting. Just like the others."

Chris watched as the captain lowered his binoculars, and his expression turned from fascination to concern.

"It's like—"

But he was interrupted before he could complete the thought as Perez suddenly guffawed, then appeared shocked as he realized he had inadvertently interrupted the captain.

"Something funny, Mr. Perez?" Captain Eckles appeared irritated, but peered quizzically at the younger man.

"No, sir." But as soon as he said it, he began to laugh. There was something in the young man's laughter that made the hair on Chris' neck stand up. He watched as Perez took a deep, stuttering breath, apparently trying to get himself under control.

"Mr. Perez?" the captain repeated.

Finally, as if unable to contain himself any longer, Perez guffawed. It was an echoing, sonorous exhalation of a belly laugh that had the man bent over slapping his thigh at whatever it was he found so hilarious. The bridge crew wasn't large, just over a dozen people, and Perez's laughter drew the attention of everyone else in the room. Chris looked around to see if the others were as freaked out as he was, but to his alarm, most of them began to smile with the young man.

From his station at the back of the bridge, Chris watched as Perez stood and pointed to the cetaceans thrashing about in the ocean ahead. The man took a deep breath, struggling to keep himself together as he tried to explain what he found so amusing. "Flip... Flipper..." he laughed again, then turned to face Captain Eckles. "Flippers flipped out!"

There were other hoots of laughter as he shouted again, "Flipper's flipped, Flipper's flipped, Flipper's flipped!" Without warning, Perez swung his binoculars into the captain's face. Eckles went down with a cry of pain, Perez atop the bigger man slamming the lenses into the man's head over and over.

Pandemonium erupted throughout the bridge. Chris started forward to pull Perez from the captain's limp form, but as he moved forward, he saw other fights breaking out all around him. Instantly, he saw the thing that chilled his blood. Every attacker, all over the bridge, each and every one of them, was giggling insanely. And there were many more people laughing than not. In fact, only seconds after that furious initial attack, Chris was the only person standing who wasn't laughing.

One by one, the laughing faces turned his way. Chris thought briefly about trying to reason with them, but the expressions he saw showed little in the way of sanity, and he knew he had no chance. Chris Tallant lunged for the door, running for his life as the rest of the bridge crew chased after him with gleeful destruction in their eyes.

Heart pounding, Tallant raced down the stairs, taking them three at a time. The corridors were lined with passengers going to and fro about their normal frivolous cruise business, and he ran through them, more terrified than he had ever been in his entire life. At first, he managed to avoid most of them, weaving through the light foot traffic at breakneck speed, but the farther he went, the more dense the foot traffic was, and he quickly found himself pushing people out of his way in his panic. He bounced off a young woman in blue jeans and a white, sequined blouse.

"Hey!" she protested.

"Run!"

Irritation turned to confusion as she realized something was wrong. "What? Are you all right?"

There were shouts behind him. Some were shouts of indignation and anger. Some were shouts of laughter.

Over it all, he could barely make out the raucous chant of, "Flipper's flipped! Flipper's flipped!"

Tallant wanted to cry out when he heard more laughter in the crowd. Some of the passengers must have thought it was some kind of joke. Perhaps a spontaneous show of some sort... street theater on the high seas. Whatever the reason, he heard many of them begin laughing.

He grabbed the woman in front of him. "They're crazy! Run!"

Brows furrowed, she looked at him in confusion. "What?"

He shoved her ahead of him, trying to get her to understand the danger that was blossoming behind them.

"What the hell are you doing?"

"No time, lady. You have to run!"

"Get your hands off me!" She began slapping at his arm. "Help!"

All around them, people moved out of their way, and to his horror, Tallant saw many of them begin to smile.

He couldn't make her understand. Couldn't make her believe there was any danger in the few seconds they had. He grabbed her arm and tried to pull her along with him, but she struggled against him.

"Help!" she screamed. "Help!"

Others around them watched, no doubt confused at the sight of a uniformed crew hand trying to pull a young woman down the hallway. The woman clawed at his arm, raking her nails along the skin, and he jerked his hand back.

He couldn't save her. She didn't know she needed to be saved. None of the people around him understood. So he took the coward's way. He ran on.

As he shoved his way through the milling crowd, the volume of the voices behind him rose. There was more laughing… more screaming. And he couldn't be sure, but he thought he could hear the young woman's voice join those of the screamers.

As soon as he hit the deck below, he cut sharply around the first corner he came to and looked for something to hide behind. Nothing.

Ahead, he could see pockets of normalcy along the ship. But there were also pockets of laughter, and those areas turned immediately into rioting throngs of insanity. People—running, panicked, angry, fighting, laughing, people. People fighting for their lives. There were screams of anguish and anger, but above it all was the incessant sound of maniacal laughter. Whatever this was, it was spreading rapidly throughout the ship.

Chris shoved his way through the riot, pushing away everyone, laughing or not. All he wanted was to get away from everyone… to hide.

A scene caught his eye… a man swung a length of wood, something he had salvaged from some broken piece of furniture. He screamed his defiance at several laughing attackers, hitting them with his makeshift weapon, but all his screams did was draw more attention to himself, and as Chris looked on, the man fell beneath more of them.

Looking for a way through the churning crowd, Chris began to panic. He shoved people away, heading toward the elevator. The only thing he could think of was to get into an elevator and get to the lower decks. If he could get to the crew quarters, there was a chance that the insanity hadn't made it past the general populace. Even if that wasn't the case, there were fewer people below decks, so it should at least be easier to hide.

Chris dodged through the crowd until he got to the elevator. He hit the button and ducked behind a large decorative potted plant, waiting for his salvation to arrive. He didn't hear its arrival over the screams of the crowd, but he saw a laughing group of teens pour out of it. As they dove into the fray, Chris jumped up and ran into the newly emptied car. He pressed frantically at the button to close the doors even as he reached for his ID badge with his other hand.

After an agonizing wait, the doors slid shut. He shoved his ID card into the slot on the panel, and selected the restricted D2 button that would take him to the floor where his quarters were located.

He sobbed with relief when the elevator began to move.

CHAPTER 15
AUGUST GRAPPIN
THIS IS A FAMILY CRUISE

Gus eventually caught Cindy in a darkened corner of the pool, and he had to wonder if he'd really caught her, or if she had let him catch up in the place of her choosing. He had to admit that the dark corner was about as good a place as the waterpark offered. He smiled as he swam up to her. They were in the deep end of the pool now, and Cindy had to hold onto the wall.

He put his hands on either side of her. The exertion of the chase in the pool had taken more out of him than he had expected. He felt lightheaded, drunk. He grinned at her, suddenly leaning in and kissing her hard.

Cindy moaned into his mouth, grinding against his thigh. She reached down to the bulge in his swim trunks and gripped him hard. He laughed.

"That's enough, you two." The lifeguard scowled at them. "This is a family cruise."

Gus ignored him, laughing as he pawed at Cindy's bikini top.

"Hey! I said that's enough! You can't do that here." The man dropped into the water beside them and reached to pull Gus and Cindy apart.

Cindy laughed at him, and threw herself forward, suddenly clawing at the man's face. He screamed in pain as one of her nails tore into his eye. Gus thought this was hilarious. He grabbed the man's head and slammed it into the side of the pool. He and Cindy giggled as the blood from the man's scalp wound began to spread through the pool. They let go, and the lifeguard's unconscious form slipped facedown into the water.

Gus grabbed again at her breast, giggling as he did so. "I like tits!" he shouted at the top of his lungs. Several other kids around him laughed as well. There were also screams, but most of the kids were laughing and shouting. For a brief moment, Gus felt like there was something wrong. Wasn't there something…?

The thought left as quickly as it had come. After that, all that mattered was the laughter. Maintaining the high that accompanied the laughter. Finding anyone who wasn't laughing. Making them laugh. Or using them to make others laugh.

Cindy pulled herself out of the water, and Gus noticed with interest that one of the straps on her bikini was untied. It had come loose, leaving her left breast exposed, giving him the first glimpse he'd ever had of a real live breast. He guffawed at the sight and pulled himself up to follow her out of the water.

CHAPTER 16

Transcript of emergency radio call from cruise ship Bahama Queen to US Coast Guard Search and Rescue unit based out of Freeport, Texas
Sunday, November 20 – 10:53 AM

BAHAMA QUEEN —…an emergency. Please someone respond!

USCG DISPATCH — This is Coast Guard Search and Rescue out of Freeport. Please identify yourself.

BAHAMA QUEEN — There's some kind of outbreak here—

USCG DISPATCH — Sir? Who is this?

BAHAMA QUEEN — I'm sorry. (voice sobbing) They're killing everyone! Everybody's going crazy.

USCG DISPATCH — Sir? I need you to iden—

BAHAMA QUEEN — My name is Johannes Karlsson. I am third engineer on the Bahama Queen, and the rest of the crew— (more sobbing)

USCG DISPATCH — Mr. Karlsson? What's going on, sir? You said someone was killing people. Who is it?

BAHAMA QUEEN — They're laughing and… and… (undecipherable).

USCG DISPATCH — I'm sorry, Mr. Karlsson. What are they doing?

BAHAMA QUEEN — I was on watch when they started laughing… they began beating people with… with anything they could grab… (more sobbing)

USCG DISPATCH — Mr. Karlsson, is there someone else there I can speak with?

BAHAMA QUEEN — There's no one else down here. No one sane. I'm hiding in the Engineering Control Room. (pause) Oh, God. They're outside! They can see me through the glass!

(loud, repeating, booming noise in background)

BAHAMA QUEEN — Oh God. (mumbling)

USCG DISPATCH — Mr. Karlsson, what's going on? What is that noise?

BAHAMA QUEEN — They're beating the glass. It's breaking. It's not supposed to break. Oh God. They're going to get in.

USCG DISPATCH — Do you have someplace you can hide?

BAHAMA QUEEN — (undecipherable)

USCG DISPATCH — What was that?

BAHAMA QUEEN — They can see me. They'll know where — (sound of glass falling and breaking) Oh my God! They're coming in! (Many voices laughing in the background) Please don't let... (screaming)

[Transmission ends]

CHAPTER 17
CHRIS TALLANT
ELEVATOR HATCH

The elevator traveled only a few seconds before the lights went out, and the car jerked to a halt. The car went pitch dark for a short time before the red emergency light in the ceiling flickered to life.

"No!" Tallant jumped forward and hit the D2 button over and over, trying to will the car back into motion.

He was stuck. Worse, he was stuck, and terrified, in a motionless elevator, with nothing but the faint red illumination of the emergency lighting as he tried to come to grips with the fact that his dream job had turned into a nightmare only Dante himself could imagine, all in a matter of a few minutes. He hit the call button on the panel, but the line was silent. Did it tie into the power system somehow?

There was no way for him to know for sure, but it didn't seem likely. After all, a power failure was what had trapped him in the elevator to begin with. Who would design an emergency system that would quit working as soon as the elevator did? But he was having trouble thinking straight. His heart pounded in his chest, and his lungs heaved as he gasped for breath so rapidly that he sobbed as the oxygen entered his terrified body.

He told himself it was simple exertion, not panic, that made him tremble. And his eyes were just blurry from exhaustion, not tears. He forced himself to take more trembling breaths, sucking oxygen deeply into his lungs, and trying to calm his trembling nerves.

"Don't panic!" he told himself. "There's no one after you right now." He looked around the elevator once more. "And for the moment, at least, you're safe."

It was true. He assessed the elevator anew, seeing it now not as a trap, but rather as about as safe a place as he could hope for, considering the riot he had just escaped.

But that drew his attention back to the sounds on the other side of the steel doors. The agonized screams, and insane laughter, and the pounding in his chest rose again. His breathing increased again, and his hands started shaking once more. His hands shook as he tried to wrap his head around his situation, and it became too much. He sank to the floor of the elevator, squeezed his eyes closed, and covered his ears, trying in vain to block out the sights and sounds replaying in his mind. At some point, his mind simply refused to accept any more of the insanity. The faint shouts and screams faded into nightmares of bloody binoculars and laughing dolphins.

CHAPTER 18
CHARLES GRIFFE
STONE-COLD SOBER

Charlie must have passed out, because he woke up staring into the vomit-filled toilet. The stench of partially digested lobster thermidor and whiskey caused him to gag once more, but there was nothing left in his much-abused stomach to heave, and he had finally managed to raise his aching head off the porcelain rim of the commode.

The muzak piping in through the bathroom speakers ripped through his pounding head like a jackhammer, but he fought his way to his feet. He fumbled for a moment with the lock on the stall door, but finally persevered and staggered to the row of sinks. It only took him a few minutes to rinse his mouth and scrub the puke off his face. He stared into the mirror at the disheveled reflection, focusing for the moment of the splatters of partially digested lobster humidor on his collar. *You look like hell. And it's all her fault. She made a fool of you. You* let *her make a fool of you.*

"Damned bitch!" It was her who had whined about dinner, who had turned down a ninety-dollar fucking lobster dinner—her who had run off crying when he'd said he didn't want to go dancing. Hell, it was her who'd wanted to come on the fucking cruise, not him! And now here he was, drunk in a bathroom in the bar of a cruise ship he didn't want to be on in the first place. He slipped off his soiled dinner jacket, making sure to hide the pale stains as he draped it over his arm.

In a worse mood than he could remember being in, in a very long time, Charlie opened the door to go back out to the bar. He froze before the door was open more than a few inches, sure that there was something wrong with his eyes. Or perhaps he was just more plastered than he thought, because the sight before him surely couldn't be real.

There was no way that the bar had really turned into a slaughterhouse full of bodies while he was passed out in the bathroom. He blinked. Then blinked again, willing his eyes to shed this macabre illusion and show him the mundane reality he expected. But no, the carnage remained, and there were about a dozen teens laughing hysterically as they beat the few remaining victims with bottles evidently acquired from behind the bar. Charlie's eyes widened, and he was quite suddenly stone-cold sober as he realized that he was witnessing a mass murder in progress. As quickly as possible, he closed the door to where there was only enough of an opening to peer through.

In the far corner of the room, a young boy, about fifteen or sixteen years old, swung an electric guitar over and over, beating one of the jazz musicians to his knees before the neck of the guitar finally broke. Then he rammed the splintered neck into the man's abdomen and pointed, jumping up and down, laughing excitedly.

An old woman came staggering into sight from across the room. She was sobbing hysterically, clearly terrified as she glanced back over her shoulder into the room behind her. Charlie heard the laughter of her pursuers and he ducked back out of sight, pulling the restroom door almost closed. Peeking through a half-inch gap, he watched in horrified fascination as six or seven teens caught the woman and knocked her to her knees. An attractive young girl in a string bikini swung a bottle at the old woman's face, and Charlie's eyes locked for a second on the picture on the label, where a seventeenth-century privateer stood on one leg, the other foot raised and resting possessively on a barrel of rum.

His trance was broken as the bottle slammed into the woman's cheek, and she shrieked in anguish. It was a terrified wail, more horrifying than anything he had ever before heard, and Charlie choked back his own scream as something flew from her face. He envisioned a piece of her jaw ripped from her skull and thrown flying at him. It was harder still for him to remain silent when he saw that there appeared to be a full set of teeth lying on the carpet before him, until he realized it was a set of dentures. He looked back at the poor woman, and he saw momentary hope in her eyes as they locked onto his own. For a split second, Charlie's heart trip-hammered in his chest and he feared she was going to give away his hiding place. That fear, and the hope in her eyes, evaporated as the girl in the bikini did her best Mickey Mantle imitation, slamming the bottle of rum into the back of the woman's head so hard that the bottle broke, half of it flying into the face of one of her companions. They all seemed to think this was hilarious, even the boy whose face the glass had cut, and the old woman dropped like a marionette with severed strings. From where he cowered, Charlie could see her empty eyes staring sightlessly at the spreading pool of scarlet as her life's blood leaked from her mouth and nose onto the finely tiled floor.

Another shout drew his attention to where a different group of teens dragged the bartender onto the bar itself and began beating him with whatever they could get their hands on. Charlie froze, unsure of what to do. He was a big man, in relatively good condition. Should he run in to help the poor bartender? The teens were facing away from him. He could jump them from behind, probably knock several of them down. They were only kids, after all. Jump in, kick a little ass, and drag the man out of the crowd before they knew what happened.

Or you could run.

He looked around to consider his options. The restrooms were near the entrance to the lounge, and Charlie bolted without a second's hesitation. He was running toward the elevators when the lights went out. All the lights, all the music piping through the speaker system, all the elevators — all suddenly lifeless.

"Shit!" Charlie watched helplessly as the indicators on the elevators went dark. Dim red lights now lined the room and corridors, the only light available to in the otherwise pitch darkness. And he was suddenly aware of the sound of laughter as the doors to the bar opened behind him. The gang was coming. Whether they had seen him leave, or it was just a coincidence didn't matter. He had no doubt that he would meet the same fate as the people in the bar if they caught him. Next to the elevators, a door sported an emergency exit sign. Charlie slammed his shoulder into the door and raced down the stairwell.

CHAPTER 19
CHRIS TALLANT
GET YOUR ACT TOGETHER

Time passed. He wasn't sure how much, but it was long enough that his body ached when he stirred on the dark floor of the elevator car. The dim emergency light didn't cast enough light for him to see what time it was. And the act of trying made him wince at the long bloody streaks on his arm. He wondered if the girl who gave them to him was still alive.

The shouts and screams outside the elevator seemed to have diminished for the moment. He realized that while the elevator car might be a safe enough refuge for now, he couldn't continue to hide in it. And the idea that he was hiding at all, shamed him into action. "Come one, Tallant. Get your act together." He got to his feet and took a deep, shaking breath. "You're a freaking second mate on this ship, dammit! So get your sorry ass out of this elevator and get some help!"

Taking a deep breath, he stood and looked up at the ceiling. He knew there was a hatch up there. Everyone had seen them in movies. It only took a minute for him to manage the delicate balancing act of straddling the handholds on either side of the elevator car and moving the light covers out of the way. Once they were down, he spotted the hatch easily. He pushed.

The door lifted a fraction of an inch, then stopped.

"What the hell?"

He tried again. He heard a telltale rattle that told him the door was locked from the outside. "Son of a bitch!"

So much for the movies.

He thought about trying to pry open the elevator doors. Was it worth the risk? After all, he might open the doors into the middle of the riot.

"Do you have a choice?" he asked himself. "Besides, all you have to do is open it an inch or so to see what's outside."

He put his fingers into the tiny gap in the door and strained. They parted slowly, but part they did, and Tallant groaned as he saw nothing but painted steel before his straining face. He was trapped between floors. He let go and stepped back. "You're screwed, Tallant. Well and truly…"

The words trailed off as he looked down and saw the red of the emergency lighting reflected off a shiny surface near the bottom of the closing doors. "Yes!" He shoved his hands back into the gap and pulled again. Sure enough, there was the inside of an outer door. He had stopped at the top of a floor, and the shine of steel revealed his salvation.

Shoving the inner doors open, he placed his left foot against one side, dropped to the floor, and shoved his shoulder against the right so he could get to the outer doors at the bottom. It was a bit of a balancing act, holding one side open with his foot, the other with his shoulder, all while sitting on his right foot and prying the outer doors open with his hands. It was awkward as hell, but he managed to open them a few inches and dropped his head down to peek through the opening. There was barely enough room to see anything. In fact, he was afraid for a moment that there wasn't enough room for him to fit through the gap. The screaming and laughter was still there, but for the moment, it was far enough away that he risked pulling the door open farther, and as the gap widened, he was able to see that there was, indeed, enough room to slide through. It would be a close thing, but he figured there would be a few inches to spare.

Moving slowly, he pulled harder, putting enough of a gap in the outer door that he could see into the corridor outside. And still there was no outcry nearby.

Looks like the coast is clear, Tallant. Now move your ass.

Still holding the inner doors with foot and shoulder, he shoved the outer doors far enough apart that he could catch the left one with the same foot holding the inner door, and slid his right leg out through the gap. Wriggling clumsily, he slid onto his back, one leg holding the elevator doors, one leg hanging out into the corridor, and bracing the opposite doors with his shoulders, he shifted his hips farther into the corridor, and slipped his right arm through as well.

Walking his shoulders across the floor of the elevator, he tried to get his head through next. But no matter how he tried, there was no way to bend his neck enough to get his head out without letting go of the doors with his shoulder. He was going to have to let go with his left leg and slide out feet first as the door began to close, pivot his body, and push himself out, all while the door was closing.

And if he got hung up, he ran the risk of breaking his neck as his body dropped and his head stayed inside the elevator.

Laughter down the corridor reminded him that time was a luxury he couldn't afford. Taking several deep breaths, he exhaled to minimize his chest, swung his left leg out, pivoted on his butt and slid out, scraping his back on the edge of the elevator floor and banging his forehead on the door as he slipped free. He collapsed to the floor awkwardly and fiery agony on his back told him he'd likely lost some skin, but that concern was overridden as stomping footsteps and laughter sounded to his right.

Whipping his head that way, he saw three men running past. One of them saw him lying on the floor and stopped in his tracks. He pointed and screeched laughter, as if seeing Tallant on the floor was the funniest thing the man had ever seen. His companions must have noticed he had stopped because they joined him in a matter of seconds.

Ignoring the pain in his back, Chris scrambled to his feet and ran without thinking. The wide, brightly carpeted stairway was in front of him and he didn't hesitate. He took the stairs two at a time, only realizing after the second step that he was heading back upstairs instead of down. Laughter behind told him there was no going back.

Chris ran for his life.

CHAPTER 20
AUGUST GRAPPIN
FROLICKING

Gus followed the girl with the single free breast as she, and a growing number of other teens from the pool, cavorted through the ship. They joined with groups from the ship's game rooms, putt-putt course, and other entertainment venues on the upper decks. They danced and played, occasionally encountering someone who didn't understand.

When that happened, they would try to play with the newcomer, showing them how much fun they were having. Sometimes, the new person would join them in their frolicking, laughing and dancing alongside the family. Other times, a newcomer wouldn't understand, no matter how hard everyone played with them. But even then, there was entertainment.

CHAPTER 21
CHARLES GRIFFE
A STUDY IN RED

Charlie could hear his pursuers as they poured into the stairwell two floors above him, and his chest tightened with panic. He fumbled at the wall before him and felt a door handle. Yanking the door open, he lunged from the pitch darkness of the stairwell onto Deck Fifteen.

The sight of electric lights ahead befuddled him for a moment, and he paused, confused. Evidently the power outage didn't cover everything on the ship. Sounds of laughter and footsteps from the darkened stairwell above reminded him of the gravity of his situation. He wasn't terribly familiar with the layout of the ship, and was more than a little bit startled at the sight of a series of side-by-side outdoor basketball courts before him. The miniature, stadium-style lights illuminated the fight that was playing out on the nearest of the three courts. A group of about a dozen teens wielding golf clubs, milled about a smaller group of four men dressed in gym shorts. The teens shrieked in joy as they pounded the men.

One of the adults appeared to be holding his own. He had managed to avoid most of the gangsters, and held one of them before him as a shield. Charlie heard the hooting and laughter of his own pursuers, reminding him again that he had a decision to make. Should he chance the deck before him, or try to outrun them down the stairs for another deck or two?

The sound of shoes slapping hard on the stairwell behind him caused him to turn. One of the kids, an older teen with a silver ring in his lower lip, had leapt over the railing of the stairs and onto the landing behind him. Without thinking, Charlie stepped out onto the court and turned to shove the door closed behind him. He cursed as the pneumatic door closer kept him from shutting it quickly enough, and the kid behind him slammed his shoulder into it, knocking Charlie backwards. There was no way he was going to be able to keep them out. He would have to chance the basketball courts.

He stepped away just as Lip Ring grabbed his sleeve. Charlie heard someone screaming like a little girl, and he jerked his arm back in a panicked attempt to extricate himself from the kid's grip. The annoying screaming was distracting, and he wished whoever it was would just shut the hell up. Wide-eyed and terrified, he yanked his arm repeatedly, finally breaking free, and turned his head to the basketball court to see every head in the area turned to look at him.

Over it all, he heard his dad's voice, *"Stop screaming, you pussy!"*

The malicious laughter from the thugs increased as they looked his way, pointing at him and slapping their knees as Charlie realized that Dad was right. The incessant screeching was coming from his own burning throat. Embarrassed and furious, he managed to bring his shrieking down to a whimpering keen as he turned back to the leech that once again tugged at his sleeve. Anger and shame gave him strength, and he jerked his arm free, kicking at the kid with all his might. Lip Ring fell back, and Charlie ran into the chaos of the basketball court.

Laughing at him, a kid with what Charlie now realized was a putter from a miniature golf course, lunged toward him. At the same instant, the sounds of the rest of the gang from the bar on Deck Seventeen told Charlie that his pursuers were pouring in from the stairwell behind him. He decided there was no time to hesitate. He dropped his shoulder and drove into the kid before him just as the putter slammed down. Dropping as he did was all that saved him. He felt the shaft of the club hit his back, but the actual head missed him, and Charlie's tackle did its job.

The kid went sprawling, and Charlie barely slowed. His high school football days briefly entered his mind as he sprinted through the crowd. Two more club brandishing youths ran at him, and he feinted left, then right. Their putters tangled together as he left them in his wake.

"Over here!" To his left, Charlie saw the only remaining adult survivor of the brawl on the basketball court, frantically doing his best to fend off the advancing crowd around him. The man desperately spun to keep his captive between himself and the clubs of his attackers, but it was no use. Even as Charlie watched, the other kids continued to swing at him, uncaring of the fate of their companion. One putter smashed into the man's arm where he held his human shield in place, while another drove into the shield's skull, caving it in and spraying blood all over the man holding him.

All the while, they continued to laugh and cheer. But not so loud that he couldn't hear the man's desperate plea. "Help me!"

Charlie didn't pause. He darted away from the crowd… away from the man who fought hopelessly for his life. There was a gap in the crowd behind the attackers who were paying attention to the easy prey as he began to scream for his life, and Charlie drove through. He dodged and spun when he could, avoiding contact, doing his best to avoid drawing attention to himself. And whenever he couldn't see an opening, he made one, slamming his adult frame through the smaller teens like a wrecking ball.

He'd never been so effective in football, but his desperation and larger size gave him a clear advantage. *If only Coach could see me now.*

Finally, he cleared the mob and turned triumphantly. Self-congratulation gave way to disbelief, then desperation as he saw that his dash through them had attracted the attention of just about every teen who wasn't already directly engaged in pounding the life out of the screaming man who had finally collapsed to the polished floor. The number of his pursuers had now swelled well past the original crowd in the stairwell, adding the thugs from the court to their number, and Charlie now had nearly thirty maniacally laughing teens hot on his tail.

He looked ahead. The end of the outermost court was before him. A set of double doors in the wall beneath the Observation Deck was his only hope of escape. Panting a bit now, Charlie glanced behind at the raucous pursuit. Looking ahead again, he calculated he would barely make it to the door ahead of them.

God, please let the damned things be unlocked.

He reached the doors and pushed. For a panicked second, nothing happened. Then he realized they opened toward him. Bracing against the left door, he yanked the right one open and slipped inside. He pulled the door closed with all his weight, straining against the pneumatic door stop. He got it closed and looked out the inset glass window at the mob just as they hit the doors. Charlie braced his feet and pulled, desperately trying to keep them closed, but he knew there was no way he could win a tug of war against so many of them. Ironically, there were so many teens pushing forward that they impeded one another's progress as the ones in front tried to pull the doors open, even as the ones behind pushed forward.

He looked around frantically for something to slide through the door handles, and his eyes stopped on a mop in a rolling cart at the wall behind him. But with the constant pull from the other side of the door, the mop might as well have been on the moon. There was no way he would be able to let go of the door to reach it, without the jeering horde pouring in behind him.

Then he noticed the door on the other side of the room. It was a single door, not another double like the one he was currently frantically trying to keep closed. Straining to maintain status quo for the moment, he looked once again at that door. He looked at the mop. His feet began to slide, and he knew he was losing the battle to keep the doors closed. Taking one last straining breath, he yanked the doors inward once more and then let them go.

He turned, took the three steps to the mop, grabbed it by the handle, and used it to slide the rolling container of water toward the kids as they rushed into the room, tripping the first few to make it through. Hanging onto the mop, he sprinted to the door across the room, yanking it open, then slamming his weight into the door again. *Damn these pneumatics!* He got the door mostly closed and shoved the mop through the door handle, getting as much of it behind the doorframe as he could before he turned and ran the ten feet to the short stairway to the Observation Deck above the basketball courts.

The door behind him boomed once, twice, and on the third time, he heard the snap of the mop handle as the door came open. But he was already at the top of the stairs by then, and emerging onto the deck above. He looked around as he ran. There was no time to stop and analyze his options. He was figuring this out as he ran.

There was a short metal railing surrounding the raised observation area where people could watch the various activities on the deck below.

Beneath him and behind, were the basketball courts. The courts were surrounded by the outer hull of the ship to one side, the wall with the doors through which he had entered, the wall with the double doors through which he had just escaped, and a Plexiglas wall down the length of the courts opposite the ship's hull. On the other side of the Plexiglas was a huge drop-off, where several decks of cabin balconies overlooked the ship's central boardwalk below.

There was no escape that way. Charlie kept running. He didn't know where he was going other than away from the stairs behind. Teens began pouring from the stairwell like ants from a carelessly kicked anthill. And in the meantime, Charlie saw he was running out of Observation Deck ahead. There was a partition surrounding a small raised platform ahead, and lacking any choice, he drove himself toward it. Six short steps up, and he found himself standing on a precipice overlooking the boardwalk below. Frantic, he looked back and saw the kids less than twenty feet away.

He looked down and saw several nylon harnesses with the words Zip Line embossed on them. Beside them were half a dozen metal contraptions that looked like pulley rollers with handles to either side. The label on the wall identified them as trolleys. He looked up. Sure enough, a metal cable hung just over his head, and extended across the vast open emptiness above the boardwalk nine decks below.

The first of his pursuers reached the steps below him. He did a double-take at the boy's hair... shaved on the left, bright purple on the right as he giggled up at Charlie. There was obviously no time to strap on a safety harness. Charlie snatched one of the trolleys off the hook and slammed it into the kid's head, knocking him back into the growing mass of pursuers, slowing them for the split second Charlie needed to slide the open bottom of the trolley over the cable. Seating the trolley wheels firmly, he kicked up the safety bar between himself and the emptiness, and launched himself into the air.

Desperately, he clung to the handles of the trolley, hoping his grip would hold as he flew through the darkness into whatever awaited him at the other end of the zip line. Once again, Charlie screamed like a little girl.

He screamed as he shot away from his pursuers.

He screamed as he clung to the trolley for dear life, flying through the inky blackness over nine decks of emptiness, terrified that his grip would fail and he would plummet to his death.

And that thought made him more conscious than ever of his fragile grip on the handles of that trolley, and he felt every muscle in his hand reflexively tighten until he feared they would cramp and make him fall anyway. That made him scream even more.

He screamed until he slammed into the padded wall at the other end of the zip line, and fell unceremoniously on his ass just in front of the entrance to Deck Sixteen's starboard side mini-golf course. He looked back, wide-eyed and terrified at the abyss he had just crossed, suspended by little more than wishful thinking.

As he looked, movement to his left reminded him that his pursuit was still on the move. He scrambled to his feet, forcing his shaky legs to move him forward once more. He appeared to have gained at least fifty yards on his pursuers, and he saw the Plexiglas double doors that led to the snack bar just past the putting green before him. He sprinted for the doors, snatching up a couple of putters laying on the ground as he staggered past. Slipping through the doors, he pulled once more against the pneumatic door-closer until he was able to slide the putters through the handles. He finished just before the first of the kids reached the door.

Charlie was startled to recognize the kid. Purple Hair was evidently faster than his companions, and reached the door several seconds before the rest of the crowd. Charlie jumped back, as the wide-eyed, laughing thug yanked on the door, only to have it catch against the improvised door lock. He looked down at the putters, then grinned at Charlie through the clear plastic.

"Clever little piggy!" He cocked his head to the side, eyes wide and utterly lacking in any semblance of sanity. "Little pig, little pig, let me in!" Then he shoved his face into the Plexiglas, flattening his nose as he squealed like a frightened piglet. "Squee! Squeee!" The pig imitation mixed with laughter as the kid alternated between the two. He bled profusely from an open wound on his forehead, and Charlie realized it was from where he had hit the kid with the zip line trolley. As Charlie watched, the teen deliberately smeared a crimson trail across the

Plexiglas, violet locks sticking and mixing with the blood, spreading it even more across the door. Charlie was momentarily hypnotized, watching the macabre scene as Purple Hair giggled and oinked, all the while painting his obscene abstract art project——*A Study in Red, A Painting with Blood on a clear canvas, using human hair on plastic.*

He was startled out of his reverie as the other teens arrived in a seething mass, slamming into the doors and the clear plastic walls of the snack bar. They laughed, evidently finding the first kid's piggy imitation hilarious, and they began to do the same. Within seconds, dozens of teens were giggling and squealing at him, and the hair on the back of Charlie's neck raised at the eeriness of the sound. He backed away until he stumbled against a table and turned to look around.

He studied the snack bar, nearly sobbing with relief at the sight of the starboard side stairwell on the back wall. As he wove his way through the tables scattered across the floor, his pursuers began pounding on the wall, and Charlie briefly wondered how long he had before the Plexiglas broke. He looked back at them as he reached the stairwell. The doors still held, but it looked like the putters were beginning to bend. Charlie shouldered through the door and down the stairs once more.

WEDNESDAY
NOVEMBER 23

CHAPTER 22
LT. CDR FRANK JAMESON
JAYHAWK 6152

"Bahama Queen, this is Coast Guard Search and Rescue. Please respond. Over." Jameson waited several seconds more before trying again. "Bahama Queen, this is Jayhawk Rescue Helicopter Six One Five Two with Coast Guard Search and Rescue out of Freeport, Texas. Please respond. Over."

Again, there was no response. He peered out the portside window. It was dark outside and visibility from the helicopter was pretty limited, but the huge glowing slick of bioluminescent plankton gave him enough light to plainly see the outline of the cruise ship.

Jameson looked quizzically at his copilot. "Still no chopper?"

Visalli shook his head. "Nothing I can see. And no response to queries. It's like they never existed."

"Yeah, well transmissions from their landing say otherwise."

That shut Visalli up. They had all heard the recordings. Everything had sounded normal and Jayhawk 6075 had reported that everything on the Bahama Queen looked fine from the air. They said thermal imaging showed a lot of people on the decks, dancing and running about "like there was a big party." That had all changed when they landed on the helipad. The recording from that point sounded frantic, and Luke Murphy, a long-time friend, had shouted into the radio that they were being swarmed by people rushing onto the pad. Gunfire sounded in the background before the recording ended.

That was less than three hours ago, and Jayhawk 6152 had been scrambled within minutes. Jameson was determined to find out what had happened to Luke. He turned to his co-pilot. "Anything on thermal?"

"Affirmative. The decks are crawling with people."

In his helmet, Jameson heard Collins mutter from behind, "Just like Six Oh Seven Five reported."

Jameson started to snap at Collins, but held his tongue. They were all jumpy. There was something off about this rescue, even beyond the fact that 6075 seemed to have dropped off the face of the planet. Everything about this one felt wrong.

He flew over the helipad as Marsha McNeese lit it up with the spotlight.

"Holy shit," she exclaimed, forgetting for the moment that they were being recorded back at base.

"Is there a problem, Six One Five Two?" The voice came over their headsets, and McNeese grimaced at the reminder that they needed to remain professional.

Jameson glanced back at her and answered for them all. "Negative, Freeport. However, there appear to be several bodies on the helipad below us. Looks like confirmation that Six Oh Seven Five was forced to open fire."

"Understood. Are you going to be able to land?"

Jameson looked around below. He couldn't see anyone moving on the pad. "McNeese, give me some light farther out on the decks."

She did, and he could see a surge of people running toward them.

"I can make it if I go right now. I need clearance now if I'm going to do this."

"Roger, Six One Five Two." There was a pause of about two seconds. "You are cleared to land. You are cleared for weapons hot. Only fire if threatened." Jameson heard Collins open the weapons locker behind him as he and McNeese readied for landing.

Jameson kicked the rudder and dropped the Jayhawk toward the helipad. "Roger that, Freeport. Six One Five Two landing now."

There was a clearing in the bodies toward the back of the helipad, and Jameson assumed it was where 6075 had landed. He dropped as quickly as he safely could, touching down as the leaders of the mob swelled onto the landing pad. Jameson yelled into his comm. "Collins, McNeese, go!"

He glanced back as the two crewmen slid the starboard door open and jumped onto the pad, openly brandishing their weapons. Jameson switched control of the spotlight and hoist camera to his console so he could see what was going on.

On his screen, he watched McNeese step toward the crowd, while Collins dropped to a knee, covering her from behind.

But the surge of bodies washing onto the landing pad made Jameson curse. There were too many to handle if things went south on her. "This looks bad. Visalli, back them up on the door gun."

His copilot unbuckled and ran back to the open doorway even as Marsha shouted at the crowd. Jameson heard every word in his headset as she spoke calmly at the rushing crowd. "Hold it right there, folks. We're here in answer to a distress call we received. We need to see…"

But the crowd *didn't* hold it. They didn't even pause. They rushed forward, unphased by her words, or the threat of her weapons, and the situation went south before she ever had a chance.

"Commander?" Jameson heard the confusion in her voice as she called back to him.

He looked at the screen showing the wave of people as they rushed at her. The lead runners were close enough for him to get a good look at their faces, even through the camera lens. They were laughing hysterically as they rushed forward, and his heart skipped as he saw that a few of them had blood spattered on their faces and clothing. "Protect yourself, McNeese! Open fire!"

She raised her M16, but still she hesitated. Jameson understood her reluctance. These were civilians, after all.

"McNeese!" He sought to ease her conscience. "Open fire, Lieutenant, that's an order!"

Through his helmet, he heard her beg one last time. "Wait," she implored. When she no longer had any choice, she opened fire. "God help me."

But He didn't. Jameson watched on the screen as the first civilian hit her in a tackle even as she shot him. Off balance, she fell, but threw the man off and scrambled to get back up. She made it back to one knee when another man hit her. She looked up as he hit her, and Jameson saw her thumb her rifle to full auto and pull the trigger. A storm of bullets dropped several of the mob at her feet.

"Collins!" she yelled into the comm. Jameson felt a second of pride in his crewmate as he heard her voice. Her fear was gone for the moment, and she was all business. "There's too many. They're not—" One of the men in front swung something, and her helmet rang with the impact. Still, she refused to go down. Jameson watched as she continued to fire short bursts, fighting back to her feet, and for the next few seconds, she managed to push back the tide.

Then her rifle went silent, and Jameson realized she had emptied her magazine.

He watched in horror as she turned, trying to run back to the Jayhawk. She only made it a few steps before she was tackled again, and disappeared beneath the leading edge of the crowd.

They all froze for a second as McNeese screamed into their comms, "Collins! Oh shit, they're—" Another scream, guttural and incoherent, told them she was still alive, and for a second, the thought made Jameson wonder if that was necessarily a good thing.

Through the eye of the hoist camera, he saw one of the men in the crowd swinging something at the curled up body on the deck, and he realized that the man was beating McNeese with her own rifle.

Collins was yelling into his comlink. "They're killing her!" He fired into the crowd. "They're ripping her to pieces!"

"What the hell?" Visalli's voice came over the comm.

Jameson called back to him, "Visalli, how bad is it?"

"I can't see her, and there's a damned mob coming at us."

Watching as the mob surged up the gangway and onto the pad, Jameson immediately knew what had happened to Luke and the crew of 6075. In his mind's eye, he saw the crowd rushing onto the helipad. There were hundreds of them. More than enough to shove a helicopter off the pad and into the ocean below.

Jameson called out, "Collins, can you get to her?"

"Working on it, Commander."

In their helmets, McNeese's cries grew weaker, even as Collins ran forward, new magazine in his M16. In less than five seconds, he sent thirty rounds into thirty bodies, and his rifle ran dry again. He fed it again, pausing only for the few seconds it took to slam another magazine into place before he opened up. He moved forward slowly, steadily, laying waste to the front line of the crowd.

From the vantage of the hoist camera, Jameson could see over their heads to the endless mass shoving forward from the deck below. He saw Collins pause again, backing up a few steps as he grabbed for another magazine. It was a heroic effort, but Jameson could see that there was simply no way Collins could possibly have enough ammunition to stop them all. For every person he dropped, three more surged forward. At the rate things were escalating, Jameson estimated they had about twenty seconds before the crowd overran Collins.

"Visalli, what's the holdup?"

"Feed belt's misaligned. Give me a second!"

"Collins doesn't have a second."

He looked again at the screen and made a decision. "Collins, fall back. Get back on board!"

"Negative, Commander." Collins came into view through the starboard side front window, firing as he laid down suppression fire. "McNeese is still out there!" Collins yelled.

Heart pounding, he struggled to maintain some semblance of calm as he called back to base. "Freeport Base, this is Jayhawk Six One Five Two declaring an emergency. We are in danger of being overrun. Civilians on board are…" he hesitated. "They're laughing while they rush us. No hesitation. It's like they don't care whether or not they get shot."

He'd barely finished that short report to base, before he turned. "Come on, Visalli! You're the only one with the angle to do her any good."

Visalli cursed, and slammed the feed belt into place. As Jameson watched, the man's expression changed from frustrated concentration to fierce determination. He yelled out, "Collins, hit the deck!"

At Visalli's yell, Collins threw himself down, and the big door gun whirred into action. Within seconds, nothing on the helipad moved. There was a pile of bodies at the gangway leading from the deck below, and it seemed to be blocking access to the helipad… for the moment, at least.

Jameson yelled orders. "Collins, find McNeese and get back here. Visalli, keep that hole plugged!"

A new voice came over their headsets. "Lieutenant Commander Jameson, this is Captain Hopkins of Naval Intelligence. I need you to bring back one of the civilians from that ship."

Jameson blinked. "All due respect, Captain, but I don't know you, I'm not in the Navy, and I don't take orders from you. Please clear this channel for official Coast Guard business." Damned squid. He might be a captain, but he had no idea what was going on out here.

"Commander Jameson, this is Under Secretary Michael O'Connor of Homeland Security. You are to comply with Captain Hopkins' request."

Before he could reply, yet a third voice came through his helmet. It was his commanding officer, head of the Search and Rescue base in Freeport. "Lieutenant Commander, this is Captain Thomas. Sorry, Jameson. This comes from the top. You have to get one or more of the civilians back here. They think terrorism might be—"

"Captain Thomas, that's enough."

Jameson was pissed enough that some squid was trying to give them orders, but now some Homeland bureaucrat was backing him. And making everything all cloak and dagger, to boot? What the hell was going on? Why were all these heavy hitters monitoring his operation?

"Jameson?" Captain Thomas said. "Do you copy?"

Jameson growled. "I copy." He looked at the hoist cam and saw Collins lifting McNeese into a fireman's carry. Even as he watched, the bodies plugging the gangway onto the helipad fell forward as they were shoved out of the way from behind.

"Visalli, I said keep that damn hole plugged."

The door gun thundered again and more bodies slumped over the pile.

"Lieutenant Commander Jameson, I need you to confirm your orders."

Pissed off beyond anything he had ever felt before, Jameson snapped into his comm, "I'll get you your damned specimens. Now clear the fucking channel! This is a combat situation, and I don't need you pinheads squelching my communications!"

"Commander! You will—"

"Piss off or I'll take off from here the second my man gets back on board and consequences be damned! Do you read me?"

There was a slight shift to the Jayhawk and Collins called out. "I'm aboard, Commander."

"How is she?" Jameson turned to look and saw Collins shake his head. He looked at the limp body, and was sickened at the ravaged mess the mob had left. Jameson gritted his teeth as he saw that she was missing an eye, and her throat had been ripped out.

"Damn it!" He took a deep breath. "Visalli, start letting them through."

"You sure?"

"I'm sure. Keep 'em thinned out, but we need to get some guinea pigs for the brass."

He watched his screen as the pile of bodies were shoved aside again, and the horde once more flooded onto the helipad.

Jameson kicked the rotor speed up. The rotor wash of the Jayhawk could produce winds approaching hurricane strength, and he intended to use that to help keep most of the approaching mob back.

"Let one or two of them through. Knock 'em out when they get on board."

"Roger that." Visalli's tone left no doubt that he didn't like the orders any more than Jameson did, but he was a professional. Collins didn't answer.

Jameson increased rotor speed up to the point that the Jayhawk was barely over the helipad. He increased and decreased the RPMs, making the helicopter bounce up and down over the pad, and incidentally increasing and decreasing the wind gusts blasting through the mob. Many of them lost their footing, tripping others as they went down. Approximately a dozen managed to keep moving forward.

Jameson heard Collins snarl. "Come on, you laughing bastards. Let's get this over with." The sound of machinegun fire diminished as fewer laughing civilians were able to move toward them. He kept his eyes on the crowd, bouncing the Jayhawk to push more rotor wash at them to keep most of them at bay.

"Let that lead one through." Jameson heard Visalli yell at Collins. "Commander, keep us steady for a minute."

Jameson dropped back onto the helipad and lowered the RPMs on the rotor. But he kept an eye on the crowd. More of them managed to climb back to their feet, bracing themselves against the reduced wind speed. He heard grunts from the cargo area and glanced back just as Collins slammed the butt of his M16 into the head of a man reaching toward him. "That's for McNeese, you son of a bitch." The man shook his head and reached again. Collins hit him two more times before the man dropped. Collins and Visalli dragged the man into the Jayhawk, and Visalli began tying the man's hands behind his back with a length of nylon rope he had prepared.

Jameson looked back to the mob pouring back onto the helipad. "Any others close?"

But three more men had already leapt into the hold while Collins and Visalli worked on the first one.

"Shit!" Collins jumped to his feet. "Commander, get us in the air!"

Jameson didn't need to be told twice, and he spun the rotors up and lifted off the pad. The Jayhawk lurched to starboard, and he knew some of the mob had jumped onto the struts. "We got hitchhikers on the starboard strut!" he yelled, but Collins and Visalli were grunting and shouting as they fought the three boarders. Jameson drew his sidearm and made sure he had a round chambered. He didn't want to fire in the confines of the helicopter, but the cargo door was still open, and he suspected there would be more boarders in a few seconds.

To make matters worse, he had those assholes back on the mainland shouting questions at him. He ignored them for the moment, and concentrated on the doorway. Sure enough, a hand reached up to the floor of the cargo hold, and another laughing face appeared as a man pulled himself into aircraft. Jameson made sure he had a clear shot and pulled the trigger. There was a slight lurch as the Jayhawk lost a few hundred pounds of extra weight. If his shot went through the man, it went through the open door and into the sea.

Meanwhile, Collins and Visalli struggled to bring the other three under control. Visalli kicked one of them back, and Jameson saw the man pass in front of the open door. His shot clear, he fired again, and the man toppled out the door.

His men were able to get the last two under control after that, and within minutes, there were three unconscious men tied up on the cargo deck of the Jayhawk.

He called back to them, "Everyone all right?"

Visalli moved to get the med kit. "Yeah. We're all right. I'm going to sedate these mother fuckers, though."

"Lieutenant Commander! Report!"

Jameson recognized the voice in his helmet as that of the Naval Intelligence officer. *Hopkins, wasn't it? Yeah, that was it... Captain Hopkins.* He bit back the retort he wanted to give the man, swallowed, and took a deep breath. "Jayhawk Six One Five Two is air born with three..." He hesitated. What were they? Hostiles? Subjects? "...civilians. They are currently unconscious, restrained, and my medic is working on sedating them."

"That's excellent work, Lieuten—"

Jameson continued, interrupting the Captain. "We lost McNeese. They just ran over her and beat her to death... tore her damned throat out! So you want to tell us what the hell is going on here?"

There was silence on the line for a moment. Finally, Hopkins came back. "Sorry, son. It's classified."

"Classified my ass! Those people back there are fucking insane! They didn't show any hesitation at running straight at my crew even when they were being shot at. They didn't even slow down! Hell, the three we have restrained on board are still laughing. They're unconscious, but still laughing! No one acts like that!" Jameson realized he was yelling, despite his earlier determination to remain professional.

"Lieutenant Commander Jameson, control yourself! You are ordered to take those civilians directly to Houston Methodist Hospital. There will be a special detail awaiting your arrival at the helipad there. You will make best speed and get them there safely. Do I make myself clear?"

Jameson swallowed back his anger and took another deep breath. He would maintain his professionalism. "Yes, sir," he growled. "Crystal clear." He plugged the new destination into the NAVSAT. "ETA is two hours, twelve minutes. Jayhawk 6152 out."

CHAPTER 23

AUGUST GRAPPIN
WONDERFUL AND TERRIBLE PLEASURE/PAIN

Laughter. Pain. Disorientation.

All Gus's feelings were jumbled. No. Not jumbled. They were fused. He had realized it on some primal level when the man had smashed him in the face with the metal thing at the wire thing. What was it called? He used to know…

Zip… something. It was right on the tip of his tongue. He shook his head. It didn't matter. All that mattered was the wonderful and terrible pleasure/pain feelings, and the laughter.

And the feeling that the man with the metal zip thing had given him was exquisite. He had found plenty of other people here on the big boat, and they had given him some small satisfaction as he and his new friends had played with them. But none had hurt him like the big man had. The big man reminded him of his father. The love/hate feelings were so much alike.

He needed to find the man again. Find him and thank him properly.

CHAPTER 24
CHARLES GRIFFE
CLOWNS TO THE LEFT OF ME

"Pick the cruise, Charlie." Charlie mimicked Felicia's words under his breath. "We've never been on a cruise before." He trotted down the shadowy, smoke-filled corridors of the Bahama Queen. "Shoulda taken the damn movie tickets."

He glanced at his watch. *No wonder I'm so damned tired.* For most of eighteen hours now, he had played this deadly game of hide and seek with various groups of homicidal teenagers. He'd seen dozens of bodies and dodged several groups of laughing gang bangers. He didn't know if they were all from the same gang or not. None of them seemed to be wearing any colors. Still, he was certain that was what must have happened. Rival gangs on a cruise liner had somehow met and begun terrorizing the rest of the ship. It was the only thing that made any sense.

He briefly wondered how Felicia was doing, and imagined her cowering in their cabin, terrified at the chaos in the corridors. He had to admit, he was a little conflicted at the thought. On the one hand, he felt a certain smug satisfaction at the thought. But another part of him realized it was a real dick feeling... like something his dad would say.

It'll do her good to go through something like this on her own for a little while. Show her what it's like to have to face the world without you to take care of her.

"Shut up, Dad," he muttered. "You're just proving my point." For the moment, he had more important things to worry about than his dad's warped version of how the world should be run—like how he was going to stay alive. The kids hooted and shouted their laughter as they patrolled the corridors, and Charlie didn't think he was going to make it down to his and Felicia's cabin on Deck Seven. Not today, anyway. He was exhausted, terrified, and he'd been playing cat and mouse with the gang bangers all day. Sooner or later, his luck was bound to run out.

He ducked behind a display case as another group of raucous teens darted across the intersection ahead, banging loudly on the walls as they ran. Once they passed, he eased forward, peeking carefully around the corner. He watched them pass by the dim light of the rising sun filtering through a few windows along the way. Those patches of sunlight and the red glow of scattered emergency lights were the only light available in the inner corridors of the ship. He'd been running and hiding all night, and it was just too dangerous to stay in the hallways. He needed to find someplace to hide and rest.

He watched as the teens rounded a corner, oblivious to his presence. Once they were out of sight, he jogged down the corridor in the opposite direction.

The upper decks were smaller, and had been overrun with teens who attacked other passengers without hesitation. Throughout the night, he'd seen too many fights where older, terrified adults had been swarmed and beaten to death by mobs of teenagers. Luckily for him, those fights had also presented opportunities for him to slip out of sight. On each deck he had emerged from the stairwell, trying to slip down the corridor to find some sort of authority figure. Each time, it had taken only a few minutes to find that the gang bangers had gotten there before him and he'd been forced to retreat back to the stairs.

He'd finally made it down to Deck Twelve. Twelve was the one of the highest living quarter decks, filled with more than three hundred passenger cabins. It was several times larger than the upper decks had been, so he had expected to easily find someone to help him. Unfortunately, it was nearly as bad as those upper decks had been. As soon as he emerged from the dark stairwell, he had heard the screams and knew he was screwed. But with laughter on the stairs above him, he'd had little choice. He had to find someplace to hide.

There was a single bar on the deck, *The Grotto*. Charlie huddled out of sight behind the counter, trying his best to block out the sounds of screaming and rioting that echoed throughout the ship.

***

A nearby scream awoke him, and he was startled to realize he had managed to fall asleep. He rubbed the sand out of his eyes and pressed the button on his watch. *Eight fifteen.* With an exhausted sigh, he left the scant safety of his hideaway, creeping through the morning shadows until he finally made his way back to the emergency stairwell. It was dark as hell in there, but it also seemed to be the best way to travel without being seen.

Carefully feeling his way down the darkened stairs again, Charlie only made it down a single floor before he heard the door above him slam open, the hooting and laughter of several voices was accompanied by the flickering light of a torch of some kind suddenly flooding the stairwell. Had someone seen him enter?

That don't really matter, does it? Time to get the hell out.

Charlie was tired of his dad being right so much of the time. But now wasn't the time or place to argue the point. He yanked open the door and entered the shadowed hallways of Deck Eleven.

By the dim light, he could make out silhouetted forms running up and down the hallway, though details were impossible to discern. But over it all, the incessant laughter played, an increasingly horrifying soundtrack to the horror movie that this cruise had become. There wasn't time to think about it. He had chaos all around, but almost certain death pursued from the stairs behind him. He ran to the hallway on his left and tried a cabin door. *Locked.* He trotted farther down the corridor, intent on putting as much distance between himself and whoever emerged from the stairwell behind him.

A few moments later, he slowed and looked back. The emergency stairwell was lost in the blackness behind him. *Good enough. If I can't see them, they can't see me either.* He slowed to a safer trot, concentrating on sticking to the shadows. The sounds of screaming and laughter echoed eerily throughout the ship, and all Charlie could think of was getting out of sight. He had to find a place to hide. But again, each cabin door he tried was locked from within. He moved down the corridor and slowed as he noted a flickering light ahead on the right. Shouting from the same direction caused him to slow even more until he was almost crawling as he came to the railing that overlooked the open air park four levels below. He eased forward, looking upwards at where he had ridden the zip line over the park several hours before. And though the line was hidden in the darkness, he nevertheless shuddered at the memory.

He looked down at the source of the shouting and lights, and after a few seconds confusion, he shook his head at the sight. There must have been hundreds of them, teens with liquor bottles and clubs dancing and shouting around several large fires. Fires. They had piled chairs, and desks, and apparently just about anything else that they could burn, and the crazy, stoned little shits were actually stupid enough to start fires on a ship! Like it was some sort of insane camping trip! He started to step back into the shadows when outraged shouting below drew his attention back to the macabre party. As he watched, a group dragged a thrashing man into view. He was bruised and bleeding from an open wound on his forehead, but that didn't seem to slow his struggles.

"Let me go, you little shit!" he shouted above the jeering of the crowd. "Let me go or I swear to God, I'll kick your fucking little ass." Charlie had always found threats like that amusing. Dad had taught him that they were the mark of a weak man. If he had been in any position to kick anyone's ass, he wouldn't have been trussed up like a Thanksgiving turkey in the first place. That didn't seem to have occurred to him, though, as he continued his rant. "I'll rip your little throats out and skull fu—" Without hesitation, the teens tossed him on one of the fires. They tittered wildly while he thrashed about in the flames, screeching as his skin began to blister and char, finally rolling out of it and making it to his feet. Screaming in agony, the man ran down the corridor, his burning clothes lighting a path down the darkened halls. Several drunken teens chased after him, and they all ran out of Charlie's angle of vision. They must have caught the man quickly, because his shrieks increased in volume and frequency for a few seconds before they suddenly came to an abrupt end.

Charlie quickly dropped back out of sight, wide-eyed and breathing heavily from what he had seen. The brutality in the jazz bar had been bad enough, and he'd had no illusions about the bodies lying all over the corridors. But until now, he'd been treating this whole nightmare like some sort of high-stakes game. Granted, the stakes were life and death, but he had never really doubted that he would win. After all, he was smarter than any teenaged gang banger.

But seeing what they had done to that man on the promenade below had sent a shock through him. To blithely throw someone into a fire like that. Even worse, to laugh while they did it? That was a whole new level of bat-shit crazy.

It brought back the memories of a night twenty-three years ago.

And it terrified him.

That's 'cause of the way it all happened, though, ain't it? You ain't exactly the innocent little bystander, are you?

No, he wasn't. He remembered with crystal clarity how his mother had chased him through the house, waving her bottle as she staggered after him. How even at the age of nine, he had learned to dodge and toss things in her path. How she had tripped, shattered glass and booze spilling across the tile floor in the kitchen. And the candles.

He hadn't known what they would do. Mom kept a plate of scented candles burning on the kitchen counter, and Charlie had simply seen it as another object to throw in her path. But suddenly, she was screaming, thrashing about on the floor. Her nightgown and hair turning into a raging torch, her skin blistering, charring... just as the man on the boardwalk below had done.

And nine-year-old Charlie had run into the pantry, hiding, covering his ears to the sounds of his mother's tortured screams... trying to block them out with screams of his own. And oddly enough, he recalled kneeling beside potatoes... that the potatoes were just beginning to rot, filling the pantry with their own cloying stench of decay. But he had filled his lungs with their stink willingly, because even that was better than the acrid scent of his mother's burning hair.

The rest of the night was nothing more than flashes for him. He recalled Dad yelling. Screaming. Crying. Pulling Charlie from the pantry and into the yard as the house burned.

The firetrucks and police cars.

The funeral home.

The neighbors had sympathized, making all the noises about how she'd always seemed so nice. But Charlie had seen the look in her eyes as she'd chased him. It wasn't *nice* that he'd seen in those eyes. It was insanity. And when she had died in that fire, he hadn't mourned like his father. He'd kept it inside, but he was relieved. And that relief had bred a mixture of guilt and anger that had put him at odds with his father and had haunted their relationship until the bitter old man had died four years ago.

It had taken years of medication and sessions with various therapists to get past it, but Charlie had eventually come to understood that death itself wasn't so much the thing to be feared. No, it was the *how* of death. He'd thought about it a lot—far too much to be healthy, especially for a young boy, and for many years, Charlie's soul had been tortured with the sounds of screaming.

And to this day, the smell of rotten potatoes made him puke.

Really? You kill your mother, and all you can remember is how the damned potatoes smelled?

Dad's voice brought him back to the here and now. "Shut up, Dad!" Charlie gripped his aching head, wishing his father would leave him alone. He looked around frantically. Had he said that out loud? Did anyone hear him?

For the moment, at least, he appeared to be safe. But the smell of burned flesh brought so many memories back. Memories he'd managed to repress for so long. Memories of pain and anguish.

And of guilt.

But the sight of those kids throwing that man into the fire had brought it all into focus for him. *That will* not *happen to me.* His sudden conviction filled him with purpose. No more taking chances. No more recklessness. All things eventually came to an end. This gang war or terrorism, or whatever was going on was no exception. It, too, would come to an end. All Charlie had to do was outlast it. It was time to find someplace to hide.

But where?

Get into a cabin, you stupid little shit.

It was true, the corridor was lined with cabin doors, but like hotel room doors, they were designed to close and lock automatically. Having tried several of them on this macabre journey through the ship, he could vouch for how well that design functioned. He had yet to find a single cabin door opened or unlocked.

"In case you haven't noticed, I've been trying that, old man," he muttered.

Tittering from the darkness in the corridor behind him caused him to jerk to his feet. It wasn't terribly close, but it was the first indication he'd had that he wasn't alone in the area. He had to move.

Ducking low in the darkness, he crept up the corridor, occasionally stepping over small groups of corpses, constantly aware of the low laughter in the corridor behind him. As he left the noisy bonfire party behind, he kept trying the handles of cabin doors, each time with no more luck than the time before. It was difficult to judge in the darkness, but he figured he had made it more than halfway to the fore of the ship when he heard more laughter ahead. He froze. The lines to an old song came unbidden to his mind;

Clowns to the left of me,

jokers to the right...

Turning back the way he had come, Charlie listened carefully for movement in the darkness, but the pounding of his heart made it impossible to concentrate. He knew there was someone behind him. He just didn't know how far back they were. He was fairly certain they were farther away than the new threat ahead of him, though. He started moving back aft.

Within a couple of minutes, he could hear the sounds of the laughter to the fore of the ship fading, but the group aft was getting closer. A deafening bang sounded from farther down the hallway, followed by the sound of something large breaking into smaller pieces. Desperately, Charlie tried another door, then another. All of them were locked. Sticking to the shadows, he moved through the dark corridor away from the noise, trying to balance the distance between the laughter before and behind. With each passing moment, both sets drew closer.

Looks like your luck's run out, boy.

"Fuck you, old man." Charlie frantically tried each door he passed, and just as he began to fear his dad might be right, he stumbled over his salvation. A leg stuck out from a cabin door, holding it ajar. It was hardly the first body he'd come across, but he hesitated a second at the smell of this one. The stench of urine and feces in the hallway indicated that the interior of the cabin was likely to be much worse, and he didn't know if he could stand prolonged proximity to such a disgusting odor. Then laughter sounded from the darkness behind him, and Charlie decided there were worse things than a foul-smelling cabin. He pushed again at the cabin door, struggling to shove the dead weight of the body out of the way.

He strained mightily against a door that didn't want to budge, the body evidently wedged against something inside.

Come on, you little wuss. Put your back into it.

He put his hands to his ears and shouted at the voice at the top of his lungs. "Shut the hell up!" The area all around him was suddenly silent for a brief second, and his eyes widened as he realized how his shout echoed in the corridor. Suddenly, the laughter resumed, sounding almost frenzied now as it drew rapidly nearer.

"Damn you, Dad. Now see what you did?"

Still blaming me for your fuck ups, huh? The voice dripped sarcasm.

Stealth was no longer an option, and Charlie threw his weight into the door over and over again, moving the body inch by inch. He made enough headway that he could get his head through the door now, and looked forward into the darkness. The cabin was nearly pitch black, and he saw nothing. But he could hear rapidly approaching laughter from outside. Behind him, he heard a shriek of hooting laughter and jerked his head back out. Less than fifty feet away, three dark shapes ran drunkenly toward him. With terror, Charlie recognized the one in the lead. The kid's purple hair identified him, and it was obvious that they had seen him.

Charlie screamed and slammed into the door again and again until he suddenly felt something give and he stumbled inside. He turned to close the door and panicked when it wouldn't shut. He slammed it twice, and each time it stopped before hitting the door jamb. The laughter was almost on him when he looked down and noticed the dead man's shoe blocking the door. He kicked it away and shoved the door closed, throwing the thumb latch for the privacy lock just as it shook with the impact of something, or someone, slamming into it. He jumped back, heart pounding, steeling himself for another blow. For a second nothing happened, and he leaned in, listening. Then he heard a scratchy, high-pitched voice. "Little pig, little pig, let me in." Purple Hair seemed to find himself amusing because he started laughing again.

It sent a shiver over Charlie's skin. In the back of his mind, Charlie had thought that anyone capable of committing such atrocities as he had seen had to be insane. Something about that voice eliminated any doubt.

Boom!

Charlie yelped and jumped back as the door shook again.

"Little pig, little pig, let me in!" The door began to shake within its frame as Purple Hair, and the others with him, started pounding emphatically, yanking on the handle to get it open, all the while laughing merrily as if it were all a huge joke.

Suddenly, the rattling stopped, and for some reason Charlie found the silence in the cabin more unsettling than the rattling. What are they up to now? He didn't know if it was him or his father wondering, and he didn't have much time to think about it.

BOOM.

Charlie nearly screamed as the door served as a drum head to something or someone slamming into it. He jumped to his feet and started to stumble across the room when his feet tangled in something unseen in the near-darkness. He tumbled to the floor, landing in a wet patch of carpet that smelled of urine.

BOOM.

He jumped again, pushed himself to hands and knees, and gagged when his hand slipped in something that felt like raw hamburger with a thin coating of slime.

BOOM.

Sobbing now, Charlie carefully drew himself to his feet. *Don't try to hurry it. Take your time. Careful and slow is faster than falling every few feet when you trip your clumsy ass over something in the dark.* Charlie was too terrified to argue at this point.

BOOM.

The darkness in the cabin was almost tangible, and he felt slowly forward with his feet. *Where am I? Portside? Starboard? Is this an interior cabin, or ocean view?* His foot brushed against something on the floor, and he was fairly certain it was another body, but was afraid to bend over to confirm it. Charlie had a mental image of one of those teenagers laying a trap, waiting for him to come within reach so he could reach up and lock his fingers around Charlie's throat.

BOOM.

He thought he heard a slight splintering and kept moving, arms outstretched, feeling inch by inch with hands and feet as he made his way across the cabin to the wall opposite the door. After what felt like more than an hour, though, he knew it could only have been a couple of minutes, he felt heavy fabric against his left hand.

BOOM.

There was definitely a splintering sound with that impact, and Charlie turned to face the fabric on the wall. He felt with both hands until he found the end of the curtain and slipped behind it fumbling at the latch to the sliding glass door to the balcony. He sobbed with relief as he slipped into the morning light and welcoming fresh sea breeze.

Laughter sounded from below, and Charlie drew back from the edge of the balcony railing. Running footsteps and shouting approached from below on the right and faded after a moment to the left. He peered forward slowly and saw several people running on an outdoor track several decks below. They disappeared around the curve of the track, and he turned his attention back to the situation at hand. Screams again tore through the air interrupting his concentration as a woman's shriek of terror turned to pain and torment.

BOOM.

Behind him, the door shook in its frame as Purple Hair and company did their best to break it down. He didn't have much time, and as far as he could see, there was only one chance of escape. He craned his neck over the railing. Below him were several more levels of cabin balconies, stacked one atop the other like layers of a gigantic cake. All he had to do was crawl over the railing, let himself down the outside of the balcony wall, and swing himself into the balcony below.

Without missing. That was the important part. If he missed, he would have several decks to regret his actions before he splattered on the jogging track below.

The cabin door began to make splintering noises as Charlie swung a leg over the rail.

CHAPTER 25
CHRIS TALLANT
FINDING THE KEY

His head hurt, the strip of skin he'd scraped on his back burned with every step, and his stomach reminded him with a gurgle that he'd missed at least two meals. It seemed like hours since he'd rested, and he was so far past exhausted that it wasn't funny. Chris grimaced at the poor choice of words that flashed through his mind. Despite all the laughter he'd heard, *nothing* about recent events struck him as funny. He would never have thought it possible, but the sound of laughter was rapidly becoming synonymous with fear and pain.

So far, he'd managed to avoid large groups of the crazies, as he'd begun thinking of them, but had to fight his way through single adversaries twice. The first time had been sometime in the night, shortly after he'd escaped the elevator. He'd been scared out of his mind, but had stumbled across the man while running from a larger group. It had been either fight the lone crazy or wait for the group behind him to catch up. He'd plowed ahead, shoving the wide-eyed lunatic against the wall and punching him with a rapid combination of strikes that had surprised him with their effectiveness.

Tallant had never been much of a fighter, but the man had gone down with hardly any resistance whatsoever. He didn't know if he'd simply caught the man by surprise, or if he, like Chris, had no experience in the pugilistic arts. Either way, the encounter had boosted his confidence so that when he'd run across a second lone crazy, he'd barely slowed as he attacked the man.

Afterward, he'd felt the bruising on his knuckles, and determined to find something to use as a weapon. So far, he hadn't had any luck, though it appeared several of the crazies had, as more often than not he saw them swinging chair legs, bats from batting cages, putters from the mini-golf course, and various other clubbing implements.

Now, several hours later, with sunlight beginning to peek in through various exit doors in the hallway, he flitted from shadow to shadow, keeping to cover as much as possible. He found fewer and fewer lone crazies. They seemed to be congregating together, reminding him of herds of wild animals. And he found no more normal people. On occasion, he would hear screaming somewhere in the ship, signaling to him that he wasn't truly alone. But they, like him, were obviously hiding from the roving bands of predators.

What he did find in plenty, was bodies. Dozens—no, hundreds of bodies. They were scattered all over the corridors. Some were barely touched, but most were bloody messes of torn and beaten hamburger. The scope of the carnage shook his sense of reality. His hands trembled as he looked at the outcome of the unbelievable events of the previous night.

Laughter from behind prodded him farther aft, down the shadowed corridor. Laughter was the enemy, and he strove to avoid its source at all costs. Trotting several yards down the corridor, he dropped down to hide behind a large potted plant, waiting for the laughter to fade once more. He closed his eyes, allowing the exhaustion to have him for a moment.

***

The gurgling of his stomach brought him back to consciousness. His eyes snapped open, and his heart pounded at the realization that he'd fallen asleep. He couldn't afford sleep right now, especially out in the open like this. It was a miracle that laughing monstrosities hadn't stumbled across him and beaten him to a pulp. He had to find shelter. Trapped on the upper decks as he was, though, he had no access to any. No place where he could safely lock himself away from the roving bands of death that roamed the ship.

A loud growl from his stomach reminded him rather sharply that he had another priority as well. Food and shelter. Those were key.

With that thought, he suddenly knew what he needed.

Creeping quietly down the halls, he tried to avoid looking too closely at the butchery, while scanning the bodies *en masse*. Exhausted, hungry, and scared out of his mind, Tallant knew he had to find food and shelter soon, or his body was likely to join those strewn so carelessly about the ship. And somewhere, likely hidden in plain sight around him, was the key to finding both.

When he finally found it, he was elated… until he saw the poor man's head.

When he'd been a child, his family had had a pair of Siamese cats. He'd been six or seven years old, and didn't remember much about them except that they were very temperamental cats, and that they'd had a litter of kittens. One kitten in particular, he remembered very well.

He'd named the little ball of fur Patch, and unlike the adult cats, Patch was affectionate and playful. Little Chris and Patch were inseparable for weeks, playing about the yard and flower beds. Mom had fussed at both of them more than once when they'd trampled through her geraniums.

He remembered one day when the family was getting ready to go somewhere. They piled in the car to go, he didn't recall where. But he would never forget the scream of the kitten as the car rolled over him. Dad stopped immediately, and Little Chris had jumped out before Mom and Dad could stop him. The sight of the tiny twitching form, blood streaming from its every orifice, had horrified him. But the thing that truly haunted his dreams for weeks to come, was the sight of Patch's eyes… how the pressure of the vehicle rolling over his body had popped them from his skull so that they hung by little streamers of blood and tissue.

Now, back in the charnel house that the Bahama Queen had become, Tallant relived that horror as he looked at the body of one of the ship's stewards. The white shirt, beige vest, and black tie gave proof to the man's position on the ship. But his head…

Tallant vomited what little contents his stomach contained onto the carpet beside him. When he was finished, still shaking from the exertion, he forced himself to search the body until he found the treasure he sought. It was strange, how much relief such a small thing could bring. But sitting back on his haunches, Chris stared at the little plastic rectangle as if it were a holy relic. His shoulders sagged with blessed contentment, if only for a moment.

Laughter sounded once more, prompting him back to his feet... back to the horrific reality of flight. But at least now, he had an escape.

Calmly, Chris walked down the hall a few yards, unlocked the door to a passenger cabin, and stepped inside. The door clicked audibly as it locked behind him.

CHAPTER 26

LT. CDR FRANK JAMESON
SPECIAL DELIVERY

"Houston Methodist, this is Jayhawk Six One Five Two inbound. Do you read?"

"Loud and clear, Six One Five Two. We've been expecting you. What do you have for us?"

Jameson hesitated. If this was classified, then it wasn't likely that the higher ups would want him blabbing about it on an open channel. And he had no doubt the channel was being monitored. "Special delivery. I was told you knew what to expect."

The woman on the other end sounded irritated. "We haven't been told much of anything. Makes it sorta hard to do our jobs, you know?"

"Understood, Methodist. We've been told there should be a Dr. Sondheimer meeting us?"

"That's what we heard, too. But she called in. She's caught in morning traffic." The voice was clearly irritated.

"And she hasn't briefed you on what to expect?"

"Only that we need to take contamination precautions."

"Well, all I can tell you is that we have three patients from a cruise ship. We have them sedated for now, but all three exhibited altered mental states."

"Altered how?"

"Tendency for extreme violence." He hesitated, unsure how to communicate the insanity he and his crew had witnessed. "Hell, I'm not a doctor. They're bat shit crazy."

"So what... drugs?"

Jameson thought back to the hundreds of people on the Bahama Queen who exhibited the same symptoms. "Not likely. There were too man—"

There was a sudden rush of static on the line.

"Say again, Six One Five Two. You broke up."

But Jameson knew the static wasn't simple line interference. That was someone warning him, telling him he was skirting too close to the "classified" part of the mission. "We're almost there, Methodist. Have your crew meet us at the helipad. You'll need three gurneys with isolation bubbles and one body bag on hand."

There was a pause. "Isolation bubbles and a body bag? Holy shit. What the hell *are* you bringing us?"

Another squelch of static.

"This is Jayhawk Six One Five Two. ETA, five minutes. Out."

CHAPTER 27
LINTON BOWERS
SCENARIO 3-4-8

Linton fumbled in his shirt pocket for his Bluetooth as he drove down the highway. The thing was uncomfortable as hell, and he couldn't stand to wear it all the time, but that meant every time his cell rang, he had to rush to get it on his ear before whoever was calling hung up. This time, he made it by the third ring. "Bowers here. What can I do for you?"

"Hey, Linton. It's Emmet."

Linton's heart skipped a beat. Emmet Pismire's real name was Chris Van Duyne, and he was Linton's contact at the Office of Naval Intelligence. He had taken the unusual alias several years back, even before he'd joined the Bee Hive. He'd never explained it to anyone, only hinting that it had to do with his interest in prepping. Most people simply dropped it politely at that point, but Linton had once looked it up online. He'd found that the Emmet was actually a heraldic emblem, also known as "the ant and the pismire." There were pictures of shields with all sorts of designs on them. The one thing they all had in common was that they incorporated the emblem of the ant somehow.

"Ant man! How are you?"

Emmet sighed. "I really wish you wouldn't call me that."

"Yeah, whatever. Wish in one hand and spit in the other. See which one gets filled up first."

As they spoke, Linton began negotiating through traffic to pull his pickup off to the shoulder of the road. He hadn't heard from his friend in a couple of weeks, but that wasn't unusual. Emmet often worked long hours and didn't like to call people when he thought they might be sleeping. And he never had time to call during working hours. Linton knew his friend would never call in the middle of the day like this if it weren't important. "So what time is it, buddy? Aren't you supposed to be working?"

"Just slipped out for a quick break. My watch says it's about ten after nine. What's the matter? You late for your mid-morning nap, old man?"

Linton chuckled as he looked at his watch. It showed nine thirteen. "Old man? I'm an old man now?" As he said this, he pulled to a stop and opened his glove box.

"Five years older than me, anyway. I can damn near hear your arteries hardening over the phone."

Linton forced a laugh, despite the chill that went up his spine. He was actually only a year older than Emmet. "Whatever. So did you just call to insult me, or what?"

"No, I just wanted to know if that invitation for Thanksgiving dinner was still good."

Mind whirling, Linton thought quickly. There had been no invitation, so he knew this was part of a carefully constructed conversation. He pulled the Bee Hive manual out of the glovebox and laid it on the seat beside him. "Sure. You gonna be able to make it?" He pulled a pen out of his shirt pocket and started scribbling notes.

9:13 - 9:10.

5 yrs. – 1 yr.

"Yep. Managed to swap my leave with a buddy."

"Sounds great. Looking forward to seeing you again."

"Me, too. So I'll see you guys Thanksgiving morning sometime between seven and nine."

"All right, we'll keep an eye out for you."

7-8-9. He circled the eight.

There was a slight pause before Emmet replied. "Thanks for the invite, Linton. I really appreciate it. Tell everyone I'm looking forward to seeing them all."

"Will do. See you then."

"Later."

Linton killed the connection and took a deep breath.

Tell everyone I'm looking forward to seeing them all.

Heart pounding, Linton sat for a moment. Bee Hive protocol was pretty simple. It had to be, since the Hive was mostly civilians. Treat all phone conversations as if they were being monitored. When passing your information, do it in a specific format to answer four questions.

First, what kind of scenario you are dealing with? Second, do you have a recommended course of action? In other words, is it a bug out, or a bug in situation? Third, in the case of a bug out, what location makes the most sense as a gathering point? And finally, who does the crisis affect? Who needs to take action?

The Bee Hive manual only consisted of forty-three pages divided into five sections. Sections one through four covered each of the four questions. Section five consisted of maps, checklists, rally points, and contingency plans to help keep members of the hive organized in times of crisis. Linton was pretty sure he already knew what Emmet had just told him, but he wasn't leaving anything to chance.

What kind of scenario? He looked at his first note—*9:13 - 9:10.* That was a three-minute time difference. He turned to section one and went to scenario number three. The caption read *Confirmed Global Pandemic, Extreme Mortality Rate.*

He turned to section two, *Recommended Action Plans,* then looked at his notes again. *"Five years older…"* A four year difference.

Action plan #4 - Bug out recommended within seventy-two hours. Bug out can be recommended for any number of situations, from localized climatologically instigated emergencies, to more serious and widespread conditions. For any of the bug out action plans, see section three for a list of Bee Hive locations.

Assuming bug out, what location? Section three, *List of Possible BOLs.* He ran a shaking finger down the list, already knowing what he was going to see. *"…sometime between seven and nine."* His finger stopped on location number eight. *Bee Hive bunker retreat south of Winnie, Texas.*

The bunker was a fully stocked and maintained location that was as self-sufficient as they had been able to afford. It had enough freeze-dried food to last a group of twenty for three months, a low-wattage photovoltaic system, with enough solar panels to charge the batteries from complete depletion to full charge within a few hours—not that they ever wanted to let the batteries get that low, water filtration and storage, and an air filtration system. It was the most secure location they had.

Obviously, Emmet thought things were going to get bad—about as bad as they could get.

For the last part of the equation, Linton didn't need to consult the manual. Chris hadn't minced any words in telling him who needed to take action. *"Tell everyone I'm looking forward to seeing them all."*

"Tell everyone..."

Linton opened the glove box again and pulled out a prepaid cell phone. He knew it wasn't truly untraceable, but it would take more trouble to track than there was any reason to suspect anyone would put forth. At least, that was the idea. He dialed the number he had long ago memorized. A woman answered on the second ring. "Hello?"

"Lima Bravo."

There was a slight pause. "Echo Kilo."

Linton felt a little silly with the security designators, but he was the one who had set up the protocol. "Start the phone tree. Bravo, hotel, mike, three, four, eight."

Another pause. "You realize it's just a few days before Thanksgiving, right?"

"Yeah. Can't be helped. This is serious."

"Not a drill?"

"I only wish."

"All right. What branches of the tree should I shake?"

"All of them."

"All of them?"

"You heard me. All Hive members."

"Holy shit."

"Yeah." He could hear her tapping keys on a computer in the background.

"Got it. Three, four, eight. What is it?"

Linton sighed. "Just pull the manual and look it up. Send me the confirmation list by six o'clock."

"Will do."

"All right. I'll see you soon." He started to hang up.

"Hey, boss?"

"Yeah?"

"This really isn't some kind of drill, or a test or something, is it?"

"I don't think so. The intel is from a trusted source."

"Holy shit."

"I think we already covered that."

"Yeah, sorry. I'll start making calls."

"Thanks." He hung up.

Sitting there on the side of the road, Linton stared for a while into space. Finally, he looked into the rearview mirror at the haunted eyes staring back at him. "God help us," he told his reflection. "It's really happening."

* * *

Erin Kazmark, security designator Echo Kilo, looked up scenario three four eight as she'd been told. A minute later, her hands were shaking. *Confirmed Global Pandemic, Extreme Mortality Rate.* "Holy shit," she said for the third time in as many minutes. She turned to the last page in the manual and called the first number in the list.

A woman answered on the fifth ring. "Hello?"

"Echo Kilo."

"Romeo Papa." Her voice sounded weary and irritated.

"Bravo, hotel, mike, three, four, eight."

The woman on the other end of the line sighed, then broke protocol. "Seriously? It's Thanksgiving week. Besides, we just had a drill two weeks ago. Jesus, Erin. Some of us don't have the resources to keep this stuff up."

Erin understood. Membership in the Bee Hive was a commitment. There were annual dues, required training sessions, internal testing, minimal gear requirements, and a commitment to serve at least one weekend per quarter on maintenance and upkeep on the group's gear. It wasn't for everyone. But it looked like they were at the point where it could all prove its value.

Erin wasn't supposed to say anything that might risk the group's security, but she sensed that Rita's resolve was about gone, and it was more important than ever that she stick it out a little longer.

"Rita?"

Rita chuckled bitterly into the phone. "Don't you mean 'Romeo Papa'?"

"No, I mean Rita Post," she said. "I'm talking to you as a friend now, Rita. This isn't another drill. This is where all the drills pay off. It's big. I can't say anything more than that over the phone. Hell, you and I both know I'm not even supposed to say that much, so please just check the manual. The code again is three, four, eight. Look it up before you make any decisions."

There was a short pause.

"It's really not another drill?"

"Looks like it's real enough that I'm scared to death. Please don't quit now, Rita."

Another pause, and Erin wondered if she'd managed to reach her friend in time. Finally, Rita answered. "All right. Romeo Papa. Message acknowledged."

The line went dead, and Erin breathed a sigh of relief. She looked at her list. The next name was Peggy Bisard. She dialed the number.

"Hello?"

"Echo Kilo."

"Papa Bravo."

"Bravo, hotel, mike, three, four, eight."

"Message confirmed. Scenario three four eight."

CHAPTER 28
AUGUST GRAPPIN
FEELING

Gus ran through the hallway leading his group. They had found so many new friends. Some joined them. Others didn't. But even those who didn't join contributed to the euphoria that was *feeling*. The big man with the metal thing had given such exquisite feeling that Gus felt compelled to seek him out. He had found many others, but so far none who had given him such sublime pleasure/pain.

He vaguely recalled some modicum of pleasure when his mom told him about the cruise. Even more when he had groped black bikini girl and seen her breast. But the closest he felt to the new pleasure/pain ecstasy was in the heat of fighting. Those were the times when his heart pounded, pumping euphoria through his veins.

Of course, there were still things that bothered him sometimes – quiet nigglings in the back of his hindbrain that sometimes made him think that something was missing. Like the fact that he kept trying to do things with his hands that it seemed they should be able to do, but the dexterity was no longer there. And there was a concept that bounced around in his head… the paradoxical idea that he didn't remember things like he should, but couldn't remember why it was important.

But he could use his hands well enough to wield the length of wood—to impart pleasure/pain to those he came across—to grant them *feeling*. And he could still understand some of the old words and concepts from before. Many of his troop couldn't. They were reduced to pummeling and clawing with their hands, and biting when they could get close enough. Somewhere deep within, Gus knew he would eventually join them in this primal frenzy of anger and delight. He didn't know if one way was better or worse, but for now it didn't matter. All of it was secondary to the drive for *feeling*.

CHAPTER 29
CHARLES GRIFFE
RAG DOLL

Wake up, asshole!

Charlie started at the voice and realized he had fallen asleep. He winced at the painfully bright flood of sunlight pouring into the cabin through the shattered balcony door. It had been the only way for him to get in, and while he had feared the sound of breaking glass might draw attention, he had feared being caught out on the open balcony even more. He'd reasoned that he could easily escape into the hallway if Purple Hair and his gang figured out where he had gone, and so he sat on the floor by the cabin door watching and waiting for gang bangers to come climbing down from the balcony above.

Now, sunlight in his eyes let him know that exhaustion had finally overtaken him, and he stood stiffly from where he leaned against the door. He checked his watch.

Two fifty-six.

He'd slept through the morning and into the afternoon. Stretching his back, he looked around the cabin. A softshell suitcase lay unzipped, but closed on the bed. He walked over and flipped the top open. It was a woman's suitcase, filled with nice clothes, makeup, two bikinis that hinted at a nice figure, and slinky lingerie. He picked up a frilly bra that left little to the imagination. Nice, but the owner obviously wasn't as well-endowed as Felicia.

Charlie was startled to realize he was genuinely concerned about her, his anger from the night before completely gone. He wondered whether or not she was still alive.

You should hope so. It would be a real shame to lose a hot piece like her.

"She's not just a piece of ass."

True enough. She's got a helluva rack on her, too.

Charlie could practically hear Dad smile. "Fuck you, old man. She's better to me than you ever were."

Aw, poor Charlie. Did I hurt your feelings? I'm sorry. I didn't know that you really loved the stupid cow.

"I'm not having this conversation with you right now." And no matter how much his father provoked him, Charlie ignored the jibes. Checking around the cabin proved fruitless as far as providing any sort of weapon, though he did find two small bags of trail mix in the suitcase. He shoved one in his pocket, and the second one lasted all of thirty seconds as he ripped it open and shoved its contents into his mouth. It was only a few handfuls, but at least it quieted the growling in his stomach for the time being. He'd been making do with pretzels, peanuts, and whatever other munchies he could find in bars or vending machines since this insanity had started. He went to the sink in the restroom and turned on the faucet, cursing when all he got was a tiny trickle of water that lasted about three seconds and then was gone. He cracked the door open, peeking into the corridor.

The scene outside was a stark contrast to the night before. Sunlight streamed in from the open atrium in the upper decks, illuminating the horror of death and destruction spread as far as he could see. There were bodies and worse, body parts, strewn about as far as he could see. Thick, black smoke filled the corridors, and through it all, he could still hear the screaming and laughter that told him the rampage was ongoing. He thought again of Felicia and wondered how difficult it was going to be to get to her. Their cabin was on Deck Seven. He was startled to realize that he wasn't sure what deck he was on at the moment.

"Nine or Ten, I think. Should only be a few decks away." Three decks would normally be a matter of walking a few minutes down a couple of staircases. But it had taken him more than twelve hours to travel half a dozen decks. Travel time under these circumstances was subjective, to stay the least.

He eased out of the room, sticking to the shadows as much as possible. He soon came across a directory sign that confirmed he was on Deck Ten. Charlie trotted carefully through the shadows toward where he thought he remembered the stairwell was, but screams and laughter from that direction stopped him. He hugged the wall and eased forward slowly, so as not to attract any attention. There was an open area ahead, brightly illuminated by the sunlight streaming in from above. For this stretch, there were no inside cabins and there was no way he was going to be able to make it across unseen. He could see over the railing to the Promenade Deck, two levels below. Straight ahead, past the open stretch was another darkened corridor, but Charlie could see several people milling about, dancing and laughing.

"Damn." Hugging the walls, he headed back the way he had come. Along the way, he stopped at the directory sign again, looking for another route. He traced his finger along the corridors away from the stairwell, recalling as his fingers hit it that there were another pair of stairwells at the fore end of the ship. With a goal in mind, he increased his pace.

It took him nearly fifteen minutes to travel from shadow to shadow to the forward stairs. Along the way, he dodged two groups of thugs, but eventually he saw the foredeck ahead. He knew from the diagram that the forward stairwells were just around the next corner, but the sound of laughter told him that there was more than escape waiting for him ahead.

Charlie crept slowly to the corner, peeking around, ready to run in the opposite direction if there was any sign of discovery. His eyes were drawn immediately to the sight of a group of teen boys shoving a young girl around their circle. Her left eye was bruised and swollen, and her bottom lip was split. Blood poured from her nose onto her *Bahama Queen* T-shirt. One of the boys giggled, slapped her in the face, and kicked her to another of his buddies. The girl staggered, so abused and bedraggled that she barely even groaned as she was beaten.

Charlie's heart dropped as he saw that they were near the far emergency stairwell. There was no way he was going to get past them and through the door. By the sunlight coming in from above, he saw one of the large, sweeping intra-level staircases that flowed from one deck to another. He could probably get there and make a dash down those stairs before they got to him, but he knew they would be right behind him, and he had no idea where he would go once he reached the bottom of the stairs. Plus, kids that age were almost certain to be faster than he was. No, his best chance for survival wasn't in speed, but rather in stealth. He had to make his way by hiding, or by tricking the killers.

He brought the directory sign back to mind. There was the main staircase, restrooms, and the port and starboard forward stairwells. Port *and* starboard. He could see the main stairwell, and the door to the emergency stairwell behind the thugs. The port stairwell. That meant the starboard stairwell was just around the corner from him. He couldn't see it because he was behind it, and he could probably make it before the thugs could get to him, but there was no way he would make it without at least some of them seeing him.

Again, stealth, not speed. A rise in volume pulled his attention back to the gang across the causeway. The girl they were brutalizing suddenly lost her apathy and started screaming at the top of her lungs, while the boys all bent over her doing something. Charlie watched while they shuffled about, heads bobbing as they grabbed the girl, struggling to hold onto her as they lifted. The girl managed to kick one of the boys in the nuts, dropping him to the floor. Charlie winced as the boy doubled up into a fetal curl, facing away from the action. The others ignored him, and as Charlie watched in horror, they raised the girl over their shoulders and tossed her over the rail.

The girl's screams rose in pitch for a second, then she was gone. The boys all stood, hanging over the railing, pointing and laughing, and to his horror, Charlie could still hear the girl crying, though now her voice carried more pain than fear. He remembered that the Promenade was only two decks below, so it wasn't surprising that she had survived the fall. But her voice told him she was definitely hurt. The boys rushed to the main stairway, obviously intent on reacquiring their play toy.

This was his chance. Watching the boys head down the stairs, he waited until the last in line rounded the corner, passing out of sight. He crept to the banister and peeked over. The girl lay on the wooden surface of a shuffleboard deck, right leg twisted at an unnatural angle. She was dragging herself across the floor trying to escape. Then the first of the boys reached the bottom of the stairs and slowly approached her.

"Please," she begged between sobs, "no more."

The smiling boy chuckled. "More-no-more-no-more…" His raspy mutter faded into insane titters. He reached out and stroked her hair tenderly. Her sobbing diminished as he continued to stroke her hair, chuckling the entire time. As the other boys arrived, they slowed, gathering around her. At some unspoken signal, the first boy grabbed a handful of her hair and yanked. The raucous laughter was back in an instant, and the others roughly pulled her to her feet.

Staggering on the broken right leg, she fell into one of them. Charlie winced as the boy kicked her in the stomach. They laughed and shouted as she screamed, until Charlie couldn't tell the screams from the laughter.

Suddenly, there was a crushing weight on his back and he fell forward, hitting his head on the railing. He saw stars for a moment, but struggled against his attacker, the hoarse laughter an incessant and terrifying soundtrack in his ear. Stunned, dizzy, and if he were to be completely honest with himself, terrified of dying, Charlie thrashed as his attacker squeezed. He heaved himself up as the arm tightened around his neck, and his vision began to swim.

Come on, boy. If there's one thing I taught you, it's how to fight.

Throwing himself backwards, Charlie landed on the floor again, his entire body weight landing on his attacker. The arm loosened, and Charlie dug his chin into the crook of the elbow and bit.

The laughter in his ear became shrill, and the arm loosened enough for Charlie to get a good grip on it. He yanked and spun to face his attacker. It was the kid that the girl had kicked and left rolling on the floor. Charlie had forgotten him as he watched the attack below. Now the kid launched himself at Charlie again. Charlie swung. It wasn't pretty. There was no finesse to his punch. But it was the punch of a frightened, two hundred thirty pound man hitting the jaw of a kid about half his size.

His attacker dropped like a lead balloon. Charlie panted and his hands shook from the adrenaline rush. His heart pounded in his ears, and it took several seconds for him to realize that the kid, even while unconscious, was still chuckling quietly.

Well, that's more than a little disturbing.

"You think?" Cries from below interrupted his argument with his dad, and Charlie ran back to the railing. The gang below was still beating the poor girl.

Ain't nothing you can do, boy. Get the hell out of sight.

Charlie turned toward the stairwell and stopped at the sight of the unconscious thug on the ground. He grinned, and he felt his dad's approval.

Well, there might be one *thing you can do.*

Charlie heaved the kid over his shoulder and walked to the railing. Taking careful aim, he shoved his burden into the empty air, just as they had done to the poor girl. The kid rag dolled as he fell, limbs flailing limply until he hit three of the kids below.

Good shot, boy! That'll teach 'em you don't fuck with the Griffes.

"Shut up, Dad," Charlie muttered for the umpteenth time. He looked over the rail. Two of the kids he hit weren't moving. Neither was the kid he had tossed. The others pointed up at him, and a second later they were rushing for the stairs. "Oh shit." Charlie bolted for the stairwell, starting down. He briefly entertained the idea that they would go up the main stairway while he passed them in the enclosed emergency stairwell. Unfortunately, the thugs had other ideas. Evidently, not all of them had gone up the main stairs. Laughter below told him that there were several of them in the stairwell below him.

Charlie turned and headed back up the stairs. His father's voice chided him as he went. *Aren't you getting tired of hiding like a scared little pussy?*

"Like I have a choice?" Charlie was getting tired of the constant criticism, but Dad had always been like that. And even a nagging partner was better than having to face the nightmare of this cruise alone.

Well, you're running in the wrong direction, dumb fuck. You're supposed to be going downstairs.

"Yeah. Well, why don't you tell that to the kids chasing me? Maybe they'll stand aside while I go past."

The noise below him sounded frighteningly close as he clambered up the stairs as quickly as he could. The flashing red LEDs was really not enough to make quick progress a possibility, and he had to concentrate on making sure his feet planted properly on each step. He had become very familiar with the stairwells since this nightmare had begun. There were fifteen steps between decks. He had it memorized, and this simple fact led to a process. Down eight steps, grab the handrail, jump and swing one hundred eighty degrees around the landing to the lower seven steps. Those last seven steps put him on the lower landing, just to the left of the exit. He had done it so many times over the last two days that the routine was instinctive by now—eight steps, turn, seven steps, door. This let him concentrate less on his surroundings, and more on where he placed his feet. It was like running on autopilot, and he was able to speed through the emergency stairs much faster that way.

But the very routine that had saved him time before, was nearly his undoing this time. Eight steps, turn, seven steps, door. Lather, rinse, repeat. But that was the routine for going *down* the stairwell.

So when his foot hit empty air, rather than an eighth step, he staggered for a second. It only took a second for him to realize his mistake, but it shook him.

Autopilot off. If he'd had time, he would have taken a minute to gather his shaken confidence, but the shouts, laughter, and clambering footsteps behind him gave him no chance to regroup. He turned around the landing and scrambled up the next seven, *no eight*, steps to the deck above.

His foot tripped on the edge of the eighth step and he fell to his knees. Scrambling on hands and knees, he moved to the door on the right. But the door wasn't there. And the raucous sounds of pursuit drew closer. Charlie climbed quickly to his feet and spun in the darkness. The red emergency light blinked again and he saw stairs before him.

No time to think about it. He headed up as quickly as he could, repeating his mantra under his breath. "Eight steps, turn—"

No, you're going up *now, stupid.*

The old man was right. "*Seven* steps, turn. Then eight steps, door."

Only the door won't be on your right if you're going up, will it?

"That's right. It should be right in front of me at the top of the stairs."

That's my boy!

Charlie grunted at his father's praise. There was once a day when he would have reveled in it. Now it simply irritated him. His foot reached the seventh step, and he gripped the handrail tightly, used his momentum to maintain his speed as he pivoted on the landing just as the red light blinked back on, and confirmed his process. And still the sounds of his pursuers grew louder.

"...five, six, seven, landing."

Sure enough, there was the door, right in front of him. He shoved his way out of the stairwell. The sign outside the door confirmed his dad's words. He was back up on Deck Twelve. "Shit."

He ran across the causeway from the starboard stairwell, past the open staircase, over to the port side of the ship. He ran into the shadowy corridors on the opposite side from where he had been earlier. He had no sooner turned the corner out of sight when he heard the stairwell door slam open, and footsteps pounding up the main stairway. He stopped around the corner, peeking back the way he had come. Four teens exited the stairwell he had just been in, and half a dozen more ran up the main stairwell, whooping and hollering. A bang on the wall around the corner from where he was watching reminded him that there was a second emergency stairwell, and he was hiding right behind it.

Charlie tore down the shadowy corridor as quickly as he could, stumbling on occasion over barely seen obstacles. At one point, he fell over something soft and rubbery. He looked back and saw an arm on the blood-soaked carpet. The rest of the body was nowhere to be seen.

Charlie choked back the bile and scrambled to his feet. Peering back down the corridor seemed to show that he had lost his pursuers, but he couldn't afford to take that for granted. He moved on up the hallway. His pace was like that of an elderly speed walker doing laps at the mall, but any faster and he would be running blind in and out of inky shadows.

And through it all, the laugh track played.

Ahead, the corridor opened into one of the wide public areas of the ship that offered restaurants, bars, or entertainment venues. It also offered a swath of bright sunlight from the open atrium above. Charlie hesitated at the edge of the sunlight. Moving forward would immediately expose him to anyone watching from the shadows.

He spent several minutes frozen in place, watching the shadowy places between doorways for movement. Was there someone there, watching the shadows as he was, waiting for their prey to expose themselves? The longer he waited, the more nervous be grew, convincing himself as each moment passed that movement on his part would be tantamount to suicide.

Was that a hand on the wall near the bar across the causeway? He peered intently at the shadow on the wall, watching for it to move.

Dammit, you little pussy! Shit or get off the pot, for fuck's sake.

Whether or not he liked how Dad said it, the old man had a point. Standing around waiting on something to happen wasn't going to accomplish anything. So where to?

He saw a sign across the hall. *Library.* Yeah, that should do. He sprinted across the brightly lit open area and pushed into the darkened room. "Oh, shit."

His illusions of hiding among the books were dashed the moment he entered the room. Where he had imagined racks upon racks of tomes, the dim red light in the ceiling revealed the library of the *Bahama Queen* to be a relatively small study area with bookcases around the walls. It's only furnishings were a dozen or so chairs, and a large table in the center. He turned to leave just as a scream sounded outside the door. He backed away and looked around the darkened room. The emergency light left most of the area in shadow, but there was an especially inky black space that seemed to blend into the far wall. Hoping for an office or other alcove, he quietly trotted across the carpeted floor of the library. Deeper in the darkness, he found another exit and opened it. His path was beginning to get pretty confusing, and he had some misgivings about getting any farther away from the stairwell, but a banging on the door at the other end of the library pushed those doubts aside. Charlie slipped out the back exit, easing the door closed behind him.

Through the gloom, he saw the faint reflection of another frosted glass doorway about fifty feet ahead. Looking left, then right, Charlie crept across the open intersection to the doors, hoping for someplace to hide. Slipping quietly through the doors, he shook his head. "I think I might be spending too much time in bars," he thought. The remains of a large mirror hung precariously behind the bar, a huge, reflective jigsaw of deadly shards. Stepping forward, Charlie felt something crunch beneath his shoes and saw that the carpet was covered with bits of glass. Broken bottles and mirror bits interspersed with slicks of various liquids that made his footing uncertain.

When he saw the bodies, he almost turned and ran. The blinking red light illuminated the sight, making it all the more macabre. Only the sounds of laughter and screaming out in the halls kept him moving through the dark room. He slid his feet forward, trying to move as quietly as possible, minimizing the crunch of glass as much as possible, though the idea of anyone being able to hear it over the litany of curses, laughter, and screams outside was almost ridiculous.

He crept through the darkness, looking for the exit that he knew had to be there, but his eyes kept flicking back to the bodies on the floor. Edging around a pool of blood that spread from the open mouth of a dead brunette, Charlie concentrated on getting out of the room as quickly as possible. His back to the bar, he stepped carefully over the dark stain and just as he set his foot, a hand snaked around his mouth and firmly shut off the scream that tried to erupt from his throat. A second hand grabbed him by the shoulder and yanked him off his feet into the darkness behind the bar.

CHAPTER 30
LINTON BOWERS
IS YOUR UNDERSTUDY ANY GOOD?

It had taken several hours to make all the arrangements, but he wasn't too concerned. Michelle was in San Francisco, so her day was a few hours behind him. That, plus the late hours she put in when she was on the road, and he knew she wouldn't be awake until almost noon. That gave him time to call in to work sick, get back home and hit several internet travel sites. The holidays made his quest for a ticket nearly impossible. Nearly, but not quite. The gods were with him, and he was able to find a seat.

He made the call. "Hi, baby. How's the show going?"

"It's okay, I guess. Wish I was back there with you, though."

"Funny you should say that."

"Why? Something wrong?"

"I'm afraid so. Is your understudy any good?"

"Yeah, she's really good, actually. So what's going on? You're starting to worry me."

"I think you need to get home right away."

"What's wrong, Lint? Is someone hurt?"

This was where things could go badly. "Sorry, baby, but it's your dad. He's taken a turn for the worse. They don't know if he's going to make it through the night." Linton held his breath, hoping Michelle wouldn't give it away.

After a short pause, she replied cautiously. "Is it really going to happen that quickly?"

"There's no way to know for sure, but it looks like it's going to be really soon, and I don't want you halfway across the country when he goes."

Michelle sighed. "I'll see how quick I can get a flight back. This close to Thanksgiving, it's liable to—"

"I've already got one for you. There's an e-ticket in your name in your mailbox. Your flight leaves at 4:20, with a connecting flight in Phoenix. You get into Hobby Airport at 11:30."

She paused. "Lint, what's going on?"

"You need to get home as quick as you can."

"But—"

"Sorry, baby. I have to go. Just promise me you'll make that flight?"

A heavy sigh told him she was getting irritated. "Sure. I promise."

"Thanks. I'll pick you up at the airport." As he hung up, Linton exhaled a breath he hadn't realized he was holding.

CHAPTER 31
GUS
CONNECTION

Laughter. Frustration. Confusion.

But always laughter. Gus had almost caught up to the big man. He giggled at the memory of the man's face as he had seen Gus. The big man recognized him. If only Gus could just get him to laugh, he would know how much fun they could have together. He had tried to let the man know as he had chanted at the cabin door. He'd waited for the man to get the joke. Waited for him to respond with "not by the hair of my chinny chin chin."

It would have been hilarious! The big man would have laughed, and perhaps he would have hurt Gus again. It could be agonizingly wonderful, that pleasure/pain. They would have been close again.

No, that wasn't right. They weren't close before. So they couldn't be close again.

But they would be close like he had been close to his father. Gus shook his head, confused again.

But it didn't matter. There was a connection between him and the big man, Gus knew that. He would find him again.

CHAPTER 32
CHARLES GRIFFE
I THINK IT'S THE SLICK

Charlie thrashed about, kicking and pulling ineffectively at the hand over his mouth. His heart pounded, and all he could hear was his own muffled shrieking. He inhaled the scent of… peanuts? And he blew snot from his nose as all the air from his screams was rerouted to his nostrils. *Oh shit, oh shit, oh shit. This is it. I'm gonna die. Some little fucker is gonna rip my throat out and I'm gonna…*

"Shhh. Come on, buddy. Would you please shut the hell up?"

The words finally filtered through, and Charlie realized that whoever held him from behind was trying to get him quiet. More importantly, though, the owner of that disembodied voice *wasn't* trying to kill him. He calmed himself, and stopped his screaming.

"That's better. If I take my hand away, can you keep quiet?"

Eyes still wide in fear, Charlie nevertheless nodded. The hands eased off of his mouth and shoulder, releasing him, and Charlie scrambled away from the hidden stranger. He jumped from behind the bar, and spun to try and get a look at the man who had grabbed him.

"What the fuck do you think you're doing, grabbing me like that?" he shouted.

"Shhh," he hissed. "Keep it quiet, buddy! You want to attract those things in here?"

Charlie had to squint to make out the faint silhouette of the man hidden in the darkness. "And how do I know you aren't one of them?" He'd seen too much insanity tonight to trust a stranger, and he kept edging away from the other man.

The man shook his head in the darkness. "I'm not laughing."

The apparent non-sequitur took Charlie by surprise. It tickled his brain a bit, seeming almost to make sense, but he didn't have time to think it through. He had to get away from everyone. He had to get to safety. But the laughter reference tugged at him. "Laughing?" he asked.

"Yeah. Haven't you noticed? All the crazies are the ones that are laughing."

Charlie backed slowly away. "Yeah, well, I think you might be a little crazy yourself." The back of his thigh brushed against a table behind him and he edged sideways toward the other doorway.

"Think about it. Have you seen anyone that's gone nuts that isn't laughing?"

It was true. "No." He stopped moving for the moment, willing to let the man explain.

"I think it's the slick."

The slick? All right. He'd had his chance. Charlie began backing away again. The man might not be laughing, but neither was he making any sense. What the hell was the slick? "Yeah, well, I think you're probably right. But I really need to go, so good to meet you and all that, but I think I'm gonna—"

The man stood and held up his hands. "Wait a sec. I know how it sounds, but it's true."

"Okay. But I really need to go."

The man stepped forward and Charlie panicked. "Keep away from me!"

He froze and held up his hands. "Shh! Keep your voice down! You want them to—"

But they already had. The doors back at the entrance where Charlie had come in flew open, and three laughing men squinted into the shadows at Charlie and his anonymous companion. One of the crazies, as the man had called them, pointed at Charlie and giggled with glee. Charlie didn't wait. He ran to the door behind him and slammed it open, the other man right behind him.

"This way," the man shoved Charlie to the right, and without any better ideas, Charlie didn't fight him.

They ran a few yards and came to one of the wide, open staircases that flowed from one deck to the next. Bright sunlight lit their way, and

Charlie got his first good look at the man. About a head shorter than Charlie, the man wore black slacks and a white shirt with some kind of emblem on the lapel. He pulled past Charlie and led him at a sprint down the open staircase to Deck Eleven. Charlie struggled not to stumble as they flew down the stairs. The commotion was drawing more attention, though, and more laughter sounded from the shadows around them.

Charlie and his new companion ran into the shadows of the corridor between the port side cabins. *Is it port? I'm too mixed up now, can't tell where I am.* Charlie heard more laughter from the staircase behind, and saw the three men who had chased them out of the bar coming down the stairs. The man shoved Charlie around another corner, and they plunged back into shadow. Almost as soon as they rounded the corner, the man stopped in front of a cabin door. Nearly falling over his companion, Charlie hissed, "What the hell are you doing?"

But the man simply inserted a card into the lock on the door, and pushed through. Charlie followed and they closed the door behind them. Pressing their ears to the door, they listened as the laughter approached, and when it paused outside, Charlie held his breath.

"Heh, heh, heh, heh, heh..." The incessant litany sounded less like laughter, and more like a small, engine, idling in park and waiting for someone to kick it into gear. After only a few seconds, the sound moved away from the door, gradually diminishing into the background noise of cackling and screams that occasionally sounded throughout the ship.

Charlie sighed with relief and then glanced at his companion. Light from the balcony let him see that the man was staring intently at him, as if wondering if he had made a mistake. It began to piss Charlie off. "What?"

He's wondering if you're worth the trouble you caused him.

"Shut up!" Charlie hissed at his father without thinking. He backed away from the other man, eyes narrowed, unsure of what to expect from him, but the man made no move, as if aware that Charlie was on the verge of panic.

"I didn't say anything," he said.

"No, I..." Charlie had to ignore his father. Things were getting confusing. "Sorry, I must have heard a scream outside." He shook his head. "All the damn screaming and laughing. The whole damn place has gone insane."

He waited to see if the man would accept his excuse. His eyes narrowed for a moment, watching Charlie quietly. Charlie stared back. He could see him more clearly now, and he absently glanced across the room to see bright sunlight filtering through the curtains at the balcony. He turned back and saw the other man's eyes still on him.

Man's gonna try to stare you down, see if you'll punk out first.

Charlie clenched his jaw, determined to ignore his father this time, and backed to the middle of the room. They stood that way, simply staring at one another for a second, each assessing the other. The white shirt Charlie had noticed earlier bore epaulettes on the shoulder, and Charlie recognized it as a uniform. He guessed the man was with the cruise line.

Still, neither of them seemed ready to speak just yet. Charlie started to get pissed, and he felt his father grin. And that was enough to make him take a deep, calming, breath. If the old man thought getting pissed off was a good idea, then it was bound to be bad.

That's a hell of a thing to say about your dear old dad.

Charlie stepped back and finally figured that if the man had wanted to do him harm, he'd already had plenty of opportunities. He nodded to the man. "Ah, I guess I should thank you."

With that simple acknowledgment, the man seemed to relax the slightest bit. "Not a problem." He eased away from the door, still moving slowly and deliberately. He pointed to a chair. "Mind if I sit?"

Odd thing to say. "Not my room," Charlie replied.

"Not mine either. I just opened the first door I saw once we got out of sight."

Charlie's eyebrows arched. "How did you manage that? Every one I've tried has been locked." But even as he asked, he knew what the answer would be. His brain finally began to kick into gear, and he began putting pieces of the puzzle together. The uniform, opening the door the way he had... "Oh yeah, you're part of the ship's crew, aren't you?"

The uniformed man sat down and nodded. "I am. But that's not how I got in. My key would still only work on my own door and work areas." He raised a plastic card, waving it in the faint sunlight. "But a steward's key is different. And the steward I got this one from isn't going to be needing it anymore." He averted his eyes, looking uncomfortable for the first time since Charlie had met him.

Charlie started to ask if the steward had already been dead when the man had lifted the card, then decided he probably didn't really want to know. "Well, thanks anyway."

The man nodded. "No problem." He slowly leaned forward and extended his hand, as if afraid of spooking Charlie. "I'm Chris. Chris Tallant."

Charlie hesitated, considering the hand before stepping forward and grasping it in his own. "Charles Griffe. Call me Charlie."

The man nodded. "All right, Charlie it is then." They each stepped back after they shook, as if they still didn't know whether or not to trust one another.

Charlie cleared his throat nervously. "So, what did you mean back there?"

Chris cocked his head quizzically. "Back where?"

"You said something about a slick."

The other man nodded. "Yeah. That." He rubbed his face in both hands before looking back up. "It's going to sound pretty crazy."

"And a gang war on a cruise liner isn't crazy enough?"

Chris looked at Charlie as if trying to figure out where to start. Finally, he just shook his head. "I think it's even crazier than that. You might want to sit down for this."

Charlie cocked an eyebrow, but sat on the edge of the bed opposite the crewman.

"I was on the bridge yesterday when we saw a big phosphorescent slick in the Gulf," Chris began.

Charlie interrupted immediately. "You were on the bridge?"

"Yeah, I'm a navigator." He paused again. "Anyway, we saw this huge phosphorescent slick in the Gulf. Even the captain mentioned how unusual it looked. And there was this huge pod of dolphins. They were thrashing around like crazy, churning the water... it looked like they were fighting... killing each other. Never seen anything like it."

"Anyway, we were watching the dolphins through the binoculars when Jesse, he's an apprentice, started pointing and laughing. He says something like 'Flipper's flipped.' A couple of the other guys started laughing at his joke, and then Jesse pulled the binoculars away from his face. I got a good look at his eyes when he did, and I swear to God, he looked terrified. But it was like he couldn't stop laughing."

Chris went silent for a moment, and Charlie thought he had finished. "Well, ah… that's really—"

He started up again as if Charlie hadn't said a word. "Then Jesse smashed Captain Eckles in the face with the binoculars. And all the sudden, everyone else was either laughing or running." Silhouetted shoulders rose in a slight shrug. "I ran."

Charlie waited again for him to continue, but this time, it looked like Chris had gotten lost in his thoughts. Charlie reflected on what the man said. It made a certain amount of sense. It *was* true that everyone Charlie had seen who had been attacking someone had been laughing. "So you think whatever is going on is making people laugh… and then kill each other?"

"Yeah, I do." The man sounded like he had already made up his mind. "Look, I know how it sounds, but you weren't there. You didn't see—"

"I saw plenty," Charlie interrupted. He stared at the carpet as he recalled some of the horror. "I saw kids killing an old woman and a bartender. I saw them laughing while they beat people to death on the basketball courts. While they chased me all over the upper decks." He shuddered. "I saw them throw someone on a fire while he was still alive."

Chris was silent for a moment. "I guess everyone saw some pretty hellacious stuff."

Another shriek sounded outside. "They still are," Charlie corrected.

The two men were quiet for a bit. Then Chris turned back to Charlie. "Kids?" The question brought Charlie back.

"What?"

"You mentioned kids attacking?"

"Yeah. Teenagers. They killed everyone in the bar I was in. I tried to sneak out, but they saw me. Chased me down the stairs and I've been running or hiding ever since."

"Huh. I hadn't thought about the kids." The man's voice sounded sad.

"What do you mean?"

"I just hadn't thought about the upper decks having all those kids on them. I suppose it makes sense. That's where the pools and playgrounds are."

Charlie remembered the girl in the string bikini. Dentures flying from an old woman's mouth. "I don't know if it was drugs, a gang initiation, or what, but…"

He trailed off, watching as Chris shook his head. "It's not just kids."

"What?"

"Remember those guys who chased us out of the bar upstairs? They weren't kids."

That brought Charlie up short. Chris was right. They had been adults.

"And the bridge crew certainly weren't kids."

Somehow, that depressed Charlie even more. "That's all I saw at first. The only adults I saw were getting the shit beat out of them. I just figured it was some kind of gang war. Wasn't until I got down here to Deck Ten that I heard any adults laughing."

"Eleven."

"What?"

"We're on Eleven now. Twelve was where we met in the bar. We came down the stairs to Eleven."

"Does it really matter?"

"Sorry. Guess I'm a bit of a stickler for that kind of stuff." Chris rubbed the back of his neck as if it ached. "So what's your story?"

"What?"

"I told you what happened to me. How did you end up in that bar?"

"Got into a fight with my old lady at dinner…" He stopped to think, "I guess it was two nights ago now." He shook his head. "It doesn't seem that long ago, but I guess it has been."

"What happened?"

"She's a woman."

Chris cocked his head quizzically. "What?"

"She was just being a bitch." *I really feel like dancing.* In his mind, Felicia's voice blended into his father's. The old man laughed. *Told you she was a fucking cow.* Charlie clenched his jaw against his retort. "So I went to the bar on Seventeen." He rubbed his eyes and sighed. "Had too much to drink and passed out in the bathroom. When I woke up, there was a gang of kids in the bar." He went silent, remembering again. Dentures on the carpet.

"I'm sorry, buddy. Is she dead?"

"What? What the hell do you mean?"

"Your wife. I figured since she wasn't with you..."

"We're not married, but as far as I know she's still alive." If he were perfectly honest with himself, Charlie hadn't thought much beyond finding a place to hide. He had been too pissed at Felicia to even begin to think about her well-being. But that was something people tended to look down on you for saying.

"So where is she?"

Charlie didn't like the shift in the other man's tone. It sounded too judgmental for his liking. "I don't know. Last time I saw her, she was running out of *Le Trône de la Mer.* Like I said, we had a fight."

Chris simply stared at him, patient and unflinching, waiting for Charlie to continue. It made him uncomfortable. "What?"

"Aren't you worried about her?"

Nosy little prick, ain't he?

"Of course I am," Charlie snapped. But to himself, he thought, "Why are people always worried about *her*? What about me? I'm the one who was almost killed." He stopped himself mentally, torn when he realized what he'd been thinking. But it *was* her fault he was in this predicament. It *was* her who had insisted on the damned cruise in the first place, wasn't it?

That's right, boy. Don't forget who got you into this shit in the first place.

"Sorry," Charlie stumbled over the word, momentarily unsure if he was speaking to Chris or Dad. He knew though, even as mixed up as he was, that agreeing with Dad was a sure sign he was on the wrong track.

You should be, Dad growled.

At the same time, Chris just nodded. "No problem."

Charlie grabbed his head. The conversation was getting too confusing.

"So you're going after her, I imagine." Chris made it sound like a question.

"Well, yeah. I guess."

"You guess?"

This fucker's really startin' to piss me off.

Charlie had to agree with his dad.

"Yeah, of course I'm going to get her."

Sanctimonious prick is judging you, boy. He's looking down at you just like those uptight sons of bitches at the dinner table.

Looking in the other man's eyes, Charlie couldn't tell whether Chris was judging him, or if his view was being skewed by his father's words. Either way, though, Charlie had dealt with that kind of person before. He knew how to deal with them. Tell him what he expects to hear. Wait for the right opportunity, and find a way to subtly prove just how wrong he was. Not in a gloating manner, but in a subtle, yet superior way. "I figure she probably headed down to our cabin on Seven." It sounded reasonable. He expanded, "That's where I've been trying to get to. I need to make sure she's all right." He looked away, trying to play the part of the worried paramour.

"Well, let's give it a few hours for things to calm down out there. We can get a little rest and then see about getting down there."

Charlie jerked his head back up. "We?" He didn't like the way Chris was starting to take over. "Look, buddy. I appreciate you getting me in here and all, but I still don't know you. And what makes you think I need your help getting to my cabin?"

Chris arched an eyebrow. "You want to go back out there on your own?"

"I was doing all right before I found you in the bar."

The man was silent for a moment before he spoke again. "Well, I suppose I can't keep you here." He waved at the door. "Good luck."

Charlie's heart thudded, thoughts suddenly muddled as the man called his bluff. As long as Chris had that master key, Charlie had to admit that travel on the ship was much too dangerous. It had taken him two days to get from Seventeen to this cabin on Eleven. Two days!

Frustrated for the moment, Charlie sighed. "All right. I guess I could use the help."

CHAPTER 33

FORUM POST FROM H-TOWNDATE.NET

<u>Harvey Corpseman - 9:16 AM</u>
WTF? Had some weird shit going down at the ER this morning. Quick rundown…

06:00 Coast Guard brings in three victims. No word where they came from. All hush, hush. I get assigned one of them with instructions to keep him sedated.

06:15 While pt was unconscious, I went to get some meds and equipment.

06:17 turn around and see patient standing by the sliding glass door fixated on me with the weirdest grin. Totally freaky.

06:18 I return to room, try to shake off the feeling. After all, the guy's just smiling, right? I try to coax pt back to his bed, but he just cocks his head like a puppy would, and all the time he's just grinning like it's all some big joke to him. I try to get firm with him. You know, like you would with a kid who's misbehaving. Pt started laughing and attacked me. I was in the military for two tours, and I know how to handle myself, so I punched him in the ribs in a way that almost always ended the fight in the past. Not this guy, he just bounces off the wall and jumps at me again. I hit him again, harder this time… nothing. This guy continues to look at me like I'm a damn cheeseburger. By now, the scuffle has attracted the attention of the other ER nurses and they come to help me. It took 12 of us to hold him down for long enough to get restraints on him. Added face net and a butt load of anti-psychotics and sedatives.

06:30 Patient is finally out

06:55 pt moved to safe room n psych ward heavily medicated, and tied down.

Notes: not one time did this guy tried to punch, slap, kick or strike me in any way. All he was trying to do was to bite. But here's the REALLY weird part – this guy was giggling like a drunk school kid the whole damn time!

I'm completely freaked out.

Death Eater - 9:30 AM
Lot of crazy crap going on out there. Stay safe HC

Griggs - 9:36 AM
What did tests show? Keep us posted.

Harvey Corpseman - 11:01 AM
They don't even seem to know what to look for. Some folks are suggesting something like the old bath salts drugs from a few years back. Thing is, they're telling me they don't have the ability to test for it. Got a call from a buddy at UCSF in California, and he said they've got three more cases just like this one. Said they had Nat'l Guard roll in and they were starting to take over the place. That was the last thing he said before the line went dead.

Whole damn hospital just went offline.

What is this shit? Does the government know something we don't? Is this a virus? A biological weapon that leaked? Who knows? What I do know is over the last week, we've started hearing about more and more of these cases. They keep telling us it's drugs, but that just doesn't ring true. Now, all over the country ER nurses and doctors like myself are wrestling these people unprotected, thinking its drug related.

What if it's really viral? How does it spread? Are we at risk? Bite, spit, breathing?? What does it take to get it? I'm getting sick to my stomach thinking about this.

Gotta go. Pulling a double, and this place is getting weird.

<u>BARBIE GURL - 11:34 AM</u>
My suggestion is to have zombie kit on standby. LOL!
STUD MUFFIN' and Griggs like this post.

<u>Holy Roller - 11:43 AM</u>
Prolly high on some new designer drug. For now, you guys have him restrained. Just watch him and maybe when he comes down he can tell you what drugs he took… or not.

Please keep us up to date.
Stay safe, Harvey!

<u>G-DAWG - 11:55 AM</u>
I remember that bath salts scare. That was some scary shit.
Who decides to grab mama's bath salts and snort them to see what's going to happen? Jeez… people really have too much time on their hands.

<u>Griggs - 12:10 PM</u>
You do realize they're not really bath salts, right? That's just the name someone slapped on a new drug.
Internet says they're made up of some substances that there's supposedly no way to test for. That doesn't sound right though. I mean, once you know what chemical you're looking for, you should be able to test for it, right?

<u>OLE FOGEY - 12:16 PM</u>
Griggs, You are correct… There are ways to test for ANY Chemical Compounds… What the Talking Heads are saying, is that there is NOT a simple Idiot-proof Test Strip type Test for these compounds, so maybe not a kit test at your local hospital. But any Good Forensic Lab can determine if these compounds are present in a blood sample, fairly easily.

<u>NKOTB - 12:27 PM</u>
What Ole Fogey said is right. Tissue sample run through gas chromatography will find damn near anything.

Tin Foil Joe - 3:02 PM
I think the gooberment is experimenting again. They're placing these new drugs out there to see what effect they have on us. Don't rely on the CDC.

I don't envy you for working in an emergency room, you are basically on the front-lines when these odd illnesses appear. You do have your gut instinct and your knowledge of what is normal or not. Please keep us updated.

G-DAWG - 4:14 PM
  QUOTE - Tin Foil Joe said:
  Don't rely on the CDC.

Smart… very smart.

ADMIN - 5:38 PM
Harvey Corpseman – How about an update? Did he come down from whatever it was?

Harvey Corpseman - 9:19 PM
Ok update! It turns out that my patient with the giggles was transferred to another section by military uniforms they told me. This freaked me out, there are only two people that can sign a transfer. The nursing house supervisor, and the ER charge nurse. I was the charge nurse and I know I didn't sign him out. I spoke to the supervisor and he didn't know anything about it, either. And there's nothing in the log about any transfer.

WTF???????

End of story, this guy is a ghost. Even worse, rumors are that some of the staff are infected, too. This is scary shit, but I've been on shift for 18 hours. Time to let someone else worry about it. L8rs guys.

G-DAWG -10:30 PM
…can't wait for the movie.

…Bottom of Form…

CHAPTER 34
ERICA CHAPMAN
THE DAY BEFORE THANKSGIVING

It was November twenty-third, the day before Thanksgiving when Erica finally found herself with nothing left to do. It had been several days since she'd taken a break, and it suddenly occurred to her that she was alone, tomorrow was Thanksgiving, and she had no one with whom to share the holiday. She turned on the television in hopes of keeping the loneliness at bay for a while. After an hour of humorless laugh tracks, she found herself flipping through channels again. Pausing on one of the cable news channels again, a news headline scrolling across the bottom of the screen caught her eye. She read it twice before accepting that she hadn't misread it.

Millions dead throughout Central Africa. All travel to the following nations is suspended—

The list was frighteningly large. She recalled the conjecture on the news about a pandemic in Uganda and realized that for once the talking heads had actually gotten something right. "Holy shit."

She picked up her cell phone. "Call—Ross—mobile."

"Did you say—call—Ross—mobile?"

"Yes."

"Calling."

CHAPTER 35
CHARLES GRIFFE
SEVEN, TURN, EIGHT, DOOR

Charlie awoke to a gentle shaking as Chris poked his shoulder. "Come on, buddy. Time to get going."

"Hmph?"

"Time to go get your wife."

Charlie sat up with a groan. The sofa wasn't the most comfortable of places to sleep, but he had been uncomfortable sleeping on the bed with another man. He wiped the sleep from his eyes and stretched. "Not my wife," he mumbled.

Chris rolled his eyes. "All right. Your *woman*, then." He handed Charlie a bottle of water from the room's mini-fridge. "Sorry, but this is all we have for dinner."

Charlie put his hand on his pocket, feeling the package of trail mix.

Ain't no need for that. That's yours, and he ain't done nothing but look down his nose at you since you helped him get out of that bar. Screw him if he's hungry. He can find his own food.

The old man was right. Charlie opened the bottle and took a deep swig from the cool water. "You sound like you have a plan?"

Chris nodded. "I do. Not really anything that has to do with getting your... look, I can't keep calling her 'your woman.' That just doesn't sound right. And you really seem to have a problem with calling her your wife. So would you just tell me her name so we can both be happy?"

Charlie nodded. "Sure. Her name's Felicia."

"All right then. I don't necessarily have a plan on how to get to Felicia any easier than what you were already doing. But maybe with two of us, it'll go a little easier. We can watch each other's backs. And it occurs to me that once we have her, there will be three of us. And if there are three of us, there are bound to be more."

Charlie noted that the man was careful to stay positive, avoiding any mention of the possibility that Felicia might already be beyond saving. He didn't know whether to be grateful for the man's consideration, or irritated at his assumption.

"So why does it matter how many of us there are? The old 'strength in numbers' thing?"

Chris nodded. "The more of us there are, the less vulnerable we are."

Charlie's scoffed. "So we can't feed ourselves, and you want to find more people?"

Chris shrugged. "Okay, so there's still a few bugs to work out. For now, let's take it a step at a time." He nodded at the door. "Let's go get Felicia."

Together, they approached the door of the cabin, looked at one another, and by unspoken agreement both put their ears to the door. After a second, Charlie whispered, "You hear anything?"

Chris shook his head. "You?"

"Nope." He pulled his head away and placed his hand on the door knob. But he couldn't bring himself to turn it. In his imagination, Purple Hair stood on the other side, waiting to pounce.

Chris looked at him quizzically. "Something wrong?"

Shaking his head, Charlie took a deep breath, turned the handle, and cracked the door enough to see into the hallway. It was darker than when they had come into the room. There was nothing as far as he could see, though he couldn't see very far in the inky blackness. He glanced down at the watch on his wrist. *Twelve minutes after eight.* He blinked, trying to figure out how many days he'd been running. Everything was so jumbled, and he was so exhausted that everything was running together.

A scream filled the night and Charlie jumped back, half shutting the door before it registered that the sound was too far away for anyone to have seen him. He eased the door open and stepped into the dimly lit hallway. Far away telltale laughter indicated that unless they were fast or lucky, whoever had screamed would probably be doing so again soon. Chris eased into the hallway beside him. He leaned in close to Charlie and whispered, "Which way is your cabin?"

Charlie pulled back with a sneer. "I already told you. Deck Seven."

"No. Which direction, fore or aft?"

Charlie thought for a moment. "Cabin seventy-five, thirty-eight. It's on the starboard side near the front."

"And we're aft port side, four decks up. That's a long way to go. How have you been getting between decks?"

"Stairs."

"Are you crazy? The stairways are way too open."

Charlie shook his head. "I've been taking the emergency stairwells."

"I tried that. They were too dark, and with all the crazies, I was afraid of getting caught in there and not knowing how to get back out before they caught me."

"Seven steps, turn. Eight steps, door."

"What?"

"There's a pattern that makes it easier. Go down seven steps, then turn around on the landing. Then eight more steps and the door will be right in front of you. It's still slow, but it's a lot safer than trying to make your way out in the open."

Chris nodded. "Smart."

They rounded the corner slowly, senses straining for any indication that someone was watching them. Seeing nothing, Charlie turned to Chris. "Let's go."

"Wait. It's seven, turn, eight, door. Right?"

"That's it. And it's not like there's no light. The emergency LEDs flash every five or ten seconds."

"Five or ten seconds in pitch dark can seem like a really long time."

"Yes, it can."

See? He ain't no damned hero. He's just as scared as you are.

Charlie bit his tongue, determined to ignore his father's comment. He nodded to Chris. "You ready?"

Chris took a deep breath. "Guess we're gonna find out. Let's do it."

Charlie rounded the corner and scanned ahead. Nothing. He hugged the wall, moving quietly to the next corner, peeked around, and signaled for Chris to join him. "The door to the stairwell is just around this next corner," he whispered.

Chris nodded.

"Remember—seven, turn, eight, door."

"Got it."

They entered the stairwell and pulled the door closed behind them. Just as the door closed, the red emergency light flared, then dimmed. By that brief light, Charlie saw the way before them was empty. He felt his way forward to the first step, finding the edge with his foot. Very quietly, he snapped his fingers to let Chris know where he was, then reached out with his hand until he felt the other man's sleeve. He dragged him to the handrail, placing his hand on it before taking the first step downward.

Red light flared again, but Charlie resisted the temptation to look up, instead concentrating on counting out his steps. ...*six, seven, turn, one, two three...*

He heard Chris stumble and curse behind him.

"Shh," he hissed, reaching back. He felt his way up the man's sleeve to locate his ear, then leaned in close. "Sound echoes in here."

"Sorry."

Charlie turned back to the stairs, but now he couldn't remember where he was on his count. He waited for a few seconds for the next flare of the emergency light. There! Four more steps to the next door. He reached the landing, then turned to head down another flight. *Seven steps, turn. Eight steps, door.* Another turn, another seven steps. Another turn.

Suddenly, a bright flare of white light nearly blinded him. At the same time, a scream sounded from right in front of him, jolting him out of his trance. He looked up to see a young woman with wild eyes, bedraggled hair and a torn floral shirt, her arm a blur as it flickered toward him. He caught sight of a reflective something in her hand as he threw himself backward. At the same time, Chris stumbled into him from behind. There was a searing agony as the glittering object in her hand sliced across his chest from sternum to right shoulder as he fell to the stairs. He heard Chris growl and jump past him, followed by the sounds of a scuffle.

The light served to silhouette the struggle before him, as the screaming grew in volume, accompanied by Chris grunting. Charlie heard Chris strike the woman three times before the screaming stopped. Then all he could hear was the high-pitched keening of someone trying not to scream.

His father's voice echoed in his head. *Shut up, you damned pussy!*

Charlie clamped his mouth shut and took a deep breath. He looked to where Chris's silhouette shifted, reached toward the little light source on the floor, and pointed the light at Charlie. "You all right?"

He stood and stepped toward where Charlie lay on the stairs and Charlie saw his eyes widen. "Oh hell."

Chris stepped carefully past the limp form on the floor. "How bad does it hurt?"

"What?" Charlie was still trying to catch up to what had just happened. "How bad does what…" He hissed as he tried to sit up. "Oh, fuck me with a blowtorch!" He felt like someone had poured acid on his skin and started to raise his right hand to touch it, but that movement increased the pain. "Son of a bitch!" He raised his left hand with no problem. He reached out with his left hand and grabbed Chris's shoulder. "Help me up."

"I don't know if you should move." Chris sounded doubtful, and Charlie wondered just how bad he looked.

"Well, I'm sure as shit not about to stay here." He tried to keep his voice low, but the pain made it hard to concentrate.

He felt Chris's hand tentatively feel its way up his sleeve and stopped him. "Not my right hand." He grabbed Chris's hand with his left and grasped the man's forearm. "There. Now pull."

He hissed as Chris helped him to his feet, and he felt rivulets of blood running down his chest and soaking into the torn rags of his shirt.

Then a door below them slammed open, and laughter poured into the stairwell. "Shit. Shut off the light." Charlie turned and headed back up the stairs as the stairwell plunged once more into darkness.

"What about her?"

Charlie shook his head, forgetting for the moment that Chris couldn't see him. "Leave her."

"We can't just leave her. They'll kill her."

"And she tried to kill me. Forgive me if my give-a-shit meter is running a bit low." Footsteps and laughter pounded up the dark stairwell from below. "Look, there's no time to discuss this. If you try to carry her, they'll catch you both. Leave her, and we live."

He turned back up the stairs as red flared once more. He heard Chris grunting behind him and turned back to see the man lifting their attacker over his shoulder and step toward the stairs. "You stupid fucking son of a bitch! What the hell are you doing?"

Leave him, boy. He made his choice.

Charlie hesitated, then stepped back down the stairs with a growl.

Damn you, boy. You're as stupid as he is.

Charlie reached out with his left hand until he felt moving cloth on his fingers. Chris grunted as he lugged the woman's dead weight. Charlie felt heavy denim beneath his fingers and grabbed a handful of Levi's, attempting to lift some of the weight off his companion's shoulders as they scrambled up the stairs. And all the while, laughter and giggling gained on them from below.

They reached the landing as the emergency light flared again, and Charlie opened the door just enough to see outside.

And what are you gonna do if some of those fuckers are outside the door?

Charlie didn't have a ready answer to his father's question, but the question was moot. There was no one there. He yanked the door open as the laughter from below got closer. "This way!"

Chris huffed his way through the door, and they turned the corner toward the shadows of the portside corridor of cabins once again. As they approached the final corner before the long row of cabin doors, two giggling forms, a man and a woman in torn and filthy clothing, rounded the corner. Giggles turned to shouts of glee and laughter as they broke into a run. Charlie growled and dropped his weight, running at them as he had the kids on the basketball court. He slammed his shoulder into the man, screaming with the agony it brought to his wound, but he dug deep and lifted the man off his feet and slammed him into the railing over the atrium. Grabbing onto the railing with his left hand, Charlie drove his shoulder forward one last time, and the man plummeted over the rail. He watched as the man hit the floor three decks below and lay still. He had no sooner taken a sigh of relief than the laughing woman landed on his back.

Nails raked at his face and she leaned in to bite his neck. Charlie screamed and punched over his shoulder with his left hand, hitting her repeatedly before she could really sink her teeth into him. But her weight pulled him off balance and he struggled to stay on his feet.

"Fuck it." He spun and threw himself to the floor, landing on top of her, driving his elbow into her body as he did. He felt something crack, and knew he had just broken at least one of her ribs. And still she laughed. He slammed his elbow backward again and again feeling another rib crack. But she refuse to relinquish her death grip on his neck.

"Watch out!"

Charlie turned to see Chris staggering toward him, the unconscious woman still draped across his shoulders. His eyes widened as he saw Chris draw back his foot. Charlie just had time to turn his head as Chris kicked his attacker in her face.

Her grip went limp and Charlie rolled to his feet with a hiss. "Come on. The others are going to be pouring out of—"

The door slammed open, making his point. He and Chris, and Chris's unconscious burden, stumbled around the corner. "Where's the key?"

"Shirt pocket." Chris was too winded to say more, and Charlie reached into his pocket. He jammed the card into the first door they came to and yanked it open. They fell inside and shut the door quickly, but quietly.

Charlie held his breath as they listened to the crowd of laughing maniacs run past in the darkened hallway, and only after they had passed did he let his head drop to the floor.

CHAPTER 36
LINTON BOWERS
I'VE BEEN HEARING THAT A LOT

Linton met Michelle at Hobby Airport's baggage claim area. She smiled thinly at him when he caught her eye, and the two of them navigated the living river of people milling about the overcrowded airport. When he finally reached her, they drew each other close and hugged. Then Linton took her bag and guided her toward the exit. "Come on, babe. Let's get out of this crowd."

She nodded and the two of them wound their way through the throng of pre-holiday red eye fliers, eventually making their way to the parking garage outside the exit. They were quiet until they got into Linton's pickup, but as the doors closed and he started up the engine, she finally started the questioning that he had known was coming.

"You mind telling me what's going on?"

"Sorry, babe. It's sort—"

"Why did you have me bail on the show? This was my chance to show the choreographers what I can really do. It might have gotten me out of the matinee shows and into the starting cast."

"I'm sorry, but this is impor—"

"And why would you bring up my dad? You know how—"

But it was Linton's turn to interrupt. "It's important!"

The fact that he raised his voice to her was enough to quiet her down. He never yelled. Never. Linton was a big man, six foot, three inches tall, and two hundred forty pounds. He'd been in the Marines for three tours and had seen too much of the suck to let minor things bother him. For him to get this close to losing his temper now must have stressed just how serious he thought things were. She got quiet for a moment, working to keep her own temper, willing to wait for him to continue and to let him gather his thoughts.

Linton, on the other hand, concentrated on negotiating through the rush of traffic leaving the airport. He remained quiet as they drove through the exit booth and he paid the parking fee.

He'd had plenty of time to think about Emmet's veiled information. He looked around him at the line of red tail lights as people waited at the traffic light. If what Emmet had communicated was correct, there was a good chance that most of the people in the cars around him would be dead in weeks. The thought was nearly impossible to wrap his head around.

A few minutes later, they were out of the airport and pulling back onto the streets headed home. Once he was out of the airport holiday traveler traffic, Linton began to relax a little.

"I know you haven't always been on board with the Bee Hive," he started, "but it looks like there's a real situation brewing."

"Really, Lint? This is what you brought me home for?" But she quieted again when she saw his knuckles whitening on the steering wheel. "Sorry."

"Emmet called. He's got some inside intel. Shit-hit-the-fan stuff. And it's evidently scary enough that he's bugging out with us."

"Bugging out?"

Linton looked over at her. He could see that she was taking him seriously now. She knew that of all of them, Emmet Pismire had the most to lose by overreacting. Things had to be grim, indeed, if he was willing to risk blowing a promising career in Naval Intelligence. More than that. He was evidently willing to risk prison.

"So what is it?"

"He couldn't give details over the phone. All he was able to pass on was that it has something to do with a global pandemic. That whatever it is has a very high mortality rate, and that we need to get everyone to the bunker within the next three days. Two days now."

Michelle was silent. Linton assumed she was thinking through the implications of what he'd told her. It had been a low blow, invoking her dad to bring her home. She'd known he was lying, of course. Her father had been in a boating accident last year. He had been fishing on Lake

Conroe and some drunk in a jet ski had slammed into him. He had spent two months in a coma while Michelle had been forced to watch him wither away.

Linton had tried his best to support her emotionally through the ordeal. He remembered how much it had hurt her to have to sign the papers that let the hospital disconnect her father from life support. Even worse was that the man had held on without life support for almost an hour, chest heaving as his body instinctively struggled for air. At the end, his eyes had flown open, and the old man had stared sightlessly at the ceiling as his last breath left his chest. Michelle had buried her face in Linton's chest as her father had passed away, and for several months she'd had nightmares in which her father had accused her of killing him.

In bringing that memory back to the surface, Linton had hoped to stress to her the importance he placed on getting her home. And it had worked. But that didn't mean she wasn't going to be pissed at him for doing so. From the corner of his eye, he watched her anger fade as she thought through the implications.

"All right. So what do we do?"

"I've already got the bugout bags in the back of the truck. I also have some gear packed up at home. For now, we go home and get some rest. We'll wait to hear from Emmet tomorrow and hopefully he'll be able to give us more details."

"What if something happens before we hear from him?"

"Then we head for Winnie. Erin's already notified the Hive members, and everyone is supposed to be there by tomorrow."

She was silent for a few more minutes before asking, "This isn't another drill, is it?"

Linton shook his head.

Her shoulders slumped. "Holy shit."

"Yeah, I've been hearing that a lot."

CHAPTER 37

Interview with Dr. Shiri Sondheimer at the CDC Quarantine Station
Bush Intercontinental Airport
Houston, Texas
Recorded November 23rd following the Bahama Queen Coast Guard
rescue
Recording presented to the Joint CDC/WHO Emergency Commission
investigating the Kampala Syndrome Pandemic

Two men come on screen on one side of a clear glass wall. The first man, dressed casually in khakis and a polo shirt, takes a seat in the plastic chair placed there before the recording began. He opens a small tablet computer and turns it on. The second man is dressed in a military uniform, and stands to one side, barely within the frame of the video.

On the other side of the glass, a young woman in blue scrubs sits in a similar chair. Hers however, is behind a small desk on which a small pot sits on a pad. Steam rises from the spout, as it does from the coffee mug beside it. There is also a folder from which the edges of several sheets of paper protrude sitting before her.

The interview begins:

"Dr. Sondheimer, we appreciate your seeing us so promptly. My name is John Markham, and I've been asked to record this interview with you as part of the CDC investigation into what happened on the Bahama Queen."

"Of course." *Dr. Sondheimer picks up the coffee mug and sips. She sets the cup back down, and appears lost in thought for a moment.*

The man in khakis clears his throat. "Dr. Sondheimer?"

She looks up at the faces before her, her own face drawn and weary. "Apologies. I haven't slept in almost two days. Let me begin by saying that this is not going to be good news."

The man in the chair nods. "I suspected as much." *He waves a hand at the camera.* "For the record, would you start at the beginning?"

Sondheimer shuffles through the notes before her and selects a particular page. She skims through it, apparently refreshing her memory before she speaks. "In the pre-dawn hours yesterday morning, the Coast Guard was sent to investigate a suspected outbreak of Kampala Syndrome on the Bahama Queen, a luxury cruise ship in the Gulf of Mexico. The cruise line's home office contacted them after they lost communication with the ship. At almost the same time, the Coast Guard received a garbled transmission from one of the crew indicating that some of his fellow officers had... his words were that they had 'gone crazy.' The transmission ended abruptly, and all attempts to re-establish communications failed. The ship lost power shortly after that, and the Coast Guard immediately launched an investigation.

"The first helicopter they sent out reported that they saw large crowds of people dancing and laughing on the decks. Upon landing, they reported that they were under attack. Recordings of the transmission revealed that there were several people laughing in the background while various weapons were being fired. It's unknown what the fate of the helicopter was, as all communications were lost, and the helicopter wasn't there when the second one was sent. Analysis of the recording, however..."

The man on the outside of the quarantine wall nods impatiently. "Excuse me, Dr. Sondheimer. We've read that report and heard the recordings, too. Could we skip ahead to the autopsy? We're more concerned with what caused the death. Was it the result of a disease? If so, where did it come from, is it contagious, and just what is our level of exposure?"

Sondheimer shakes her head. "Very well." *She shuffles through the folder, finally pulling out another page.* "Subject number eight was..."

"Wait." *The man begins tapping quickly on his tablet computer.* "Number eight? I thought the second helicopter only retrieved three people from the cruise ship."

"They did. According to the reports I received, they managed to capture, restrain, and sedate three people. Those three were initially brought to Houston Methodist Hospital." *She looks up from her notes.* "Methodist has one of the best virology research departments in the area."

Markham nods, types something into his tablet, and waves his hand indicating that she should proceed.

"All three subjects brought back acted erratically, laughing and attacking any person they saw. Kampala was suspected, so I was sent to meet the helicopter. Unfortunately, I wasn't able to get there before they did, and since the nature of the outbreak was being kept quiet, the ER crew brought the patients from the helicopter into the ER. Not knowing what to look for, all their reports showed was that the subjects were obviously mentally impaired, and extremely violent. When several of the staff began to exhibit similar behavior, they initiated quarantine procedures. I arrived just as they were locking down."

"And that's when you had them transported here?"

Sondheimer nods. "For the last few weeks, the CDC has been made aware of the rapid spread of a disease or condition known as Kampala Syndrome, named after the city in Uganda in which the first controlled study was attempted. We received only preliminary reports from the WHO base there before the communications blackout two days later. As far as I know, there have been no other reports.

"I had seen those initial reports from Kampala before they went silent, and recognized the similarity in reported symptoms. I felt it was imperative that we get these people into isolation as quickly as possible. By this time, there were seventeen of them."

"Why did you feel it necessary to move them?"

"While Methodist Hospital is a fine virology research facility, they aren't as well equipped to quarantine large numbers of infected patients as we are here at the CDC. Seeing how quickly we went from three patients to seventeen, I felt the more secure facility here was more appropriate."

Markham nods again, indicating that Sondheimer should continue.

"This afternoon, subject eight managed to break free of his restraints. He attacked the physician who was attempting to take a blood sample. Clawed the man's eyes out and bit through his carotid. The guard on duty was forced to shoot the subject, but we were unable to save Dr. Johnson." *With shaking hands, Sondheimer takes another drink.*

"Which is why we are here, Doctor. You reported that you performed an autopsy on the subject, and that there is significant damage in some areas of the brain?"

"Not precisely."

The man sits back in his chair and cocks his head. "I beg your pardon?"

"There is no evidence of actual damage to the brain. Rather, there is evidence of considerable change in the neural pathways of the subject's brain."

"But I was told that only happens when there has been a traumatic event to the brain, or severe swelling, such as that caused by encephalitis or a cancerous growth."

"Someone has briefed you pretty well." *Sondheimer nods.* "That's usually true. In fact, I did notice similarities between the patient's brain, and that of someone suffering from viral encephalitis. However, there was no swelling of the tissue, no tumors, and no evidence of trauma."

The man is silent for a moment, apparently thinking about her statement. "All right, Doctor. You've told me what wasn't there. So what similarities *did* you see?"

"In the cases you mentioned—cerebral edema, trauma, or cancer—rerouting the neural pathways is the body's attempt to bypass a damaged, or non-functioning portion of the brain. In the case of Number Eight, it appears to be the work of an unknown virus."

"I'm confused, Doctor. Didn't you just say that there was no evidence of a viral infection?"

"No. I said there was no evidence of cerebral trauma or swelling as is typically caused by a viral infection. However, the routing of the neural pathways is consistent enough between the subjects studied, that it must be considered a symptom in and of itself."

"You said subjects. I thought you had only autopsied the one."

"Two actually. I also performed an autopsy on Dr. Johnson. Both subjects showed abnormal density in the white matter of the brain."

The man sighs. "And white matter is...?"

Dr. Sondheimer furrows her brows. "I'm sorry, but I assumed the CDC was going to send a specialist."

"I am a specialist, Doctor. Just not in neurobiology."

"Do you mind if I ask just what your specialty is?"

The man shakes his head. "I'm afraid I'm not at liberty to say. But let's get back to this white matter."

Dr. Sondheimer purses her lips, appearing to think for a moment. "I don't suppose you know anything about computer networks?"

"Let's assume I do."

"Well, the human brain consists of two types of tissue: grey matter and white matter. You can think of the grey matter as a data center consisting of hundreds, or even thousands of servers. The white matter, then, would be the network cables connecting the servers to one another. And when something goes wrong with one of the servers, the body attempts to reroute the network cables around the damaged computer, allowing the information to continue flowing to the rest of the network."

The man nods and waves her on.

"In the cases of Number Eight and Dr. Johnson, it appeared that there was an unusual amount of white matter in cross sections of the brain, so I decided to test for unusual axon activity with a white matter scan."

"A what?"

"Sorry, it's a relatively new type of scan, a neuroimaging technique that allows us to see microstructural properties of the brain's white matter. Basically, it lets us see what parts of the data center are communicating with what other parts. And in this case, we found some fascinating, and terrifying neural activity.

"There seems to be unusual activity in the limbic system, the nucleus accumbens, ventral pallium, the orbitofrontal and anterior cingulate cortex, the hypothalamus and septum pelluci—"

"Doctor? Once again, we are not neurobiologists. However, it seems to me that you're describing functions in a living brain. I don't follow how you could have found this out during an autopsy."

"That's correct. We sedated the other infected subjects and tested them."

"Of course. I'm sorry for the interruption. Please continue."

Sondheimer shuffles through her notes again. "It appears that this virus is rewriting the neural pathways of the human brain to create a kind of feedback loop between parts of the brain that shouldn't be linked. The end result is that the subject becomes disoriented, as if they were intoxicated, and increasingly aggressive and violent. Yet the condition also creates a kind of euphoria, and stimulates the... what most people simply call the pleasure center of the brain. The cognitive ability of the subject is suppressed, and the axons tying it to the pleasure center are, for lack of a better term, cross-wired with the areas of the brain that typically report pain." *She takes another deep breath.* "And all of that is tied in to the reward centers, so that the more aggressive and violent the person becomes, the more pleasure they feel, and the cycle turns into an addiction for them."

There is silence for a moment on both sides of the glass when she is finished speaking.

"Have you been able to determine the vectors?"

She holds her hands out in a gesture of helplessness. "All vectors."

"All?"

"Yes. Preliminary tests show a better than ninety percent transmission rate via body fluids, and nearly as high for air-born dispersal." *She looks up from her notes and clasps her hands before her, waiting for further questions from the men on the other side of the glass.*

"Do you have any recommendations on how to treat or stop it?"

She shakes her head. "It's too late to stop it. From what I can tell, it was too late to stop it weeks ago."

"What do you mean?"

"I mean that rerouting the neural pathways of the human brain doesn't happen overnight. These people were initially exposed weeks ago."

"But that's not possible. The people only got on that cruise ship a few days ago. You yourself told us that the people from the hospital were only exposed yesterday."

Sondheimer nods. "Yes, I did. But from what I can tell, that wasn't their initial exposure. I believe that there is a sequence of events that triggers Kampala Syndrome. The viral exposure is only the beginning. It's like shingles."

"Excuse me?"

"For the last few decades, we've had a vaccine for Chicken Pox. But before that, it was simply accepted as a given that about ninety-five percent of children would contract the disease before the age of eighteen."

"I'm sorry, but are you telling me that this virus is some... some new strain of chicken pox?"

"Please just listen. Chicken pox was so accepted that parents would often have pox parties when one of their kids caught it. They would let the other parents in the neighborhood know, and those parents would often purposely expose their kids just so they could get it over with on their own schedule, and not have to worry about it in the future."

"And what does...?"

Sondheimer holds up her hand. "For many people, chicken pox wasn't the end of the problem, though. It was just the first presentation of a three-stage disease. For about one out of every three adults, the virus reactivated after many years of dormancy. It was triggered by some sort of lowering of the immune system, whether excessive emotional stress, another illness, excessive use of corticosteroids, or any number of other immune inhibiting situations. At that point, the virus came back in another form. We call that form shingles.

"I believe Kampala Syndrome is similar in its makeup, except its initial stage is less obvious than anything else I've ever seen. Other than possibly a few headaches, I don't think there are any external symptoms. And like shingles, the later instance lies dormant in the body until a triggering event.

"This is still speculation, but I believe Kampala's first stage doesn't really go dormant. Instead, it continues to replicate within the body. Since there are no real external symptoms, no one is aware that they are being turned into living incubators until the exposed person reaches a tipping point."

"What sort of tipping point?"

"There's no way to know for sure. Best guess? A certain level of exposure, a density of the virus within the body, followed by a triggering event."

Markham is silent, typing notes into his tablet. He finishes, then looks back up at Sondheimer. "And the trigger?"

"Once the tipping point has been reached, it appears that the actual trigger is simply becoming amused by something."

"Excuse me?"

"Laughter releases various neurotransmitters into the body. Once critical mass is reached, the serotonin and dopamine released by a bout of laughter triggers the rerouted neural pathways and the person succumbs to full-blown Kampala."

The two men look at one another before the seated man tries another question. "Dr. Sondheimer, if what you say is true, then there are people who are already infected and don't currently show any symptoms."

Sondheimer nods.

"How could you possibly know this?"

She takes another drink from her glass. Her hand shakes as she sets the glass back on the desk. "Because once I realized how long it would take for the cerebral changes to take place, I began to suspect. So I tested everyone in this facility. Without fail, every one showed the same results. And I've personally seen three of my people succumb to the syndrome. Each time, it was after they began laughing or made some sort of joke."

"Doctor, there has to be some way to stop this virus."

She shakes her head. "No, there doesn't. Not anymore."

Markham shakes his head sympathetically. "Dr. Sondheimer, I appreciate how wearying this discovery has been for you. Finding that your entire facility has been infected has to be…"

Sondheimer slams her hand down on the desk. "You still don't get it! It's already too late! Maybe we could have stopped it a month ago, or maybe even as little as a few weeks ago. That's assuming we would have recognized it for what it was, and been able to find an anti-viral that was effective on it. But not now. Now it's too late." *She looks intently at him.* "Don't you see? We've had this disease for weeks now, and we never even knew it. All of us! How many times a week do you get a headache? Three? Four? More?

"Well for the last few weeks, maybe longer, any number of those headaches could have been this thing winding its way through your brain, rewiring you without your knowledge."

The man pushes his chair back and stands. He leans in close to the glass. "You aren't just talking about the ship. Or the hospital. Or even your facility here. You're talking about the world?"

Sondheimer sits back in her chair and nods, beginning to smile at Markham. "Finally! Now you understand. This thing has been in the air we breathe for some time now. We just didn't know it. Some people will exhibit symptoms sooner than others, some will be more resistant. Hell, some might even be immune. Some people with certain mental conditions have reduced dopamine levels, so that might make them more resistant. But the fact is, it's all guesswork at this point. And it's too late to do anything about it! We're all screwed." *Dr. Sondheimer begins to laugh.* "All of us, all over the world. Screwed!" *Her laughter continues, and the cameraman, realizing something is wrong, zooms in on her face. The look of terror in her eyes is at complete odds with her maniacal laughter. The screen freezes on her expression of horror.*

THURSDAY
NOVEMBER 24
THANKSGIVING DAY

CHAPTER 38
CHARLES GRIFFE
"A WASTE OF PERFECTLY GOOD BOOZE"

"Hey, Charlie. You awake?"

"What?" He hadn't even been aware he was falling asleep.

Chris's voice came from the darkness behind him. It sounded like he was on the floor, too. "You awake?"

"Yeah. How long was I asleep?"

"I don't know. I fell asleep, too. You all right?"

Charlie could hear the other man shifting in the dark. "No thanks to you," he growled.

"What do you mean? I saved your damned life!"

"Which wouldn't have needed saving if you had left her there like I told you."

"Well, for what it's worth, I'm really grateful that you didn't." The woman's voice caused Charlie to open his eyes and squint into the darkened room. He thought he could see a slight movement in the dim light, but gave up trying to see any details. He felt a moment of guilt at what he'd said, then shoved it aside.

"Yeah? You have one hell of a way of showing it. You trying to gut me, or what?"

"You scared me! I thought you were one of them!"

Charlie let his head drop back and closed his eyes. "Whatever."

A few seconds later, "Well, I'm sorry."

He heard her move toward him. Suddenly light flared in the room as Chris turned the flashlight back on.

"Good! I was afraid you left it."

"Oh. Yeah, I guess this is yours." The light shifted from Chris to the woman. She stepped over in front of Charlie, and reached toward him.

"What the fu…?"

"Shh." He felt her pulling gently at his shirt. "Don't be a baby." As she spoke, she tugged the shirt free of the dried and drying blood on his chest.

"Ouch!" His shirt was stuck to the wound in places, and extremely tender. "What the hell did you cut me with, anyway?"

"I wrapped a piece a broken mirror in some cloth and sort of made a knife out of it."

Charlie looked down at the cut across his chest, seeing the wound for the first time. He winced, "Guess it did the job."

She poked lightly at the wound. "Sorry, but I think you probably need some stitches."

Chris knelt beside her. "You a doctor?"

"Nope. My mom is a retired nurse, though."

Charlie snorted. "Got that on your resume, do you?"

"I watched her treat every bruise, cut, and concussion me and my brother had when we were growing up." She gently peeled more of his shirt away. "I even saw her save a man's life on the street after he got hit by a car."

Charlie hissed as the shirt and dried blood tugged at the edges of the cut.

"Can you move your arm?"

He raised his right, wincing as he did. "Yeah," he hissed. "Hurts like hell, but I can move it."

The light in his face faded as she and her flashlight moved to the faux wood dresser where she began going through the drawers. "If I can find a first-aid kit…" She began pulling out clothes and other items, tossing them unceremoniously onto the bed. After a moment, she sighed. "No such luck."

Charlie heard her open and close the cabin's mini-fridge and sat up, wincing as he did. "Don't worry about it. I'll survive." Chris helped him to his feet and the two of them walked over and sat on the bed.

She stepped back to them. "Hold this." She handed the light back to Chris and laid a few folded T-shirts on the bed beside Charlie. She held up a small glass bottle, opened the lid, and poured the amber liquid onto one of them.

Charlie knew what was coming, and attempted to make light of it. "That's a waste of perfectly good booze." He smiled.

Without warning, the woman slapped his face. "What the hell was—?"

"Don't smile. Don't laugh. Don't even think about anything funny!"

"What?"

"We don't know what's making everyone go crazy here. We don't know if it's something in the food, in the water, in the air... if it's a bacteria, or a virus, or a curse from God Himself. All we know is that the crazy people are the ones who are laughing. So don't laugh. Got it?"

Fuming, Charlie rubbed his cheek. "You seriously think I'm going to go crazy if I just smile?"

"I don't know. And that's the point. None of us knows."

You gonna let this bitch talk to you like that, boy?

Charlie started to snarl back at her, but Chris piped up. "She's right."

"What? You're seriously buying into this shit?"

"I'm buying into the fact that we don't really know what's causing this..." he waved his hand, "whatever it is. And she's right about the fact that the crazy people are the ones that are laughing. We already talked about that. So what does it hurt to be extra careful?"

Charlie shook his head. "You're both nuts." But the woman had succeeded in changing his mood. He no longer wanted to smile. He turned back to her, nodding at the whiskey-soaked T-shirt. "Fine. Do it."

She leaned in. "This is probably going to sting a bit."

It did, but Charlie's anger at her overrode the pain. He ground his teeth and glared at her.

Chris broke the silence as she wiped at Charlie's wound. "So what's your name?"

"Tabatha Haddix. Tabby." She wiped more blood away, dabbing at the open cut.

"Good to meet you, Tabby." Chris said. "I'm Chris Tallant, and the guy you slapped—"

"And tried to cut open," Charlie added.

"...is Charlie Griffe."

Tabby nodded. "Well, thanks, Chris."

"For what?"

She turned to face him. "For not listening to your friend here and leaving me to die on the stairs."

Chris nodded. Charlie simply grunted.

Tabby finished cleaning his wound and tore the other two shirts into wide strips, ripping carefully in a spiraling strip that reminded Charlie of the way he'd seen his father peel an apple. When she was finished, she began wrapping the strips around his chest and over his right shoulder. When she was finished, the cut was covered. "Like I said before, you really need some stitches, or at least some butterfly bandages. But without a first-aid kit, this is the best I can do."

She took the light back from Chris and turned to the closet. After a moment of rummaging, she pulled something off a hanger. "Here we go."

She held out a blue denim button up and helped Charlie slip it on. "How's that?"

The sleeves were a little short, but Charlie figured he wasn't going to be posing for a fashion magazine anytime soon. He eased his right arm up slowly. "Hurts, but I'll make do."

Tabby nodded. "Good." Her eyes narrowed and she looked unflinchingly at Charlie. "Now, Charlie? I'm only going to say this once. I'm sorry I cut you. I panicked, and I reacted. But I'm not about to walk on eggshells around you. And I'm not going to spend any more time apologizing. So I need to know right now, are we all right? Or do I need to leave you two and find my own way once we leave this room?"

There she goes again. Woman's too damn pushy. You need to put her in her place, boy.

Charlie sorted his thoughts from his father's words for a moment. Then he nodded at her. "Far as I'm concerned, we're good."

Pussy!

Tabby nodded. "Good." She walked back to the mini-fridge and pulled out two bottles of water. She tossed one to each of them before grabbing a third one and twisting the cap open. She took a swallow and wiped her mouth with the back of her hand. "So what's the plan, then?"

"We're trying to get Charlie back to his cabin on Deck Seven. He's got... someone... that we think might be trapped there."

"Wife?"

Charlie rolled his eyes and Chris waved him off before he could say anything. "Just call her his girlfriend."

She was silent for a moment. "How do you know she's still alive? Or that she's not..." Her voice trailed off as she apparently realized what she was saying.

There was an awkward silence as the three of them stared at the floor before Charlie cleared his throat. "We don't." He looked up at her and set his jaw. "We don't know if she's dead or alive... or a fucking laughing lunatic like the others. But I have to find out." He took a swig from the water bottle. "Chris says he's coming with me, so that leaves you. Are you in or out?"

"I'm in. But that brings us back to my original question: what's the plan?"

"We're on Deck Nine." Charlie turned to Chris. "Right?"

Chris nodded. "Port side. We need to get to starboard, up most of the length of the ship, and down two more decks."

"How?" Tabby clearly wasn't willing to let them skate by on the matter.

Chris looked at Charlie, evidently willing to let him take the lead on the matter.

Charlie shrugged. "You remember where you were when we ran into you?"

"In the emergency stairwell?"

"Yep. Between Decks Eight and Nine. We started on Deck Eleven."

"So down the stairwell, then across the width of the ship, and along almost the entire length of the ship? Are you crazy?"

Bitch, bitch, bitch... all she wants to do is complain. Just like your mother. Nothin' but a whinin'—

"So don't come." Charlie was gruff, angry at his father, angry at Tabby, and especially angry at the pain the cut across his chest caused him. But he was also tired of being put on the defensive again. First, Chris had questioned his motives, now Tabby was questioning his methods. If they didn't like his plans, they could quit their complaining and offer up a better suggestion. Otherwise, they should just shut the hell up and get out of his way.

You tell 'em, boy!

"Shut up, old man." The words were out before he could stop himself, and both Chris and Tabby looked at him askance.

"What?"

"She reminds me of my old man," Charlie covered. "Always complaining, but never offering up any better solutions." He faced their newest companion. "*Do* you have a better idea?"

Tabby appeared to be taken aback. "N-no."

"Then how about you shut the fuck up and get out of my way." With that, Charlie pushed past them and went to the cabin door.

CHAPTER 39
AUGUST GRAPPIN
HUNGER

Other than pleasure/pain, hunger seemed to be the only recognizable sensation in his life now, and the smell of chocolate made Gus's stomach growl loud enough that some of his friends had laughed and pointed. He giggled with them as they ran through the demolished area that had only days before been a huge dining hall. Reaching the source of the wonderful smell, Gus yanked the glass doors to the large pastry display open hard enough that the one on the right snapped off its hinge and fell to the floor, bouncing once on the carpet before it broke. Chuckling his pleasure to the group, Gus snatched at the object of his immediate attention and began answering the need of that most primal urge, hunger.

He'd been giggling and moaning with pleasure as he stuffed handfuls of chocolate cake into his mouth for a few minutes when he looked up to see a blond woman crouched beneath a table about thirty feet away. She stared at Gus and his friends through wide eyes. Unmoving as she was, Gus almost missed her amidst the tangle of overturned tables and chairs. Her eyes darted from Gus, to his friends, to the food, then back to Gus. Gus guffawed, pointing and slapping chocolate smeared hands at his companions, drawing their attention to the woman.

"Waldo!" he wheezed.

The woman leapt to her feet, clutching something in her hand and threw it at them as they started moving toward her. The dinner plate struck Gus in the shoulder, and the sensation sent a thrill through him. He laughed and chased after her, hoping she would do it again. His nervous system had been so corrupted by this time, that it interpreted any feeling at all as pleasure. The more intense the stimulus, the greater the pleasure.

As he ran, he rubbed the bruise where the plate had struck him, shoving his thumb into it in an attempt to squeeze out more pleasure as he ran after the woman. But there was no more feeling to be had. He chased after her. The woman slung chairs behind her, tripping Gus, and many of his friends. She slammed through the double doors at the entrance to the dining hall and turned left down the first hallway. Gus was back on his feet in seconds, chasing after her.

He ran through the doors, turning to follow as she raced up the corridor. She was fast, but Gus was faster. He easily outdistanced his friends, gaining quickly on the woman. He was only seconds behind as she turned right at the next intersection. He could hear his friends hooting behind him as they followed.

Gus staggered as he tried to negotiate the corner, his feet clumsier than they had been before everything had become so funny. His shoulder hit the wall of the hallway as he turned after the woman. He righted himself and kept going, but he had lost ground. She was farther ahead now, and the light this far away from the outer windows was dim. He stumbled again, tripping over the body of a man. Caked blood covered the face, and the mouth was oddly contorted. Gus slowed, stuck his tongue out at the dead man, and laughed even louder. He turned his full attention back up the dim corridor to see the woman had pulled ahead again. His friends came up the corridor behind him.

Far ahead, well beyond the woman he chased, Gus could hear even more laughter. More friends were coming. The woman cried out, and her high-pitched wail was comical in Gus's ears. He could hear her sobbing as she ran.

She put on a burst of speed, and Gus could see her shine a light at a door. She ran a few doors farther and stopped. Slipping something from her pocket, she slipped it into the door, opened it, and slammed the door closed scant seconds before Gus got to her.

Slapping his palm loudly against the door, he heard her scream inside. He giggled. Misfiring synapses vaguely reminded him of a similar situation he'd been in recently, and he stopped for a second struggling again for the memory. Laughing aloud, he recalled the line.

"Little pig, little pig, let me in!"

Laughing and hooting, his friends arrived, and together they all began beating down the door.

CHAPTER 40
LINTON BOWERS
"I TRULY HOPE I'M WRONG."

Picking Michelle up from her red-eye had put them getting home at well after one in the morning, and they were exhausted. Linton didn't even remember setting the alarm on his phone until its irritating beep woke him at ten-thirty. Groggy, opened his eyes and immediately shut them against the blindingly bright morning sun that streamed in through the bedroom windows. Eyes still closed, he slapped blindly at the nightstand until he found the phone and shut the alarm off. "Michelle? Time to get moving, babe. Let's…" His groping hand found that the spot in the bed beside him was empty. He forced his eyes open to find that his wife wasn't in the bed. "Michelle?"

"I'm gettin' too old for this." He lay there for a moment, staring at the ceiling, trying to gather the willpower to get up. He remembered pulling all-nighters in the past, or nights when he'd stayed awake into the wee hours of the morning, only to get up after two or three hours of sleep. Now, only a decade or so later, he was beginning to feel the ache in his back when he didn't get at least six hours. He'd barely slept since he'd heard from Emmet, unable to relax until he got Michelle home. He never slept well when she was on tour, but ever since getting word that they had a bugout scenario, he hadn't been able to relax at all.

Last night had gone a long way to catching him up, and he was only mildly exhausted. Nevertheless, it was better than he'd felt in a few days. Rubbing his face, he swung his feet out of the bed, groaning as he stood up. The faint sound of the television drew him to the den where he found Michelle standing in front of the flat screen. She held a cup of coffee as she watched one of the cable news channels. "There you are. I was looking…" His voice trailed off as she turned toward him.

He and Michelle had been married for seven years, and he'd known her for three years before that. One of the things that he treasured in her was the fact that she was such a strong woman. He'd seen plenty of his buddies in the Marines who had married pretty, timid, young women who had hung on their arms and doted on their husbands' stories of glory. Trophy wives who married the big, strong, man in uniform. But as often as not, those marriages didn't last. Sooner or later, reality intruded. Military life was a hard life.

Linton had been so lucky to find a kindred soul in Michelle, a quiet warrior spirit who was strong enough to cut through the emotional crap that life dished out, put her head down, do whatever needed to be done, and deal with the consequences later.

In their years together, he'd seen her happy and sad. He'd seen her show concern, and on occasion, he'd seen her angry. Those were times he dreaded, almost as much as he looked forward to the mischievous, lustful look she showed in the bedroom. But the look in her eyes now was something he'd never seen. For the first time since he'd known her, there was genuine fear in her eyes. "What is it?"

"They're saying there's some sort of outbreak in Africa. Estimates are that there are millions of people dead."

"Millions?" Linton walked numbly to stand beside her and together the two of them watched the talking heads comment somberly to each other as film footage of burned villages played behind them. All travel to Africa was suspended. All American travelers returning from Africa were to be quarantined by the CDC until they were cleared.

"This is it, isn't it? This is what Emmet was talking about."

"Holy shit." His heart thumped in his chest. It was one thing to plan for "what if" scenarios. It was quite another to see one playing out. "Yeah. I'm pretty sure it is."

Michelle watched the screen until it switched to the Thanksgiving Day parade in New York. She raised the remote and shut it off. "Okay, so what do we need to do?"

"The truck's in the garage. We pack all the canned food, gasoline, and weapons in it and wait until we hear from Emmet."

"How long?"

Linton glanced at his watch. "Let's have some breakfast and pack. If we haven't heard from him by noon, I'll give him a call."

"That won't get him in trouble?"

"I'll just be checking to see when he's going to be here for Thanksgiving dinner."

Michelle nodded. She sipped her coffee as she headed into the kitchen. "Bacon and eggs?"

"Sounds good."

Linton's phone rang as he was loading the last of the five-gallon gas cans in the back of the truck. He didn't recognize the number, but answered it. "Lima Bravo."

"Happy Thanksgiving, Lint." If he didn't know the man so well, Linton might have been fooled by Emmet's almost cheerful voice. "You guys still up for another guest at the table?"

Linton sighed in relief. "Sure thing. You on your way over?"

"Yep. I'm in a cab as we speak. Looks like I'm about…" There was a muffled discussion as Emmet covered the phone with his hand and spoke to someone. "Cabbie says we're about twenty minutes away from your driveway."

"Sounds good. See you when you get here."

Michelle was at the garage door with another box of canned food when he looked up. "He's on his way?"

"Yeah. Twenty minutes."

She handed him the box. "What then?"

He heaved the box into the bed of the truck. "Then we see what he has to say."

It was only fifteen minutes before a cab pulled into the driveway and an exhausted-looking Emmet Pismire stepped out. He slid a heavy duffle bag out of the back seat, handed the driver some bills, and walked to the door. His expression was somber as he hugged Michelle and slapped Linton on the shoulder. They all walked inside. "You guys ready to pull out?"

Linton nodded.

"Good. We probably don't really have to go right away, but it's better to be ready, just in case."

"It's that epidemic in Africa, isn't it?" Michelle asked.

Emmet nodded. "It's not just in Africa. It's spread into Europe." He walked into the kitchen and helped himself to a cup of coffee. "So far, we think we've kept it contained here in the US, but there's no way of knowing how long that'll last."

Linton swallowed. "So what is it? Ebola, anthrax… what?"

"We don't know. This shit has spread so fast that they haven't had time to figure it all out."

"That's kinda hard to believe."

He shrugged. "I'm sure someone somewhere knows what it is, but it's not common knowledge yet." He pulled up a chair at their breakfast table and sat staring at his coffee. Linton and Michelle sat across from him. Michelle put her hand on his arm. "Emmet? You're starting to really scare me."

Emmet nodded. "Good. I wouldn't want to be the only one in the room that's scared shitless." He took another sip of coffee before looking up at them. "I'm real sketchy on what's going on. Truth is, I'm not supposed to know any of this. But with all the buzz, it's hard to miss that there's something big happening. And you know how I can't keep my nose out of things.

"So I've been putting things together from different sources. There have been disaster recovery plans that are being brought out of mothballs, about three times as many high-level reports have been coming in than usual; high level encrypted stuff to the higher ups. There's been a lot of other traffic, too. Stuff from FEMA, the Coasties, World Health Organization, and the CDC. Day before yesterday, I saw COOP advisories coming in."

Linton blew a deep breath out through his mouth. "Wow."

"COOP?" Michelle looked from Chris to Linton.

"Continuity of Operations Plan," Linton said. His eyes never left his friend's. "It means the government is planning to start rotating key officials into secure bunkers."

Emmet nodded slowly. "Combine that with the other traffic, and it's not hard to figure out that this epidemic overseas has really spooked the higher ups."

"So with all this going on, how did you manage to get out? I mean, security has to be insane right now."

Emmet looked at his watch. "By now, it probably is. I left last night."

Linton furrowed his brow. "So?"

"The COOP reports were for Colonel Stafford's eyes. But the colonel was out sick a few days ago and he had me covering for him. I saw those reports in his desk, I stepped outside and called you on my burner. Then I developed a cough and left for the day."

Linton shook his head. "Holy shit, Emmet! They're gonna be on you like white on rice."

Emmet shook his head. "At some point, they'll try to call me. Eventually, they'll send someone to check on me. There will be some buzz, and they might even pull the records on my phone. But I called you from the burner. So, not finding any suspicious activity on *my* cell, they'll track the phone's GPS. At that point, they might even contact someone in New York to find out what I'm doing there."

"New York?"

Emmet shrugged. "My phone might have accidentally fallen out of my pocket and into a ream of paper that was sent to a New York publishing house."

"I don't get it."

"Did I ever tell you I thought about writing a book one time?"

"What the hell are you talking about?"

"I found out that there was a lot more to getting a book published than just sending a manuscript to a publisher. In fact, when you send an unsolicited manuscript to one of the big publishing houses, it usually sits in their slush pile for weeks before anyone even looks at it.

"Ah!"

"Yeah. I figure if they actually send someone to find me, they'll just find the phone in New York at first. If they don't then it'll be at least a couple of weeks before anyone opens that package. By then, the battery will have died anyway."

Linton nodded. "You're taking a hell of a risk, buddy."

"Yeah, but from what I saw in those reports, the government's about to have a lot more to worry about than one AWOL sailor. I doubt they'll even remember my name in another few weeks."

"So what's the plan, then?"

Emmet yawned. "Well, I don't know about you, but I'm beat. I've been on the road all night. How about we grab a few hours of rest while we can and head for the bunker this evening?"

Linton nodded. "I'm pretty well rested, but you catch some z's in the guest room. Michelle and I will finish packing the truck. Maybe catch some more news." He looked at the time on his phone. "Wake you at six?"

"Sounds good. The bunker's what, two hours away?"

"A little less."

"So with everything packed, you could get up at six, fix a quick bite, and be out the door by six thirty?"

"Yeah, and at the bunker around eight o'clock."

Linton showed his friend to the guest room, and Michelle brought him some blankets and kissed him on the cheek. He looked surprised.

"What's that for?"

"You risked a lot to help us."

Emmet shrugged. "And you guys have offered me a place to stay."

She looked at the small bed, then back at him.

"That's not what I'm talking about, and you know it. If this all goes down the way it's starting to look like it will, that bunker is going to be one of the best places to try and ride things out."

"You really think it's going to happen?"

"It's already happening in Africa, and starting in Europe. I think it's only a matter of time. And I don't know how much time."

Michelle pressed her lips into a thin line and started to turn. But Emmet wasn't through.

"You know, if I'm wrong… if this doesn't happen, then I'm going to be hunted down eventually. They'll find me, haul me in as a deserter, and if I'm lucky, I'll spend several years in prison." He looked her squarely in the eyes. "And even with that, I truly hope I'm wrong."

CHAPTER 41
ERICA CHAPMAN
THANKSGIVING MORNING

What began as a melancholy Thanksgiving Thursday got progressively worse as the morning passed. The lawyers wanted Erica out by Friday, so she'd already packed what few personal belongings she still had at the ranch into her old mini-van in preparation for the trip home. According to the documents she'd signed, their representatives would be by in the morning to *facilitate the transfer of ownership* on the ranch. She assumed that was legalese for kicking her out and taking the keys.

She worked on a final cleaning of the house, mainly to keep herself distracted. But as she cleaned, she kept running into reminders of the years she and Uncle J had spent together. And as morning faded to afternoon, so too did melancholy devolve into outright depression. By late afternoon, she realized she had finished cleaning long ago. At that point, all she was really doing was wandering from room to room, looking at pictures and knick-knacks, all the while getting more and more depressed.

I need to get out of here for a while. Her stomach growled agreement, reminding her that, despite bone-wearying depression, the body still required its due. Checking the time, she was startled to find it was already late in the afternoon. *So then, food.* That decided, she grabbed her keys and left without further planning. Erica had long ago decided that planning was overrated, anyway.

She had cause to second guess that philosophy half an hour later, as she aimlessly drove around Katy, looking for someplace to eat. It took only a few minutes to remember that her dining options were going to be limited on Thanksgiving. And of those places that were open, she had to choose between fast food, and restaurants so crowded that many of them had lines waiting in the parking lots. She absolutely refused to have fast food for Thanksgiving. The very thought seemed almost sacrilegious. She figured there had to be someplace she could go where she could walk in and have a semi-traditional turkey dinner without having to wait for an hour.

Salvation appeared in the guise of an IHOP that perched in the corner of a shopping mall parking lot. Surprisingly, there were quite a few cars parked out front, giving testament to the fact that it was open. Yet, there was no evidence of the huge crowds she had seen at some of the other diners. *Finally. Something going my way!*

She should have known better. There was a half hour wait before they had a table cleared for her. Twenty minutes after being seated, she looked at her plate in fascinated disgust as a sea of giblet gravy congealed around an island of factory pressed turkey resting on a bed of soggy dressing. *Christ on a stick, I was actually eating this?*

She dropped her fork, appetite gone for the moment, and looked around at the crowded diner. There was an old couple sitting at a booth across the room, almost shouting as they tried to hear one another over the constant din of clinking dishes and shouted orders between the wait staff. Erica watched as busboys, waiters, and waitresses frantically scrambled to keep ahead of the holiday rush.

Shaking her head, Erica pushed away from the table, paid at the register, and left the bustling restaurant. She'd wanted to get away from the quiet depression of Uncle J's ranch, but being thrust into such a crowd wasn't quite what she'd had in mind.

By now, the day was done, the sun long gone below the western horizon, and she had some serious reservations as to how much more of an ass-kicking she could take from the world. Uncle J's death, the loss of the ranch, the state of her personal life... and all just in time for the holidays. *No wonder so many people commit suicide this time of year.*

She walked across the darkening parking lot towards her old van, diligently checking her surroundings as she went. It was another of Uncle J's lessons. *Pretty girl like you, you gotta keep your eyes open. Muggers look for folks that ain't payin' attention.* She'd always blushed when he complimented her, but the lesson held, nonetheless. As a result,

Erica was one of those people that tried to sit with her back to the wall, and made sure she knew where the exits were when she walked into a room. She still heard his voice, "Some folks call it paranoid. I just call it payin' attention."

Whatever you chose to call it, it was part of her now. As she scanned her surroundings though, a movie marquee caught her eye. The AMC 20 across the mall parking lot was open, and it suddenly occurred to her that she really didn't feel like going back to the empty ranch house. She checked the marquee to see if any of the titles looked interesting.

While there were twenty screens, most of the titles ran on more than one, and severely limited her options. *Gambit,* the latest X-Men movie, was playing on four screens, and *Avatar 2* took another four. Besides those blockbusters, there was Mila Kunis's latest romantic comedy on two screens, *The Bourne Betrayal* on three screens, and *Star Trek 4* was beginning to die down and was also down to two screens. But the new animated movie *Grump* was taking up the slack with three more screens. The only movie that even looked like it was slightly holiday themed was *Hell's Holiday*, and it looked like the writers had managed to combine Halloween and Christmas into one singularly bad movie.

She was briefly torn between the romantic comedy, and the latest in the Jason Bourne franchise, but considering the state of her own love life, she sure as hell didn't feel like seeing a rom-com. No, an action flick was just the kind of distraction she needed. Not seeing the need to take the car just to cross the parking lot, Erica opted to walk the hundred yards to the theater.

There turned out to be just over half an hour before the seven forty showing started, so she bought her ticket, a box of chocolate-covered peanuts, and a diet soda. Seventeen dollars and fifty cents later, she wandered around the lobby looking at the cardboard cutout advertisements for upcoming movies. *Star Wars: Episode 9, Expendables 4*, and the upcoming release of a new movie called *Bay's End* that looked like a rip off of the old King movie *Stand By Me*. Erica shook her head at that one. "Typical Hollywood," she thought. "Not an ounce of originality in the whole damn town."

She noticed patrons beginning to exit the previous viewing of

Bourne Betrayal and made her way over to wait in line with the rest of the milling Thanksgiving crowd. The exiting moviegoers seemed excited as they walked out, so her hopes were high that this would be better than the last movie she'd seen.

Fifteen minutes later, she sat near the front of the theater, simply too lazy to climb too far up the stadium seating. She fought briefly with the box of candy before breaking a nail on the faux perforated thumb hole. At that point, she'd had enough and bit into the box, ripping the end of it off with her teeth. *Take that you little shit!* And with that unfortunate choice of descriptor for her chocolate-covered peanuts, the lights dimmed, and the preliminary movie trailers began.

After fifteen minutes of previews for coming attractions, the familiar Jason Bourne theme music finally began, and she settled in while Matt Damon fought his way through a wall of the worst marksmen in the world. It always amazed her that the hero in a Hollywood production could walk through a building full of men wielding fully automatic machine guns, and take them all out with nothing more than a small pistol, all while never taking a hit or even breaking a sweat. She shook her head, wondering if she was going to regret her movie choice.

About half an hour into the movie, she heard laughter from the theater next door. It sounded as if the antics of Mila Kunis and her entourage were funnier than the TV commercials had let on. Turning her attention back to the screen before her, Erica watched as Jason Bourne set his plan in motion. Another round of muted laughter came from the other side of the wall, and this time it was accompanied by what sounded like a scream. It was distracting enough that she cocked her head to the side, listening more intently. Another wave of laughter, and more screams sounded. She looked around and saw several other people that seemed disturbed as well. Two men got out of their seats and walked down the stairs toward the entrance. As they passed Erica, she heard them muttering about having management turn down the volume next door so they could enjoy the movie. They rounded the wall at ground level and walked back toward the entrance.

Erica knew immediately when they reached the entrance. Everyone must have known, because the volume of the laughter—and of the screaming suddenly trebled, and she finally realized that something was horribly wrong. One of the two men came backpedaling back into sight just below her with that deer in the headlights look that said that he knew something was wrong, but didn't have any idea how to react. That was when a small group of people tackled him and began kicking him as he screamed. One of the men laughed maniacally, and straddled the man, punching and scratching at his face. To Erica's horror, the attacker then leaned over and bit into the man's cheek, ripping a mouthful of skin off with his teeth. The man's screams intensified, and Erica's skin crawled as she froze in her seat, unable to process what she was seeing. The others, two more men and a woman, pulled the first maniac off the man on the floor and Erica thought at first that they had regained their sanity.

She was wrong—terribly wrong. Rather than giving the poor man relief, they immediately began kicking him where he lay in a fetal curl, crying on the sticky cinema floor. The woman of the group took one of her heels off her foot and knelt beside the man. She began beating him with the heel of the shoe, tittering the whole time, until to everyone's horror, the man quit screaming and she rolled him onto his back. Erica could see he was unconscious, just before the woman drove the heel of her shoe through his eye and twisted it. Her companions thought that was hilarious, and the first attacker turned toward Erica, chuckling maniacally past a hunk of cheek.

She screamed.

Just about everyone in the theater screamed. The laughing maniac who had locked eyes with Erica launched himself over the first row of seats below her, eyes never leaving hers. She grabbed her purse and scrambled over the back of her seat into the row behind her, trying to escape higher into the stadium seating of the theater. The rest of the theater erupted into a panicked madhouse as people screamed and left their seats, trying to put as much distance between themselves and the demented attackers on the ground level. Erica glanced back at the two-legged hyena chasing her, and thought distance was probably a pretty good idea. Two steps gained her a little room as her pursuer struggled to climb over the seats. Two more steps and she dared hope she was in the clear. And just as that thought entered her mind, her feet hit a puddle of soda on the sticky floor. She didn't even have time to scream as she went down, cracking her elbow on the back of one of the seats.

CHAPTER 42
LINTON BOWERS
"LOOKS LIKE KEITH IS DRUNK AGAIN."

The screeching of wheels followed by the unmistakable sound of an automobile accident brought Linton out of the garage and into the house. From the kitchen, Michelle looked at him, concerned.

"That sounded close!"

Emmet came out of the guest room and the two of them walked toward the front window. Linton noted that his friend held a pistol in his hand, finger parallel to the barrel. He didn't know whether to be more concerned that Emmet had thought to keep his weapon beside him as he slept, or that he hadn't thought to grab his own.

They drew opposite corners of the drapes away from the window to look at the scene across the street. By the fading light of the evening sun, Linton could see that his neighbor had driven his car into the garage, without bothering to open the garage door first.

Neighborhood kids had interrupted their street ball game to gather around and gawk.

Linton shook his head in disgust. "Looks like Keith is drunk again."

"What happened?" Michelle's voice from behind startled him.

"Keith Gray drove his car through his garage door." He watched as Keith's neighbor from just next door trotted over to see what had happened. The neighbor called something out that Linton wasn't able to hear as Keith staggered out of his garage, stumbling over a crumpled section of sheet metal, and fell to his knees in the driveway. Just then, Linton's phone alarm began beeping. He let the drapes fall back into place and pulled the phone out of his pocket. "The idiot just got off a DUI last month." He shut off the alarm. "I thought he was smarter…"

"What the hell?" Emmet interrupted.

"What?" Linton looked over at Emmet, who was making a face as if he'd just realized he had eaten something from the north side of a south-bound dog. "What is it?" He and Michelle moved to the window together just as they heard screaming from outside. Michelle got there first and gasped. Linton pulled the drapes above her open. His eyes widened at the sight before him.

Keith's next door neighbor had reached him in the driveway, and Keith had latched onto the man, drawing him down into a grotesque embrace as he bit into the other man's shoulder. This was no ordinary bite either. Keith was doing his best to rip a hunk out of his would-be rescuer, worrying his head from side to side as the other man screamed for help.

Emmet was already running to the front door and Linton started to join him.

"Wait, guys!"

The men stopped at Michelle's call. "What?"

She pushed the drapes closed and stepped back. "There's more of them."

Linton stepped to the window as the sound of children laughing sounded from the front yard. The sound was accompanied by screams of other children, and the distinct sound of a screaming woman. He drew the drapes back just enough to peek outside, but not enough to draw anyone's attention. Linton got the feeling he was caught up in an episode of The Twilight Zone. Reality had simply shifted on him in that same, macabre way that the old television show had done and his senses simply couldn't be trusted. There was no way he was actually seeing a group of pre-teens dragging a grown woman to the sidewalk.

The group of ball players from across the street was laughing uncontrollably, kicking the shrieking woman or beating her with baseball bats. A solid-sounding thud accompanied a wooden bat impacting her skull, and the kid who swung it hooted with glee.

"Holy fuck!" Emmet stepped back from the window. Eyes wide, he looked at Linton and repeated himself. "Holy fuck, Linton. Did you see... those little shits killed..." He turned around and walked into the kitchen. Linton and Michelle followed him.

"Emmet? What kind of disease was on those reports? Is this it?"

Emmet simply stared at him, eyes unfocused.

"Emmet!" Linton stepped forward and shook him. "Snap out of it, dude. We don't have time for you to freak out."

His friend blinked and nodded. "Yeah. But holy fuck, man. Those kids just killed that woman."

"So is it the disease?"

"What disease?" Linton could see he was still having difficulty processing what they had just seen. He couldn't blame the man, but they didn't have time for it, either. Out of the corner of his eye, he saw Michelle leave the room.

"The disease that has everyone in ONI in a panic."

Emmet blinked for a second, seemingly trying to gather his thoughts. "I'm not sure. It's something they just called Kampala Syndrome. No one seems to really say what it does. They just know that it..." His eyes finally met Linton's. "Shit. This has to be it. One of the reports mentioned altered mental states. I just thought they meant people got disoriented or something like that."

Linton shook his head. "Well, I'd say those people's mental states are sure as hell altered."

Michelle came back into the kitchen carrying a small canvas duffle and Linton's shoulder holster with his Glock. She handed him his pistol rig and reached into the duffle. She pulled out a gas mask and held it out to Emmet. She looked at Linton. "I think it's time to go."

Linton finished snapping his shoulder holster into place and took the second gas mask. He held it in his hand looking at it. He felt a little foolish at first, but noticed Emmet strapped his on without hesitation. She pulled out a third mask as more screams sounded from outside, followed by the sound of breaking glass. Linton and Michelle looked at one another then hurriedly followed Emmet's lead.

Linton adjusted the mask to where he could see relatively well. From their drills, he knew the masks they had chosen would sacrifice very little in the way of peripheral vision. That was one of the reasons the Bee Hive had settled on the Israeli M-15 mask. But that didn't mean they were comfortable, by any means. Still, if that bug... virus, or whatever it was had already reached the streets outside, a little discomfort seemed a small sacrifice to make. He went into the bedroom and grabbed a light hoodie, slipping it on over the holster, leaving it unzipped most of the way, for easy access to his pistol. "Everybody tight?" Emmet and Michelle both nodded, confirming a good seal on their masks.

"Voicemitter check?"

"Check here." Michelle's voice sounded a little tinny through the mask's voice amplifier, but the volume was good.

"Emmet?"

"Check."

Linton nodded. "Michelle, you have your pistol?"

She raised her jacket so he could see the twin to his own Glock 17 strapped to her hip. As with most of their equipment, members of the Bee Hive were encouraged to use the same pistol so that parts and ammunition would be interchangeable.

He glanced at the pistol Emmet carried. It was a Glock 19. Not quite the same as his own, but it was close enough that they could at least use the same ammunition.

"So what's the plan?" Emmet asked

"Truck's already packed. We get the hell out of Dodge." He headed to the garage door as they spoke.

"Not to sound ungrateful or anything, but please tell me we have more than these three pistols?"

"Get in the truck and you'll find company in the back seat. Now can we go?" He opened the door that led to the garage and they climbed into Linton's extended cab pickup.

"Nice," Emmet said as he climbed into the back. He grabbed the AK-47 from where it laid in the seat.

Linton and Michelle climbed into the front, where Michelle had another one waiting. Linton looked back at Emmet. "Ready?"

Emmet nodded. Linton turned to his wife. "You ready, baby?"

She yanked back on the charging lever to her rifle, checked the load, and nodded. "Ready."

Linton thumbed the garage door opener and turned the engine key. Looking out the rearview mirror, he saw kids from the street turn at the sound of the garage door. Laughing and hooting, several of the ball players began to run their direction.

"Come on, Lint. Let's get out of here."

"Gotta wait for the door to open all the way." But by the time he said it, the door was up far enough to get the truck out. He hit the gas and squealed the tires as he hurried out of the garage. One of the kids slammed a bloody baseball bat against the rear of the truck as it backed out. Linton jumped a bit at the sound, but kept accelerating. Swerving a little as they reached the street, he slipped the gearshift into drive and stomped on the gas. The pickup lurched forward and they left the gang of laughing kids behind them.

"Holy crap," Emmet said.

Linton and Michelle just looked at each other. Behind her mask, Michelle's eyes were wide and she seemed to be breathing heavily. Linton realized his breathing was just as panicked, and he imagined his eyes were every bit as wide as hers. He looked back at the road before them and made an effort to slow his breathing, taking a series of deep, calming breaths.

He looked back at Michelle and was about to say something when her eyes widened even more and she screamed at him. "Look out!"

Linton slammed his foot on the brakes instinctively, even as he swiveled his head around. A delivery truck screamed past them, barely missing the front bumper. "Shit!" The delivery truck swerved, clipped the rear end of a parked car on the street, swerved to the other side of the street, and plowed headlong into another parked car. The front of the truck pushed up, over the trunk of the other car, and ground to a stop in a cloud of steam.

Linton started to get out to check on the driver, but Michelle put a hand on his arm and shook her head. "I saw his face."

At first, he didn't know what she meant, but as he watched, the door of the delivery truck opened and a man dropped to the ground. He was laughing hysterically.

Linton looked both ways, making sure there was no other more oncoming traffic, and pulled away from the man before he got close.

They saw two other accidents before they even got out of the neighborhood. The road out of the subdivision was perpendicular to the interstate. They all sat for a moment, looking at the madness before them.

"Oh my God!"

From the back seat, Emmet echoed Michelle's sentiment. Cars were racing at breakneck speeds; some trying to avoid accidents, while others were intentionally ramming themselves into any vehicle in front of them, moving or not. And anytime Linton saw a face, they were either terrified, or laughing uncontrollably.

"You're not thinking about getting on the freeway, are you?" Emmet asked.

Linton shook his head. "Not anymore."

He pulled onto the feeder, driving parallel to the interstate. "You guys watch for other laughers."

"Laughers?"

Linton shrugged. "Fits, doesn't it?"

Emmet nodded. "I guess."

"So watch for traffic coming out of side roads."

As the evening light began to fade, they continued up the I-45 interstate northward. "You sure you want to go this way?" Michelle asked. She flinched as the sound of another wreck sounded from the nearby freeway. She looked past Linton, toward the sound. In the fading light, Linton saw the flickering of flames reflected in the lenses of her mask.

He didn't bother looking. He'd seen more accidents in the last five minutes then he'd seen in his whole life before tonight. There was no doubt in his mind now. The Kampala Syndrome had spread to the United States.

CHAPTER 43

KEN HOLTZAPFEL

THE INTERSECTION OF HOLY SHIT AND WHAT THE HELL

When the blonde waved him down, Ken briefly considered passing her by. His shift had ended more than an hour earlier, and he was tired. But she staggered a bit as she tried to flag him down, and tipsy passengers often tipped well, especially on holidays.

He swung to the curb and waited as she climbed in. "Where to, ma'am?"

"How mush would it cost to get me to Tomball?"

He did a quick calculation in his head. "About forty bucks."

She peered drunkenly into her purse, head weaving unsteadily from side to side as she reached in and pulled out her wallet. After a moment of squinting at the wallet's contents, she smiled up at him. "Oh, good! I got it covered."

Ken pulled into traffic. "Well, then how about we get you there?"

"I think tha's a good idea."

He slowed as they approached a red light. "What's the address you're heading to?"

She seemed to concentrate for a moment before answering. "Nineteen, six, forty Turalosa... no, Turlar..." She cursed. "Tu... la... ro... sa. Drive."

"Tularosa Drive?"

"Yeah! Tha'shit!" She giggled. "'M sorry! I said shit! I meant," and she slowed, carefully enunciating each syllable once more, "to... say... that's... it." She sighed as if she had just completed a great undertaking. "Shorry. Think I'm a li'l drunk."

Ken looked up and smiled at her in his mirror. "Then it's a good thing you took a cab, right?"

"Thank you!" She slapped the back of his seat enthusiastically. "Tha's what I told my hubsan. Hubsan?" She shook her head. "My husband. He got all pissed that I got a little teeeeny bit drunk an' he wouldn' come pick me up."

Traffic started moving again and Ken eased his way through downtown Houston. "So what were you doing downtown?"

"Came down to a spor's bar with a girlfriend to a Patriots party."

He raised an eyebrow. "You're a football fan?"

"Bet chur ass!"

"And a Patriots fan."

"Yup."

"So why isn't your girlfriend driving you home?"

The blonde sighed. "She got lucky. Some guy had th' right pickup line an' I tol' 'er to jump on him b'fore he got away."

"You're a good friend."

"Thank you! I am, aren't I?" She leaned forward and peered at Ken's name placard. "Holtzapple?"

He grinned. "Holtzapfel. But if it makes you feel any better, you got closer than most people do on their first try."

"Thank you, again. I'm sure sayin' that a lot, aren't I? Thank you, Ken Holtzapplefull. Again."

Ken didn't bother correcting her. "You're welcome. Again." He pulled to a stop at another red light.

"Well, Ken Holtzaff... Holtzap, fel... Ah hell. I'm sorry. I'm totally screwing it up. But I'm Angela, Ken with the unpronow-sable last name. Angela Montgomery."

"Pleased to meet you, Angela. A few more blocks and we'll hit the freeway." The light changed to green and he pulled forward. "After that, I figure we'll have about twenty minutes until we get—" Just as he entered the intersection, a blur of headlights appeared from his right, and a Houston Metro bus plowed into the traffic stopped perpendicular to his lane.

"Holy shit!" Angela exclaimed. "Did you see that?"

"Sure did." Bright lights in his rear view approached rapidly, and Ken saw a pickup plow into a car three cars behind his cab. It started a chain reaction that shoved all the cars forward. If Ken hadn't already been moving forward, his cab would have been caught in it. He stomped on the gas, moving away from the chaos behind. Some redneck must have been watching the bus instead of the road.

Another horn, and another car plowed into the rear of the pickup.

"What the hell?" Angela said it for him.

A third accident? Ken didn't know what was going on, but he thought it was a question better addressed from somewhere else. Somewhere far away from the crazy drivers at the intersection of Holy Shit and What the Hell. He blew through the next intersection without regard for the speed limit, weaving through traffic as he concentrated on putting some distance between himself and the craziness behind him. Just as he thought it would be best to slow down, headlights swerved to his left as another vehicle veered toward him. "Hang on!" It was all the warning he had time to give before the cab lurched and his airbag deployed.

There was a moment of shock as his head was slammed back and his senses were a jumble of spinning lights, horns, and screaming.

CHAPTER 44
ERICA CHAPMAN
THANKSGIVING MOVIE MADNESS

"I'm in hell," Erica thought. "That's the only logical explanation." Less than an hour earlier, she'd been opening a box of candy with her teeth while her movie started. Now, she lay face down in a puddle of soda, stunned and wondering why her elbow hurt so much. Maniacal laughter from behind reminded her, and she turned to look over her shoulder as the tittering lunatic climbed over the rail below, all the while chewing absently on what had only moments before been part of a screaming man's face. The only thing that kept her from gagging was the near certainty that if she took the time to vomit, she would be the next victim of the clambering clown.

There was a split second of despair as she contemplated her fate. *No! This is not how I am going to die!*

With that galvanizing thought, fear turned to anger and she rolled onto her back to face her attacker just as he stepped over the seat. Laughing maniacally, cheek eater leapt at her as she raised her leg to kick him. At the same time, a deafening clap of thunder sounded, and the man's head blossomed a slick, wet geyser of gray matter. He fell on forward lifelessly, and she scrambled out from under his body, trying her best to ignore the sticky wetness leaking from his head.

Another boom, and one of the other laughing maniacs dropped. Erica looked to the source of the noise and saw a man three rows above her with a pistol braced in both hands. He fired again and the laughing woman who had driven her heel through the first victim's eye dropped where she stood. The final attacker stood, pointed at the man with the pistol and laughed louder than ever. "Hey!" he guffawed. "Guns don't kill people! People ki…"

The pistol boomed again, proving him wrong. "Ma'am? You all right?"

Erica sat up from the sticky floor and felt a wet patch on her back where the spilled soda had soaked through her shirt. There was more stickiness on her arm and face, and she wiped it absently, only realizing when she looked down it wasn't soda. That realization instigated a rebellion somewhere in her digestive tract, and she barely managed to lean over the seat in the row below her in time to heave her IHOP Thanksgiving Special all over it. She found herself having a hard time absorbing everything that had happened in the last few minutes, and she could only imagine how she looked as she scrambled to her feet, wide-eyed and blood-spattered, wiping vomit from her chin.

The theater was utter pandemonium, with people screaming and crying. Through it all though, Erica heard a voice behind her, closer than the others. "Ma'am?"

"What!" She spun so quickly she nearly fell again. The man with the pistol was climbing carefully over the seats toward her.

"What? I mean, that man was... you just shot..." She stopped for a second, realizing she wasn't making any sense. But people were still screaming, and it was distracting her. "But you killed... he was chewing someone's face!" *Nope. Still not making sense. Get it together. See if you can't make a complete sentence.* Erica took a deep breath and found something she could wrap her head around. She glared at the man who had just saved her life. "What are you doing with a gun in a movie theater?"

"I beg your pardon?" He stopped on the aisle one level above her.

"You have a gun in public. Isn't that illegal?"

The man looked at her like she was crazy. "You mean the gun that just saved your life? That gun?"

She looked down at the pistol in question, idly noting that his finger was now off the trigger, lying flat above the trigger guard. She pointed at the weapon in question. "Yes! You just shot those people!"

"Jesus H. Christ, Lady! I just saved your damned life!"

He was right, but she was trying to process too many things at once. People were beginning to calm down some, at least no one was still screaming, though there was still plenty of sobbing and shouting. Erica saw three men running down the aisle toward the bodies on the floor. And through it all, Matt Damon calmly beat his way through yet another assassin. It was all simply too much to take in.

Realizing she was approaching overload, she decided to focus on one thing at a time. She whirled back to her rescuer. "Why do you have a gun in a movie theater?"

"Jesus, lady. You're welcome!" The man simply shook his head and turned away, walking down the aisle toward the group gathering around the bodies. She heard him muttering to himself as he passed, but all she could hear for sure was "…ungrateful bitch."

At that point, another man jumped up from his seat a few rows back. "You wanna know why he has a gun? 'Cause this is Texas, bitch!" The man was obviously impressed with his own wit, because he bent over and slapped his knee, hooting at what he apparently thought was a hilarious joke.

When he looked back up, he was still laughing, but there was horror in his eyes.

A woman sitting two seats down from him started to laugh at the same time, and a similar look of terror hid behind her eyes as well. Erica barely had time to scream a warning to the man with the pistol before they were on him, chuckling and punching and kicking. She saw the pistol go flying as he fell to the floor, and Erica slipped her purse strap around her neck and climbed over the seats into the next row without thinking.

The aisle was narrow, and the attackers were having a hard time finding room to really lay into their victim. The woman was in front kicking and giggling, while Mr. "This is Texas" was behind her, trying to get his shots in as he could. Erica ran up behind them and found her opening. Without hesitating, she kicked the man from behind… as hard as she could… directly between his legs.

His deep chortling laughter momentarily turned to shrieks a full octave higher as he doubled over and grabbed his crotch. Still crouched in pain, he nevertheless turned and reached toward her. She kicked again, this time introducing his teeth to the sole of her tennis shoe. His head snapped back and he dropped like a sack of potatoes. In the meantime, her erstwhile pistol-wielding rescuer found himself with one less attacker and managed to power back to his feet. The laughing woman clawed at his back and he cold cocked her, dropping her beside her companion. "What the hell is going on here?" he screamed. He looked as freaked as Erica had felt just moments before, and ironically, she finally felt more sympathy than animosity for him.

"I wish I knew." She looked around at the bodies, both unconscious and dead, with a growing sense of dread. Other than the sound of Jason Bourne making a motorcycle perform gravity-defying stunts, the theater was finally relatively quiet. There were no more screams or shouts. So why did she suddenly feel the chill of death crawling up her spine?

Looking up, Erica saw nearly all the other moviegoers staring at her and her guardian angel. Almost as one, they began to chuckle. Mr. Pistol and Erica looked at each other. She pointed to where his gun had fallen. "Now might be a good time to pick that back up."

He ran to scoop up the firearm from the floor, and she was right on his heels. Looking back, she saw the horde rushing them, their insane laughter like nails on the chalkboard of her sanity. "Hurry, hurry, hurry!"

Pistol Pete grabbed Erica's arm and pulled her along. Together, they sprinted down the steps to ground level and turned the corner to run toward the lobby. Just as they turned the corner, a mob crashed through the theater entrance—all of them laughing. Mr. Pistol raised his arm and fired three times into the crowd. Three bodies dropped, but the others didn't even pause. Erica looked back up at the other pursuers swarming over the seats in the theater behind her. "This way!" She pulled Pistol's arm to get his attention.

He looked at her over his shoulder, and she pointed to the emergency exit under Jason Bourne's right foot. Pistol led the way, crashing into the door with his shoulder so hard that Erica was convinced that it would have buckled even if it had been locked. The door slammed open with a hollow boom and the two of them burst free into the open air of the parking lot. They didn't slow for a second, determined to put as much distance as possible between themselves and the insane laughter behind them. "Where's your car?" he asked.

"Across the parking lot, in front of the IHOP. Where's yours?"

He shook his head. "I rode with a friend."

"Well, where's he?"

"Chasing us. You kicked him in the balls while he was trying to kill me."

"Shit. Follow me." She sprinted across the concrete. Her stride ate up the ground, using muscles conditioned by years of lacrosse, and she reached into her purse as she ran. Not daring to slow down and look, she felt around in the bouncing purse until she found her keys. *Don't drop them! Don't drop them!* She held firmly onto them as she found the door remote. "Still with me?" She didn't turn to look.

"Still… here," he panted. It sounded like he was only ten or fifteen feet behind.

Erica pressed the unlock button on her clicker and the parking lights of her van blinked twice. "See the car?"

"Yeah."

She hit the door opener and the side door slid open. "Take the back seat on this side. I'll drive."

"Got it."

Seconds later, she slammed into the door, jerked it open, and threw herself inside. She hit the close button for the side door, and her new companion dove inside as it began to shut. She looked beyond him and for a second she froze. There must have close to a hundred of those… things chasing them. *Must be everyone from the whole damned theater.* There was a click as the door behind her closed and a shout from the back seat. "Lock the doors! Lock the doors! Lock the doors!"

His shout shook her out of her stupor, and she hit the lock button just as the first of the crowd hit the van. The first one at her door slammed his hand into the window hard enough to cause her to shriek, but it held. He shoved his face up to the glass and tittered wildly. The next arrival behind him, grabbed him by the head and smashed it into the window hard enough that both cracked. The first attacker slid to the ground unconscious, leaving a trail of blood on the now cracked window.

"Start the car, lady! Start the damn car!"

She jerked, then fumbled the key into the ignition just as the bulk of the crowd got to them. They wasted no time slamming the old van, slapping it with open palms or fists. Several of them used their neighbors as makeshift battering rams, smashing them into the windows in an attempt to break in. Within seconds, they had the entire vehicle rocking back and forth, and it suddenly occurred to Erica that if they manage to roll the van completely over, they would be dead shortly after. She cranked the engine and put it in gear, but hesitated. There were several people, or whatever they were, in front of the van.

There was the sound of breaking glass and the volume of the laughter increased. "Floor it, lady! Get us the hell outta here!" That was followed by the deafening boom of his pistol.

Erica's ears rang as she closed her eyes and hit the gas. And nothing happened. There were simply too many of them pushing back against the hood. She slammed the van into reverse and punched it again. This time they moved, and she felt the wheels roll over something that felt like a bag of mud. Looking into the rearview mirror, she saw Pistol Pete taking aim at another of those laughing monstrosities as it began to pull itself through the broken back window. "Save your bullets," Erica told him, and accelerated backwards, slamming into a pickup truck in the row behind us. The creepy crawlie's laughter stopped as his body was crushed between the rear hatch and the pickup. She threw the stick back into drive, slamming her foot to the floor. This time, they had momentum on their side, and the mob never had a chance. The van plowed through them, and she tried not to think too much about the lurching of the van as the tires rolled over several bumps.

There seemed to be more cars in the parking lot than there had been when she'd first gone into the theater, and she realized that people were starting to gear up for the Black Friday sales at the mall. She accelerated down the lane at what would normally be considered an unsafe speed, trying to gain enough distance to safely turn and head toward the street exits. She glanced into the rearview and saw that the crowd was about fifty yards behind us and smiled. *We're going to make it.* "Hang on to something back there. I'm gonna have to make a sharp turn ahead."

"Do whatever you need to do. Just get us the hell out of here."

She slammed on the brakes as she approached the end of the row of vehicles, and yanked the wheel to the right. There was a crash of falling boxes and breaking glass from the back of the van, followed by some inventive cursing. "Holy shit, lady. What the hell is all this crap back here?"

She'd forgotten about all her belongings from Uncle J's house, but she didn't have time to worry about it at the moment. Her braking and the turn had let the throng behind them regain some ground. Erica watched in the mirror as they cut across the parking lot at an angle to intercept the van. As she watched, they swarmed like a rushing tide over and between the vehicles that she'd had to maneuver around, and for a moment, she feared they were going to catch up.

Then she hit a straightaway and punched the gas. Taking a deep and shaky breath, she steered toward the main exit from the mall.

CHAPTER 45
LESSLIE LAMPHERE
EAT AT JOE'S

"You folks have a great Thanksgiving, okay?" Lesslie Lamphere handed the customer his order and turned to look at the last sheet on the pickup list. It was six thirty, and they were supposed to have closed Joe's at six, but there was still one order waiting on a customer pickup. She figured she would give the guy until seven to pick it up. Joe had given her and Barry permission to take the extra overtime, and it wasn't like she had anyplace she needed to be. Neither did Barry, evidently.

He poked his head out from the back. "That the last one?"

"One more."

The man sighed. "Well, hell."

"Why don't you go ahead and leave? I can cover this last one."

"Nah. I still have a little bit of cleaning I need to do." He turned, heading back out of sight. "Besides," he called over his shoulder, "I couldn't deprive you of my sparkling personality."

Lesslie smiled. Barry Begault had been flirting with her for weeks now. He presented it as if it were all a joke, but she could tell. He was about as subtle as a hand grenade. And if she was honest with herself, she was flattered. The problem was that she just wasn't ready for another relationship. And she definitely wasn't ready to start one at this time of the year. The holidays were always a tough time, but this was going to be her first season without Gabe, and it was all she could do to keep from melting into a puddle of tears at the thought.

Barry knew this, and was enough of a gentleman to keep his distance. She appreciated that about him. And it wasn't like she wasn't attracted. But it was going to be at least a few more months before she could even look at him without comparing him to Gabriel, and that wasn't fair to him. It wasn't fair to her either.

The jingle of the bell told her another customer had come in. She looked up to see a young couple walking toward the counter. "Welcome to Smokey Joe's. You here for a pickup?"

"Yes," the man spoke for them. "We're the Rileys. The order is under the name of Doug Riley. Sorry we're so late, but the traffic out there is unbelievable. We passed four different wrecks on the way here."

She raised an eyebrow at that. "Really? Big pileup?"

This time it was the woman who spoke. "That's the weird thing. They weren't anywhere close to each other. It was really four wrecks in four different places. There's just all kinds of craziness out there."

"Oh man, that sucks. I guess that just shows you, no matter how bad you think the holidays are, it can always be worse." Lesslie pulled up the last ticket and rang it up on the register. "Okay, Mr. Riley, I show you ordered one smoked turkey, a spiral cut ham, two orders of yeast rolls, half a pound of fried okra, six baked potatoes all the way, and two cherry pies. That sound right?"

"Sure. What's the damage?"

"It's gonna be one-thirteen, twenty-seven."

The man handed her a credit card.

"Will there be anything else?" She asked it automatically, hoping he would say no.

"No thanks. Dinner's already gonna be late. I just hope they have the wrecks cleared on the way home. If it takes me another hour to get home, my wife's gonna cook me!" He laughed.

Lesslie handed his credit card back to him, along with a pen and receipt. "Well, let's get you out of here and on your way."

But Mr. Riley didn't take the pen. He simply stood there, looking at her, chuckling. "She's gonna cook me!"

His wife also seemed to think that was funny, and the couple turned to Lesslie, as if waiting for her to get the joke. Brows furrowed, Lesslie saw something in the man's expression that was off. His chuckle turned to a laugh, getting louder as he stood there. But it never made it to his eyes. She looked at the woman, and saw the same expression of humor below the eyes, coupled with terror deep within them.

She drew her hand back from where she had been trying to hand him his receipt. "You all right?"

The man shook his head once, as if trying to clear his thoughts, then grabbed at her hand as he giggled.

"Barry!" Lesslie yanked her hand back out of the man's reach.

"Come back," he laughed. "I said come back here, and the customer is always right!" The man began climbing over the counter while the woman ran around.

Lesslie screamed and ran into the back. "Barry, help!"

She hit the swinging door to the kitchen, to find Barry poking his head around the corner of one of the large stainless warmers.

"What's—?" His eyes went from concerned to fearful as he saw the man chasing Lesslie through the door. "Hey!" Evidently something in Barry's mind identified the man as a threat, and his eyes went dark. He stepped out from behind the warmer and moved toward the man. Lesslie ran past him and turned.

"Buddy, you need to get the hell out of here."

That was when the man's wife came through the door as well. Both of them were still laughing uncontrollably. Barry reached to the bench behind him and picked up one of the many large butcher knives they used to cut the barbecue. Lesslie knew just how sharp they kept those blades. She reached out and grabbed one, too. Barry waved the knife at the man. "I ain't kidding, mister. You get out now or I'll call the cops."

The man stopped and laughed even harder, though he seemed to be struggling to get words out. "That's not, heh hee. Not a phone!"

Before Lesslie or Barry either one could reply, Mr. Riley threw himself at Barry. Barry screamed, pulling back even as he reflexively shoved the knife toward the threat. The blade slid into Riley effortlessly, but the man still didn't stop. Barry screamed again, yanked his knife back, then plunged it again into the man.

Lesslie's eyes widened in horror at the sight of Doug Riley's blood pouring onto the floor even as he continued to claw his way past the blade and reach for Barry's throat. But his movements were less coordinated by the second, and she could see he was dying. The woman behind him was another matter. Mrs. Riley dove past her dying husband and latched her teeth onto Barry's bicep. He screamed again, releasing the knife buried in the now motionless Mr. Riley and staggered back under this second attacker's onslaught.

Her teeth released their purchase on his arm, and the smaller woman crawled up his body and bit his ear. She didn't bite his earlobe, or some other specific part of his ear. Lesslie watched dumbfounded as the woman stuffed Barry's entire ear into her mouth. Barry's shouts turned into shrieks as she clamped down, and Lesslie wanted to gag as she saw his ear come away in the woman's mouth.

She saw her friend collapse in pain, and the crazy lady clawed at his face, even as she chewed on his ear. Still, Lesslie hesitated. A little voice in the back of her mind tried to rationalize that she couldn't stab the woman for fear of cutting Barry, but deep down she knew she was simply too terrified of taking another person's life to take action. She cried in frustration as the woman clawed at her friend, leaving bloody streaks on his face.

"Lesslie!"

He looked at her, his eyes pleading for her help, and finally she moved in with her knife. Attacking from behind, Lesslie drove the knife deep into the woman's back. She pulled it back and was sickened when the meat surrounding the blade resisted with a sucking sound. She yanked, then drove it home again, then a third time.

She must have hit something vital that last time, for the woman finally fell. She rolled onto her back, looking at Lesslie, blood spraying lightly from her mouth as she continued to cackle, even as she died.

Barry coughed, and Lesslie turned her attention to her mangled friend. "Barry?" she sobbed. "Barry, are you okay?" She knew it was a stupid question, but she didn't know what else to say.

He looked at her with tears in his own eyes, and she thought how strange they looked on her friend. She had never seen a man cry like that. Of course she'd never seen a man get his ear chewed off, either. "I been better, darlin'." He dragged himself into a sitting position and leaned back against the warmer. He lifted a shaking hand up to the side of his head, touched a fingertip to the ragged skin where his ear had been, and hissed in pain.

"Don't do that!" Lesslie chided. "Hang on while I call 911." Thankful she kept her phone in her left pocket, she dug into her pocket with her clean hand. Her right hand was coated in Mrs. Riley's blood. As Lesslie punched in the digits, she noticed how much her hands were trembling. She put the phone to her ear, irrationally self-conscious of the fact that she still had an ear when Barry didn't.

The answer was immediate, and the man's voice sounded almost frantic as he answered. "Nine-one-one. Please state the nature of your emergency."

"My name's Lesslie Lamphere and I'm at Smokey Joe's..." She stopped herself. They wouldn't care about the name of the place, they would want the address. "We're at the intersection of Nebraska Avenue and I-45 South. We were just attacked by two—"

"Were they laughing?"

A chill when up Lesslie's spine at the man's interruption. "How did you know?"

"Ma'am, we're not sure what's going on, but you need to keep away from them. We have reports coming in from all over. All I can tell you is to not approach them, and don't let them bite you. We have a lot of reports of them trying to bite people. Lock yourself in and wait for help. We'll get someone there as soon as we can."

"But they're dead. We killed them."

"Were you injured?"

"No, but my friend was. She bit his ear off."

"She bit him?"

Lesslie was getting frustrated. "She didn't just bite him. She bit his ear completely off!"

"Ma'am, you need to get away from all of them. You say you killed the attackers? Did you get any of their blood on you?"

"What?" She looked down at her blood-soaked apron. Blood ran down her right arm and dripped from her hand. "Yes. Yes I did."

There was a pause. "Lock yourself in the building and stay away from the windows. Don't let anyone else know you're there. We'll get someone there as soon as we can."

"We're going to need an ambulance. My friend is..." The line went dead. "...bleeding." She swallowed nervously.

"They on the way?" Barry wasn't looking at her, staring instead at the warped reflection in the side of the stainless refrigerator in front of him.

"Yeah," she lied. "They said it might take a while, though. It seems there are a lot of these attacks going on."

Barry turned to her. "No shit?"

"That's what they said." She put a hand on his face and turned his head to get a better look at his ear. Or rather, where his ear had been. She pushed down the gorge that threatened and tried to smile reassuringly. "Let me see what we have in the first-aid kit and I'll clean this thing up for you."

She started to leave him and stopped as he groaned. She laid a sympathetic hand on his shoulder. "You going to be all right while I'm gone?"

He shook his head and chuckled. "Do I look all right?"

His chuckle turned to a chortle, then a full-blown belly laugh. Lesslie's skin crawled as she saw the horror in his eyes. "That's not all that funny, is it?" But he kept laughing. Then the terror in his eyes changed to anger and he launched himself at her.

CHAPTER 46
CHARLES GRIFFE
GAINS AND LOSSES

Chris's master key made things easier, allowing them to simply pop into the nearest cabin whenever they saw or heard any pursuit. The problem was that the crazies seemed to be getting much quieter. Charlie didn't know if it was because they were becoming stealthier, or if they were actually going hoarse from all the yelling and laughing. Either way, it was getting harder to hear them coming.

They also found more traveling companions—people who hadn't succumbed to laughter. The first two joined them shortly after they had left the cabin on Nine. They had heard the trampling of a large group of crazies running through the corridor before them and had slipped into a cabin just a few doors up the hall from where they had started. They found an elderly couple, Merl and Celina Errington, cowering inside. They'd spent almost an hour resting in the cabin, exchanging stories, and in the end, the couple had elected to join them. Charlie had been none too happy, as he was sure the old man and woman were bound to slow them down, but he'd had little say in the matter.

They entered the stairwell, now five strong, and Tabby's flashlight gave them surer footing in the darkness. They quickly found that it also made them a target. They were halfway between Decks Nine and Eight, with the Erringtons moving a bit slower than the others, when the sound of footsteps and low chuckles began to rise from the darkness below. Chris was in the lead and cursed as he skipped down the stairs to the door. "Hurry! Sounds like they're still a couple of decks below." He pulled the next door open enough to peer out, then opened it all the way. "We get out here."

Tabby helped Celina down the stairs, and Charlie brought up the rear, all the while pushing back thoughts of shoving the old couple down the stairs. But all five of them made it out and hurried to the shadows of the starboard cabins. As was quickly becoming their modus operandi, they rounded the corner, and as soon as they were out of sight, Chris opened the door of another cabin.

They all slipped quickly inside. Merl and Celina sat heavily on the bed, and Charlie rolled his eyes.

Look at those old farts. One flight of stairs and a thirty-yard sprint and they're suckin' air like fish outta water. I'm tellin' you boy, they're gonna get you killed.

Charlie bit back his sharp reply. He didn't need the others thinking he was crazy.

But ain't you, though?

His mouth went dry at that thought. He hadn't needed the meds in years now. Of course, he hadn't had dear old Dad talking in his head for years, either. The fear of that particular line of thought was interrupted as Tabby slipped past them and opened the curtains at the balcony. The pale light of daybreak faintly illuminated the cabin as Charlie turned to Chris. "Well, at least we're on the right side of the ship now."

Chris nodded. "One more deck and up the length of the ship."

Charlie drew closer to Chris and lowered his voice. "You think the geezers can make it?"

Chris looked over at them. "We'll just have to take it easy on them. There's not that much farther to go. They'll be all right."

The sound of breaking glass interrupted them, and Charlie spun to find Tabby squatting over the remains of the dresser mirror, carefully picking through the pieces. She made a satisfied noise and pinched a long sliver between her thumb and index finger. Charlie remembered what she had cut him with and nodded. He turned back to Chris. "Probably not a bad idea."

Chris nodded, and the two of them walked to the mess and began poking through the broken glass as well. Charlie found a piece that looked like a crooked dagger and picked it up. He turned and saw Tabby rummaging through the closet. She pulled out a pair of jeans and used the piece of mirror to slice long strips out of the denim. Wrapping the base of the mirror, she created a safe handle for her makeshift dagger and nodded.

Apparently satisfied with her project, she looked up to see Chris and Charlie watching her. She tossed them the remains of the blue jeans and the two men followed her lead, cutting strips of cloth to wrap around their own weapons. As he worked on his weapon, Charlie thought he heard a tapping. He froze, listening for the noise to repeat itself.

Chris saw him and stopped moving as well. "What?"

Charlie shook his head, "I thought I—"

There it was again. "Did you hear that?"

Chris nodded and signaled Tabby to come over.

Merl called from where he and his wife sat on the bed. "Wha—?"

"Sh!" The tapping sounded once again. Tabby, Chris, and Charlie walked to the wall where Tabby had broken the mirror. Before Charlie could stop her, Tabby reached out and tapped lightly on the wall. Immediately, there was a response. Then the tapping changed to a quick pattern. It was one that every kid in the world learned at a young age: three fast, three slow, and three fast.

"SOS?"

Charlie rolled his eyes. Chris had a talent for stating the obvious.

Tabby shone the flashlight along the wall. "What are you doing?" Charlie asked.

"Looking to see if this is a suite with an adjoining door."

"You what?" Charlie couldn't believe it. "You don't know who or what's doing the tapping. For all we know, it might be a bunch of crazies on the other side of that wall."

She shook her head. "I don't think so. I don't think they have that much sense left. I mean, I haven't even heard any of them speak, have you?"

"As a matter of fact, I have." Charlie recalled Purple Hair taunting him from the other side of the cabin door as he and his cohorts worked to break it down. *Little pig, little pig, let me in.*

She looked surprised at that. "You have?"

"Yeah. And it was creepy as shit."

Chris nodded. "I have too. And he's right. It's pretty messed up."

Tabby looked a bit less sure of herself at that. Chris shrugged. "It doesn't really matter. This isn't one of the suites that join like you're talking about."

The tapping sounded again. "So what do we do about that?"

Charlie shrugged. "Nothing."

"But it's probably somebody trying to see whether or not we're crazy! They probably heard us break the mirror and are hoping it's someone normal over here."

Charlie shook his head. "How the hell do you jump to that conclusion?"

"Well, how would you explain it?"

"I wouldn't explain it. Hell, lady, I can't explain anything that's happened on this damned cruise. But just because I can't explain it doesn't mean there isn't a shitload of crazy ass people out there killing anyone that ain't a member of their happy little band of lunatics."

Further argument was interrupted when the tapping sounded again. This time, it was from the cabin door.

They all looked at one another as the tapping at the door repeated. Charlie tightened his grip on his newly fashioned weapon as Chris moved toward the door. Charlie took a deep breath and followed the man, Tabby close behind. The navigation officer leaned forward and put his eye to the peephole.

"Well?" Charlie whispered.

"One person. It's pretty dark out there, but it doesn't look like he's laughing."

"Should we let him in?" Tabby asked.

Charlie held up his shard of mirror. "There's three of us and one of him." Chris nodded and turned back to the door. He hesitated for another second, they yanked the door open, grabbed the man standing outside by the lapels and pulled him into the cabin before he could resist. Charlie slammed the man against the wall and shoved the sliver of mirror against his throat while Chris shut the cabin door as quickly as he had opened it.

"Hey, hey, hey!" The man from the corridor raised his hands, fear recognizable in his eyes. "No need for all this!"

"Who are you?" Charlie growled.

"Sh-Shane. Shane Kemmerling. I heard the glass break and thought I heard people moving around. I didn't hear any laughing, so I figured I would see if you were…" He fell silent.

"What? See if we were what?"

"Normal?"

Tabby put a hand on Charlie's arm. "Let him go, Charlie. He's not infected."

Charlie swallowed and nodded. The man was frightened, but hadn't so much as smiled since he'd been dragged into their cabin. It turned out that Shane wasn't alone. His girlfriend was in the cabin as well, and as soon as they made sure it was safe, they brought her over as well. Before the day was out, they found three more couples and a lone young boy, bringing their number up to fourteen.

CHAPTER 47
LINTON BOWERS
US OR THEM

"Well, crap."

"What's wrong?" Emmet asked from the back seat, leaning over so he could see out the front windshield.

"Looks like our luck just ran out."

Ahead of them was an exit ramp from the interstate that dumped traffic from the freeway, and the insanity of the interstate was spilling onto the feeder. At least half a dozen cars were piled up ahead, and even as they watched, another car came flying off the freeway at full speed. Linton stomped on the brakes as the racing sedan clipped a pickup at the edge of the pileup, spun halfway around, and rolled over several times until it was hidden from their view behind the pileup. Smoke began to waft up from behind the wreckage, while all around the mangled mess of automobiles, people jumped and laughed.

"Can you get around?"

Linton looked at the wreckage on the left. "Maybe. If I—"

Before he could finish, flames sprang up from the wreck. "Oh crap."

Michelle pointed to a gap on the right side. "You might be able to get through over here, but if you're going to do it, you'd better go now, before one of those tanks explodes."

Linton hesitated only a second, then hit the gas. "You guys might want to get down." Michelle and Emmet stayed where they were, though, and Linton didn't have time to worry any more about them. As he got close to the flaming pile of cars, some of the dancing menagerie from the street began to run at the truck. Linton reached blindly for the electronic door locks and made sure they were all secured. He slowed as a couple of the dancers jumped in front of him, laughing and slapping their hands on the hood.

"What are you doing?" Michelle practically shouted at him.

"What do you want me to do, run them over? They're still people! Besides," He eased forward as more and more of them gathered around the truck, shoving them back with the truck's sheer mass, "it's not like they can really stop us."

And he was right. They could laugh and dance and slap the hood all they wanted, but his heavy-duty pickup would not be denied. Of course, there was also nothing to keep the lunatics from climbing into the bed of the truck, either.

"Linton!" Emmet drew his pistol and aimed at the two people, a man and a woman, climbing into the back, over the tarps covering all their supplies. "What d'you want me to do, man?"

Linton looked in the mirror and cursed again. The woman pawed at the tarp and pulled back a corner to reveal several boxes of food. Giggling, she ripped open the box and hefted a large can of fruit cocktail over her head. Eyes wide with glee, she threw the can into the back of the truck, cracking the sliding partition window. Her companion found that just as funny as she did, and staggered over to the box she had opened for a projectile of his own. Linton looked beyond their passengers and confirmed the road was clear. "Hang on!" He hit the brakes, and slammed the truck into reverse. The two passengers pitched toward the cab of the truck, stumbling over the uneven footing and into the cab. The woman went over the top and landed on the hood before sliding off as Linton accelerated backwards in the street.

The man, however, had managed to hang on and was banging his fist into the already-damaged rear window. Linton hit the brakes again, causing the man to stumble backward, and then threw the truck back into drive and punched the gas. Still giggling, the man fell backward over the tailgate.

Linton swerved to miss the woman, who was limping as she came toward them. Once past her, he bounced the truck over the curb and into the grass to the side of the fire. Another man ran at them and Linton swerved slightly, clipping him and knocking him to the ground.

"Son of a bitch!" Linton didn't know if he cursed himself for hitting the man, or at the man for rushing at them. Either way, he had hit a man, and he hadn't stopped. His life had just taken a darker turn than he'd ever had to deal with.

When they were almost even with the fire, another man ran laughing at them from the other side of the pileup. Linton saw him, saw the fire, gauged the distance between the fire and the brick wall beside the business on the right, and saw that there was no way he was going to miss the man. He had to decide: was he going to stop, or was he going to run the man down?

That was his turning point. *It's us or them, Lint. Us or them.*

He hit the gas. The impact of the man on the hood wasn't as bad as he had expected. He was only going twenty or twenty-five mile an hour, so it wasn't like his truck was going to cave in. But the sight of the man's head flopping forward and hitting the hood wasn't something Linton was going to be able to forget for a long, long, time.

They were several miles past the wreck before Linton realized Michelle was crying in the seat beside him. His hands ached from clenching the steering wheel so tightly, and he realized that he didn't remember any of the drive since hitting that man. He looked down at the speedometer and saw that he was driving too fast for the feeder road he was on, and he hadn't been paying the slightest attention to any traffic.

He eased off the gas and checked his mirrors. Seeing no traffic, he looked over his shoulder at Emmet. "You okay?"

His friend swallowed. "Yeah. You?"

Linton shook his head. "I don't think I'll ever be okay." He reached across and grabbed Michelle's hand. "But we'll work it out, right?"

Her sniffling sounded strange through the diaphragm on the mask, but she nodded. "Sure." Unable to wipe her eyes through the mask, she squeezed them closed repeatedly to clear her vision.

Around a curve in the road, Linton saw another pileup. His chest tightened at the thought of a possible repeat of earlier events. He slowed the truck as he saw more people jumping around in the street. "Emmet, call up a map on your phone and find us another route."

"You got it."

The crowd around the wreck started running their direction.

"You just passed a neighborhood a minute ago," Michelle suggested. "Maybe there's a way around through there."

Linton nodded and began backing up around the curve. He found the entrance to the neighborhood just where Michelle had said it would be. He turned in and headed away from the wrecks. "How you doing on that alternate route, Emmet?"

"You just made it a lot harder. Doesn't look like there's a way through here."

"Even off road?"

Emmet ran his fingers on the screen of his phone. "Maybe. It looks like there might be a field you can cross into the next neighborhood. Take the second left up ahead."

The second left had several people running between houses, most of them laughing. Linton sped past quickly, and they found a wooden barrier at the end of a dead-end street. Across the field behind it, they could see a row of fences; the backs of the homes in the next neighborhood.

"Is there another street over there?" Linton asked.

Emmet squinted at his phone. "Doesn't look like it. You're going to have to go through some fences."

People running behind them convinced Linton that there wasn't any time to worry about the legalities of driving through someone's fence. "Hang on."

He crashed the barrier and headed across the field.

CHAPTER 48
ROSS MAYFIELD
SLEEP

One of the only bonuses to Ross's condition was the fact that he always had a good supply of medications on hand, including anti-depressants and sleep aids. He seldom ever used the anti-depressants. They left him with a mental fuzziness he didn't like. It made it too difficult for him to maintain that keen edge of mental control that was so important to him. But the sleep aid was another story. His doctor was under the impression that Ross used them all the time, and so prescribed him ninety days at a time. And Ross filled those prescriptions every ninety days, even though he only took them a few times each month. Every doctor he had seen had told him that the only treatment was finding the right combination of drugs. They claimed that there was no behavioral treatment for his very rare variant of cataplexy.

But Ross hated the way all the drugs made him feel. It was the control issue again. So he politely filled the prescriptions as he was supposed to, and the extra pills filled several bottles that he kept in his dorm room.

He'd found that he could make a bit of extra cash under the table by selling the stuff to fellow students who used uppers during the day to keep up in classes. They often needed something to balance them out at night so they could get to sleep, and Ross became known as the guy who could get it. He didn't really think of himself as a drug dealer. For that matter, he didn't even think of himself as a user. He sold one item, and one item only. He sold "Zs". As for use, he only used two drugs; the occasional Z, and grass.

After a sleepless night during which he'd been unable to take his mind off of Erica, he'd found himself getting more and more depressed.

When he realized he was in danger of losing control, he considered taking the anti-depressant. But he finally decided that all he really needed was to get some sleep.

It was a self-admitted fault in his character. Ross had a tendency to sleep whenever he felt depressed. He didn't know whether it was a part of his cataplexy, or just an emotional retreat. Either way, all he wanted to do when he felt the gloom coming on was curl up and sleep it off like some sort of emotional hangover.

It was pitiful and childish, but he really didn't care. Between Erica having left without so much as a "kiss my ass," his parents being out of the country, and most of the campus being deserted for the holiday, he figured he was entitled to a little childishness. So he'd finally given up as the sun was beginning to rise and he'd swallowed a double dose of Z.

He slept until he heard the laughter and shrieking in the dormitory hallways, groaning at the latest personal affront that the heavens had thrown at him, rolled over in his bed, and pulled the pillow over his head. Unfortunately, it seemed that he had reached the point where his mind and body were in disagreement with one another. His mind demanded that he shut it all out and go back to sleep. Perhaps tomorrow would be a better day.

But his body was already fully rested. He peeked out from under his pillow and looked at his alarm clock. It was seven o'clock. He'd slept all day. No wonder he couldn't go back to sleep. More laughter sounded outside. It was accompanied by the sound of several people running past his door, hooting and cackling in amusement at something. He sat up and sighed. Opening the drawer in his nightstand, he pulled out the baggie and papers, and began rolling himself a joint.

He'd begun smoking pot a few years ago after reading about other narcoleptics and cataleptics who'd had great results with it. To his great surprise, it had worked wonders for him. When the state of Alabama had made the marijuana extract CBD legal, he had tried that too. And while it had helped, he had already invested the time into learning how much pot he could smoke without losing control. That was the key for him: getting just enough in his system that it would help keep the cataplexy at bay, but not enough that he risked losing control of himself.

Ross lit the joint and took a deep drag. He held his breath for a moment before repeating the process. After half of the joint was ash, he pinched it off and dropped the remainder back into the baggie. More laughing distracted him, this time from the quad outside his window. He knew there would be a few people like him who stayed on campus for Thanksgiving, but he hadn't anticipated having to contend with so much noise. Didn't they know he was busy in here trying to sulk?

He tossed his baggie back into the nightstand. As he did, he glanced at where his phone lay plugged into its charger. An indicator flashed on the screen. He opened the screen and saw that he'd missed two calls. How had the phone not awakened him?

Looking at the bar at the top, he wanted to kick himself. *You silenced the damned thing so it wouldn't wake you, you dumb ass!* He pressed and held the one on the number pad, hitting the built-in speed dial button for his voice mail.

"You have *one* unheard message. First message, sent *yesterday* at *eight, twenty, three, pee, em* from *Erica mobile*." There was a short tone followed by Erica's voice, "Hi Ross. Hey, umm… it's Erica." He heard her sigh into the phone. "Sorry, that was a stupid thing to… you recognized my voice, though, didn't you? Of course, you did. Look, I'm sorry I had to leave town so abruptly. Uncle J died and I had to come back to Texas to take care of things. I found out about it right after we had our fight. No, that's not fair. We didn't have a fight. I just got pissed off and left. You didn't do anything wrong." There was a short pause before her voice continued. "Listen, I know I left things on a bad… Never mind. We'll talk it out later. What I really called you about was the news. I know you don't usually watch TV, but you really need to watch the news. Or maybe look it up online or whatever works best for you. There's something going on in Africa, and some folks are saying it might be spreading. Supposedly there's an epidemic or something. They're saying that millions are dead." She paused again, and Ross imagined her on the other end of the line trying to think of what to say. "Baby, I'm so sorry I got ma—" Her voice was cut off in the middle of whatever she was going to say.

What the hell? Then he recalled that he'd set his voicemail to only give callers sixty seconds for their messages. The messaging system then told him, "To repeat message, press *one*. To delete, press *seven*. To archive, press *nine*. To hear more options, press *star*."

This was one of those times when someone in one of the silly movies Erica watched would likely fling his phone across the room. He wondered whether there was really an emotional satisfaction for some people in seeing a five hundred dollar piece of electronics shatter into dozens of pieces. It was something he would never know first-hand. He couldn't afford the loss of control.

Instead, he took a deep and calming breath, once more sinking into the near meditative state he strove for. It was relatively easy at the moment, having just awakened from more than thirteen hours of sleep, followed by half a joint. What was harder was the deeper technique of finding his heartbeat and acquiring the more profound control of his body. The techniques that usually took him only moments, were more elusive after the weed. But Ross was patient, and after nearly fifteen minutes of meditation and deep breathing, he began to feel he had it.

He was at the point of attuning his heart to the piano tone when another bout of laughter sounded from outside. Shoving it into the background, he again reached for the tenuous link between imagined piano and heartbeat when a woman's scream sounded, as well. It was followed by a deeper voice, a male voice. A voice that shouted loudly enough that Ross could hear it even from his bedroom.

"...back! Leave her alone, you sick sons o' bitches!"

Ross got up and walked to his window just as the man started screaming. The sound raised goose bumps, and his jaw dropped at the sight in the lawn just outside the quad. It was getting dark, but there was still enough light for him to make out the scene below. Five men and a couple of women were beating and clawing at a young man on the grass. A woman, apparently unconscious, lay unmoving on the grass a few yards away from them. It was impossible for Ross to see much detail, but her face and throat appeared to be little more than a wet and red mess of ragged tissue. He felt his pulse begin pounding, and immediately took a deep breath as he reached again for the piano tone. He felt the muscles of his jaw begin to weaken and his vision swam.

No, I will not lose it this time! He closed his eyes and fought for the calmness that would allow him to bypass the impending episode, feeling for a moment the fragile mental anchor as his body threatened to betray him again. *Ping, two, three. Ping, two, three. Slow it down. Concentrate on the sound.*

Another scream sounded from outside and his eyes flicked open once more, involuntarily drawn to the scene of the attack out there. The man was curled up in a fetal position as the crowd laughed and kicked at him. One of the crowd raised a large rock above his head. Laughing the entire time, he smashed it down on his victim's head. And though it wasn't possible that he could have actually heard it, the imagined sound of the man's skull smashing like a watermelon was enough to send Ross over the edge. His knees began to buckle, followed quickly by the other muscles as they all decided to betray him. He managed to angle his body away from the wall as he collapsed, and that was the last influence he was able to exert over his body. He hit the floor face first and stared at the carpet as he waited to regain control of his body.

CHAPTER 49
KEN HOLTZAPFEL
DOWNTOWN H-TOWN

Ken awoke to the rocking of his boat on the lake. The wind must have really been kicking up because it was jostling his whole body.

"Mister? Mister Holtz… ah, hell. Ken! You need to wake up!"

Ken opened his eyes to find a pretty blonde woman reaching over the back seat and shaking his shoulder. She had blood running down her face, leaking from a scalp wound behind her hairline. "What the hell happened?"

"We got hit." She nodded at the little BMW that had attached itself to the front of his cab. The windshield of the Beamer was starred in front of the driver's seat, and something dark trickled from the point of impact.

Ken blinked as he began to recall the craziness before the accident. He heard sounds outside; screaming, laughter, horns blaring. And there was suddenly the sound of another accident somewhere behind them. That spurred him into motion. He tried to open his door, but it was jammed from the wreck. "We need to get out." He scooted warily across the seat, being careful to not cut himself on any of the hundreds of squares of broken safety glass that littered his seat. He reached the passenger's side door and shoved it open, finding the blonde lady already there to help him as he stumbled into the street. He looked around, dazed. What was her name? Angela, wasn't it?

Ken's vision swam as he turned his head. "Let's get out of the street. The way people are driving tonight, it ain't safe out here." He squinted at the sidewalk across the street. Even through his admittedly fuzzy vision, something was off. People were running all around them. But it was the sounds that ran a chill up Ken's spine. There were screams, as some of the people ran from others, but there were more people who were laughing.

"What the hell?" Angela said.

He looked at his fare, then to where she pointed. On the sidewalk to the right, a woman screamed as two men knelt over her. The men were laughing uncontrollably, and as Ken watched, one of them bent over the woman and kissed her. The woman's screams increased in volume, and as the man raised back up, his face was coated in blood.

"Oh god!" Angela suddenly turned away from Ken and puked. The tart, yet sweet smell of grenadine and alcohol hit him, and he was glad she'd had the presence of mind to turn away.

Ken pulled his eyes away from the scene on the sidewalk and walked the few steps back to his cab. He reached in the open front door and withdrew his attitude adjustment device. It was an old tire iron, and he always kept it in the front seat, just in case. And if this wasn't such a case, he didn't know what was. He hefted the length of iron in his fist and felt much better. "Come on, lady. Let's get inside someplace where it's safe."

"Safe? That man just ate a woman's lips!" Angela sounded on the verge of hysteria, and if Ken had realized what the man had done before, he might have been a bit hysterical, himself. But he hadn't comprehended what he was seeing when he had watched earlier, and now he had his mind on protecting himself and Angela.

"All the more reason to get out of sight." He pulled her along, toward the opposite sidewalk. He scanned the streets around them, and the sound of another accident sounded from the corner ahead. A block behind them, the sound of an explosion caused them to spin around. Ken saw the fuel tank on one of the vehicles in the first accident had exploded.

The men who had been accosting the woman on the sidewalk jumped up, laughing gleefully as they ran toward the flames. Ken pulled Angela along again in the opposite direction. "Come on." They were in the theater district, close to the I-45 entrance ramp. As late as it was, there wasn't going to be much open, but if there was a Thanksgiving play of some kind going this evening, maybe there would be an armed guard at the underground parking garage. Ken saw a sign for The Hobby

Center for the Performing Arts, and started jogging. He tried to keep them away from the other groups of people, but there was a young couple on the sidewalk ahead of them. They laughed and ran at Ken and Angela.

Ken waved his tire iron at them. "Stay back." He didn't know what their intentions were, but they definitely weren't acting normal. On the other hand, he didn't want to have to explain to the police why he had accosted two people with a tire iron. He tried again to warn them off. "We don't want any trouble."

The couple didn't even slow. The man tackled Ken before he could convince himself that he was really going to attack. Out of the corner of his eye, he saw the woman jump on Angela. The man on top of him leaned in as if for a kiss, and Ken remembered Angela's words about a man eating the other woman's lips.

"Sorry, buddy." Ken pushed against the man. "I'm flattered and all, but I'm straight." He shoved the tire iron against the man's throat, forcing him back. He heard Angela scream and his protective instinct kicked in. He bucked his hips and jabbed the point of the iron into the man's shoulder. He shoved as hard as he could and rolled his attacker over. Scrambling to his feet, Ken swung the tire iron against the man's head and turned to Angela.

He didn't hesitate this time. He swung the tire iron again and the woman fell to the ground beside Angela. Ken reached down and helped his passenger to her feet. She had tears in her eyes, but looked more angry than frightened. "Come on."

She nodded, stepped past him, and kicked the laughing man behind Ken in the chin as he got to his hands and knees. The man dropped.

Ken nodded. *I like this woman.* They started running for the garage again. Ken reflected as they ran how quickly he had gone from being worried about getting in trouble with the police for hitting someone with a tire iron, to just being worried about staying alive. *Is that all it takes to strip civilization from a person?* He could only hope he got the chance to ponder this philosophical question another day. For now, he couldn't afford that luxury. He scanned the streets for other potential attackers. He didn't know for sure who could be trusted, though at this point, it looked like most of the violence was being done by people who were laughing. He shook his head at the thought, but another glance around them only served to reinforce that observation. For whatever reason, people were laughing, and then attacking people who weren't.

"Where are we going?"

"Hobby Center." He slowed only enough to make sure Angela was keeping up, but she was keeping pace with no trouble. He realized as he watched her easy stride that she was probably in better shape than he was. He could tell she was holding back to stay with him.

"Any particular reason?" she asked. He noted that she seemed perfectly sober now, and figured what they had seen would sober anyone.

The sound of a blaring horn from the freeway ahead was followed by the now familiar sounds of squealing rubber, crunching metal, and breaking glass. "The theaters keep armed guards in their parking lots."

"Good idea."

Screams and laughter fell behind them as they raced down the street. Ken saw the light pouring from the entrance to the underground parking ahead and altered course a bit to cut across the grass. He could only hope they would find help.

CHAPTER 50
CHARLES GRIFFE
LOSSES

Charlie followed behind Chris, the two of them leading the group as quietly as they could go. Tabby brought up the rear. He had suggested that she take that position, implying that it was too important a task to leave to any of the newcomers. The truth of the matter was that he honestly wasn't sure if he trusted her. She had, after all, come close to killing him in that stairwell. That wasn't something he was going to just forget.

Getting a group their size into the stairwell had been a major undertaking, and they'd barely made it inside before hooting and laughter told them they'd been spotted. But with fourteen people, by the time the last of them were in, the leaders were nearly to the exit onto the next deck. It had been a mad dash to get everyone back out of the stairwell and into a nearby cabin. Even then, it had been one of the economy cabins, and barely held all of them.

But they'd made it, and managed to evade the groups chasing them once again.

Now, another hour later, they were creeping once again up the hallway, moving as stealthily as a group of fourteen frightened people could move. Less than five nerve-wracking minutes later, Tabby whistled once from behind. It was their prearranged signal for Chris to open a cabin. Two more sharp whistles let them know he needed to hurry.

Charlie looked back and saw movement in the shadows. He saw Tabby brace herself for a fight in the middle of the corridor, gripping her mirror shard tightly.

All pretense of stealth gone, Chris ran ahead. "Here, this is one of the luxury suites!" He keyed the door open, and started ushering the group inside. If they moved too slowly, he grabbed them by the arm and shoved.

Charlie nodded approvingly and moved back to see Tabby still set to make her stand. Past her, a barely-seen mass of movement deep in the shadows of the darkened hallway told him there was a rushing mob heading their way. He ran up and tapped her shoulder. "Let's go!" Chris hissed at them to hurry and they ducked inside well ahead of the laughing troop behind them.

"Did they see you?" Chris asked.

Tabby shrugged. "Hard to tell."

Chris whispered to Shane, signaling him to come listen at the door while they checked the cabin. It was one of the larger affairs, and as they moved into it, sudden movement caught Charlie's eye. One of the latest people to join their group was Scott Ward. They had found him and his wife back on Deck Nine shortly before the near disaster in the stairwell, and Charlie really didn't know much about them.

But he recognized his balding head and full beard as Tabby whipped the flashlight in the direction of his shout. He spun frantically as a giggling woman dressed in a soiled baby doll nightie, bit and clawed at him from behind. Before anyone could get to them, she plunged a long, polished fingernail through his eye and laughed as she swirled it around. As she and Scott fell to the floor, she leaned forward, latched onto his ear with her teeth and yanked her head back. She grinned and drooled around a bloody earlobe as Charlie dove at her, dragging her off her victim.

Scott twitched on the cabin floor, blood and something thicker than blood running down his cheek. Charlie and the pajama-clad crazy struggled across the cabin floor, and she turned her nails on him, scratching his face as she sought his eyes. But before she could do more than rake at his face, Tabby stepped in, plunged her mirror shard into the woman's throat and twisted it. The throat spewed crimson, and the woman dropped to her knees, lips drawn back into a snarl as she reached for Tabby and fell forward. She died within seconds, still crawling toward Tabby.

The whole attack happened so quickly that both Scott and the crazy woman were dead before Scott's wife realized what had happened. It was immediately evident when she caught on, though. Her screams pierced the room.

The old man, Merl, grabbed her and covered her mouth with his hand. "Lady, you gotta stop that! They'll hear you!" But she was inconsolable and her screams continued. And though they were muffled by the man's hand, they were too loud to escape notice if there were any crazies in the area.

Boy, you best do something or she's gonna get us all killed.

Dad was right. Charlie looked at everyone else, but none of them seemed ready to do anything but make shushing noises at the woman. "Oh, for fuck's sake."

He grabbed the woman by the shoulder and spun her out of Merl's grasp. He winced a bit as the action strained the wound across his chest, but he couldn't afford to worry about it. He had to shut the grieving woman up. Deciding to start with a minimal action, he smacked his open palm across her face. It wasn't a gentle slap, by any means, and it rocked the smaller woman back into Merl's arms. But the important thing was that it was effective. That hand across her cheek brought instant silence, not only from the sobbing woman, but also from everyone else in the cabin. They looked at him as if he had committed an atrocious act. "What?" he hissed. "You want to have more of those crazies pounding down the cabin door? None of you had the balls to do what needed to be done, so I had to. I could have just knocked her out. Just think about how well you would have liked that." He fought to keep his voice low, but his anger threatened to override his common sense. "And now you want to make me the bad guy? Well fuck you. All of you!"

There was shocked silence in the room, except for the grieving Mrs. Ward who still sobbed, albeit much more quietly, as she stepped across the cabin and knelt to cradle the head of her husband. Charlie sat back down on the bed, rubbing his hand gently across the cut across his chest. Tabby approached and he glared at her. "You come to tell me I'm an asshole, or what?"

She shook her head. "I came to check on your cut." She knelt on the floor before him and shone the light at where his shirt oozed small dark spots.

She started to reach for his shirt, but the sight of the wet, crimson streaks on her arm caused Charlie to pull back. "Hang on a minute. Not that I'm not grateful, but I don't think I want you touching me with that blood all over you. We still don't know how this shit is being spread, but I'd guess mixing infected blood with my own might be a good way to get sick, don't you?"

Tabby pulled her hands back. "True enough. Give me a minute." She went to the mini-fridge and pulled out a bottle of water. Chris joined her and the two of them took turns washing the blood from where it stained their skin. Then Tabby grabbed one of the mini bottles of whiskey and poured half over her hands before handing it to Chris and walking back to Charlie. "Better?"

"Yeah, thanks." He winced a little as she pulled his shirt back from his chest.

"Looks like you're bleeding again." Without turning, she called out in a loud whisper. "Can someone open the balcony drapes? Let's get some air in here."

Charlie heard the curtains slide back and the click of the lock. Seconds later the door slid open, letting the cool ocean air in to clear out some of the funk. Tabby called back over her shoulder. "Chris, can you bring me another bottle of whiskey? This cut is looking a little infected."

Charlie looked down, nearly going cross-eyed as he tried to see where she pressed on the wound. "Infected?"

"Don't worry. It's just a little inflamed. Should be fine as long as we keep it cleaned."

Chris handed her another bottle from the mini-fridge, as well as a wash rag. He looked at Charlie. "You okay?"

"Yeah." But he hissed and jerked away as Tabby applied the alcohol-soaked rag to his chest.

"Sorry," she said.

"It's all ri—"

He was interrupted by a shout from the old woman in the group, Celina. "Allison, no!"

Charlie jerked his head around as Tabby gasped. Chris bolted around the bed, but they were all too late. Allison sat on the balcony rail, looked back at them, and just before Chris got to her, leaned backward. She didn't scream, didn't make a sound at all as she fell out of sight. Chris leaned over the rail and his shoulders sagged. He turned back to them and shook his head. "She's gone."

Tabby moved toward the balcony. "Are you sure the fall killed her? Maybe she's—"

Chris shook his head. "This cabin is one of the luxury suites. The balcony goes past the jogging track and out over the ocean. She's gone."

They didn't have much else they could do at that point. They threw the other bodies into the ocean and sat for a while in silence.

CHAPTER 51
ERICA CHAPMAN
EARLY BLACK FRIDAY

The world had obviously gone insane. That was the only way Erica could wrap her mind around the idea of a raging mob of laughing killers chasing her van through the mall parking lot. You wouldn't ordinarily think that outrunning them would have been too much of a problem, what with her driving a van like a madman. But as she drove up the aisle toward the mall proper, another group of people poured through the entrance and into the parking lot. She did a double take as she noticed a few mostly naked women in the crowd, bare breasts bouncing in the cold November night. "What the hell?" then she noticed the sign above the entrance and understood. *Victoria's Secret Early Black Friday Sale.*

A woman wearing a shimmering red baby doll nightie trimmed in white faux fur tackled another woman, beating her with the pale white arm from a store mannequin. Heart pounding, Erica slowed as the riot spilled into the lane of the parking lot. Then the mob saw the van and began hooting and laughing as they rushed toward it. "Shit!"

"What's wrong?" Her pistol-waving benefactor leaned up between the front seats so he could see out the windshield.

"There's more of them coming out of the mall."

"Punch it!"

A kid in a leather jacket left the mob. He raced straight at the van, waving the support beam from a chromed metal clothes rack over his head. Several of his companions noticed, and joined him in his attack. As he drew nearer, Erica saw a haunted, out-of-control, insanity in his eyes—the same look she'd seen in the eyes of Mr. This-is-Texas back in the theater.

"Lady, you're slowing down!"

"I don't have a choice," Erica yelled back. "He's running to get in front of us. I'll hit him."

"And if you don't, they'll be all over this van in ten seconds. Punch it!" He reached across and pushed her knee down on the gas pedal. She thought only a second about fighting against that pressure, but the reality was that he was right. She allowed the van to accelerate, pretending to herself that she was helpless to stop it—that the hand on her leg was forcing her actions.

At the last second, she swerved away from the kid, popping up over a parking block and scraping down the length of a convertible. The van bounced enough that the hand on her knee released its grip, opting instead to use its powers for good—namely to grab the back of her seat to brace her passenger as the van bounded wildly for a few seconds while they sped past the rest of the crowd. She looked ahead and saw more people rushing out of the various mall exits. Some of them laughed, some of them screamed in panic. Most of those screaming were quickly overrun by the pursuing horde.

She yanked the wheel to the right at the first chance, steering away from the exit ahead, heading instead to the outskirts of the parking lot in an effort to put as much distance between herself and the mall as was possible. She looked once more into the rearview mirror, saw it was working.

"You're going the wrong way! The exit's the other direction!"

"It's a mall, damn it! They generally have more than one way out, you know." Her passenger shut up at that and she glanced again in the mirror. They were finally putting some real distance between themselves and their pursuers. Another thirty seconds, and it began to look like they were in the clear. She looked in the rearview mirror and saw that the mob seemed to have lost interest in pursuit and was busily milling about the parking lot and beating on parked cars. Hands trembling, Erica reached into her purse and withdrew her cell phone. Taking care not to drop it, she dialed 911 on the keypad. "Nine, one, one. Please state the nature of your emergency."

It wasn't until she opened her mouth to speak that she realized she had no idea what to say. "I… there were people at the theater… they all started laughing… and they killed a man…"

"Ma'am, did you say they killed someone?"

Erica found her eyes blurring and knuckled back the tears with the back of her hand. She sniffed. "Yes, they killed a man. And one of them started to eat his face!" There was silence on the line for a second.

"Ma'am, are you all right?"

Erica took her eyes off the road for a second and stared at her cell phone in disbelief. "Am I all right?" She put the phone back to her ear. "Of course I'm not all right! There's at least a dozen people dead back there at the movie theater!

"Wow. That must have been a really bad movie!" And the voice on the other end began to laugh.

Erica really didn't handle it well. She screamed and threw the phone. It bounced off the passenger side door and landed back in the passenger's seat beside her. She beat her fist against the steering wheel. She evidently reacted badly enough that the poor man in the back seat started to yell.

"Hey, lady! Whoa, whoa, whoa, whoa! Watch where you're going!"

Looking up through teary eyes, she saw she had veered toward the hedges surrounding the parking lot. Only the fact that there were hardly any cars this far out in the parking area her from turning them into a traffic statistic. She jerked the wheel back to the right and slammed on the brakes, coming to a full stop.

"What's wrong?"

Not trusting herself to speak, she simply pointed to where her phone lay on the passenger's seat.

"What? Something wrong with your pho…" but he went silent as the sound of laughter and gunfire sounded from it.

More pops sounded from the phone, and she stared at it as if it were a rattlesnake waiting to strike. After several more gunshots and a lot of shouting, they heard the laughter of several people. Then one voice got closer than the others. It was a woman's voice, and she shrieked at something she seemed to find absolutely hilarious. It was the creepiest laugh Erica had ever heard in her life, and she shivered at the rustling sound of someone moving the phone or headset coming through the speaker. Then a freakishly cheerful voice came across the line. "I'm sorry, but the number you have dialed is not a working number." The voice giggled again before screaming into the line, "So hang up the damn phone! Hee, hee, hee..." The line went silent, and the screen on the phone lit up. *Call ended.*

Erica knuckled the tears back and took a deep, shuddering breath, then turned to look at the man in the back. His eyes were wide as she picked up the phone and placed it in the console. She looked in the mirror again and saw that the mob in the parking lot was spreading and a small splinter of them were running toward the van again. She took one more calming breath and put the van back into drive. A few hundred yards later, she saw the back exit just ahead on the left. Speeding past the hedge row that bordered the parking area, she breathed a quick sigh of relief, daring to think they were safe.

She should have known better.

They were still fifty yards from the exit when a Ford pickup bounced across the esplanade that separated the inbound traffic from the outbound. Erica slammed on the brakes as the truck veered toward them and watched as an obviously terrified red-headed woman drove past, eyes pleading for help she knew they couldn't provide. There were half a dozen crazies standing in the bed of the truck, hooting and beating their hands on the top of the cab.

But that wasn't the worst of it.

As she went past, Erica could see a teenage girl in the cab with the woman. The woman was trying her best to fend off the lunges from the teen, whose hair was the same tint of red as the driver's. She was bound to have been the driver's daughter, and that made it even more terrifying when the girl latched on to the older woman's hand with her teeth and bit down. That was all Erica saw as the pickup sped past.

"What the hell is going on?" The voice from behind startled Erica. She had been so intent on the poor woman's plight that she had momentarily forgotten about her passenger. She glanced briefly back at him, and saw that he was watching the woman too, as she drove past. She realized he wasn't really expecting an answer, so she bit her lip and shook her head. She breathed a sigh of relief as they finally reached the exit and she anticipated leaving the insanity of the shopping mall.

A blaring horn sounded to her right and she slammed her foot on the brake, throwing her passenger, as well as several boxes of personal belongings, toward the front seat as another pickup truck sped past. At first, she thought the driver was trying to flee the chaos. But as he flew past she saw the now familiar maniacal grin on his face. He laughed and pounded incessantly on the horn as he passed, plowing unheeding through a small crowd of people just before he rammed headlong into an oncoming SUV. The rear wheels of both vehicles lifted momentarily into the air as the forward momentum was transferred to the only other direction physically available. Blood splattered the side window, and the driver of the SUV hung halfway through the shattered windshield. Erica thought she could see him moving as a torrent of steam from the crumpled radiators obscured her view. Her mind reeled as she tried to make some sort of sense of this, and something clicked.

"Oh God, oh God, oh God, oh God!" She reached forward and shut off the air conditioner, slapping the dash vents closed as she did so.

"What are you doing?"

"It's gas. It's got to be some kind of gas."

"What?"

"Maybe a terrorist attack, or a lab accident." She looked back at him.

"What the hell are you talking about?"

"There must be something in the air that's driving people crazy. It's the only explanation that makes any kind of sense."

He scrambled over the console between the seats and dropped into the passenger's seat, reaching for the dash vents that were out of Erica's reach. "You think this will keep it out?"

"I don't know. You have a better idea?"

He licked his lips, looking nervous for the first time since she'd met him. Of course, she'd met him less than ten minutes ago. She looked back outside at the mayhem in the street. What she saw out there made the parking lot seem tame by comparison. Masses of people chased one another through the street, weaving between too many multi-car pileups to count. They formed a living, amorphous mass, flowing between vehicles, congregating in frantic groups as they found a victim, hooting, screeching, kicking. There were hundreds of them, and as they hunted, for there was no other word for what they were doing, they emitted a constant, horrifying, frenetic tittering.

Erica looked once more at the wreck they had just witnessed, distracted by the mayhem in the streets. The SUV had caught fire, and as flames began to spread throughout the vehicle, someone emerged from the passenger door. To her utter horror, she saw it was a man with a burning jacket, and though she wasn't able to hear him over the cacophony of screaming and laughter, she could tell that he wasn't one of the laughing horde. There was no maniacal rictus of insanity on his face, only pain and panic as he flailed about trying to get his jacket off. Suddenly, the horn of the SUV began blaring, startling her. At first, she thought the driver might also still be alive, but his body still hung lifelessly halfway through the windshield. She realized then that the fire must have shorted the wiring, causing the horn to sound. It had the unfortunate side effect of attracting the attention of everyone in the area. And everyone in the area was Erica, her passenger, and the mob of crazed killers in the street. Almost as one, they turned toward the SUV. It was only a split second from seeing the SUV, to seeing the screaming man in the burning jacket.

The mob rushed him, and he was immediately buried beneath their mass. "Holy shit." Pistol Pete's voice was quiet, his words more an expression of fear and dismay than a curse. Erica had no answer. And as bad as that was, she found things could always get worse. As she watched, a pair of revelers emerged from the mob, each brandishing a torch. "Where did they get torches?"

"Those aren't torches."

"What? Of course they…" That was when she noticed the lower halves of the burning brands were flopping loosely as the men cavorted about—and they had fingers. One of them ran to another wrecked vehicle and tossed the arm in the back seat, starting yet another car burning. "I think I'm gonna be sick."

"No time for that, ma'am." He directed her attention back to the main mob that was beginning to disperse. A few of them ran madly through the street, their clothing ablaze from where they had gotten too close to the SUV, or to the now smoldering carcass that lay in the middle of a shiny pool that reflected the light from the streetlights. Looking where he pointed, Erica saw several individuals split off from the rest of the mob, hooting and laughing as they noticed the van's headlights pointing at them, apparently attracted as moths might be. As they ran, they attracted the attention of others, and in short order, there was another mob rushing at the van. "Time to go, lady. We gotta move it!"

Erica gulped and put the van back in gear, spinning the wheels as she pulled onto the street proper and drove away from the mayhem. They had come out of the parking lot by way of the back exit, and as they raced along the back road behind the mall, Erica was thankful for the relatively empty street ahead. Turning right at the next corner, she saw another empty street. But as they approached the next, another car raced past the intersection. There was someone clinging to the top of the car, grinning madly as he reached in through an opened window and yanked on the driver's hair. They flew past the intersection and out of sight before Erica could see how their particular scenario ended, but as they reached the corner, she saw that there were plenty of other shows to watch.

This was the main thoroughfare. At this point, they were less than a mile from Interstate 10, and from there, it was a matter of about ten more miles to the safety of Uncle J's. All that stood between them and the ranch were several blocks of high-end strip centers, independent department stores, and a hotel. And of course, all the people who raced about in the parking lots of these temples to the gods of commerce, chasing or being chased.

Squealing tires drew her attention to an old Ford pickup that screeched through the parking lot of a drug store across the street, hitting at least four people. At this distance, Erica couldn't tell if the driver was laughing or not. In all honesty, she was past the point of caring. She spun the wheel to the right and pulled onto the main road toward the ranch. There were several wrecks in the street ahead, but she thought she should be able to weave her way through them easily enough.

Her passenger turned to look out the back. "Gotta move it, lady. We're attracting attention."

Erica didn't bother looking to see where their pursuers were. After what she'd already seen, it was incentive enough to know they were coming. The first wreck blocked the outbound side of the street, but she was able to get the van onto the grassy median, making it with minimal scraping of the undercarriage. She dropped back to the concrete, eyeing the next obstacle. It was a four-car pileup, one car burned, upside down atop the others. She briefly wondered how it had happened, then recalled the crazed driver of the pickup as he intentionally drove headlong into the SUV. Burning fuel pooled across the median ahead, burning the box hedges and decorative landscaping that grew there. Her only option was to cross the median again, driving into the opposite lane. It didn't seem to matter, though. There was no oncoming traffic to worry about. She slowed to hop the curb once more, and as she did, she heard a thump, followed by insane cackling as one of the crazies slapped his hands against the side window in the back.

Her passenger raised his pistol and aimed somewhere behind them. "There's only one right now, but in about thirty seconds, we're gonna have a whole crowd of 'em on us again. Can you get us out of here?" She was about to reply when blinding lights from the parking lot across the street distracted her. She raised her hand to block some of the glare and the blaring of a horn quickly grew louder.

"Shit! Hold on to something!" Erica screamed to be heard over the sound of the horn and cut the wheel to the right. She stomped the gas pedal to the floor, fervently praying that she would be able to get them out of the path of the four-wheeled missile. The van bounced off the median and back to the street, lurching forward as the tires found purchase on concrete. Erica glanced in the mirror and nearly cried in frustration when she realized it wasn't going to be enough. "Hang on!"

She noted with a certain level of detachment that it was the same Ford pickup she'd seen in the parking lot just a few minutes earlier. Then it slammed into the rear quarter panel and spun them around. She saw stars as her head was thrown back by the force of the airbag, and boxes dumped their contents, turning them into painful projectiles that flew about the interior of the van. Erica heard her passenger curse before something hit her head. She struggled for a second, trying desperately to hold on to consciousness, and though she could hear various sounds around her, her brain couldn't seem to process them. Her eyes refused to stay focused, and she caught the scent of hot radiator fluid and steam just before things went dark.

CHAPTER 52
LINTON BOWERS
THIS MIGHT GET HAIRY

Michelle made a sound of disgust as they rounded the corner and saw the fire ahead. By this time, they had been on the road for more than an hour, but had hardly made any progress on their trip at all. It was dark now, and the fire lit the surrounding area like a beacon. "Another wreck."

Linton sighed. "Emmet, you got another route ready?" He saw a light come on in the back seat as his friend called up a map on his smartphone for the eighth time.

After a minute, he leaned over the seat and showed Linton and Michelle his phone. "Guys, it looks like it just isn't going to happen this way. We've tried every route available to get to a clear spot on I-10. Between the craziness on the actual freeway, and all the wrecks blocking the feeder, I don't see this route working for us."

Linton pulled out the Bee Hive Manual and turned to the maps in the back. He turned on a pocket flash and checked his notes. He'd plotted a variety of routes to the bunker, but all of them depended on somehow getting north to I-10. So far, they hadn't even come close. "Dammit!" He slammed the manual closed and took a deep breath to keep his frustration in check. "All right. Either of you have any suggestions?"

"I do." Michelle took the manual from him and opened to the Houston area map. She shined her own flashlight at the page, studied it for a moment, then pointed to a location on the I-45 feeder. "We're about here, right?"

Emmet and Linton looked. "That's where my phone says we are," Emmet agreed.

She traced a path northward along the freeway to where it intersected with Houston's 610 loop. "And your plan was for us to go north to 610, ride the east loop north to I-10?"

Linton nodded. "Or possibly pass the 610 loop and go straight up to where 45 intersects I-10, or any of the smaller roads that lead up to ten."

Michelle nodded. "What if we head south?" She traced a route with her finger. "We could go back to Sam Houston Parkway, cut over to 146, and take it up to I-10. That gets us there without having to go close to Houston."

Linton looked at the route she proposed. "That's quite a bit out of our way, babe."

"But doesn't it have a better chance of having less traffic?"

He nodded. "Yeah, I guess it does. What do you think, Emmet?"

Emmet shook his head. "I'm not from around here. I'm just along for the ride. I'll go with whatever you guys decide."

Linton looked at the map again, willing something to pop out at him that didn't involve sacrificing what little ground they had gained. But the more he looked at it, the more it appeared his wife was right. "All right. Let me find a place to turn around."

Emmet cleared his throat. "There is one little detail I feel obligated to point out." He tapped the filter on his gas mask. "These filters don't last forever. How many replacements do we have?"

Linton pointed to a bag in the back seat across from Emmet. "Each filter should last about four hours, and we have two replacements for each of us. That should give us plenty of time to get to the bunker."

"We just passed the Monroe underpass a minute ago," Michelle offered. "We can turn around and get over to the southbound side there."

Linton nodded, did an illegal three-point turn in the feeder, and headed back the way they had come. Minutes later, they were southbound on the other side of the freeway. Weaving their way through the insane maze of wreckage that Houston's streets had become, Linton slowed even more. "Is that what I think it is?" He was afraid to come to a full stop, for fear that some of the infected people outside would try to climb aboard the truck again, but he slowed as much as he felt was safe as they approached the conflagration ahead. Emmet leaned over the back seat and peered through the windshield, and Michelle leaned forward as well.

It was Michelle who spoke first. "Is it a passenger jet?"

Emmet cursed. "Could we have any worse luck? I mean come on! Aren't we having a hard enough time? God decides to drop a damned plane in the road?"

As they got closer, Linton could see that it was, indeed, a small passenger airliner. They had just pushed their way through another pileup at the last exit ramp a mile back, but the feeder ahead was completely blocked by the smoldering fuselage. The jet had crashed into the building across from the freeway, and the wreckage was scattered across the feeder and partially onto the interstate itself. What was left of the building, as well as scattered pieces of the aircraft, sputtered with flames, and Linton knew it was likely his imagination, but he thought he could actually smell the stench of burning jet fuel, plastic, and flesh. It wasn't likely though, that he would be able to smell much through the filter on his mask.

"Must have been coming in to Hobby."

Linton nodded agreement. They were only a few miles from the airport. Michelle was undoubtedly correct.

He slowed even more, trying to buy time for them to figure out what to do. Before he could ask Emmet to check the map, Michelle pointed to the left. "There's an entrance ramp. Maybe we can get past on the freeway?"

They had noticed that much of the traffic on the freeway had come to a standstill. Linton figured most of the infected had already wrecked their vehicles. But he had also seen many of them wandering about on foot in the middle of the freeway. He didn't relish the idea of trying to weave between the maze of accidents and people, and now burning airplane wreckage, that was scattered about the interstate. But he didn't see any other way to get past.

He slapped his hand against the steering wheel.

"Calm down, brother. It ain't like we have any sort of choice in the matter. We just gotta keep moving forward."

Emmet was right, and Linton took a calming breath. "Yeah." He steered for the on ramp. "There's a lot of people wandering around on the freeway. Keep your doors locked and weapons drawn. This might get hairy."

"Like it hasn't been already?"

"Point taken." He pulled up the ramp and onto the freeway.

CHAPTER 53
ROSS MAYFIELD
COMMUNICATION

The man had stopped screaming by the time Ross began to regain control of his body. Weak and shaky, Ross pushed himself to his hands and knees. He was still wobbly, but he crawled over to his bed and climbed onto it. He grabbed weakly at his cell phone and hit 9-1-1. The phone rang twice before rolling into a fast busy signal. Looking at the screen, he saw a "circuits are busy" message.

What the hell? He tried again, with the same result. The only time he'd ever seen that message was in 2005. His dad had been overseas when Katrina had decimated the Gulf Coast. Ross and his mother had been at home in Mobile, and she'd wanted to call and let Dad know they were all right. But no matter how many times she tried, she'd been unable to get through. Ross recalled being amused that she seemed to take the lack of cell service as a personal affront.

He realized now, though, how helpless she must have felt to be in the midst of an emergency and unable to contact anyone. And that triggered his realization that there was something momentous going on—something much larger than two deaths in the quad outside. He recalled Erica's message, "…there's an epidemic or something. They're saying that millions are dead." He thought about the man outside. He kept tight rein on his emotions this time, and when he was sure he could handle it, he stood slowly and went back to the window. Sure enough, the light from the gas lamps in the quad revealed two bodies lying in the grass.

A small group of students stood laughing at the dorm across the lawn, throwing rocks through windows. Could this be the epidemic?

Something that drove people crazy? He needed more information. Walking away from the window, he brought up the call log on his phone again. Erica's number was at the top, and he hit the call-back icon. Once more, a fast busy was the only sound he heard.

He cursed and became aware of the rise in his heart rate. *Deep breaths, Ross. Feel your heart. Control it.* He got it back under control and tried to think. Text her! He remembered learning that SMS texting used a different frequency or some such. He started typing.

ERICA ITS ROSS. U THERE?

He waited a few minutes before assuming she wasn't going to reply.

WHEN U GET THIS, CALL OR MSG BACK. CRAZY SHIT GOING ON. WANT 2 KNOW UR ALL RIGHT.

"So now what? Can't call anyone. Erica's out of town. Parents are out of the country." That gave him pause. Were they all right? What about Alex? What about any of his friends?

For the next several minutes, he sent text messages to anyone he could think of. But Ross really didn't have a lot of friends, and within ten minutes, he was at the end of his contacts list. Sitting there, he tried to think about what he could do next. His stomach growled, reminding him that it had been almost twenty-four hours since he had last eaten. Since money wasn't a problem for Ross, he almost always ate out. He thought about the crowd outside. *Well, I'm not going outside with them running around.* He had a few energy bars in his gear bag, and was pretty sure he had some noodle pouches in the pantry. There was bottled water in the refrigerator. It wasn't much, but he figured he wasn't in any danger of starvation. Not before the police arrived, anyway.

That thought gave him pause. When *would* the police arrive? Erica had mentioned millions dead in Africa, and there was apparently enough going on locally to flood the cellular network. He hadn't been able to get through to the cops, but surely someone else had. How would he know?

Of course!

He hopped up and opened his laptop. While it was powering up, he went to his gear bag to get a couple of the energy bars. Reaching into the bag, he paused at the sight of his *dao*. Even thinking of carrying it made him feel a bit foolish. Until he remembered the bodies outside. He grabbed the energy bars and the *dao* before moving back to the laptop. He munched one of the sweet, nutty bars as he got online and checked some of his social media sites.

As he read, his appetite was suddenly forgotten. People from all over were reporting scenes similar to what he had seen outside his window. Many of them had seen worse. There were estimates of tens of thousands of attacks all over the country.

His cell phone chimed, distracting him from the screen. He had a text.

GOT UR MSG. STAY THERE. COMING OVER. —ALEX

Ross closed his eyes and sighed with relief. Alex was all right. If he was okay, then this couldn't be all that bad, right? But the irritating little voice in his head chided his logic. "Then why hasn't anyone else replied?" the voice asked.

Ross had no answer to that. He took another bite of the energy bar and waited.

CHAPTER 54
KEN HOLTZAPFEL
PARKING GARAGE

They could see that the security guard's booth was empty before they ever reached it, but Ken could see that there were hundreds of cars in the garage. He panted as they approached. "Looks like there's a play going on tonight." He looked back the way they had come. People still ran through the streets, but it didn't appear that any of them were coming after the two of them. "Maybe we can find someplace to hide."

They ran down the ramp and began to weave their way through the sea of parked cars. About halfway across the garage, Ken heard hooting and laughter behind them. Looking back at the ramp, he saw a dozen or more people shouting and laughing as they ran down the ramp. He pulled Angela down beside him and they hid behind a sedan. His heart was pounding and his legs shaking. He was in pretty good shape for a man his age, despite having a sedentary job. He used the gym at his apartment complex three nights a week to counter the effects of riding in a cab all day. But he was approaching his sixth decade of life, and there was only so much that the gym could do for him.

Angela peeked over the hood of the sedan and dropped back immediately. "Are they... crazy?" she asked him.

"I got no idea. Figure we should watch them a minute to see."

They didn't have to watch for long. A large man in a Stetson kicked at a sports car as he passed it. The car alarm went off and the volume of laughter increased immediately. The crowd began to shout and giggle as they began attacking the car. Most only had their hands, but one of them, a young woman in hooker heels and a "come and get it" skintight dress, started swinging her purse at the car over and over. The strap on her purse broke after a half dozen swings or so and its contents went flying across the garage.

Keeping low, Ken pulled Angela toward a bank of elevators on the opposite wall. The posters beside the elevator doors advertised the current play, a stage adaptation of the old Christmas movie, *Scrooged*. It was billed as "the side-splitting comedy smash of the season." Ken cursed to himself. He wasn't in the mood for any more laughter tonight.

"Up or down?"

Angela looked confused. "What?"

"We can either go up to the street level, or deeper below into the lower garage levels."

She appeared to think about it, then shrugged. "We already know what's on the street. And I don't know about you, but I'm not in a big hurry to get back up there."

Ken pressed the down button, and the door slid open with a loud ding. He looked back at the crowd that had been busy beating up the sports car. "Shit."

Sure enough, the sound of the elevator had caught their attention, and they were running toward them.

"Let's go, lady!" Angela was ahead of him as they piled into the elevator. She pressed the lowest level and then hit the "close door" repeatedly.

"Come on. C'mon, c'mon, c'mon!"

Ken readied his tire iron, hoping the fact that only a few of their attackers would be able to get through the door at the same time might help him. For a brief second, he even contemplated stepping out of the elevator to try and hold them off while Angela escaped. But he realized that stepping through the door would trigger their sensors, making their closure take even longer. As the mob in the garage made it to the last row of cars between them, the doors slid closed.

"Shit!"

Her outburst caught him by surprise. "What?"

"I left my purse in the cab. My phone was in it." She started crying. "I'm gonna die and I can't even call my husband." Now that the immediate danger was past, she was beginning to sob in earnest, and

Ken didn't know whether to pat her on the shoulder or hug her. Neither action seemed appropriate.

Before he could do either, the doors dinged again and slid open. He gently took her arm and pulled her toward the doorway. "Come on, Angela. We need to find someplace to hide."

She sniffed and nodded. "S-sorry."

"Don't worry about it."

The young woman let him lead her out of the elevator. He tried to think of someplace they could hide, but they had effectively trapped themselves four stories underground. There was insanity in the streets above, and they had been forced to choose between fighting and hiding. Ken looked around. The fourth sub-level was mostly empty, housing only twenty cars or so. Everyone else had evidently found parking on the upper levels. Ken began trying car doors as they moved across the floor, and got lucky on the fifth try. It was an older model Cadillac, and the owner had left it unlocked.

"Here, Angela. Get in here and keep your head down." It was evident that she was spent. She offered no resistance as he put her inside. He started to close the car door when she put her hand out to stop him.

"Where are you going?"

"Just going to keep an eye on things while you rest."

She swallowed, then nodded, laid down in the back seat, and let him close the door. Ken looked inside at her, nodded as she looked up at him, then turned back toward the elevators. Sooner or later, their pursuers would figure out which floor they were on, and when they came through those elevator doors, Ken was determined that he was going to stop them before they could hurt that girl.

The problem was that they didn't come by way of the elevator. Ken's grand plan of attacking them before they could clear the door was squashed as soon as he heard their laughter coming down the car ramp. *Oh crap!* There was no way he could confine them to a narrow area on that ramp. There was no way he was going to win a fight like this.

"Ken?" Angela shouted from a hundred feet behind him.

"Quiet!" He hissed, but he knew it was probably already too late. If her shout hadn't let them know what level they were on, his reply probably had. He started running back toward the car he had left her in.

"But I hear—"

"I know." He reached the car, where she had opened the door and was climbing out. "No, get back in and stay hidden."

"But—"

"No matter what you hear, you stay hidden. With any luck, they won't find you and the cops will get here in a few hours to straighten this crap out. Just stay hidden until you see the cops, all right?"

"I can't leave you out here alone," she protested.

"I'm gonna try and lead them away. I'll get them to follow me onto another level, and then I'll lose them and hide just like you are." Angela hesitated, and Ken pushed her back inside. "Remember, you stay hidden no matter what."

He closed the door as the approaching laughter forced him to turn back to the ramp. He trotted back toward the sounds, earlier feelings of despair gone now. He would win. He would keep them from that woman. No matter what.

It was obvious that they saw him as soon as they began coming down the ramp. He was still running at them, not wanting to be anywhere near Angela when he had to fight them.

There was no finesse to their attack at all. They simply charged, trying to roll him over with their numbers. Ken was smarter than that, though. As he rushed at them, he juked to the left at the last minute, swinging his tire iron into the head of the first person he came to, spinning, and swinging again at the next.

They all seemed to react a bit slowly, reminding Ken of someone who'd had a few drinks too many. Some stumbled as they tried to track his change in direction, and one actually spun so fast that he dropped to his knees, though he was back up almost immediately. The first one Ken struck dropped immediately, but he had caught the second one in the side of the neck and the man kept coming.

Ken skipped back, moving out of range, and ran past the mob, back up the ramp. They turned to follow him and he let the leaders get close, then reversed direction and slammed the pointed end of the tire iron through the shoulder of the first. He'd been aiming for the man's throat, but missed in his hurry to get in and out. Still, it dropped the man for a moment, and Ken was able to lure them farther up the ramp. If he could lead them all away from Angela, he figured she had a decent chance of lasting until the cops came.

One of the crowd was faster than the rest, and was almost on Ken before he realized the man was there. If not for the man's panting laughter, he might have managed to get a hand on Ken. But his laughter betrayed him, and Ken swung the iron hard and low as he ran. The man collapsed, and Ken could only hope he had managed to break the man's knee with his wild strike.

At any rate, it was another attacker down.

But Ken was tiring quickly, and the mob wasn't deterred. He made it to the top of the ramp, and the level ground gave him an added burst of speed. He gained a little more ground, but his breath was labored, and his pulse pounded in his ears. The elevators were a hundred feet or so ahead of him. He glanced over his shoulder. The lead pursuers had fallen behind a bit. He estimated that they were another hundred feet behind. *It might be enough.*

He put everything he had into the sprint for the elevator. He hit the button, looking back at the laughing mob as he prayed for the elevator to arrive quickly. They were still fifty feet away when the door slid open. He jumped inside, hit the button, and stood ready at the door, ready to engage the first person who breached the doorway.

He almost sobbed with relief as the door slid closed just before the first laughing face reached him. Panting, he raised his tire iron as the elevator slowed, ready to strike at anyone waiting as the door slid open. But there was no one. He looked over at the Cadillac where he had left Angela. It appeared untouched. He thought for a second about climbing into the car with her and trying to hide. It was a tempting idea, but he knew if that mob didn't find him in the open, they would probably start looking for him in the few cars down here.

Weary but determined, he trotted back to hide beneath the ramp as the sound of laughter drifted down from above.

CHAPTER 55
ERICA CHAPMAN
DEALERSHIP

"Lady?" The shouting pulled her out of the darkness. "Come on, lady. We gotta get moving. They're coming!"

Erica looked at the stranger. "What?" He was familiar, and there was a reason he was frantic, but for the life of her, she couldn't remember why. He slapped her. "Hey!" She pulled back in anger. "What the hell?"

He nodded. "Good. Come on, we gotta get out of here." He reached across and unsnapped her seatbelt as she tried to shake the cobwebs from her head. There was a noise from outside and she turned dazedly to see a crowd rushing toward them.

Oh, that's nice. Must be people coming to help us. She squinted to try and focus better. *Wonder why they're all laughing?* The sound was like fingernails on the chalkboard of her mind, and it brought her memory back at once. She gasped. "What happened?"

"We wrecked." He unsnapped his own belt and opened his door. "Not really a good time for explanations." He held a hand out to her. "Come on, let's go!"

She started to open her own door, but it wouldn't budge. There was a pickup attached to the rear of the van, the metal crumpled and twisted where they intertwined. The driver of the pickup was laughing and slapping his hand against the steering wheel, uncaring as he bled profusely from a long gash on his forehead. Looking past him, she saw the crowd running toward them and they, too, were laughing hysterically.

She grabbed her purse out of habit, and scrambled across the console toward the passenger door where the stranger with the pistol waited. As she stepped out of the wreck, something caught her eye, and on impulse, she reached down and yanked the length of aged, yellow wood from where it was wedged between the passenger seat and the door frame.

"So help me God, lady, if you don't get your ass in gear, I'm gonna leave you!"

Erica looked around. "Where to?"

He pointed to the Nissan car lot across the street. "We need new wheels." She couldn't argue his logic, but she had her doubts that they were simply going to be able to walk in and grab a car. Lacking any better idea though, she sprinted for the darkened glass building at the center of the lot. For the second time in an hour, she tested her legs and lungs, easily outdistancing her new partner once again. Purse bouncing against her hip, lacrosse stick pumping in the air with each stride, in less than a minute she was racing through shiny new Sentras and Altimas that reflected the lights from the street lights and spreading fires.

"What about the door?" she panted.

There was no answer from behind, and she looked back over her shoulder to see him raise his pistol. "Hey!" She ducked as he fired into the glass pane to the right of the dealership's front door. The glass splintered, and he fired twice more. The pane finally succumbed to gravity, falling and scattering shards all over the floor and sidewalk. She changed her destination accordingly and never slowed as crystalline shards crunched beneath her feet. An electronic alarm sounded as she entered the building, evidently triggered by a motion detector. There was a darkened hallway directly ahead, dimly lit by the streetlights a block away, and she immediately began trying doorknobs. Loud crunching over the klaxon of the alarm announced the arrival of her pistol packing partner.

"They're about thirty seconds behind me." He spoke loudly enough to be heard above the alarm.

"Then come here and help me find an unlocked door."

He started jiggling doorknobs on the other side of the hall. The third one Erica tried opened. "Got one!" she hissed at him. She glanced up the hallway to the broken glass in front. Their nearest pursuers were still in the parking lot, but rapidly approaching the building. She didn't have time to see more, as her companion shoved her into the darkened office and quietly closed the door behind them. The darkness seemed absolute, and the sound of the alarm in the showroom overloaded her hearing. It was an odd sort of sensory deprivation in which the only things she could hear were the alarm and the pounding of her heart. She bit back a whimper. The blood pounding in her ears had her convinced that one of those things outside was going to hear her heart beating and come pounding through the door. Images of what they had done to that poor man in the SUV came back to her, and she struggled to keep herself under control.

She gasped as she felt a pinpoint of pressure on the back of her thigh and her heart trip-hammered and skipped in her chest. She slapped her arm back and the lacrosse stick slammed against wood, the sound of it reassuring her that there was nothing wrong with her hearing. Somehow that made her feel better, and she got her panic under control. Reaching down, she found her assailant to be the corner of a wooden desk and smiled as an idea occurred. "Hey," she spoke just loudly enough to be heard above the alarm, "help me move this up to block the door."

"Move what?"

She heard him moving toward her and felt his arm brush against her back. She grabbed it, and forced it down to the desk. "We'll need to lift it so they don't hear."

He grunted, and moved away, down the length of the desk, briefly cursing as he stumbled against something. After a second, she felt the other end of the desk lift.

"Got it."

Erica lifted her end and the two of them stumble-walked the heavy thing back toward the door. Laughter began to fill the air outside, and her heart pounded harder once more. A sudden, booming shudder shook the walls; then another, and another. The volume of the laughter rose as the impacts continued until she heard the sound of splintering wood, and she realized their hunters had broken into the first office.

Her butt hit the door knob, and she had to scoot to the side to help slide the desk up to block the door. As she did, more banging announced they had moved to the locked door of the office directly next door. The cacophony of the crowd outside the door grew to the point that she didn't realize her hiding partner was whispering to her until she felt his hand on her shoulder. She jumped, and bit back a scream as she felt his warm breath in her ear. "What?" she whispered back.

She felt his breath again, and was able to make out "...of here..." but the growing noise outside made whispering a ridiculous waste of effort.

Evidently, he came to the same conclusion. "Screw this," she heard him say aloud, and the room was suddenly lit with the flickering of warming florescent lights. Erica squinted in the sudden brightness.

"What the hell are you doing? They'll see the light!"

"This door is next anyway, and I need to see what I aim at." He had his pistol drawn again, and had it loosely aimed at the door.

"How many bullets do you have?"

He nodded. "Good point." He pressed something, and the bottom of the pistol slid into his hand. She saw the shining brass of a bullet at the top of it as he turned it to look at the back. "Looks like I have maybe half a dozen rounds in this one." He slipped "this one" into the left pocket of his jacket, and pulled something from inside it. It was a twin to "this one" and he slid it into the pistol, then nodded. "Eighteen now."

Sudden banging on the door caused her to jump. Heart pounding, she looked frantically around the office for something else to prop against the door. Her eyes lit on the credenza on the back wall. "Help me with this." The door was beginning to rattle within its frame, and she knew it wouldn't take long for the howling freaks outside to break in. He saw what she was after and nodded, holstering his pistol. Luckily, the wooden credenza was smaller than the desk, and so was light enough for them to lift onto its mate, adding more weight to the makeshift barricade. She looked around for anything else to put in the pile, but the only other furniture in the office was the chairs. She briefly considered it, but wasn't sure if they would fit between the top of the credenza and the ceiling. "Holy crap!"

The banging and screeching was so loud now that she had to yell to make herself heard. "Follow me," she shouted, pointing to the barricade. He looked at her like she was crazy as she climbed atop the desk.

The desk that blocked the door.

The door that was in the corner of the office.

Right next to the wall.

She clambered onto her knees on the credenza and poked her lacrosse stick up, lifting one of the acoustical tiles in the ceiling and sliding it to the side. Her prayers were answered as she saw a large enough area to climb into. She was startled by a hand on her leg. "No way that ceiling's strong enough to hold us."

"I know. Help me up."

"But…"

"All we have to do is climb over this wall and into the next office. Now hold me steady while I get a tile out next door."

He looked at her like she was crazy, but the banging on the door didn't leave room for argument. He held her waist as she pried up a tile on the other side of the wall. "Got it. Let me go now." The banging and shouting was so loud she had to shout. He let go, and she shimmied up, onto the lip of the dividing wall. "When you come across, drop the tile back in place and they might take a while to figure out where we went." He nodded, so she spun her legs around, grabbed her stick, and dropped into the office next door. She quickly felt her way to the door to make sure it was locked, and as she did so heard her partner drop to the floor behind her.

"Now what?"

Inspiration struck, and she pulled out her phone. As the screen lit, she hesitated. There was a notification that she had a text from Ross. *Do I have time to read it now?* Booming on the door down the hall decided her. There were more pressing matters at hand, just now. She swiped the screen open and called up the list of applications. Finding the one she was after, she pressed the button and the camera flash turned into a flashlight. Adjusting the bar on the side until the light was a dim glow, she aimed it around the room enough to see what they had to work with.

"Good idea. Better silence it while you're at it, though. Wouldn't be a good thing to have it ringing while we're in here."

She nodded. "Now, help me move the desk."

They repeated the process three more times, leaving their pursuers farther behind each time, and the noise level dropped as they did so. They finally reached an office where the light of her phone revealed nicer furnishings than the others had had. They were a much higher quality, and the room was decorated with paintings and a wet bar. "Must be the big guy's office."

Mr. Pistol only grunted and headed for the desk. Erica laid her phone atop the desk and sighed. This one was heavier, and it was all she could do to lift her end and move it a few steps at a time. They finally settled it beside the wall, and as Erica looked up, she noticed her companion's attention was focused on something behind her. She turned to see what he was looking at and saw a metal box on the wall. It was about a foot wide, and two feet tall. "What is it?"

"I think it's a key lockbox."

Comprehension dawned. She pulled the handle on it, but it didn't budge. "It's locked."

He immediately started going through the drawers of the desk. "Maybe the boss is careless with the keys?" Erica grabbed the phone and shone the light where they could see in the drawers better.

But they had no such luck. Tucking the pistol into a shoulder holster, her companion went to the box and ran his hand along the top of it. "Damn!" Then he cocked his head and put his hand back on top. He seemed to tighten his hand then grimaced. He put his other hand up beside the first, tightening it as well, then bunched his shoulders and pulled. With a crunching of drywall, the box came loose from the wall, anchor bolts and all.

Erica arched her eyebrows. "Wow."

He shook his head. "Cheap drywall. No big deal."

Down the hall, the screaming mob had evidently given up on trying to figure out how they'd gotten out of the lit office, and were now attacking the next door. "Now that you have it off the wall, can you open it?"

"Not here," he said. "But I have an idea. For now, let's keep going the way we were."

They clambered over the wall again, and this time found themselves in a restroom. "Shit."

"What is it?" Erica asked.

"Public restrooms don't usually have locks."

She turned her phone toward the door and saw he was right. They could still hear the insane giggling from down the hall, banging and screeching. "Now what?"

He handed her the lockbox, drew his pistol, and walked toward the door. "Turn the light out."

"What the hell are you doing?"

"Relax, lady. I'm just going to take a peek."

She turned off the flashlight app. "It's Erica."

"What?"

"My name's Erica Chapman. No need for you to keep calling me 'lady.' With everything that's going on…" She let it trail off.

She heard him grunt acknowledgment. "Call me Matt."

She opened her mouth to reply, then stopped. What was she going to say? Pleased to meet you? Under the circumstances, it just seemed inane. Seconds later, she saw a sliver of dim light and heard the volume of the eerie laughter increase as Matt slowly opened the restroom door. It opened farther and she saw him stick his head out, then he stepped back and she heard the quiet hiss of the pneumatic door closer as he let it shut behind him. Erica turned the phone back on. "What did you see?"

He looked grim. "There must be thirty or forty of them out there. A bunch of 'em are working on breaking down the doors, others are running around the showroom tearing stuff up. There's no way we're gonna get past 'em all."

Erica swallowed. "I don't suppose you have any more bullets than what you mentioned earlier?"

"No ma'am, I don't. Never expected to be fighting off a whole town full of zombies."

"Zombies?"

"Well, whatever the hell they are." He shook his head. "Anyway, I do have an idea. But it's risky."

"Riskier than staying here and waiting for them to get to this door?"

"Not when you put it like that. Outside this door, just a few feet down the hall to the right, is the entrance to the garage. If we're quiet, we can probably get to the door without anyone seeing us."

Erica swallowed at the thought of stepping into that hallway. At the same time, she knew that each minute brought their pursuers closer and closer. "All right. Let's go."

He shook his head. "Not quite that simple. The door is one of those heavy, metal things. There's a chance it could make some noise when we open it."

"So we either wait here for them to find us, which they *will* do eventually. Or we go for the garage where we might have a chance." Erica looked at him. "I'd rather do something, than just wait here to die."

"All right." He took the box from her again. "Turn the light out and follow me."

CHAPTER 56
CHARLES GRIFFE
I THOUGHT YOU FORGOT ME

With shaking hands, Charlie pulled his cabin key out of his back pocket. Four days. It had taken him four days to get from the bar on Deck Seventeen back down to his and Felicia's cabin on Deck Seven. Four days since he had seen Felicia run crying from that fancy restaurant. But after all the distractions, he'd finally made it. Chris and Tabby stood to either side of him, flanked by all the others in their growing group. Everyone watched up and down the corridor nervously.

Charlie slid the key card into the door slot, and with an audible click, the locking mechanism disengaged. He pushed the door open. There was a very faint breeze filtering in from the open balcony, a peace offering from the crisp November night. "Felicia?" he called quietly. "Felicia, it's—"

With a scream, a form rushed at him from the darkness of the cabin. He had time to recognize Felicia's wild red hair as she swung a long and slender club of some sort at him.

Charlie raised his right arm to block without thinking, and was rewarded with an intense pain from the cut on his chest. It was followed by the even more intense agony of Felicia's club cracking against his raised forearm. He cried out in pain as Chris pushed past him into the cabin.

She's infected, boy. Gonna have to put her down.

Charlie dropped to his knees, pulling his injured arm into his chest, heart pounding at his father's observation.

Chris stepped between them. "Wait, lady!"

But Felicia didn't wait. With another scream, she swung her club at him as well, once, twice. She swung wildly as they pushed their way into the cabin. Chris managed to grasp the club and wrestled her to the ground. She continued to wail helplessly.

"Lady? Felicia? We aren't going to hurt you. We're with Charlie. Charlie's here."

"It's no use," Charlie spat. "She as crazy as the rest of them." The words were bitter, but Charlie was a realist. "Come on, knock her out and let's get out of here before her screaming attracts attention."

It would be a shame to lose Felicia. It was difficult in today's day and age to find a woman who really understood him like she did. Most of them were too caught up in all that feminism crap and didn't appreciate how hard it was to be a man.

He looked at the way her breasts strained her T-shirt as Chris struggled to hold her down. Such a shame. He looked speculatively at Tabby.

Nah. Too skinny. And don't forget how bad she cut you.

Charlie shook his head. As much as he hated to admit it, Dad had a point. No, Tabby wasn't right for him. Not refined enough to appreciate what he brought to the table.

"Charlie!"

With a start, he realized that he'd been staring at Tabby, and she was waving her hand in the dim dawn light.

Chris evidently wasn't as certain that Felicia was lost to them. "Charlie, she isn't like the others."

"He's right," Tabby reinforced Chris's observation. "She's not laughing."

Charlie turned back to look more carefully at where Chris sat astride a struggling Felicia, holding her hands above her head. It was true. Felicia thrashed in obvious terror, eyes wide enough that he could see them even in the dim pre-dawn light filtering in through the balcony curtains. But there was no laughter—none of the ever-present rictus that marked the crazies for what they were.

"Felicia?" He stepped closer, kneeling beside her so that she could better see his face. "Felicia, baby, it's me. It's Charlie."

Her eyes shifted to him and her screaming stopped. She looked confused for a moment and her struggles paused.

"Hey, baby. It's me. I got here as quick as I could."

She jerked her head from Charlie to Chris. She started to strain against his grip again, opening her mouth to scream.

"Felicia!" Charlie was more insistent now. "Don't scream. You'll attract the crazies."

But she didn't stop. She opened her mouth again and took a breath, drawing in to scream again.

"Don't do it, Felicia."

But he could see she was going to. Just as she started to scream, he slapped her. It wasn't often that he'd had to slap her, but on those few occasions, it had startled her into silence. This time was no different. Just as when he'd had to slap Mrs. Ward, the shock of it had stopped her. And just as when he'd done it before, the rest of his group were staring at him again, judging him. "Again? Seriously? What is it about this situation that you people don't understand? We draw attention to ourselves, we die."

There they go again. Judging you. Like they're better than you. Just because they don't have the balls to do what needs to be done. You know they probably won't survive this, don't you?

For once, he agreed with the old man. He ignored their looks and turned back to Felicia. "You're okay, aren't you baby?" Charlie saw her eyes flit from his face to Chris's, then Tabby's. Finally, they came back to him.

"Charlie?"

"Yeah. It's me, baby."

"But, your face. I didn't recognize… When did you start growing a beard?"

Charlie reached a hand up and rubbed the stubble on his chin. "There hasn't been a lot of time for shaving, baby."

He nodded to Chris, who released his grip on her hands and got off of her. "Sorry, ma'am. You had us pretty scared for a minute there.

But Felicia ignored him and leaned into Charlie's embrace. "I thought you forgot me." She sobbed into his shoulder.

CHAPTER 57
INTERLUDES

Nell Gavin was working the late shift doing maintenance upgrades on the hosting servers. It was a job that most of her friends poked fun at her for, but she actually preferred the odd hours. The upgrades pretty much ran themselves. They took anywhere from several minutes to a few hours, and all she had to do was keep an eye on the servers and make sure nothing went wrong. The thing she loved about the job was that while the updates ran, she had time to write.

Writing was her passion, and while it didn't pay as much as her main job did, she had hopes for the future. Her laptop was cranked up, and she was busy pounding the keys when the phone rang.

"Sentinel Technologies Data Center," she answered.

"Hello, my Nell. It is Francis. How are you this lovely evening?"

Nell grimaced. She had recognized Francis Kouassi's accent as soon as he'd spoken. He worked on the day shift, and was as big a sleaze ball as she'd ever seen. He was constantly hitting on the women, and she had complained about him to management on more than one occasion. Nell figured he must have incriminating pictures of someone for him to still have his job.

"What do you need, Francis?"

"I am outside the front door, and I am afraid that I have lefted my wallet at my desk. It is having my security badge in it. Would you mind to let me inside?"

"Isn't Bill out there?" Bill was the security guard that patrolled the building during the graveyard shift. He was a huge, burly man, a former pro wrestler according to the rumors.

"I have been knocking and I am not seeing him."

She didn't want to have to be in the same room with that misogynistic little prick, but she couldn't think of a decent excuse to refuse. She sighed. "Fine. I'll be down in a minute." She hung up before he could reply. Looking back at her laptop, she finished the paragraph she was working on. *Little weasel can wait a couple of minutes.* She even took an extra minute or two to read over what she had written, making sure there were no glaring errors. Finally deciding she couldn't stall any longer without being too obvious about it, she went downstairs to let Francis in.

She heard the screaming as soon as the elevator doors slid open. "What the hell?" She ran to the lobby and froze at the sight before her. Bill had returned, and was pile driving Francis into the pavement. He held the smaller man upside down by his legs, and as she watched, he lifted Francis up, and smashed him down. It must have been going on for at least a few minutes, for Francis's face and head were bleeding profusely from several scrapes and cuts.

Bill laughed as he slammed the little man into the concrete again, and Francis cried out in pain and shock as he tried to protect his head with his hands. He was only partially successful, covering his head as well as he could, but unable to protect himself fully as the weight of his entire body came down on his neck. As the security guard raised him up once more, Francis caught sight of Nell staring from inside the lobby. He screamed something, but it was so fast it was difficult for her to make it out. It took a second for her to realize he was speaking another language. "Nell! Helping me! Dear God, helping me!"

She shook her head in disbelief, and looked up to see that Bill was staring at her also. Staring, and laughing as he yelled, "Not gonna bother you no more, Nell." Then he started singing, "...no more, no more, no more, no more." With herculean strength, he slung the screaming Francis up into the air like a gardener using a hoe, then slung him down face first into the concrete. Francis stopped screaming as Bill continued to sing to Nell. "Hit the road, Jack! And don't you come back no more, no more..." The big wrestler slung the now limp Francis back and then forward this time shattering the plate glass window in the front. The glass flew across the floor of the lobby, and Bill flung Francis into the room after it.

Nell screamed. Francis was a broken bundle of bones and skin leaking blood from hundreds of tiny cuts. His eyes stared at her, completely devoid of life. It was horrible, a terrible sight to behold.

So why did she suddenly find herself laughing?

* * *

Suzanne Sargent began to giggle as she pulled into the parking lot. That crazy DJ always made her laugh. Tonight though, she couldn't seem to stop. Eyes widening as she began to realize something was wrong, Suzanne was suddenly furious at herself for not being able to stop. Then she was furious at the first thing she saw ahead of her: the telephone pole at the end of her street.

She pushed on the gas, accelerating her car over the curb, and into the pole. She laughed outright at the airbag that suddenly deployed in her face, shoving her head violently back into the headrest. There was a sudden pain in her arms, and she glanced down to find that the ultra-fast deployment mechanism had whipped open the steering column airbag cover at such velocity that it had scraped streaks of skin off her forearms, leaving small rivulets of blood running down to her arms. She laughed at the wonderful pain in her arms and neck.

Electrical wires fell from the pole, whipping around like writhing snakes as they sent sparks into the air.

And all the while, Suzanne kept her foot on the gas pedal. Though the car wasn't moving, the engine was still rattling on. Smoke began to pour from beneath the hood, soon followed by the flicker of a small engine fire. She laughed as she watched the fire spread, even when it began coming through the dash in front of her. Minutes later, the exquisite agony of flames licking at her legs sent Suzanne's screeching laughter to a new volume. It never stopped until her lungs quit functioning.

* * *

Morgan Powell cursed as another alarm went off. "Damn it! Georgie, we have another transformer out. That's seventeen in the last hour. Can you check the grid on twenty-seven, four thirty-one? I'm afraid we're getting close to another overload."

There was definitely something strange going on this evening, and she regretted switching shifts with Lanie. The power grid all over the Houston area was taking hits. She debated calling her supervisor. It would be just her luck that they end up with a major outage, and he would have her ass if that happened without her giving him a head's up. Then again, he'd have her ass if she called him after hours, and it turned out to be nothing at all.

No, the best course of action at the moment would just be to get more info.

"Georgie, did you hear me?"

Behind her, Georgie began giggling.

* * *

All over the continent, a tipping point had been reached. It was the same tipping point that had already been passed in Africa and Europe, as well as the few inhabited bases in Antarctica. It was infiltrating Asia and South America. The only place on the planet that was not yet overrun was the island continent of Australia, and the relief down under was destined to be but a brief respite. All over the world, people who were perfectly normal only moments before, suddenly erupted into laughter. That laughter was immediately followed by drunken, insane, violence. It was only a matter of timing that determined whether they found things funny and began to laugh, or were horrified at the actions of those who were laughing.

There was only one place that was immune to the plague decimating the world.

* * *

"Houston, this is ISS."

SILENCE

"Mission Control, this is ISS. Come in Mission Control."

SILENCE

"Huntsville Mission Control, we seem to have lost contact with Houston. Can you confirm communications malfunction?"

SILENCE

"Huntsville, please come in."

SILENCE

"Would someone please come in? This is International Space Station, calling on open frequencies. Is anyone there?"

SILENCE

CHAPTER 58
LINTON BOWERS
SMOKEY JOE'S BARBEQUE

Linton turned to his wife. "Let's hope that's the worst of it. Just be prepared if it's not." He sped up a bit as they continued down the freeway. Streetlights showed wrecks all over the road, but so far, he had managed to weave the truck through them with little more than a few scratches. The real problem wasn't the wrecks. It was the crazies wandering around on foot.

The first of them had shown up as he wove past the first pair of wrecked vehicles. The truck had just cleared the wreckage when two men charged it as they passed. Michelle screamed, and Linton jumped. But he was going fast enough that the men simply bounced off the truck and fell to the pavement. Looking in his rearview mirror, Linton saw them staggering back to their feet.

"Shit!" Michelle was breathing heavily in her mask. "They just jumped at us like they thought they could grab the truck. They're..." She shook her head.

"Insane? Crazy?" Linton finished.

"Yeah. I guess so."

They got past the worst of the plane wreckage within a few minutes, but the maze of wrecked vehicles spread up the freeway as far as they could see. It inhibited their speed, and Linton was in constant fear of boarders. That was the way he had come to think of the running people who kept leaping at the truck. So far, none had managed to get aboard, but it was apparent that this was their goal.

"This is taking too long," Emmet said. "We left the house hours ago, and we aren't any closer to the bunker than we were when we started." He tapped his mask. "At this rate, we won't have enough filters to get there."

"Once we get out of town, things should move faster." Linton tried to reassure his friend, but the truth of the matter was that he had been thinking the same thing.

He swerved to the left as another crazy ran at them. He completely missed them, and Linton watched in the mirror as the man loped after them.

"Look out!"

Michelle's scream drew his attention back to the road, and he swerved hard to the right as what looked like a wall of people ran at them from ahead. Before he could decide what to do, they were swarming over the truck. Linton had a moment of panic as he realized that moving forward, or for that matter, any direction, would now entail him running someone down.

Michelle screamed as one of them slammed his head into the window on her side of the truck. Wide-eyed and bleeding, the man giggled and slapped the palm of his hand against the window, leering maniacally at Michelle through the glass.

Emmet shouted from the back seat, "Let's go, Lint. Get us out of here!"

Still, Linton hesitated. Another impact on Michelle's window shook him out of it. *Us or them.* He hit the gas, sickened as several people in front of the truck fell before them, and he felt the bumps as he moved forward. He refused to look in his mirror this time as the truck moved through the crowd.

Emmet pointed to the right. "Exit ramp!"

Linton floored it and made it to the ramp before anyone could get into the bed of the truck. As they made it back to the feeder, he finally let himself look in the mirror. Dozens of people still ran after him, running down the exit ramp in their vain attempt to catch the truck. Ahead, the lights of a business complex illuminated another crowd of people running toward them.

"Where the hell are they all coming from?"

Linton didn't bother trying to answer. He accelerated, trying to get past the crowd ahead before they got the chance to block his way. It was going to be a close thing, but he thought he could make it.

He was wrong. It *was* close, and there was only one of them that got to the truck, but that one maniac didn't bother trying to grab the side of the truck. He threw himself completely in front of it. Michelle screamed, and Linton tried to avoid hitting the man, but he was already hugging the curb in his attempt to avoid the crowd. The truck popped over the curb just as the front bumper mowed the man down.

The next thing Linton realized, his side mirror was gone and his window shattered. There was a wall where his window had been, and he dazedly recognized it as the side barrier to the freeway. His ears were ringing, but he vaguely heard Michelle sobbing. He could also hear the engine of the truck. It didn't sound right. There was a loud clattering that told him that he had a serious problem. He looked over at his wife and saw that her airbag had deployed. He looked back to see that Emmet lay unmoving in the back seat. *No airbag back there.* He realized with a start that he couldn't raise his hands, looked down and saw his own airbag deflating.

Michelle was screaming something at him. His head swam as he turned it to look at her again and he fought to focus. He looked past her and his blood ran cold. The crowd was almost on them. He shoved the airbag out of the way and hit the gas. The truck squealed its protest, but pulled forward with a loping gait. Steering was damn near impossible, and he could tell he had a flat tire at the very least. He didn't care, though. All that mattered was getting some distance between the truck and the crowd chasing after it. He could worry about the truck after they were clear.

There was a small restaurant about a quarter of a mile ahead. Linton stroked the steering wheel. "Come on baby, just a little bit farther."

Smoke began to billow from beneath the hood. "Michelle? You okay, baby?"

She had stopped her sobbing when he had started moving. "Y-yes."

"Good. Emmet?"

There was a groan from the back seat. "Still in one piece. At least, I think so."

Linton sighed in relief. "All right. See that barbeque shack up ahead? I'm going to pull on the other side of it, and you two get out and get inside."

"What about you?" Michelle protested.

"Don't worry, I'll be right behind you. I just have to keep the truck moving past you before I get out." Flames began to flicker under the hood now. "The truck's had it, and chances are that it's going to attract every laughing son of a bitch in the immediate area. I have to make sure it's going to keep rolling past where we're going to hide. As soon as I get you guys out, I'm going to give it some gas and send it down the road."

Michelle began to protest again.

"Honey, we don't have time to discuss it. Grab your gear and get ready to jump!"

She looked at the flames now pouring out from the engine. Linton swerved into the restaurant parking lot and around to the other side of it. As soon as they were out of sight from the crowd, he slowed and shouted at them, "Go!"

They grabbed their bags and weapons and jumped out, not bothering to close their doors. Linton swerved, aimed the truck back at the feeder road and hit the gas. As soon as the truck was going in the right direction, he shoved his own door open, tossed out his gear, and rolled out. The impact was harder than it looked in the movies, and he fought to reorient. Through shifting vision, he saw his gear bag in the parking lot a few feet away and crawled toward it. He heard footsteps running toward him, and struggled to pull his pistol from its holster.

"No need for that, brother. Let's get you inside."

Emmet's voice angered him, even as it reassured him. He was supposed to be inside with Michelle. "Why are you—?"

"Couldn't let you have all the fun." He pulled Linton to his feet. "We'll talk about it inside. Now let's get out of sight before that crowd gets here and your brilliant plan to distract them is wasted."

Together, the two of them ran toward the barbeque shack, where Michelle and another woman held a door open for them. They got inside and had the door closed several seconds before the crowd came past the building. The truck loped to a stop on its damaged tires about a block up the road, flames now shooting several feet into the air. Linton sighed as he watched the fire began consuming the pickup.

"All those supplies," he groaned as he slid to the floor.

Michelle knelt beside him. "And we're still alive."

He looked at her. "Yeah, I guess we… your mask! Where's your mask?"

She shrugged. "Lost it when we jumped. Besides, it looks like we might not really need them."

"What?"

She waved her hand, motioning to someone else in the darkened interior. "This is Lesslie. She's been here this morning. No mask, but she doesn't seem to be infected any more than we are."

The small woman wore a greasy apron with a Smokey Joe's BBQ logo on it. She approached slowly, and Linton noted that her left cheek and eye were bruised and swollen, and she held a large knife in one hand.

"Lesslie, this is my husband, Linton."

Lesslie nodded. "Lesslie Lamphere. Pleased to… ah hell." She shook her head and turned away. She pulled a chair up from the nearest table and quietly lit a cigarette as she sat down.

Linton understood. Normal pleasantries didn't seem right. He looked again at his wife. No mask. He sighed, then pulled his mask off, too.

"What are you doing?" she gasped.

He shrugged. "You're my wife. We're in it together."

She swallowed, and he saw a tear form before she knuckled it away. She cleared her throat and continued as if nothing had happened. "Lesslie works here. She saw us jump from the truck and let us in."

The end of Leslie's cigarette flared as she inhaled. "First people I seen tonight that wasn't laughin' and tryin' to smash something. Figured it might be a good idea to have some help with all this…" She waved her hand vaguely in the direction of the back door.

Linton nodded. "Well, thanks for letting us in."

She jabbed her cigarette at their weapons. "Somethin' tells me you would have gotten in anyway. I just saved my door from some damage, is all."

Linton saw Emmet peeking through the blinds. He got back to his feet and went to join him. Looking over his friend's shoulder, he watched as the flames spread into the cab of his truck, and the mob danced and laughed around it. "Damn. That was a good truck."

Emmet let the blinds fall back into place. "I'm more pissed about all the supplies in the bed." He turned to face Linton and his eyes narrowed as he noticed his friend was no longer wearing his mask.

Linton shrugged. "Michelle lost hers." As if that explained everything.

And evidently it did, for Emmet simply nodded. "You won't be offended if I keep mine on, will you?"

"Nope."

"And since you won't be using yours, you mind if I get your filters, too?"

It would have been funny under other circumstances. But Linton didn't think he would feel like laughing again anytime in the near future. Instead, he just sighed. "Take 'em. At least one of us should stay protected."

"Thanks."

Silently, the two of them continued to watch the insanity outside.

CHAPTER 59
ROSS MAYFIELD
DYNAMIC DUO, KUNG FU STYLE

Ross waited nearly two hours, and it felt infinitely longer. It was two hours filled with hooting laughter, gunshots, and screams. It was also plenty of time to work on his meditation, since his stress levels were being tested as never before. But by the time Alex knocked on his door, Ross had a good handle on himself, body and mind.

He opened the door to find Alex standing there in obvious distress. "Sifu? What's wrong?" Realizing how inappropriate that opening was, he backtracked. "Sorry, I know what's wrong. I just mean—"

Alex pushed past him, not even looking at him. "Shut the door."

Ross did, and locked it for good measure. Alex dropped a light backpack onto the sofa and went into the kitchen. Ross followed as his friend and teacher helped himself to the refrigerator. "Got anything to drink?"

"Just what you see there."

Alex turned to him with a wild look in his eye. "Seriously? All you keep is water?"

"I usually eat out."

"Yeah, well that's probably not a good idea tonight." He grabbed a water bottle and closed the fridge. He walked to Ross's couch and sank into it. As he did, Ross noticed several things about Alex's appearance. He saw the bloody scratches on the back of his neck, others on his wrist, just beneath the cuff of his jacket. That drew his attention to the jacket itself.

"I didn't know you had a carry permit."

Alex looked from Ross down to where his coat had sagged open to reveal the firearm. "Yeah." He tugged his lapel to hide the pistol again.

"That's sorta the idea, right? Concealed carry? Emphasis on concealed." He took another swallow from his water, and Ross saw how badly his hands were shaking.

More laughter from outside caught Ross's attention. He walked to the window and looked out. A dozen or more students ran through the night, illuminated as they frolicked from one lamp post to the next. The group laughed as they went into the dorm across the quad from him. Approaching the door, one of them snatched a rock up from the ground and flung it through a window on the second floor.

"What's wrong with them?" He turned to find Alex unzipping his backpack. "It can't be gas, or we'd be affected, too."

Alex pulled a box from the pack and pulled out three shiny brass cylinders. He drew his pistol and ejected the magazine. "I don't know what causes it." He began inserting the bullets into the magazine. "All I know is one minute everything's normal," he slid the magazine back into the pistol. "The next minute, they start laughing and go crazy."

"How do you know that?" But as he asked, he realized what had to have happened. Alex was supposed to be celebrating Thanksgiving with his girlfriend. "Sifu, where's Jeanette?"

Alex looked up at him and slid his pistol back into its holster. He looked away. "It's like they're fine, then something goes wrong in their head. You can see it in their eyes... something like terror, like they know it's happening to them and they can't stop it. Then they're just gone. They're replaced by this laughing, insane... thing, and all they want to do is rip your face off."

Ross saw silent tears running down his friend's face, and felt the sudden need to concentrate on his heartbeat. After a moment or two, Alex suddenly sniffed, wiped his eyes, and turned to Ross. "So, when I got your text, it occurred to me that your little Zen master trick might help keep you on an even keel." He looked into Ross's eyes, studying him. "You are on an even keel, aren't you?"

"Yeah. I had a... a moment when I saw some people outside get killed. I lost control and had a seizure. But I'm working on keeping myself in the zone."

Alex nodded. "Good. Then that makes two of us. Everyone else I've seen in the last hour is bat-shit crazy." He stood and walked around the dorm room. "So where's the TV?"

"I don't have one."

Alex stared at him. "Are you serious?"

"Think about it. I can't let myself laugh, or I have a seizure. So no comedy. Can't let myself get scared, so no horror. Just about everything on TV is made to make you laugh, jump, or cry. Even the news gets people pissed off."

"Huh. Never thought of it like that."

Ross went to his laptop and sat down. "I was checking online earlier. Lots of people were posting about this." He called up a news site. There was only one topic, and the headline said it all: CHUCKLERS EPIDEMIC RUNS RAMPANT.

Alex, reading the article over Ross's shoulder, hissed. "Kampala Syndrome? Symptoms are uncontrollable laughter accompanied by fits of rage and violence. Well, no shit!"

Ross went to another site. "Outbreaks reported in nearly every major city. Dangerously high contagion rate. No known cure yet." He tried several more sites, but what it all boiled down to was that no one really knew anything more, although several people made all kinds of guesses. Some made the usual end of the world type predictions, others urged people to stay in their homes and tape up the windows. One that caught his eye was from someone who claimed to be an epidemiologist with the CDC. He claimed that laughter was a trigger event, and that you should try to keep from laughing at all costs. There was a short video of an interview with another doctor who explained what she had found while studying some of the first patients. Then she had gone crazy, herself. "Holy shit."

"Yeah, that's what I saw, too. But do you understand what she said about us all being infected?"

Ross nodded. "I think so. Bottom line is that this thing is already in our blood, or our head, or whatever. It's just waiting on a trigger."

"And that trigger is the thing you've spent your whole life learning to avoid. I guess you're about the safest person there is to be around."

But Ross was thinking about Erica. He pulled out his phone again. There still wasn't any reply to his text. He started typing another message to her.

"What are you doing?"

"Warning Erica not to laugh."

"You know she's probably already—"

"No, she isn't. Think about it. Laughter is the trigger. She's been busy burying the man who raised her, and settling his affairs. That's not exactly a cheerful activity."

"Okay, but didn't you say she was in Texas?"

"Yes."

"So what are you planning to do, go get her?"

Until that moment, Ross hadn't really planned anything at all. But hearing Alex put that into words, he suddenly decided. "Yes, I am."

"But you can't drive. Your condition—"

"But you can. You can drive me."

Alex was silent.

"Come on, Sifu. I have to try, and it's either you drive me, or I start walking. Maybe find a bicycle."

"You know how to ride a bicycle?"

"I'll figure it out."

Alex sighed. "All right. You and me, brother. But I need you to help me, too."

"What?"

"I need you to teach me the meditation techniques you use. Seems like that's a lot more important now than it was a few days ago."

"You got it." He stuck out his hand and they sealed the deal with a shake. "Thanks."

Alex shrugged. "No big deal. Hell, we'll probably get ourselves killed on the first day, anyway."

"Nope. I have faith."

"Never figured you for the religious type."

"I'm not. I have faith in us. We have a decent idea about what's going on. We have our training, our swords, your pistol. We know not to laugh, and we know where we're going."

"Great. We're the fucking dynamic duo." Alex sighed.

"Kung Fu style," Ross agreed.

CHAPTER 60
ERICA CHAPMAN
XTERRA

Erica put a hand on Matt's arm, and they approached the bathroom door together. Once again, the dim light from the hallway showed the opening of the door and he peeked around the corner. Turning to her, he nodded and slipped out. She followed close on his heels as he crept down the hall. A few interminable seconds later, they were at the metal door to the garage. He held up three fingers. Then two. Then one. Then he pushed the bar on the door.

The door opened smoothly and silently. Erica thanked her lucky stars as they slipped through the doorway unnoticed. She was about to let the door close and follow him into the darkness when he stopped her. "Hold the door," he whispered. "If it makes noise when it closes, they'll be all over us. Let me find something to prop it with."

She swallowed her fear and nodded, and he disappeared into the inky black of the shop. It was only seconds before he returned with a screwdriver. Turning the handle into the hallway, he let the door slowly close on the shaft, keeping it from shutting all the way. He nodded to her and she turned her light back on. Taking the lead, she held the light before them while he carried the lockbox, and they made their way across the four bay workshop. As they approached the opposite wall, Erica saw an emergency exit sign mounted above another metal door. "This way," she whispered, and hit the bar on the door.

Her heart flip-flopped as a new alarm sounded. "Damn!"

"Come on." Matt shouldered past and out the door. Outside once again, they heard car horns, screams, and the incessant laughter floating like a horrific soundtrack to the night. They were on the back side of the dealership, so they couldn't see the main street, but those sounds reminded them of the terror that was loose in the night. Erica hurried to follow her rescuer as he crept along, hugging the back wall and muttering to himself. Suddenly, he stopped, "There it is!"

He ran to a ladder on the side of the building. "That's your plan?" She looked at him in disbelief. "We'll be trapped."

He pulled the box to his chest and zipped his jacket over it. "Trust me. I have an idea."

"How are we going to get up there anyway?" Erica indicated the metal mesh cage that covered the bottom third of the ladder. It was obviously intended to keep unauthorized people off of the roof.

He drew his pistol. "Get behind me." And he aimed at the lock on the mesh door.

She hurried to duck behind him and he fired once. "All right. Climb, before we find out if any of them heard that."

She pulled the door of the cage open, slipped through, and scrambled up the ladder to the roof, banging her Bois d'Arc talisman against the rungs as she climbed. Matt was beside her in a moment. "Now what?" she asked.

For answer, he unzipped his jacket, and laid the lockbox on the roof. "Shine your light on that."

She got behind him and held the light where he could see the box. Another shot rang out and when she peeked around him, there was a jagged hole where the lock had been. He opened the box to the sight of dozens of keys. He scooped out a handful and handed them to her. "Go to the edge of the roof and start hitting the panic button on the key fobs. We're looking for one of the big trucks or SUVs. If the car you light up isn't a big one, leave the alarm blaring on it as a distraction." He grabbed another handful of keys for himself and ran to the edge to do the same. Within minutes, they had fourteen car alarms going, with the emergency lights flashing off and on. Unfortunately, the noise drew the attention of the crazies also, and they began to pour into the parking lot from all around. In no time, there were hundreds of them, screaming, laughing, and pounding on the cars as the alarms pierced the night.

"Got one," he called.

Erica hurried over to him. He pointed, and she saw their target. Then he shut it off. "Now we need to turn off any alarm that's anywhere between us and that SUV. We want all sorts of noise going as far away from it as we can get. It'll draw those… people away from where we're heading."

It actually made a lot of sense, and she hurried to go through the keys again, shutting off the closer alarms, and turning on as many others as she could. They hurried back down the ladder and Matt took the lead. Pistol at the ready, he led her to a darkened corner of the building, approaching the front of the lot. Matt held up his hand and motioned for her to get down. As she did so, a man in a hoodie and sweatpants ran past, laughing as he slapped his hands on the sides of the vehicles he passed. He was followed by another man who waved a small claw hammer over his head. Matt stuck his head out around the corner, then waved Erica forward. Together, the two of them ran hunched over to the first row of cars and squatted between a pair of Sentras. Matt raised his head to peek through the windows, then waved her on to the next row. They were halfway between the two rows when a creepy voice sounded from behind her.

"Peek-a-boo, I see you!" She spun to find a teenaged boy, dragging a tire iron through the pristine paint of the Sentra they had just left. He grinned from ear to ear, but there was nothing friendly in his countenance. He raised the tire iron and rushed at her, cackling at the top of his lungs. "Peek-a-boo! Peek-a-boo! Peek-a-boo!"

Just as he began to swing the iron, Erica checked him with the butt of her lacrosse stick, poking him hard in the shoulder just enough to throw him off balance. Then she swung the stick down across his forearm in a move that would have gotten her a slashing penalty in any game before tonight. She heard the forearm crack. Then, since she was already in penalty territory, she figured she might as well go for broke and swung the shaft around to catch him cleanly on the side of the head. The kid dropped like a rock.

She looked up to see that the altercation hadn't gone unnoticed. Half a dozen laughing lunatics started running their way. Matt shouted, "Run!" He might not be much for eloquence, but it was still sage advice. Erica turned and followed Matt through the maze of cars. She had no idea where they were in relation to the vehicle they had targeted. She had no idea how many of those crazies were chasing them, though the sound indicated the crowd was growing. All she knew was that Matt had the pistol, and he was ahead of her. If she lost him, she knew she would be ripped to pieces. That was enough for the moment.

A man in a Stetson and a jean jacket leapt out and grabbed Matt's shoulder. Erica swung the stick and caught the cowboy at the base of the skull before Matt had a chance to turn. The Stetson went flying as the man dropped. Matt grabbed her hand and they continued running. "How much farther?" she panted.

For answer, he let go of her hand and pressed the key fob. Parking lights blinked three rows ahead. The lights silhouetted the outline of four or five laughers between them and the SUV. They rushed forward even as Matt and Erica rushed at them. Matt raised his hand and fired, dropping the first two before they even got close. He hit a third one, a woman in a Christmas sweater, but she only slowed. The last one was a tall man with a beard, and he was on Matt before he could fire again.

Erica drove her stick into the throat of sweater lady, stepped aside, and swung down against her knee. She dropped momentarily, but turned to reach for Erica as she fell. Erica tried to slip past, but felt a sharp tug from behind, and fell gracelessly onto her ass. She panicked as she heard raucous cackling grow louder as sweater lady dragged her back by her purse strap. Erica swung Old Yaller wildly behind her head, but without being able to see her target, she missed. Dropping the useless stick to the ground, she struggled to get free of the leather strap dragging her down. Maneuvering the tightening strap over her shoulder and head, she slipped free of her purse and thought for a second she had escaped, then felt a hand grab her left sleeve. She screamed and reached down to find her lacrosse stick on the pavement beside her. Pivoting where she sat on the concrete, she swung and hit sweater lady on the shoulder hard enough to break her grip. She swung again, putting her lights out.

Erica looked up and saw Matt still struggling with the bearded man. The man held Matt's gun hand away from them, and gnashed his teeth at Matt's throat. Erica scramble to her feet, ran forward and swung again. This one didn't drop as easily as the woman had, but the blow distracted him enough to let Matt jab the car key into his face. The big guy batted the key from Matt's hand, sending it flying toward Erica, but he still didn't let go of Matt's gun hand. Erica swung again, aiming this time for the arm that held Matt's pistol immobile, and saw the force of her blow bend the man's elbow in a manner that nature had never intended. Matt got his pistol free, brought it to the man's chest, and fired twice.

Erica scooped up the key from where it had fallen and shouted. "I got it, Matt! We gotta go!" Dozens of them were running toward them. Erica clicked the fob again, and the two of them sprinted for the flashing lights of the Nissan Xterra in the outermost row. It was a bright yellow model, and she ran around it and yanked the driver's door open, tossed her lacrosse stick in the back seat, and jammed the key in the ignition. The SUV started immediately just as Matt yanked open the passenger door. Erica looked back at their pursuers and jammed her thumb at the locking mechanism.

"Looks like you're driving again, lady. How about we get the hell outta here?"

A loud clang startled her and she looked to her left to find one of the crazies drawing back for another swing with a golf club. *Seriously? A golf club?* She shifted into gear and stomped the gas pedal to the floor. The Xterra reacted like a champ, and the loud bang of the club on the hood of the SUV as they took off was nothing compared to the sound of screeching metal as the four-wheel-drive mowed down the chain-link fence surrounding the lot. But that fence was the only thing between them and the highway home, and Erica wasn't about to let it stop her after all they'd been through in the last hour. Part of the fence caught on the rear bumper, and the Xterra dragged it down the road, a trail of sparks illuminating their path for several yards until Erica jumped the median, crossed the road to avoid another burning wreck, and sped off down the highway.

They crossed the I-10 overpass and left the mad streets of Katy behind them. As they descended the far side of the overpass, the only sign that anything was unusual was the orange glow in the rearview mirror, an indication of the many fires burning behind them. Erica drove in silence for the first mile, unconsciously following the route back to the ranch as she tried like hell to wrap her head around what had just happened. Her passenger showed no inclination to chatter either, and she assumed he was as lost as she was.

"Erica?"

"Yeah?"

"I just wanted to thank you."

Erica furrowed her brows. "For what?"

He shrugged. "You saved my life."

"I think you have that backwards. You're the one with the gun, remember? I'd be dead several times over if you hadn't saved me."

He shrugged. "So we'll call it even."

Erica just nodded.

"You mind if I use your phone?"

She reached for her purse, then cursed.

"What is it?"

"I lost my purse. My phone was in it." *There was a text from Ross on it! Is he all right?*

After a moment of silence, he cleared his throat, "I don't suppose I could get you to take me home?"

"Where's home?"

He pursed his lips. "Back in the other direction, on the other side of Katy."

Erica shook her head. "Not tonight. I'm sorry, but I'm not driving back through that shit in the middle of the night. That's just insane."

"But you wouldn't have to go back the same way. We can skirt around town. I know the back roads."

"We don't know if it's any better than what we just went through. No, we're almost to the ranch, and there's a phone there you can use."

Matt dropped it, but she could tell he wasn't happy about the situation. But they reached the ranch shortly, and she grabbed her trusty lacrosse stick from the back seat. Going to the front door, Erica paused, then cursed.

"What?"

"My keys were in my purse."

"Need me to break a window?"

"No." She went to the front flower bed and lifted the corner brick in the border. Sure enough, Uncle J still had a spare key in the old hiding spot. She unlocked the front door and led Matt to the phone in the den. He quickly punched in a number, and she could hear the ringing of the phone on the other end of the line. After several rings, she heard a voice pick up, but it had the automated sound of an answering machine.

Matt cursed quietly and dialed again. "Come on, baby. Pick up the phone."

But baby didn't, and it went to the answering machine again.

He put the phone back in the cradle. "She's not answering."

Erica didn't know what to say. "Maybe in the morning…"

But he shook his head. "I'm gonna need the keys to the SUV."

"Listen Matt, just stay here tonight. Wait this thing out."

"Wait what out? We don't know how widespread this… whatever it is, we don't know how far it goes, how long it lasts. We don't know shit about it!"

"That's my point! Until we find out more, we need to hole up someplace safe. Tomorrow we can go check on your family and find someone who can give us some answers."

"Is this place safe?"

"It's a hell of a lot safer than what we just went through in town."

He nodded, looking around. "It's a nice place."

"Thanks. It was my uncle's."

"Was?"

"He just died a couple of weeks ago. That's why I'm in town."

"Come in for the funeral?"

"And to settle his affairs." She spread her hands to indicate the ranch. "Bank's taking it all."

"That sucks."

"Yeah."

"It's rough losing someone close to you."

Tears welled again, and she wiped them and sniffed. "Yes, it is."

"That's why I have to do this."

Erica looked up to see him pointing the pistol in her direction. It wasn't actually pointing at her, but even having it pointed at the floor near her feet was enough to make her step back. "What the hell are you doing?"

"Give me the keys. I'm taking the car."

Heart pounding, her eyes couldn't seem to unglue from that pistol. Erica swallowed. "Matt, you don't mean that!"

"Erica, I just killed about a dozen people. You know what was going through my mind the whole time? It was that I needed to get home to my wife and kids. That's the only thing that matters to me right now. So please just give me those keys before you have to find out if my family's more important to me than you are."

She pulled the keys out of her pocket and tossed them to him.

"Lock up behind me." He backed toward the door. "I'll wait 'til I hear you lock the door and then I'm out of here."

He opened the door and backed out. "I'm serious, Erica. Lock it behind me. It ain't safe out here."

He closed the door and she ran to the door and locked it. Seconds later, she heard the SUV start up outside. She pulled the blinds back from the front window and saw him looking at her. "I really am sorry, Erica." She flipped him off, and he drove away.

"Damn it!" She watched the tail lights fade down the long driveway and turn onto the main road.

After a few minutes of alternating between crying in frustration and cursing the man who had saved her life, she calmed down enough to think. She snatched the phone up and dialed Ross's number from memory. "The party you are calling is outside the network area," the automated voice informed her. "If you believe this message is in error, please hang up and dial again." She tried twice more before she growled and slammed the handset down on the receiver. The sound of the old analog phone echoed through the otherwise quiet house.

Erica looked around self-consciously, realizing she was alone on the outskirts of a town gone mad. Cursing the entire time, she checked all the doors and windows. Just because Matt had turned out to be a son of a bitch didn't mean he wasn't right. It wasn't safe out there anymore. Something had happened. The people at the theater had gone insane, then the people in the streets, and even the police station, or wherever the 911 dispatch center was. There was no way of telling how much farther it had gone.

Idiot! Of course there is. She ran into the den and turned on the television. Seconds later, she watched in horror as one report after another showed on screen, as people showed the insanity that was going on in the streets of various cities. New York City, Atlanta, San

Francisco, Los Angeles… the speculation was rampant as to what was happening. Erica saw a reporter on one of the cable news channels as he discussed the possibility of a terrorist attack with his co-anchor. They switched to a feed from Chicago where an affiliate reporter had a live report on the most recent happenings. The background changed to a city in flames as police in riot gear tried to hold back a crowd of what appeared to be hundreds of people, all of them laughing and clawing at the wall of shields.

The reporter in the foreground looked genuinely frightened as he began his spiel. "As you can see behind me, the scene here is utter pandemonium as Chicago police try to keep the crowd of rioters suppressed."

One of the anchors interjected, "Tom, does anyone seem to know what has sparked these outbreaks?"

"I've heard probably the same things that you have, David. Some say it's some sort of gas that's been released into the atmosphere, others claim it's a biological agent that escaped from a government weapons lab. I've even heard some people say it's the beginning of the zombie apocalypse. Whatever it is though, it seems to affect its victim's minds, driving them to fits of uncontrollable laughter and violence, and this is what has caused people to start calling the victims chucklers."

Erica recalled thinking of them the same way while she was in the theater, and considered it an apt description. As she watched, the camera shifted as something caught the cameraman's eye. Erica watched in horrified fascination as one of the policemen in riot gear began beating on a neighboring officer. The camera zoomed in and caught the attacking policeman's face. *Oh God!* The man was laughing. Within seconds, the line broke and the mass of chucklers overwhelmed the police.

"Run! Run!" The reporter's face was panicked, and the camera began to shake. From off camera, Erica heard a mocking voice mimicking him, "Run! Run! Whoo, hoo, hoo, hoo!" The view on the screen swung dizzyingly skyward, and briefly showed a view of Orion's Belt. Then it zoomed in on the reporter's face. It more than zoomed in, it impacted the man's face directly. It withdrew, showing a brief view of the reporter's cheek, cut and bleeding from a deep laceration. Then it zoomed in again. Withdrew, zoomed, withdrew, zoomed, each withdrawal showing more and more damage to the reporter's face until the screen went black. Even then the man's screams persisted, as did the laughter of his cameraman until the screen went back to the two stunned anchormen sitting in the silent studio.

One of the men must have suddenly realized they were back on the air because he cleared his throat and looked into the camera on set. "I'm sorry, ladies and gentlemen. We seem to be having technical difficulties."

His co-anchor looked at him in disbelief. "Technical difficulties?" He shook his head, then repeated, "Technical difficulties!" And he began to laugh. "Yeah, we're having technical difficulties all right. It looks like some prima donna reporter got greedy and kept insisting on a close up!" He jumped up and rushed at the camera leaning in to the camera, pulling back, leaning in, pulling back, and laughing the entire time. He ran back to his spot at the anchor desk and snatched up a laptop from where he'd been sitting. "Hey David! You missed your cue!" And he smashed the laptop into David's face. He raised it over his head for another strike when the screen went black, leaving Erica staring dumbfounded at the television.

Oh my God! It's everywhere.

CHAPTER 61
KEN HOLTZAPFEL
COUNTING HIS COUP

Ken took a deep breath as the first of the mob came into sight on the ramp ahead. He'd gotten well over an hour of rest, almost as if they couldn't figure out where he was. But the light on the elevator should have told them which way he went, and there was only the one floor between them. He also recalled how they were just the slightest bit clumsy. It reminded him of someone who was drunk. Not shit-faced, puke-on-the-seat hammered, but more like they'd had just a couple too many. And he definitely knew the difference. In his line of work, he'd seen all kinds of drunks, and the more he thought about what he'd seen, the more convinced he became that these people were drunk, or high on something. Even now, watching them come toward him, there were little missteps and dragging of the feet that reminded him of someone who was just a bit inebriated.

Could it be some kind of gas? He shrugged mentally. That was going to be a question for people who were a lot smarter than he was. He would be happy to just live long enough to hear about it on the news tomorrow.

He waited, conserving his strength, not moving until the leaders were within a few yards of his position. When he judged they were at the right distance, he ran to the side and once more swung his trusty tire iron. The first attacker went down, and Ken jumped back. Two more came at him, and he ducked beneath their grasping arms and stepped through, shouting as he swung at their legs. He distinctly heard the crack of breaking kneecaps and they both fell, and winced at the pain he was dealing out. But the hair on his neck stood up as he realized that even after the damage he had done to them, they were still laughing and reaching toward him.

There wasn't time to think too much about it, though, as the rest of the mob was about to reach him. He ran several steps back before turning to face them again. He hated to draw them deeper into the garage, fearing that they might find Angela hiding in the Cadillac. But there was no way he was going to be able to make another run up the ramp. Looking over the crowd, he tried to count how many he had left. It looked like there were still nine bodies jostling each other as they tried to rush him.

He stepped in and swung, spinning as he moved past them, now drawing them away from the Caddy. Two of them actually bumped into one another, and another one fell over one of their companions with the broken knee. Ken took advantage of their momentary disorientation and dropped another one with a tire iron to the head. *Eight left standing.*

"Come on, you bastards. Let's get this over with." He reversed his grip on the tire iron, holding the lug wrench end in his hand as he jabbed forward the flat, pry bar end as if it were a sword of some kind. Unfortunately, it wasn't really a sword, and the end didn't penetrate his target. It shoved him back, though, and that gave Ken a second to slam the side against the man's head. It didn't drop him, but caused him to stagger a moment. Ken hit twice more in quick succession before he was forced to jump out of reach from another attacker. He moved past them, toward the ramp once again, and had the satisfaction of seeing the man he had hit repeatedly finally fall to the concrete. *Seven.*

Ken was breathing heavily again, and his legs felt like spaghetti. *Gettin' old is a bitch, ain't it?* Two of the mob reached him at the same time and he stepped aside, getting one of them between him and the other attacker. He kicked at the man's knees to distract him, then stepped in and swung the lugged end of the tire iron into his head. *Six.*

Stepping back, Ken swung again as the second of the pair moved toward him. He missed, striking the man's shoulder instead of his head, and the man moved too close for another strike. Before he could do anything more, the man had Ken by the waist and bowled him over, landing on top of him and knocking the wind out of him. Ken shouted and bucked his hips, trying to get the man off of him, even as the man leaned in close. Ken recalled once more the sight of a man leaning in to a woman, biting down as she screamed, and spitting something into the street. He had little doubt of his attacker's intentions. Ken frantically worked the tire iron out from between them and shoved the pointed end at the man's neck. He hesitated a second at the thought of what he was going to do.

Could he really take another person's life? The sight of another laughing face coming into view over the man's shoulders decided Ken, and he shoved with all his might. Blood poured from his attacker's throat, splashing Ken's hand, running down his arm to soak his shirt sleeve. And all the while, Ken screamed in rage and fear, even as another part of his mind calmly counted. *Five.*

He barely made it to his knees before the next one was on him. It was the woman in the hooker heels, and he barely evaded her reaching nails. He swung the bloody iron again, smashing her ankle. Laughing even as she fell, she reached for him as he rose shakily back to his feet. *Four.* Ken stumbled back as the others rushed at him. There was no finesse or thought to their attack. Nothing but a brutal rush, and that incessant, insane laughter. He realized he was backing farther into the garage, and once more thought of Angela hiding in the Cadillac. Got to lure them away from there. He gulped a deep breath, then reversed direction. He stumbled briefly in his weariness, but managed to get past them as they reached for him.

Exhausted, Ken staggered a few steps farther and turned to face them once more. He barely had the strength left in him to stay on his feet, and he groaned as he saw them giggle at the game and come after him again. He backed up as they came, getting ready to brace himself for another round, when a hand grabbed his foot. He looked down to see Hooker Heels sink her teeth into his left calf. He screamed. He'd never realized how strong a person's jaws could really be, and he felt tissue rip as he yanked his leg away from her. He swung at her as he fell, but it was already too late. Even as she collapsed, Ken knew she had killed him.

The last four fell on him, laughing and clawing as they pushed him to the floor of the garage. He swung the tire iron at the closest as he fell, and felt a satisfactory crunch as a skull caved in. Part of him wondered at how quickly he had gone from crying over the taking of one man's life, to screaming in triumph as he took another's, less than a minute later. "Three!" He shouted it at the top of his lungs, counting his coup to the world. If he was going to die, he was determined that they would know they'd been in a fight, by damn!

He tried to swing again, but they were too close. One of them knocked the tire iron from his grasp, whether intentionally or not, and Ken immediately latched onto his throat. He squeezed with all his might, and he had the satisfaction of hearing at least one laughing voice go quiet for the moment. The man still strained forward though, and another laughing face appeared beside it. Ken reached for that throat also, thinking to choke that man, too. But the last man threw himself onto the pile, and the weight of three attackers was too much. Ken missed his target, and felt a sudden agony as teeth latched onto his middle and index fingers. Insane laughter in his ear let him know he only had seconds left. Crazed, giggling eyes strained against his failing arm.

Suddenly, the head lurched to one side and the eyes rolled up in their sockets. There was a scream of anger, a woman. As the man fell to the side, Ken saw Angela swing a black metallic object again, and another attacker fell. The last one finally realized there was another source of danger for him, but it was too late. Angela swung one last time, and the object that Ken now recognized as a scissor jack slammed into the man's face with a crunch of bone and cartilage as his nose broke. He dropped beside Ken on the concrete, limp and lifeless, at least for the moment.

Angela stood over Ken, panting, tears rolling down her face. "Are you all right?" She dropped to her knees beside him.

"Thanks to you, yeah." He started to push off the ground and yelped. He looked over at his mangled fingers. He hugged it to his chest, cradling the bleeding hand close to him. He held out his other hand. "Can you help me up?"

He almost fell again as he tried to put weight on his torn right calf and winced at the pain. Angela helped steady him as they looked around them at their attackers. There were still a couple of them that were conscious, but crippled, trying to drag their way toward Ken and

Angela. Ken didn't have the strength to care. "I don't think coming down here was such a great idea," he told his companion. "It just traps us if more of them come."

She nodded. "Maybe we can hole up in a building or something. Someplace with more than one door."

He nodded, and she helped him limp to the elevator. The doors closed and Ken leaned back against the wall as the elevator climbed. "There's a police depot a couple of miles up the freeway. If you can make it there, they should be able to help."

"Me? You mean us."

Ken shook his head. "With my leg messed up, I'll slow you down too much. I'll find someplace to hide, and this time, you're going to have to go without me." He looked at the scissor jack that she still clung to. Blood dripped off of the base where she had caved in the skulls of his last few attackers. "I think you can take care of yourself for a couple of miles, can't you?"

She shook her head. "That's not going to work. I'm not leaving you alone."

"I appreciate that Angela, but you have to face—" The elevator chimed and the door opened. They stared out at dozens of laughing faces. The closest to them was a young boy wearing a *Scrooged* T-shirt. Several others were dressed nicely, as if for a nice evening out at the theater. They rushed the elevator, overwhelming Ken and Angela.

Unbelievable agony tore through his body as nails and teeth ripped at him and Ken wasn't sure whether the screams he heard were his or Angela's. Teeth clamped down on his forearm and he felt muscle tear. That time, he didn't have to wonder whose screams he heard. His throat was raw and he thrashed about, trying to break free of the dozens of hands that held and pulled. He caught a brief sight of Angela, blood pouring from several scratches over her eye as more laughing people pulled at her limbs and clawed at her exposed skin. Her mouth opened and her throat worked, but if she screamed, Ken couldn't hear her over his own shrieks of agony. A laughing face rose up before him, lifting a bloody object over his head. Ken briefly recognized it as the scissor jack Angela had been carrying. The jack came down, and he didn't wonder anything at all.

FRIDAY
NOVEMBER 25

CHAPTER 62
LINTON BOWERS
MOVING OUT

Linton awoke to Michelle shaking his shoulder. "Lint. Time to get up. We need to get out of here."

"What's up? Something wrong?" He blinked against the morning sunlight, chagrined at the thought that he had slept while the world tore itself apart.

"No. The crowd outside has lost interest or something. They've moved on, and we figured it was a good time to get out."

Linton looked past his wife to see Emmet, still wearing his mask, and Lesslie, still wearing her bloody apron. "Why am I the only one still asleep?" Linton groaned as he got slowly to his feet.

"We just got up a few minutes ago. Emmet looked outside and saw that the coast was clear."

Linton shuffled over to the window and lifted a single blind to peek outside. It was morning, and other than a bit of smoke in the air, it looked like a sunny morning. He looked around, watching for movement of any sort. But like Michelle had said, there wasn't another soul in sight. He turned back, looked at Lesslie. "You work here, right?"

She nodded.

"Got a car?"

"Yeah. And I already talked to Michelle. She says you got a place that's safe from this?"

"We do. You up for a trade?"

"My car for a safe place to hole up? Hell yes."

Emmet stepped in. "Ah, Linton? I know you're the head honcho and all, but didn't you tell me that the supplies at the bunker limited the number of people you could take in?"

Linton nodded. "Yep. We have supplies to support twenty people for a year."

"And the team has already trained and drilled together, right?"

He nodded again. "Look, I know what you're getting at, but after everything we've seen out there," he nodded at the window, "do you really think all twenty Hive members are going to make it?"

Emmet nodded. "Yeah, I guess you're right. Sorry."

Linton turned back to Lesslie. "You have anything here you need to get?"

There was something in her eyes, but she shook her head. "Not anymore." She pulled a set of keys from her pocket. "I'm ready when you are."

Emmet went out first, rifle at the ready as he went to the eastern corner. Linton slipped out behind him going to the west. After affirming that the area was clear for the moment, they waved the others out. There were two cars in the parking lot. Linton looked at Lesslie. "Which one's yours?" he whispered.

She held up the electronic key fob and pressed the button before Linton could stop her. Lights blinked and the horn beeped once on a Ford sedan. "Shit. Everyone, get in before we find out if the noise caught anyone's attention."

Lesslie looked chagrinned as she realized her mistake.

"Linton?"

He turned to Emmet. "What?"

"Look at the back of the truck."

"What?" There was no truck in the parking lot.

Emmet pointed up the street where Linton's pickup had come to rest against the freeway retaining wall. "Not all of it burned."

Heart beating with excitement, Linton saw that his friend's words were true. The engine and most of the front cab were nothing but a charred husk, but most of the back was unburned. To be sure, most of their supplies were scattered all over the street, having obviously attracted the attention of the crazies last night. But there was no telling what might be left. All sorts of supplies had been packed in there. There was food, a shotgun, and several boxes of ammunition for all the firearms. If any of that was left…

He ran to catch up with Michelle and Lesslie. "Don't start the engine yet. Emmet and I are going to check the truck and see if any of our gear is salvageable."

"What if some of those... infected people see you?"

"We'll be careful. When you see us wave, come get us."

Michelle wanted to argue. Linton could see it. It was a testament to her trust in him that she held off and simply nodded.

He and Emmet looked up and down the feeder road and saw no one. They quietly ran up to his truck and started digging through the scattered boxes. After only a minute, Emmet hissed at him. Linton looked up to see him holding a heavy box of nine millimeter ammunition cradled in his left arm. He knew that box held a thousand rounds of hollow points for the Glocks. He gave Emmet a thumbs up and kept combing through the debris. There was a twelve-gauge shotgun in the truck when they had bailed out, and he was hoping to find it. But after a few minutes, he gave up. Determined that he wouldn't leave empty handed, he grabbed a knapsack that he knew was filled with freeze-dried camping food.

He waved back at Lesslie and Michelle and heard the engine crank up. It drove home how eerily silent the city was at the moment, and he looked around at the abandoned automobiles again. Who would have thought a city of more than two million people could ever be this quiet?

The Ford pulled up beside them, and he climbed in the back seat beside Michelle. He couldn't help but be disappointed at the fact that out of all the scattered remains they saw, there wasn't more of value left of the truck and its cargo. Depressed and frowning, Linton waited as Emmet climbed into the passenger seat in front. No one had anything to say as Lesslie pulled away, heading south along the I-45 feeder.

* * *

"Well that didn't take long."

Linton looked to where his wife pointed across the feeder road to the right. A large crowd milled about in the parking lot of a strip center. Several vehicles were tangled together in a big charred mess. The sound of the Ford attracted their attention, and they loped drunkenly toward the feeder to intercept the four in the sedan. Linton drew his pistol.

Michelle pointed to the left, temporarily obstructing his aim. "There's an entrance ramp," she said.

Linton looked, even as Lesslie swerved to get on the freeway. She slid past an abandoned vehicle that had rammed into the impact barrels at the entrance, and they quickly left the laughing crowd behind them. Lesslie slowed to a safer speed as they wove through the bodies and wreckage that littered the concrete ribbon before them. It was a tense and gruesome undertaking, but at least the retaining walls offered some small measure of protection from the various shopping centers and businesses along the feeder.

Emmet called up the navigation app on his phone. "Just a few miles ahead, and we should get to the Sam Houston Parkway exit."

Progress was painfully slow. "I can't believe how many accidents there are out here," Lesslie commented.

Emmet grunted, the sound transmitted through the voicemitter in his gas mask. "Based on what we saw last night, I don't think I'd go so far as to call them accidents."

"What do you mean?"

"I mean every wreck we saw seemed to have one or both parties laughing while they slammed their car into something."

"Or someone," Michelle finished.

Lesslie glanced back at Michelle quickly, before turning her attention back to her driving. "So?"

"So none of the wrecks we saw last night were accidents. They were all done on purpose."

Lesslie seemed to digest this tidbit of information. "So do you have any idea what's caused all this?"

Linton and Emmet looked at each other. Linton shrugged at his friend. If he wanted to tell, Linton would defer to him.

"I don't guess it's going to be a secret anymore, is it?" Emmet asked Linton.

"Nope."

"Well, hell." Emmet was quiet a moment before launching into a quick explanation of what they thought had happened.

"Kampala Syndrome?"

"That's what they called it," Emmet affirmed.

"And it makes everybody crazy?"

"We don't know exactly what it does," Linton told her. "All we know is that it seems to affect peoples' minds in a way that makes them act like the meanest damned drunks you ever saw."

"And the laughing?"

"We don't know. For some reason, everyone who's infected seems to break out laughing. Then they go nuts."

"Yeah." Lesslie sighed. "I saw a bit of that last night. Had a couple of customers that attacked me at the restaurant." She fell silent.

"You had to kill them?" Emmet asked, sympathy in his voice.

"No. A friend of mine killed them, Barry Begault. He saved me."

Emmet looked back at Linton, who simply shrugged.

Chris finally asked, "So what happened to him?"

Lesslie was silent.

"Lesslie? Are you crying?" Emmet's voice was full of concern.

Linton could only see the back of her head from where he sat, but he heard her sniff.

"Lesslie? What happened to Barry?"

"He was hurt pretty bad when he fought them off. He must have been in a lot of pain. But Barry was always showing off. He made some lame-ass joke. And then he started laughing." Lesslie fell silent again, maneuvering between another wreck and the center retaining wall. After a moment, she must have decided to tell the rest of her story, though. "I could see his eyes when he started to laugh. It was like something happened in his mind. Something that scared the shit out of him. And then it was like a switch flipped. He went from hurt and laughing, to terrified, and then to crazy."

She stopped the car and leaned forward, resting her head against the steering wheel. "Then he tried to kill me." And her shoulders began to shake with her sobs.

Linton felt for the poor woman, but he instinctively looked around for any signs of the infected, or crazies, or whatever they were calling them today. Michelle leaned across the seat and placed a sympathetic hand on Lesslie's back. "What happened, Lesslie?"

"He tried to kill me. I had... had the... butcher knife..." She sat up and sniffed, wiping her nose on the back of her hand. She seemed to realize that she had stopped in the middle of the freeway and she looked around, gathering her wits. On seeing that they were in no immediate danger, she turned back to look at Michelle. "He came at me, and he hit me. Threw me on the floor. He jumped on top of me, but I still had the knife."

She put the car back into drive and began their slow creep southward once more as she finished. "Knives in a barbeque restaurant are kept really sharp."

Linton recalled the knife she carried with her and swallowed. She had been through hell, and had held up remarkably well. Linton didn't know if he would have done as well. Would he have the courage to kill a friend who was attacking him? He remembered that he and Michelle no longer wore their masks. He glanced up at Emmet, still safe behind his filters. It was more likely that Emmet would be the one faced with that dilemma before he himself was. He wondered if his friend would be up to the task if it came to that.

Then he wondered whether or not he really wanted him to be.

CHAPTER 63
ERICA CHAPMAN
A GIRL'S GOT NEEDS!

Erica awoke with a start in her old bed. Sunlight streamed in through the window, letting her know she'd slept later than she'd intended. She still clutched her old Bois d'Arc lacrosse stick in her hands. She'd slept with it, drawing comfort from the dense wood, but by morning's light, it seemed wholly inadequate as a weapon. She recalled that Uncle Jimmy kept a shotgun around the place somewhere and immediately went to go look for it. As she exited her bedroom though, she froze.

Looking down the hall and through the kitchen window, she could see the cab of a bright yellow SUV. After a second's panic, she recognized it as the Xterra that she and Matt had stolen from the dealership last night. And it looked like Matt was still in it. Drawing her robe tighter around herself, she gripped her stick tighter and went outside. "Matt?" She could see him in the front seat, still sitting behind the steering wheel, and as she approached the cab, she saw he was leaning forward, forehead resting on the wheel. "Matt, is that you?" She reached for the door and stopped as she saw him move. His shoulders were shaking up and down. *Like he's laughing. Oh God, not Matt too.* She pulled her hand back slowly and gripped Old Yaller with both hands.

Then he turned toward her, tears running down his face, and she realized then that he was alone. His wife and children weren't with him, and that could only be bad news. She opened the door. "I'm so sorry, Matt."

He nodded and wiped snot and tears away with an already-soaked shirt sleeve. Taking a moment to try and get his emotions under control, he finally spoke. "I, uh… I didn't have any place else to go," he said dully. "I couldn't stay there. Not with…" He stopped, apparently lost in his memories. "Look, after last night I understand—"

Erica shook her head and put a hand on his arm. "Don't worry about it." She tugged his sleeve. "Come on inside and I'll make us some breakfast. We'll figure out what we're gonna do next."

He let her lead him inside where she sat him at the breakfast table, and started pulling food out of the refrigerator. "You okay with eggs?"

He nodded dully.

"I like mine with tomatoes and jalapeños in them. Does that work for you?"

Another nod.

Erica gave up trying to start a conversation and left him to his thoughts while she diced the veggies and mixed some eggs. Thinking it might be better to keep him busy, she showed him where the toaster was, and put him to work on the bread, then made some coffee. She intentionally kept quiet, not pressing him for details of his trip home. She figured he would talk when he was ready. But he didn't say a word until they sat at the table. Even then, it was nothing about his family. "So what's your plan? You going to hole up here and hope it all blows over?"

Erica shook her head. "I don't think it's going to blow over."

He just nodded, obviously waiting for her to continue.

"After you left me here last night, I watched the news. It looks like it's all over the country. I even saw a reporter get killed right on camera. Looked like it was his camera man that did it." She shook her head. "It's not blowing over. If anything, it's getting worse."

He threw the last of his toast onto the plate. "Shit."

"Yeah."

"So, are you staying here?"

"I don't know. This isn't really my home anymore. Legally, I'm supposed to get the last of my stuff out and be gone before five o'clock this evening." She shrugged. "Of course, the way things are looking, I seriously doubt anyone is likely to be here to enforce that particular directive." She looked around for a minute. "But this isn't home anymore, either."

He took another sip of his coffee, deep in thought. "So where *is* home?"

"I've been going to college in Montgomery, Alabama. I've sort of got someone there."

"Boyfriend?"

It was Erica's turn to take a sip while she thought it over. "I'm not really sure. We've been having some problems. I had to leave pretty quickly when Uncle Jimmy died, and I didn't let him know what was going on. Guess I didn't feel like having any sort of... confrontation."

"Sorry. You guys fight a lot?"

"Nope. Not once. Ross never gets mad."

Matt raised an eyebrow. "Sounds like a pretty understanding guy. I'd imagine you can work things out."

"Believe me, it's not understanding that keeps us from fighting."

When she didn't elucidate, he just nodded. "Sorry. Didn't mean to pry."

She shrugged. "No problem." Picking up her plate, she walked around the table to grab his. "Finished?" She nodded to the piece of toast he'd thrown down.

"Yeah, but I can get it." He picked up his plate and followed her to the sink. "So you never really answered me. What are you planning to do?"

"Things have changed. Obviously. And I think I need to get back to Ross."

"Do you even know if he's all right? How do you know he hasn't turned into one of those things from last night?"

"That's about the only thing I *am* sure of. Ross isn't one of them. He's got a condition called cataplexy. It's pretty rare, and the kind he has is rarer than most. Without all the details, it means he simply can't laugh. Anytime he starts to laugh, or cry, or experience any strong emotion, he has a kind of a seizure and his body just sort of collapses."

Matt looked at her as if she had grown a third eye. "You shitting me?"

"No. That's why we're having trouble."

"What, because you can't joke with him? That's not such a big deal."

"No. It's not just the joking. It's any strong emotional response."

"I guess that could get a little boring." But he obviously still thought she was overreacting.

"Matt, think about it. *Any* strong emotion."

He appeared puzzled, and she could see she was going to have to spell it out for him. "It's not just the laughing, and God knows it isn't the fighting. It's that the son of a bitch made me fall in love with him. He wrote all these letters, and they were so damned beautiful." She swallowed at the memory of how warm those letters made her feel—before she understood.

"I'm sorry, but I don't follow. Your relationship is on the rocks because you love him?"

"Yes. Well, no. It's complicated."

"I don't see it like that. Either you love each other, or you don't. Do you love him?"

"Yes, but—"

"Does he love you?"

"Yes, but—"

"Then no buts. You love each other, it's simple. Everything else is minor."

"Not everything. Damn it, Matt. A girl's got needs!"

"What?"

"Any strong emotional response, Matt! Get it? How would you feel if the simple act of making love caused your wife to have a seizure?" Erica realized her mistake immediately, and Matt's face froze. "I'm sorry. I wasn't thinking."

He swallowed and looked away, though not before she saw the tears begin to form. "'S okay." Turning away, he refilled his coffee cup from the pot. After several seconds, he turned back to her, eyes clear, jaw set against further emotion. "So despite all that, you're heading for Alabama?"

"Yeah." She hadn't realized until then that she'd already made up her mind. "I guess, despite our problems, Ross is pretty much the safest person I know."

"Yeah, I guess he is, at that." Matt was silent for a moment, and appeared to be thinking something over. "Listen, I know I pulled a real dick move last night, and you have no reason to want me around, but if you want some company, I'd like to come along."

She hesitated. She understood why he'd taken the truck, and truth be told, he could have simply forced her to get out when she'd first refused to take him back. But he'd seen her safely back to shelter, made sure she was inside before driving off. All in all, it was the most polite carjacking she'd ever heard of. "Yeah, I guess I'm probably gonna need some help along the way, anyway. And you seemed pretty handy with that pistol."

That reminded her. "That's right!" She brushed past Matt, leaving him looking after her quizzically as she hurried to Uncle J's bedroom. She checked in the closet, but found nothing. Turning to leave, she bumped into Matt.

"What are you looking for?"

"Uncle Jimmy had a shotgun around here."

Matt looked around the small walk-in. "No gun safe. Did he leave it loose?"

"I don't know. He only took it out when we found snakes or had a problem with coyotes or wild dogs getting into the hen house."

Matt stepped out of the closet so she could follow. He dropped to the floor and looked under the bed. "Ah hah!" He dragged out a metal case about the right size to hold a rifle or two. "I don't suppose you know the combination?"

Peeking over his shoulder, Erica saw that there was an electrical keypad recessed into one end of the case. "No, I don't."

"What was Uncle Jimmy's birthday?"

"What?"

"These things usually have a six digit combination. That naturally lends itself to dates."

"Oh. Try zero, two, one, two, four, nine."

He punched the numbers and finished with a hash mark. The keys lit up and flashed three times, and Matt tried the drawer and sighed. "Nope."

She thought for a second. "Then try zero, four, two, four, nine, five."

Matt punched them in and there was an audible click. Erica smiled sadly. Uncle Jimmy had used her birthday. Matt slid the locking lever to the right, and the cover opened a tiny bit. He pulled it down and slid the drawer out of the safe. There lay Uncle Jimmy's shotgun, as well as several boxes of shells.

Picking it up, Matt worked the action on it to see if it was loaded. Satisfied that it wasn't, he started to examine it, nodding in approval. "Pretty nice. It's a Mossberg 500. Nothing fancy, but a good, reliable twelve-gauge."

He handed her the shotgun and started laying the boxes of shells out on the bed. "Should make a nice addition to the arsenal."

She grunted. "Arsenal? You call a pistol and a shotgun an arsenal?"

Matt stood. "Okay, you're sure you're leaving here?"

"Yeah. I'm sure."

"All right." He grabbed a pillow off the bed, and stripped the pillow case off of it. Stuffing all the shotgun shells into the pillow case, he slung it over his shoulder. "Then follow me."

Erica followed him all the way outside and back to the Xterra, where he opened the back. Her jaw dropped at the sight. "Where did you get all this?"

Matt swung the pillowcase off his shoulder and into the pile of weapons in the back. "At home. It's not really all that much. Couple of rifles and six pistols. Now a shotgun."

"Not that much, huh?"

"Considering what we went through last night, do you really think it will be enough?"

He had a point. She looked back at the house, thinking about what she would need to pack and realized she had definitely decided to leave.

"So when do you want to go?"

CHAPTER 64
CHARLES GRIFFE
THE ENGINE ROOM

Chris's personal badge had gotten them past the locks on the "Crew Only" doors leading to the lower decks. Once they had made it there, the entire atmosphere changed. Everywhere had been lit by a different type of emergency lighting than they had been forced to deal with in the rest of the ship. A steady red light, allowed them to save the batteries in Tabby's little flashlight. Evidently the designers had decided that a pulse of red light every few seconds was insufficient for vital areas of the ship.

But Tabby pointed out the most startling difference. "Listen."

They all stopped, craning to hear what she was talking about. After several seconds, Charlie shook his head. "I don't hear anything."

"Exactly. No screams or laughter… not even that hoarse wheezing they've been doing lately. There's no sounds that makes you think anyone's down here at all."

Listening again, Charlie realized she was right. He turned to Chris. "Any idea why that would be?"

Chris shrugged. "Not really. Maybe anyone down here decided to move to the upper decks. Once you're out, you can't get back in without the right key card."

"But why would they go out there to begin with?"

"Not all of them did." Shane indicated another pair of bodies on the floor ahead.

"But there aren't even as many bodies down here. Why would that be?"

"Who knows?" Chris clearly wasn't worried too much about it. He started walking again. "Maybe there just weren't enough people down here to keep them entertained."

Why do you want to start looking gift horses in the mouth?

Charlie sighed. "I guess there's a reason we call 'em crazies." The group moved on. The lower four decks were the working areas of the ship, and Charlie had nearly run into Chris's back when the other man had stopped at the entrance to a huge open area. He turned and stopped them before anyone went past. "Guys, remember what we talked about with the smiling, right? Don't let yourself laugh. We don't know if that's what happens, but let's not take the chance, all right?"

Charlie thought that was an odd thing to remind them of, and peered over Chris's head into the room beyond. There was a bit of a foul stench coming from that direction, but with the number of bodies lying about the ship, they had become somewhat used to that. Then Chris stepped aside to let them pass, and Charlie suddenly understood.

They had entered the food preparation areas. It was a kitchen half the size of a football field and the sight of all that food made Charlie want to laugh. There were dozens of rows of counters, sinks, bread racks, refrigerators, ovens, utensils, dishes, and anything else one could possibly need to feed the thousands of people aboard the Bahama Queen. Charlie stepped toward one of the long counters and saw the source of much of the smell. There were hundreds of crabs, fish, lobsters and scallops rotting in the sinks. His stomach turned as he remembered throwing up the lobster thermidor on the night the madness aboard the cruise ship had begun. Choking back the bile, he continued to look around for something else to eat as the rest of the group "oo-ed" and "ah-ed" as they wandered through the foodstuffs.

The seafood was obviously not fit for consumption, but there were racks and racks of cheeses, fruits, cakes, and other non-perishables. They all sat on the floor for several minutes contentedly gorging themselves silly on cheese sandwiches and canned drinks followed by whatever fruits or pastries caught their fancy. Some of it was stale, and it was all room temperature, but compared to what they had been forced to eat over the last several days, it was a veritable feast.

Finally, after they were all sated, Chris reminded them that it wasn't the only reason they had come down to the bowels of the ship. In better spirits than he'd been in since the power had gone out, Charlie stuffed a handful of cookies into his pockets and got to his feet with the others.

As they started to leave, Tabby called for their attention. Waving a large carving knife in the air, she pointed to a drawer she had pulled open. "Might be a good idea to grab a few. Hell of a lot better than a piece of mirror."

Within moments, everyone had armed themselves with knives or in Chris's case, a large meat cleaver. "Everybody ready?"

They all nodded, and Chris led the way. They passed huge washing machines, pallets full of canned foods, toilet paper and other items for the cruise. Eventually, he brought them to the lower most deck of the ship and stopped outside a door. The sign beside the broken window read Engine Control Room. The good mood they had all shared vanished as soon as they entered.

"Shit!" Chris cursed.

Charlie picked up a shard of plastic that had once been part of a control panel. He shook his head and tossed it away. "I don't suppose we're going to get anything running in here, are we?"

"We'll see."

Felicia began to sob again. "Why would they do this?"

Charlie rolled his eyes. He'd forgotten just how much she could complain.

Chris shrugged. "Like Charlie said, there's a reason we call them crazies."

The entire control room was a wreck. Someone, or several someones, had smashed or broken anything they could get their hands on. The room was a minefield of broken glass, plastic, and oil.

Charlie reached to stand a computer monitor back up when Tabatha tugged at his sleeve. "I wouldn't touch anything."

There she goes again. Bossy bitch, ain't she?

But Charlie was beginning to get the hang of not reacting to his father's comments. "Why not?" he asked Tabby.

"Everything in here's coated with blood."

In the red light, it took Charlie several seconds to realize that the dark, viscous fluid that he'd thought was oil *was* blood, but once Tabby pointed it out, it seemed obvious.

Felicia whimpered and drew close to Charlie.

Chris spoke from the other side of the console. "Looks like they shut everything down and then smashed the controls." He reached for a large red button on the console and twisted it clockwise. The button popped up about an inch from where it had been recessed.

"What's that?" Charlie asked.

"Emergency shutoff." There was a small green button on the console next to the shutoff, and he put his finger over it. Then he pulled his hand back and turned to the others. "Before I do this, remember what I said outside the kitchen area." He pointed at the button. "If this works, we may get power again. After everything we've all been through, some of you might want to laugh or cheer or something. All I can say is don't." He put his hand back over the button. "I'd hate to have to kill any of you."

He pressed the button and they looked around. After a second, Charlie looked at Chris. "Was it supposed to happen right away?"

Chris pursed his lips. "What did I forget?" He looked around the room and stopped after a moment. He snapped his fingers. "Breaker bars!" He moved briskly to a panel on the far wall and opened it up to reveal a series of electrical breakers. "There we are." He flipped each breaker arm up and closed the panel again. Moving back to the console, he pressed the power button once again. This time, the room was immediately filled with a small hum and the lights flickered on. Charlie sighed, biting his lip to keep from smiling. Then he noticed Chris's expression. The younger man was looking around the room, and worried frown on his face.

"What's wrong?"

But he didn't answer. He just turned away from the mess and crossed to a large window on the other side of the room.

They all followed him and peered out over a room that appeared cavernous. In it rested the engines themselves. They were massive things, each one the size of Charlie's den. He waited for Chris to say something, and after a few moments of silence, Charlie cleared his throat. "All right, so what are we looking at?"

Chris spoke without turning. "Enough engine power to suck down almost twenty-five hundred gallons of fuel per hour when we're under way. Enough to produce almost one hundred thousand kilowatts of electricity, to power all the lights, elevators, electronics, galleys, the water treatment plant, and all the other systems that keep the Bahama Queen running." He turned to Charlie. "And of course, they also power the ship's propulsion systems."

Charlie just blinked at him.

Finally, Chris shrugged. "Sorry. They made us memorize a lot of the stats during our training."

"So what's the problem? They're running, right?"

"Yes, they're running."

Tabby caught on before anyone else. She looked back at the smashed consoles. "But you can't steer the ship from here, can you?"

Chris shook his head. "We had to get the engines back online first. But Tabby's right. Getting the engines started, and controlling where you're going are two different things."

Everyone in the group began to mutter.

Chris held up his hand and continued. "Now I need to get to the bridge." He sighed. "Assuming it's in better shape than the engine control room, I should be able to get us safely into port."

Tabby nodded. "So where's the bridge?"

Chris looked at her. "Deck Twelve."

Charlie gaped. "Twelve?"

"Yeah."

"And we're at the bottom? On One?"

"Yeah."

Charlie was silent a moment. "Correct me if I'm wrong, but didn't we first meet on Twelve?"

"Yeah."

"Three days ago?"

"Yeah, nearly that."

"It took us three days to get from Deck Twelve down to here. Going *down* the stairs. Now we have to go back *up*?"

"Yes." He raised an eyebrow, as if waiting for Charlie to figure something out.

"What?" Charlie found himself raising his voice. "It's still going to take us forever to get up there."

Chris just shook his head. "Not if we hurry. I figure we can make it to the elevator in about ten minutes."

Charlie looked around them at the glowing lights. *Electricity, boy.* Once more, he had to fight back a grin.

CHAPTER 65
AUGUST GRAPPIN
LIGHTS

For the first time in the last few days, he began to feel something other than constant euphoria. The pleasure/pain that occasionally escalated into an ecstatic frenzy, was beginning to fade. There was an anxiety, tinged with a frantic need to find more tactile stimulation. He tried to understand what was wrong, but thinking had grown difficult.

What was it? Why didn't he feel as much of the pleasure/pain as he had?

His throat hurt. Could that be it? He didn't think so. It was a wonderful, exquisite, agonizing rawness that ripped through him as he tried to laugh. But it wasn't the same.

He didn't understand it. In truth, he no longer had the mental capacity to understand it. All he understood anymore was laughing was good. Sharing laughter with others was good. Eating was good. To a lesser extent, finding those who didn't laugh and making them scream was almost as good.

But when there were no new people to share pleasure/pain with, he became anxious. And the constant darkness of the ship's interior made it difficult to find new people. Something in him knew there were more on board, but he and his followers hadn't seen anyone since before he had last slept.

He trotted up the dark corridor, occasionally stumbling over the body of one of the ones that wouldn't laugh. He watched closely for some sign… some indication that a new person was hiding nearby. His stomach growled, hungry once more, and he looked at one of the bodies speculatively. But no, eating one didn't seem appetizing. Not while there was still so much other food in the eating parts of the ship. Maybe it was time to go back and find more cake.

He was about to turn and go back to the food place when something changed. Change! Change was a good thing. Change brought amusement.

What was different? At first, he couldn't put his finger on it. But after a moment of concentration, he heard it. A sound like the distant buzzing of bees. He slapped a companion wheezing his fading laughter at the sound. And after a moment, they were all coughing, and wheezing their amusement as all around them, the lights flickered back into existence. Distant music lilted through the corridors as some long shut off playlist picked up again in mid song.

Hunting should get much more fun now.

CHAPTER 66
ERICA CHAPMAN
TIME TO GO

Less than an hour later, Erica had her things packed. Once she had everything in the truck, Matt took her out back and handed her a pistol. "Know how to use it?"

"Not really."

"Didn't think so. Hold it like this, grab the slide like so, and slide it back while you push the pistol forward. That chambers the first round."

"So, it's loaded?"

He sighed heavily. "Yes. It's loaded."

Over the next half hour, he showed her how to change magazines, sight, fire, and load more "rounds" in the empty magazines. Eventually, he seemed satisfied that she wasn't going to shoot her foot off and handed her two extra magazines. "Each one holds seventeen rounds. If we get in a situation where you have to use it, don't hesitate. If you're firing and it stops going boom, thumb the magazine release to change mags, rechamber a round, and keep firing."

She stared at him, feeling like someone trying to learn a foreign language. She got it, but only if she concentrated on each word, working to discern the meaning behind each sound. *Mags? Rounds? Thumb the release? Oh yeah!*

Then he handed her Uncle Jimmy's shotgun and the process started again. By the time they were finished, her wrist hurt, her shoulder hurt, and her brain hurt. But at least she was comfortable enough with the firearms that she knew how to not accidentally shoot herself or Matt. Probably.

Matt grunted in satisfaction. "You got any questions?"

Brain fried, she shook her head. She was afraid that if he showed her just one more new thing, her skull would explode.

"All right. Let's go, then. I'll take the first shift driving," Matt said. They climbed into the Xterra, and Erica set the GPS in the console. She looked around a final time as the SUV pulled away from Uncle J's ranch, knowing that she would likely never see it again. As they pulled out of the gate at the end of the drive, she sighed and faced forward. That was her old life. Careful to keep the barrel pointed away from Matt, she contemplated the pistol she now carried. So, was this her new life? This tool of death and mayhem? She was far from comfortable with it. But she was even less comfortable with the idea of being overrun by a bunch of two-legged homicidal hyenas. Matt assured her that she would get more used to it as time went on. She hoped he was wrong.

They topped off the tank at a nearby convenience store. It was eerily deserted, but the pumps were still on, so they helped themselves. Matt hung up the nozzle and the two of them looked at one another. A lifetime of conditioning made the transaction feel incomplete without at least an attempt at payment.

"Should we check to see if there's anyone inside?" Erica asked.

Matt hesitated. "If there is, you realize the chances are good that..." He swallowed, evidently unwilling to complete the sentence.

"Yeah. But we should at least look."

He reached under his jacket and pulled out his pistol. Pulling the slide back slightly, he grunted in satisfaction before slipping it back into his shoulder holster. "All right. Let's check."

They entered the double glass doors and Matt immediately called out. "Anybody here?" After a few seconds of silence he tried again. "We just got some gas and need to pay you." A few more seconds of silence and he turned to Erica.

She shrugged. "I guess nobody's home."

He nodded, then walked to the counter and looked behind it. A slight grunt, and he walked to the other side. Erica's breath caught as she watched, imagining a body on the floor back there. "What is it? What did you find?"

He looked at her, puzzled. "Nothing. Why?"

She closed her eyes in relief. "I just thought... never mind. What are you after back there?"

"I was checking to see if they had a pistol or something behind the counter. But no such luck." He grabbed a handful of plastic bags and handed several of them to her. "Let's gather up as much canned food as we can. We might need it later."

"We can't do that!"

"Why not?"

"It's stealing!"

He raised an eyebrow. "This, from the woman who drove a brand new SUV off of a dealership last night?"

"That was different. Those..." *What had they called them on the news?* "...chucklers were chasing us. It was the only way to save our lives."

Matt walked to the canned food shelf and held up a can of overpriced Dinty Moore. "Well this just might save our lives, too." He grabbed several more cans and swept them into his bag. When he noticed she wasn't doing the same, he stopped. "Look, Erica, you told me yourself that this craziness looks like it's everywhere. And we saw first-hand what's going on at least in this area. Right?"

She nodded reluctantly.

"So what are the chances that anyone is going to show up for work here and object to us taking this? And more importantly, what are the chances that we'll make it to Alabama without any food?"

As wrong as it seemed on an emotional level, she couldn't argue his logic. Reluctantly, she nodded and began loading her bags with anything she thought might come in handy. Most of it was food, but she also found shelves that contained lighters, first aid items, bandanas, and all sorts of other miscellany. The two of them gathered so much that it took them several trips to load it all in the SUV, and the back seat was piled high with white plastic shopping bags when they were finished.

Finally, well stocked for the trip, gas gauge firmly planted above the full line, and three extra gas cans full of gas strapped to the roof rack, they headed away from the ranch where Erica had grown up and toward Katy, the scene of last night's insanity. They stuck to the main highway as they approached, and things went fine at first. But as they approached town, they began to notice smoke. They passed the first accident just before the Pin Oak Road overpass approaching the Interstate. A man jumped out from behind the wreck waving a baseball bat and slammed it on the Xterra's hood. Erica screamed and pointed the pistol at him through the windshield. "Don't shoot!" Matt yelled. He punched the gas, and they swept past the man before he could swing the bat again. Erica looked back and saw that he'd been joined by three others who were chasing after the SUV, laughing the whole time. The chucklers didn't have a chance as Matt accelerated across the overpass.

"Why didn't you want me to shoot him?"

"Because you were aiming through the windshield. We're sorta going to need that."

"Oh, yeah." Erica realized she still had a lot to learn about shooting, and it looked like she was going to have to learn fast.

Once they hit the apex of the bridge, the two of them had a better vantage point. Erica's jaw dropped as they saw the source of all the smoke. Off to the left was the mall where their nightmare had begun last night. This morning, it was a smoldering ruin. There were four fire engines sitting in the parking lot, but they were abandoned. People ran about in the streets, some laughing, some screaming, all fighting.

"Holy Christ on a crutch," Matt muttered.

Erica simply nodded, figuring there wasn't much more to say. Matt turned away from the mayhem and back to the road. There were hardly any cars to be seen. No. That wasn't true. There were hardly any *moving* cars on the road. There were plenty of wrecked or stalled vehicles. They were numerous enough that Matt had to slow down so much that what would have ordinarily been a fifteen-minute drive turned into an hour of white-knuckle driving, winding through the obstacle course that was now I-10 near the mall.

"Should we get off the freeway?" Erica suggested.

Matt looked over the guardrail onto the frontage road. "Doesn't look any better there."

He was right. Cars and trucks dotted the feeder just as badly as on the freeway. Matt swerved around another abandoned car. Like so many of the others they had passed, it was by itself. There was no other vehicle, no real accident or collision. It had scraped into the side barrier and simply been abandoned.

They finally got to a fairly clear section of the freeway, and were actually beginning to make a little time when a truck on the outbound side caught Erica's attention and she tugged on Matt's sleeve. He followed her gaze and slowed down. The old pickup was the only other moving vehicle in sight at the moment. It was heading in the opposite direction, and slowed down as they approached. As it neared, Erica saw an old man in a cowboy hat behind the wheel watching them suspiciously. Finally, he must have seen what he was looking for. He stopped just before passing and stepped out of the truck on the abandoned freeway. He held a rifle in his right hand, but pointed it at the ground in a non-threatening manner. Matt stopped the Xterra and turned to Erica. "What do you think?"

"Looks like he wants to talk. And he's not laughing."

"And he's coming from Houston. Maybe he can tell us what's going on there."

They got out, pistols pointed down, and walked to meet the old man at the center barrier. Matt spoke first. "You comin' out from Houston?"

"Yeah. Everything's gone crazy. People killin' each other, settin' fires. Half'a downtown's burnin', folks are…" He swallowed. "They're laughin' while they kill each other." The old man shook his head. "I seen you headed that direction an' I figured you might oughta know what you're headin' into. It ain't no ordinary drive into town."

Matt nodded. "Yeah, we saw a little bit of it here in Katy last night, too. Erica here," he jabbed his thumb in her direction, "said she saw a news report last night that it was all over the country."

The old man nodded. "Yeah, I seen that too." He shifted the rifle to his left hand and stuck out his right. "Name's Eddie."

Matt shook first. "Matt."

The old man's hand was firm and calloused when he offered it to Erica. It reminded her of Uncle J's hands. "I'm Erica. Where you headed?"

"Got a daughter and son-in-law just this side of San Antone. Got through to my daughter this mornin' and she sounds okay for now. More than a little upset, of course, what with all this going on. Turns out her husband never came home from work last night, either. Figure I need to get out that way and make sure she stays all right. How about you folks?"

"I have a friend in Montgomery I'm trying to get to," Erica said.

The old man shook his head. "All the way to 'Bama?" He whistled. "The way the roads are right now, that's gonna be a hell of a trip." He looked up the freeway in the direction they'd come from. "Friends of yours?"

Matt and Erica turned. A crowd of about half a dozen hooting and laughing chucklers banged on abandoned vehicles with pipes, bats, and various other clubs as they ran up the freeway.

"Definitely not," Matt said. "You any good with that thing?" He indicated the rifle in Eddie's hands.

The old man shook his head sheepishly. "Ain't got no bullets. Just thought it might cause folks to hesitate before they try to pull anything."

Matt ran to the back of the Xterra. "Wouldn't be a 30.06 by any chance, would it?"

"Yeah." Eddie looked nervously back up the freeway. "And if you got ammo back there, I do appreciate it, but if not, we need to get movin' pretty quick here.

Matt pulled out one of the rifles and a box of ammo. Erica ran to the passenger door of the Xterra and pulled out Uncle Jimmy's shotgun. When she got back, the chucklers were about a football field's distance away. Matt took aim, but appeared to be waiting for a sure target, while Eddie hurriedly thumbed bullets into his rifle. Eddie brought his rifle up and sighted. "You ready?" he asked.

"Yeah. Guess that's about close enough." Matt fired a second before Eddie did, and two of the hooting attackers dropped. Two more salvos and the others were down.

The three of them were silent for a moment. Then the eerie sound of approaching laughter arose. They spun around, looking for the source, but couldn't see any others. It sounded like it came from the other side of the Xterra so they walked around it. Matt and Eddie flanked Erica as they crept around the SUV. The laughter was coming from past the truck, past the concrete barrier at the edge of the freeway. Erica gasped as she peeked over the barrier. "Matt!"

Eddie whistled again. "Ho-lee shit!"

The frontage street below was crawling with chucklers. They were pouring out of buildings across the street and running toward the freeway from side streets. Luckily for them, Matt, Erica, and Eddie had stopped on a raised section of the freeway, separated from the frontage by a high retaining wall. The chucklers couldn't scale it, but the sight of them trying was terrifying nevertheless. The sound of hundreds of people laughing and giggling was nails on the chalkboard of Erica's mind. Then it got worse.

"Guys?" Matt pointed, and one of the chucklers was scrambling up the back of another. He reached up and got within inches of the lip of the concrete barrier at the side of the freeway before the chuckler below him fell, toppling both of them to be crushed beneath the feet of the others. But another had seen, and he scrambled up the back of another chuckler. Within seconds, others were trying, and some were getting their hands on the lip of the freeway embankment and beginning to pull themselves up.

They drew back, walking quickly back to their vehicles. "Time to go." Matt handed Eddie the rest of the ammo for the rifle. "Hang on to this in case you run into any other problems."

"Sure you can spare it?"

"I got a few more boxes in back."

Eddie tipped his hat. "Well, I ain't gonna turn it down then. Thanks."

Matt nodded. "Not a problem. Good luck."

"Back atcha." Eddie sprinted for his pickup and pulled away.

Matt and Erica climbed back in their SUV and took off just as the first of the swarm scrambled onto the freeway. They easily outdistanced them, and Erica looked back to make sure Eddie got away. She saw his pickup just as it crested the overpass and disappeared from view. She turned back to face front. "Think he'll make it?"

Matt shrugged. "He's got a lot shorter trip than we do."

She thought about that. "Think *we'll* make it?"

He looked away, concentrating on the obstacle course before him. "Like the man said, it's gonna be one hell of a trip."

They crested another overpass, and Erica could see the eastern horizon blanketed by a thick cloud of black smoke. She knew the Houston skyline was hidden somewhere within that smoke. *Yeah, a hell of a trip, indeed.*

CHAPTER 67
CHARLES GRIFFE
DEEP IN THE BELLY

There wasn't room for everyone in the elevator, and most of their number weren't exactly in the best shape of their lives, so they had decided that most of their group would remain below in the relative safety of the mess section of Deck Two. Charlie, Tabby, Chris, and Shane would make the run to the bridge.

Charlie followed Chris to the elevator and watched as the man inserted a card key into a slot on the elevator panel. He noted that it wasn't the same key he had been using to get them into the various cabins.

"Let me ask you something, Chris. Why haven't we seen any help yet? I mean, this shit's been going on for almost a week already. Shouldn't the Navy or the Coast Guard or someone have already come to help us?"

"Yes, they should."

"Well then why the hell haven't—?"

"I don't know. That's been bothering me, too. There are so many damned safeguards built into this ship that you can't fart without someone at the home office knowing about it. They usually know something's wrong before we do."

"Then, like I said, why—?"

"I don't know why! Maybe they have. Maybe they already put a helicopter down on the helipad, but we were too busy hiding in the lower decks. Or maybe there's one up there right now and they're taking on passengers to go home. Hell, for all I know, there's a whole damned fleet of helicopters shuttling people on and off the ship right now.

"You were just telling me about how long it takes to go from one deck to another. But despite all your complaining, I don't think you really understand how big this ship actually is.

"The Bahama Queen is an eighteen-story luxury hotel nearly two hundred fifty feet tall, with a park and a boardwalk in the middle! Only instead of building it in Vegas or Atlantic City like any sensible person would do, we decided to strap engines on the damned thing and put it in the middle of the freaking ocean! And we're so deep in the belly right now that anything could be happening on the upper decks and we have no way of knowing it."

Charlie realized the man was right. "All right, sorry. So now what?"

Chris shrugged as the elevator door chimed and slid open. "Now we get to the bridge... and hope it's in better shape than the engine control room."

CHAPTER 68
ERICA CHAPMAN
THE ROAD WE WANT

The mid-day sun filtered through a thickening smoke as they approached Houston proper. While they were technically already within the city limits, Houston was a wide-ranging metroplex that sprawled for miles in all directions. The downtown skyline wasn't even a blip on the horizon yet, and already visibility was terrible. Between the wrecked and stalled cars on the freeway, the acrid smoke, and the occasional roving pack of chucklers that would see the SUV and pursue, it was turning into the most stressful drive of Erica's life. So far, none of their pursuers had even come close to catching them, and once they gained enough distance, the chucklers seemed to lose interest and wander off. It was as if they couldn't concentrate on anything beyond what was immediately in front of them. But Erica feared the freeway obstacle course might eventually slow them down to the point that we wouldn't be able to keep ahead of them.

As she thought that through, she wondered aloud, "Why don't they drive?"

"What?"

"The crazies, chucklers... whatever you want to call them. Why aren't they driving anymore? I mean, they talk. They seem to be able to reason well enough that they can make jokes." She wave at the abandoned cars. "All those things chasing us, and yet not a single one of them is still driving. Not one of them thinks to climb into one of the abandoned cars and turn a key?"

Matt appeared to stop and think about it, then shrugged. "Who knows? I'm just glad they haven't."

"But there's gotta be a reason. And maybe it's important."

"Maybe." He swerved around a stalled pickup and eased between the tangled wreckage of a three car pileup on the right, and another apparently abandoned minivan on the left. Erica winced as they scraped along the side of the van, snapping off its side view mirror as they passed.

Erica kept her eyes open for movement as she spoke. "They were driving last night. Why not now?"

"Not for long, though."

"What?"

"They didn't drive for long. Every one of them that we saw driving ended up wrecking, remember? It was like they didn't know what they were doing anymore."

Erica recalled the insane expression on the face of the chuckler that raced past them just before he slammed into the SUV behind the mall. "Or they were more interested in smashing something."

They gained speed as Matt cleared the tangled wreckage on the road and approached another clear area. "Maybe," he conceded.

"But if you want to start worrying about why things are happening the way they are, maybe you should ask yourself why you and I *aren't* crazy. Eddie too, for that matter."

He had a point. Last night, she had feared it was a terrorist gas attack. The news had made it obvious that wasn't likely. Something big had happened, and the news coverage made it look like it had happened everywhere.

For the next twenty minutes or so, the trip was like that. They wound their way slowly along the Interstate 10 obstacle course, making their way slowly toward downtown Houston. As the familiar skyline loomed before them, Erica started to get more nervous. She found herself looking up and to the right, watching the smoke that poured from various skyscrapers. "They seem to like fire."

Matt looked at her, then followed her eyes skyward. "Yeah." His eyes drifted back to the freeway before them. "Road's starting to come back down to street level. Keep your eyes peeled."

An apartment complex bordered the freeway to the right, and sure enough, the sound of the engine seemed to attract the attention of the occupants. At first just a few, then more than a dozen bodies began pouring out of the buildings. "On the right," she said.

He looked over, grunted and sped up, leaving the small group chasing behind them. Erica looked back at them as the Xterra passed. She was still looking back when Matt slammed on the brakes. "What the hell is…?" Her voice trailed off as she saw why he had stopped.

About a quarter of a mile ahead was a strip mall, and whether it was the sound of the engine, or the frenetic shrieks and laughter of the chucklers behind them, something had alerted a larger crowd ahead of them. Hundreds of laughing, jumping, frolicking, and running maniacs were running toward them.

Matt threw the Xterra into reverse. "This is not good!"

"Really? You think?"

But he ignored her sarcasm. "Get your shotgun ready. You might have to use it."

Erica swallowed and rolled her window down as Matt tried to maneuver the SUV around the closest wrecks in some semblance of a three point turn. She chambered a round in the shotgun, the way Matt had shown her… was it really just a few hours ago? She looked at the wrecks he was trying to maneuver through. "You're not going to make that turn in time, Matt." She pointed the shotgun at the quickly approaching crowd.

He looked away from where he had been concentrating on trying to turn around on the crowded freeway. "Shit." She saw him look back to the larger crowd coming from the opposite direction. The leaders from that group were getting close, too. "Not good," he muttered. "Not good at all."

Matt cut the wheel back the way they had been going. "Roll your window back up!"

That was all the warning Erica got, as he suddenly threw the engine back into drive and rushed the last few yards straight at the leader of the pack before them. He slammed the brakes and cut the wheel to the left just as he hit the man, knocking him to the pavement. Erica screamed as Matt, now clear of the wrecked vehicles behind them, threw the stick into reverse again, turning in his seat as he steered back through the narrow path between the other vehicles. It was the same pathway they had just passed through, only this time, Matt was driving much faster… in reverse… while several lunatics rushed at them from both before and behind.

Erica swallowed. "Matt?"

He ignored her, and the rear of the Xterra clipped the bumper of one of the already-wrecked vehicles. He didn't slow.

Erica winced as the first person in the smaller group behind them jumped into their path. The SUV jolted, then lurched as first the back tires rose, then the front, as if driving over a speed bump. She shuddered, refusing to think about what they were driving over. The rear window cracked as another chuckler dove in front of them, and he went the way of the first one. After a few more rear impacts, the back window was starred and bloody in three places, but it was clear enough to see when they cleared the wreckage.

She looked in front of them. "They're still coming."

Matt kept moving in reverse, cursing steadily as he tried to keep moving quickly enough that their pursuit wouldn't catch up. Erica looked at the outer edge of the freeway, searching for the nearest exit ramp, but there was nothing within sight. She turned back to Matt to see if he had any ideas and her eyes caught sight of a ramp on the inner lane. "There!"

He slowed and looked where she pointed. A ramp led upward, toward a high, raised section of concrete. Above the ramp was a sign that read HOV LANE - 2+ CARPOOLS ONLY. "Can you make it?"

They both looked back at the approaching mass of laughing death. "Absofuckinglutely!" Now that they were past most of the wreckage, he threw the Xterra back into drive and stomped on the gas pedal. The tires squealed as the SUV jumped forward, and Matt cut the wheel sharply to the left. He clipped another of their pursuers but didn't slow as he drove the wrong way up the freeway until he reached the ramp leading to the HOV lane. He cut the wheel sharply to the right and swung them back in the right direction, moving up the ramp to the elevated carpool lane.

Looking ahead, Erica braced her hand against the dashboard and stomped down hard on her imaginary brakes. "Matt?"

But Matt never slowed as he crashed the Xterra through the flimsy traffic gate that was designed to keep HOV traffic flowing in the other direction. Suddenly, they were in the clear and climbing up the overpass, leaving the chucklers behind them.

Eyes wide and heart pounding, Erica allowed herself to finally lean back in her seat. "Oh my God."

"You can say that again."

The HOV lane was narrower than the main interstate. As the name implied, it was only a single lane wide. But it appeared to have been almost empty when everything went to hell. There were only a few wrecks and they were simple instances of vehicles that had been driven into the concrete barrier to the side. Once he squeezed past them, Matt was able to make a little speed as they climbed the ramp, actually passing forty miles an hour for the first time since they had passed under the west loop of the 610 Freeway. Erica glanced at her watch and was surprised to realize that was almost an hour ago.

They approached the apex of the elevated lane, and it curved gently to the right. Near the top, two cars had wrecked into one another, making Matt slow down again. But there was room to make it past on the left, and Matt negotiated the tight opening with hardly any trouble. Erica looked down over the side of the freeway. They were only about thirty feet over street level, but her relief at being free of pursuit, if only for the moment, made her feel as if they were miles above the destruction below.

Then they topped the rise and downtown Houston came into view. "It was nice while it lasted," she muttered.

"What?"

She sighed. "Nothing." She looked at the smoky destruction before them. Much of the street level below was pretty much invisible, enshrouded in a drifting ethereal curtain through which she could occasionally glimpse death and destruction all over. Wrecked cars and bodies littered the streets, one as motionless as the other. Movement caught her attention at one point, and she saw a man run across the street, pursued by a crowd of dozens. The smoke from one of many burning cars hid them from her sight before she could tell whether or not he escaped.

More smoke streamed from random, jagged holes in the mirrored exteriors of several skyscrapers. Erica was so busy trying to peer through the smoke that she was caught by surprise when Matt began cursing again. She looked up, placing a hand on the shotgun again as she looked for danger. "What is it?"

He stopped the SUV, looked in the rear view mirror, and put the vehicle in park. He pointed at the GPS screen on the dash. It was flashing and a progress bar across the top indicated that it was recalculating their route.

"What's going on?"

"Come over here," he told her, then stepped out onto the freeway.

Brows furrowed, she stepped around the Xterra and joined him where he stood at the concrete barrier overlooking the city below. Glancing down, she no longer felt as if they were *only* thirty feet above the ground. Suddenly, she wanted to step back, away from the edge.

Matt pointed through the smoke to where two other strips of concrete intertwined and passed beneath them. He pointed at the lowermost one. "See that? That's I-10."

She raised her eyebrows at him. "And this is important because?"

"I-10 is the road we want to take to get to Alabama."

Erica looked back at the concrete strip they were standing on. It curved away from the interstate beneath them. "Damn. How do we get back to it?"

Matt looked back the way they had come. "Well, this carpool lane only goes two directions. And we've already seen what's behind us."

She looked down the road before them. "But this is going to take us farther away from where we want to go. And to get back," she waved her hand at the smoky streets below just as a small crowd of people ran across a street in the distance, "we're going to have to go through part of that, aren't we?"

Matt simply nodded.

CHAPTER 69
CHARLES GRIFFE
SHIP'S BRIDGE

There were several computer monitors hanging from ceiling mounts on the bridge, as well as on various desk mounts. Charlie wrinkled his nose at the stench of the darkened room. He was well used to the smell of death on the ship, and recognized it immediately. But in an enclosed room, the smell had no opportunity to disperse, and Charlie forced himself to breathe through his mouth so as to keep his nose as disengaged as he could. He cast his gaze around the room and quickly found the source of the smell. Off to the far right lay three bodies, just beginning to bloat. Chris ignored them and went unerringly to the right-hand seat at a central, U-shaped console with a desktop full of controls down the middle. He started to sit, then cursed.

"What's wrong?" Tabby asked him.

He held up what was obviously the remains of a radio transceiver. "Radio's out." He waved his hand at the console. "Monitor's smashed." He looked around the room, then got up and went to sit in front of another panel. Charlie noticed that this one appeared to be undamaged, and Chris reached behind the console and felt around for a moment. "Tabby, you still have that flashlight?"

She brought it over and handed it to him.

"Thanks." Chris dropped beneath the console for a few minutes, and Charlie could hear him doing something before crawling back out and placing the edge of his meat cleaver under the monitor's bezel. A moment of prying and the monitor slipped loose in the console. "There we go." He pulled, and the screen came completely out, wires dangling behind it.

He repeated the process back at the original station where he had started to sit earlier, and within a few minutes had replaced the damaged screen. "All right, cross your fingers." With that, he pressed a button on the monitor, then another on the console. They could hear the sound of a computer starting up, and within seconds the cruise line's logo spun into existence on the screen, followed by a logon screen.

"Yes!" Chris swung a keyboard over in front of him and typed rapidly. He grabbed a trackball on the console and clicked an icon on the screen. Seconds later, the screen was filled with something resembling a radar screen.

Charlie watched over his shoulder. "What's ARPA?"

"Automatic Radar Plotting Aid."

"So I guess it's safe to assume you know what you're doing?" Charlie asked him.

Chris didn't even look back at him. "Just another day at the office." The screen changed, zooming out to show the Gulf of Mexico coastline. "Okay, looks like we're way off course."

"How bad is it?" Shane asked him.

Chris was silent for a moment. Then he nodded. "Actually, it's not bad at all." He started to type, fingers moving confidently on the keyboard. "We've been drifting for five days and the current has been moving us closer to the coast of Louisiana." He called up another screen. "Unfortunately, there isn't any place on the Louisiana coast deep enough for the Bahama Queen to dock." Moving back to the original screen, he tapped a joystick and moved the cursor past what Charlie could recognize as the Louisiana coastline, moving farther west. "Maybe Galveston?" Fingers flew once more. "The cruise line has a port of call in Galveston, but the Bahama Queen is too big to dock there, too." A few more keystrokes and he nodded. "There we go. Did you know that Houston has a major shipping lane that connects directly with the Gulf of Mexico?" He pulled up another screen, reading rapidly through a screen of text.

"Houston? I thought that was like in the center of Texas," Shane said.

"I can see geography wasn't your best class in school." Chris frowned. "No, Houston is about fifty miles inland, and it's connected to the Gulf by the Houston Ship Channel."

"Is it deep enough?" Tabby asked him.

"According to my web search, it's just over forty-five feet deep. The Bahama Queen has a draft of forty feet. We've got room to spare." He typed for a few more minutes, called up another screen and flipped a series of switches. "Thrusters are on." He then reached across to a set of levers on the central control panel. He eased them forward and suddenly Charlie felt a slight sensation of motion.

"Are we moving?"

"We are. I've got us on course for Houston. At current speed we should get there in…" he looked at the screen, "…about five hours."

Don't you dare smile, boy. Not when we're this close to gettin' home.

Once again, his dad was right. He reached out and gripped Chris's shoulder. "Thanks, Chris."

Chris nodded. "Now let's get back to the others."

Shane led the way as they opened the door. He barely had time to scream before he was jerked forward and into the corridor where half a dozen crazies fell on him, biting and clawing at him. Charlie, Tabby, and Chris pulled back as a mob of wheezing, smiling, drooling crazies pushed into the bridge. Charlie gripped his knife in his hand and looked at his companions. "Anyone got any great ideas?"

They were both silent.

"Yeah, me neither." With a yell, he rushed forward. He hit the first one with his shoulder, driving his knife home and twisting it as he had seen Tabby do to the woman who had killed Scott. The man fell before him, and he drove into the next one. But these weren't teens, as the attackers on the basketball court had been. They didn't give way to his football style rushes as easily. His next target managed to get a hold on his shirt and pulled Charlie off balance. He staggered forward, then regained his footing just as Chris swung his cleaver down. The man's hand came off at the wrist. To Charlie's horror, that seemed to make him laugh even more, and he reached toward Chris with his other hand.

Tabby slipped in and slashed, once more going for the neck. Blood sprayed as she jumped back and slashed at another woman who leapt at her. Charlie kicked at the dying hulk Tabby had slashed and the man fell back, grinning and bleeding. He stomped on the man's chest and jumped at another attacker. Snarling in anger, he rammed the knife into the man's chest several times, feeling the blade slide on bone as it slipped between ribs.

As he pulled the knife free, something slammed into Charlie's back and the impact threw him forward, into the mob, further separating him from Chris and Tabby. He flailed about with knife and fist, and his eyes fell briefly on Shane's feebly twitching body. A ragged hole in the man's throat leaked a crimson pool onto the floor.

The sight distracted him for a second, and someone else hit Charlie from behind and he stumbled to his hands and knees, barely managing to hang on to his knife. A growling in his ear warned him of the impending bite, and he jerked his head to the side just as another body landed on him. He struggled beneath the weight of his attackers, trying to push up against them, but between the cut in his chest and the bruising of his forearm from Felicia's strike with the chair leg, he simply didn't have the full strength of his right arm. He realized he was going to go down.

Reversing his grip on the knife, he held it in his left hand like an ice pick, and gave up struggling to rise. Instead, he collapsed his right arm beneath him and spun onto his back, landing on his back with his attacker beneath him. He jabbed back with his knife, feeling the blade slide into its meaty sheath just as teeth latched into the muscle of his shoulder. He screamed, withdrew the blade and stabbed blindly behind him over and over until the teeth released their hold.

You're bit, boy. You're fucked seven ways to Sunday, now.

"Shut the hell up!" he shouted. He started to roll off the body beneath him and looked up to see an obese woman in a bloody and stained floral muumuu diving at him.

Charlie screamed as he realized his knife was still in the body of his other attacker. Four hundred pounds of muumuu woman landing on him stopped his scream as the air was forced from his lungs with a loud whoof. As he fell back again, he briefly saw his knife sticking out of the other body. It was only five or six feet away, but might as well have been across the room. He punched at his new attacker ineffectively with his left hand as he tried to hold back her gnashing teeth with his weakened right, but he was losing the battle. Straddling his hips, she used her greater weight to hold him in place as she leaned in, grinning, wheezing, teeth snapping at him, drawing closer and closer to his face. He shoved his hands out to hold her back, inadvertently getting a double handful of her massive breasts as she leaned toward him. He shifted his grip, reaching for her throat with his right hand, pulling his left back to punch again.

"Chris! Tabby! Help!" But he heard only the sounds of more fighting, incoherent shouting, and over it all, the susurrus wheezing and occasional chuckling of their attackers. And to make matters worse, the woman on top of him began grinding her groin into him in an obviously sexual manner, even as she laughed hoarsely and tried to bite at his arms.

"What the actual fuck is wrong with you?" he screamed.

Anger flared. He squeezed his right hand tight, trying to choke the life out of her, all the while swinging wildly at her with his other hand. And with each punch she only giggled more, grinding away with those huge hips.

"Well, that ain't working," he thought, and changed tactics. Giving up on trying to pummel her into submission, Charlie added his left hand to his right and was surprised to find himself unable to reach all the way around those massive jowls. Then her fingers tangled in his hair, and she pulled his head toward her gnashing teeth. More footsteps approached, and Charlie realized there was no way he would be able to hold off another attacker while his hands were buried in the triple chins of the woman dry humping him. He began to sob in helpless terror as his right arm began to betray him.

Without warning, a large black rectangle slammed into the woman's head. It withdrew out of Charlie's line of sight, then slammed down again. Bits of plastic and electronics rained down as muumuu lady's eyes rolled back in her head, and she fell to the side as Charlie frantically pushed to keep her from collapsing on top of him. Tabby stood behind the woman, the remains of the smashed monitor Chris had replaced were still in her hand.

Charlie saw movement. "Behind you!"

She spun, swinging the monitor screen at an old man who wheezed his laughter at her through a toothless mouth. This time, the screen shattered completely and the old man went down. Charlie scrambled across the floor and pulled his knife from the body where he'd left it. Staggering back to his feet, he looked around. "Where's Chris?"

Tabby pointed back into the bridge and only then did Charlie realize the two of them had made it out. "He's still in there."

Looking over her shoulder, Charlie could see at least half a dozen more crazies bunched near the navigation station Chris had recently repaired. There were shouts and curses that told Charlie that Chris was still fighting for his life in there. He shook his head. There was no way the young man was going to survive for much longer. "Poor bastard," he muttered. He started to turn toward the elevators.

His father's voice stopped him. *That poor bastard still has the keycards.*

Shit. With a grimace, Charlie took a deep breath and ran back into the bridge. Tabby followed and the two of them attacked the giggling horde from behind. Charlie yanked back on the hair of two of them and cut their throats before they even knew he was there. Tabby grabbed a desk chair from behind the console and slammed it into another one. That caught the attention of the last few, and they turned away from the meat-cleaver-wielding Chris and staggered toward her.

Charlie cut another one, while Chris got one as it turned its back to him. Suddenly, there was only the one rushing Tabby left. Chris and Charlie both fell on the man, and he collapsed in a bloody mess. The three of them stood panting, looking at one another.

"Guys?" Tabby pointed back out the door again. Charlie turned, and they saw another crowd of lunatics stumbling up the corridor toward the bridge.

Charlie, Chris, and Tabby ran out of the room. Chris stopped at the door, trying to pull it closed, but there were several bodies lying across the threshold. Charlie grabbed his sleeve. "No time!"

"But…"

Charlie yanked, and Chris staggered after him. The new crowd of attackers stomped up the port side corridor, so Charlie and his companions rushed up the starboard side, trying to gain as much distance as they could.

Tabby was in the lead, and she turned to look behind them at their pursuit. Fear showed in her eyes. "We're not going to make it. There's no time to open the elevator and close it again before they get to us."

Charlie pulled Chris up ahead of him. "Open up a cabin. Make it one on the ocean side."

"But they'll see where we go."

"It doesn't matter. Just do it!"

Chris pulled the key card from his pocket and opened the first door on the left. The three of them piled in, and Charlie slammed the door behind him, throwing the privacy lock for good measure.

"Now what? We're trapped in here and they're going to—"

A slam on the door interrupted her and she squeaked.

"They're going to bust this door down in a matter of minutes."

Charlie ran across the room to the balcony and opened the sliding door. "This way." He shoved the knife in the back of his belt and stepped to the rail. "Wish me luck."

"What?"

Without any further explanation, Charlie swung his leg over the rail as he had when Purple Hair had trapped him on his second day into this nightmare. And just like that time, the incessant pounding on the cabin door told him that time was not on his side.

"What the hell are you doing?" Chris asked him.

Rather than answer, Charlie gripped the rail and slipped the rest of his body over the side. It was much harder this time than it had been the first time. He was exhausted after the fight at the bridge, and he didn't have full use of his right arm. But he wasn't going to wait in here for them to come rip him to pieces, either.

He slid down carefully, arms shaking from fatigue, he clung to the rails as he let his feet swing out into open air. Finally, when he was hanging on the bottom rail, he swung his feet forward until he could feel the top of the balcony below. The slight swaying of the ship pushed him toward the rail, then pulled him away. Toward... away.

With his toes barely touching the balcony below them, Charlie shifted his grip, hanging precariously onto the rail with only his left hand, and slipped his weaker right hand under the bottom of the balcony to help his balance as he shifted more of his weight onto his feet. Finally, he was balanced enough. The next time the rocking shifted his weight toward the ship, he let go of the rail above, balanced for a second with his feet on the rail and his hands pressed on the ceiling above him, and jumped into the balcony of the cabin below. "Come on!" he called.

A few seconds later, he saw Tabby's legs come into sight. He stepped up to the railing, and helped guide her feet toward him. They stopped when she was still a foot away from the railing. "I can't reach!"

Charlie climbed back up, braced himself with his left hand on the ceiling again, and wrapped his right arm around her waist. "You're gonna have to let go," he shouted. "I'm gonna count to three, then you let go."

"Are you crazy?"

The ship rocked toward the cabin. "One!"

"No way!"

It rocked away. "Two."

Toward... "Three! Let go!" He pulled her toward him as she let go, and the two of them fell backward off the rail and onto the hard balcony flooring.

Charlie scrambled to his feet. Chris's feet were already coming into sight. He grabbed the man's feet and pulled them toward the railing. Seconds later, the three of them were laying on the balcony of a cabin on Deck Eleven. After a few seconds, Charlie heard the door to the cabin above crash open. He got to his feet. "Come on. They'll figure it out in a couple of minutes."

Chris and Tabby nodded and got back to their feet as well. Tabby tried to open the balcony door. "It's locked."

Charlie picked up one of the metal-framed patio chairs and swung it as hard as he could. The door shook in its frame, but the glass held.

"It's hurricane proof," Chris told him. "It's going to take more than that."

"I've already done this once, and the fun crowd in the cabin above us is gonna figure out where we went in a few minutes. And then they're gonna start trying to figure out how to join us down here. So instead of telling me how this can't work, I suggest you give me a hand and *make* it work."

It took the two of them about thirty seconds to kick the door out of its frame. It took them another minute to get out of the cabin, and into the elevator. Chris slid his keycard into the slot in the elevator and the doors closed.

* * *

"What's that?" Tabby grabbed Charlie's collar and pulled it down. "Oh, shit."

She let go and Charlie turned to face her. When he saw the look on her face, his blood went cold. "How bad is it?"

Chris looked at Charlie, then at Tabby. "What? How bad is what?"

Tabby licked her lips and Charlie took a deep breath. He unbuttoned the top three buttons on his shirt and turned back around. Pulling the top of the shirt down, he answered without looking back. "One of them bit me when we were fighting." He pulled his shirt back up, turned back to face them, and repeated his question. "Now, how bad is it?"

Tabby and Chris looked at one another. Finally Tabby answered. "It doesn't look too bad. Barely broke the skin."

Charlie nodded. "But it *did* break the skin, didn't it?"

"Yeah."

He took a deep breath, calming his nerves. "How long you figure I have before I turn into one of those things?"

Again, his companions looked at each other. Chris swallowed, then shrugged helplessly. "Who knows, man? We don't know what's causing it. I told you about that slick on the water. It could be air born, it could be something that got into some of the ship's food, it could be—"

"It could be something in the blood or saliva of someone who's already infected," Charlie finished. "Couldn't it?" He looked from one to the other. "Couldn't it?"

Tabby nodded. "It could."

Like I said boy, seven ways to Sunday.

Charlie handed his knife to Tabby. "I saw you lost yours on the bridge. Maybe you should hold on to this."

She nodded and reached for the blade. As she took it, he looked her in the eyes. "Don't you let me turn into one of those fucking hyenas. If I start laughing, you... you..."

He swallowed and Tabby solemnly met his gaze. "I will."

Charlie swallowed again around the lump that had formed in his throat and nodded. "All right, then." He turned back around as the elevator doors slid open, and the three of them stepped out to join the rest of the group below decks.

CHAPTER 70
ERICA CHAPMAN
LANE ENDS – 750 FT.

HOV LANE ENDS - 750 FT.

From that sign on, the ramp began to slope decidedly downward. Matt drove slowly as they dropped into the smoke that covered the lower streets. He and Erica both scanned the street ahead nervously as they reached the bottom of the ramp. The GPS indicated that they should turn left onto Franklin Street. Matt eased them forward and took a left, passing beneath a huge overpass.

"How far to our turn?" Matt kept his eyes on the road. His knuckles were white where they gripped the wheel.

Erica looked at the GPS. "About half a mile. Then you turn left on San Jacinto."

Matt simply nodded. On their left, they passed an older building. Smoke poured steadily from within, and Erica could see lazy flames licking through heat waves in the air out front. A three-foot-high concrete barrier bore the words UNITED ST TES POST OFFICE. She noted the missing A and wondered if it had been there before the chucklers outbreak.

There were plenty of wrecks on the road, but the street was wide enough that it would have taken a six or seven car pileup to block their way. Erica watched the street signs as they passed, confirming the route that the GPS had plotted for them. As they passed Congress Avenue, Erica let her gaze be drawn to the skyscrapers in that direction. It looked like they were less than half a dozen city blocks from the edge of downtown proper, and smoke roiled through the streets like a living thing, pouring down the embankment of Buffalo Bayou. Congress passed over the bayou, and she could see movement in the smoke. "More of them on the right."

Matt glanced over, and grunted. "Too far away to be much of a problem."

There was a huge pileup at the next intersection, but he simply hopped the curb and drove through the lawn of a bordering building. They passed another major intersection at Louisiana Boulevard, and within a few blocks, they were moving into an obviously older section of town. The buildings were an old-style brick and stonework, much different from the more modern glass and steel exteriors of current architecture. More disconcerting though, the streets were also considerably narrower.

Matt drove onto the sidewalk to get around a pileup and deeper into the old business district. Erica looked at the GPS again and pointed ahead. "Our turn should be two blocks ahead."

Two men rushed at the Xterra from behind some parked cars on the left, and Matt swerved to the right and accelerated. They passed the chucklers, and Matt was just slowing back down when a body dropped to the sidewalk to their right. Matt slammed on the brakes and if it hadn't been for her seatbelt, Erica would have hit the dash. "What the hell?" Matt blinked at the unexpected sight of the woman on the sidewalk trying to get back to her feet. The fact that her right leg refused to bear her weight without bending at an unnatural angle slowed her down, but her maniacal laughter lent an otherworldly eeriness to the scene. Apparently unperturbed, the woman leaned forward and began to drag herself across the concrete in their direction.

As they watched, a man in a torn and bedraggled business jacket, but oddly enough not wearing any pants, dropped into sight from somewhere above and landed on the woman, crushing her torso, and causing her mouth to spurt blood. Erica yelped in fear.

"What the hell?" Matt repeated, leaning forward and trying to see where the man had come from. Erica leaned toward the side window and saw another man leaning out of a third story window of the old building to their right. Meanwhile, No Pants tumbled to the sidewalk and lay stunned for a moment, but staggered to his feet after only a few seconds. He looked at Matt and Erica, grinned hugely, did a little dance step and splayed his hands at them in a comedic jazz hands movement. Then he sprinted toward Erica's door, even as the next man jumped from the window. Three other windows began spewing people, and suddenly, a crowd was forming on the sidewalk.

"Matt, let's go, let's go, let's go!" Erica screamed.

Matt shook himself out of his stunned stupor and hit the gas, pulling away just as No Pants grabbed at Erica's door handle. To her utter horror, the handle clicked and the man started to pull it open, but lost his grip as the Xterra accelerated. Panting in fear, Erica yanked the door closed and slapped her hand down on the lock. She looked over at Matt who shook his head as he drove. "They jumped out of the damned windows? Who does that?"

He raced through the next intersection and Erica glanced down at the GPS. "Turn at the next street."

Matt nodded and cut the wheel at San Jacinto. "Now go four tenths of a mile…" Her voice trailed off as she saw what was ahead of them. A jumble of burning vehicles completely blocked the street two blocks ahead of them. It wasn't a massive accident. They had simply been driven or abandoned there, and then torched. Inky black smoke flowed off of them and hundreds of revelers danced through the cloud.

Matt came to a stop just as the closest partiers noticed the SUV. There were a few cocked heads, almost as if they were trying to determine whether or not to believe there really was a bright yellow SUV idling in the street before them. Then they began shrieking with laughter and raced toward the Xterra.

"This would be a good time to go, Matt. A really good time to go!"

Matt must have thought so too. He put the shifter in reverse and started to back up. Something slammed into the back windshield, and he stomped the brake again. Erica spun in her seat to find No Pants drawing his hand back to slap his open palm against the vehicle again. Past him, through the cracked and bloody window, there was another crowd of laughing faces rushing at them.

Matt didn't need Erica to tell him to hurry. No Pants was shoved to the side as they powered past him and into the mass of his companions behind him. Erica and Matt found themselves four wheeling through the crowd from behind while a larger one rushed at them from the street before them. The SUV struggled against the mass of bodies behind them. Once again, Erica felt the sickening bounce of multiple speed bumps in the road.

She looked past the crowd behind them and saw more and more chucklers emerging from various buildings all around them. "Oh god, Matt. There's more of them."

* * *

The SUV cleared No Pants and his traveling companions, and Matt cut the wheel sharply to the right. He shifted back into drive and punched the gas, spinning the tires as they tore down the nearest clear street. Erica glanced down at the GPS, but it was busy recalculating their route. In the meantime, even more people began streaming from the entrances of buildings. "Why are they coming out now?" Erica asked.

"Must be all the noise," Matt shouted. "Between spinning the tires, and the mob chasing after us, we're getting a little loud."

Erica looked up to see a DO NOT ENTER sign in front of them. "You're going the wrong way!"

Matt blew through the intersection. "If a cop stops us, I'll apologize."

Erica swallowed, mentally kicking herself. "Sorry."

Another crowd milled about in an empty parking lot ahead and Matt turned left, again going against the light, as the laughing mob began running toward the yellow SUV. "Where are we?" he asked.

She looked at the GPS again. "You're going too fast for the thing to keep up. Every time you turn, it starts to recalculate again."

"Give me a minute to put enough distance between us and those... just give me a minute and I'll try to slow down." Matt was trying to keep calm, but Erica could see how rattled he was. Ironically, that helped her to keep calm.

He swerved left, then right to avoid more small wrecks as the road began to curve more to the left. Ahead, the wrecks became too dense and he cursed. Erica looked behind them and saw the crowd coming toward them from two blocks behind. She licked her lips. "Matt? They're—"

"Yeah, I see 'em." He drove over the concrete esplanade and into the inbound lane, cursing quietly as he was once more forced to drive back toward downtown. But there were fewer accidents on that side of the road, and he was able to make better time. They left the mob behind, driving back into the smoke.

"Any luck with that thing yet?" Matt jutted his chin at the GPS screen, reminding Erica of what she needed to be doing.

"Give me a minute." The progress bar showed that the GPS was seventy-three percent completed with recalculating their new route.

"Faster would be better. We've got more of 'em up ahead."

She looked up and saw another crowd running toward them from several of the buildings around them. "Turn here," Erica pointed to the left.

He turned without asking why, and she lost sight of their pursuers. "Now turn right in two blocks and slow down."

"Where are we going?"

"We need to get where those people can't see us anymore, or they're going to keep coming."

Matt grunted and turned left. "Good thinking." He slowed, and after another block, the GPS finally pinged that it had completed its rerouting.

"Where to?" Matt asked.

Erica cursed. "It wants us to turn around."

"Well that sure as hell ain't happening." Matt continued to drive straight.

She tapped the screen several times, taking it out of trip mode, and activating the map function. The GPS showed about a nine block grid and showed her that they were on Ruiz Street. She tapped the minus symbol on the screen to zoom out until she could see the freeway system surrounding the downtown area.

"There's a freeway up ahead," Matt said. "Can you see where the closest entrance ramp is?"

"I think there's one up ahead on the left."

"Good." He drove to the freeway and turned left, shaking his head as he saw the ramp ahead of them. "Figures."

There was a ramp, all right. But it was another exit ramp, and it rose up toward another source of billowing black smoke. He looked at Erica. "What do you think?"

She considered only a second. "We already know what's behind us."

"True enough."

Matt drove around a small, two-car accident near the base of the ramp and drove toward the smoke. As they reached the top, he whistled. "That must have been one hell of a sight last night."

In front of them, a fuel tanker had driven off of the overpass above, landed on several cars on the freeway before them, and the entire conflagration had left nothing more than a charred and twisted mass of metal and plastic. Most of the flames were out by now, though some small flickers still showed inside a couple of blackened chassis on the road. But while there was no longer any real danger from the fires, there was no way they were getting past the twisted wreckage blocking the freeway. "Looks like we're going to have to keep heading south for a while." Matt drove to the top of the ramp and turned the Xterra onto the freeway, heading southward on I-59.

They made good time for a few minutes, as the inferno behind them had blocked any traffic from making it this far on the freeway. But after only a few miles, more cars began to appear... more cars, and more wrecks. Within five minutes, they were once more driving at a maddeningly slow pace, winding their way through wrecks every few yards.

Erica put the GPS back to finding them a new route to Montgomery, and eventually, it quit trying to get them to turn around, and selected a route that took them from I-59 onto the Gulf Freeway toward Galveston. It wanted them to then cut to the 610 loop, routing around the east side of Houston and travel back north to I-10.

When the ramp onto 610 proved impassable, they rerouted yet again, once more heading farther south. This time, their goal was the Sam Houston Parkway. It was a roundabout way of getting there, but by that time, Erica really didn't care. She just wanted to get out of the nightmare that downtown Houston had become.

CHAPTER 71
LINTON BOWERS
LOSING IT

"We got runners on the right," Emmet called out. "They're moving to cut you off, Lesslie. You're gonna have to punch it."

Lesslie hesitated. "Lots of debris on the freeway. I'm not sure we can—"

"If you don't speed up, they're going to be blocking the road. You gotta move it!"

Linton leaned over the back seat to see the crowd running at them from the right. "He's right, Lesslie. It's what *might* happen with the debris, or what we *know* will happen if that crowd gets us."

"Shit." Lesslie sped up and the sedan bounced as they drove over bits and pieces of automobile wreckage. "Getting on the freeway like this was a mistake."

Linton silently agreed, but figured there wasn't any use worrying about it at the moment. There were more important things to concentrate on. He jumped at the sound as the tires threw pieces of twisted metal up to strike the undercarriage. They hit with thuds and pops loud enough to make him wonder if they weren't tearing the car apart.

"Gotta go faster. They'll be in front of us in about ten seconds!" Emmet's voice sounded a little panicked, even through his voicemitter.

Linton felt the car accelerate more as Lesslie put the gas pedal to the floor, and the car bounced more violently across the debris field. The sounds of debris hitting under the car were deafening. Michelle moved beside him, calmly drawing her pistol and making sure there was a round in the chamber. Linton nodded, and did the same.

"Not gonna make it," Lesslie said through gritted teeth.

"Yes you will," Linton reassured her. "Just don't let off that gas, no matter what."

"And if they get in front of us?"

Linton caught her eyes in the rearview mirror. "No matter what," he repeated.

She looked a bit panicked, but nodded.

"Everybody got their seatbelts on?" Linton yelled. "Lesslie, you're probably going to clip the leader. Don't stop no matter what, you hear me?"

"Oh god. I don't know if I—"

"If you stop, we're all dead!"

The frontrunner of the mob stepped out in front of them. Lesslie swerved to the left, scraping the driver's side of the vehicle along the concrete center barrier. Sparks flew, and Linton gritted his teeth at the jarring sound of metal scraping concrete just outside his window.

Ultimately, even swerving as far as she did wasn't enough. The man folded over the hood of the car with a jolt that shook them all. But Lesslie did as she had been told, and her foot never left the accelerator.

"Holy shit!" Emmet shouted, as the man hit the windshield right in front of him before bouncing violently off the car and into the rest of the crowd. Linton had a brief flash of his face as it splattered blood on the broken glass. Even as the man had died, he had been laughing.

Then they were past the crowd and tearing down the freeway. Linton felt his heart pounding in his chest, and he was breathing so heavily he wondered if he was in danger of hyperventilating. When he felt he could speak, he asked, "Everyone okay?"

They all nodded, but no one actually said anything.

Linton looked behind them as the crowd fell behind. When he felt they were in no danger of the mob catching them, he touched Lesslie on the shoulder. "That was a great piece of driving, but you can slow down now."

He watched her in the rearview as she swallowed nervously and nodded. She let off the gas and they began to slow.

"Damn!" Emmet said, following it with, "I can't believe we made it!"

Linton glanced over to see that his wife was crying. He put a hand on her shoulder. "You okay?"

She sniffed and nodded.

"We made it!" Emmet repeated, and pumped his fist against the ceiling. "Yeah!"

And he started to laugh. "We made it. We... heh... we fucking made it! Heh heh... Oh no..." He spun to look back, and through his mask, Linton could see a look of horror in his eyes. It only lasted a second, and then his friend's eyes widened and he was suddenly laughing. He jumped toward Lesslie, and only the fact that he still wore his seatbelt saved her. She screamed, swerving the car as she pulled her body against her door, straining to stay out of his reach.

But while he might not be able to jump at her, she was easily within reach of his fists. Linton reached forward, trying to restrain his old friend, but his own seatbelt held him back at first, and Lesslie screamed again as Emmet pistoned a fist at her. Lesslie's head fell sideways, and Michelle screamed as the car swerved out of control.

Linton looked up to see the rear end of a trailer just before they impacted.

* * *

He couldn't have been out for more than a few seconds, but the sound of approaching laughter jolted him awake like ice water in the face. Linton looked over at his wife. "Michelle?" He shook her shoulder and she groaned. "Michelle! Wake up, they're coming."

Her eyes flicked open at that. She blinked a few times and fumbled with her seatbelt.

"You all right?"

She nodded as she grabbed her pack and rifle from where they had fallen to the floor. She looked up, and gasped. Linton followed her gaze to the front seat. Lesslie sat, eyes closed, twisted against the driver's side door. She was still and unmoving, and blood seeped down the window behind her head. He reached over the seat and checked her pulse, confirming what he feared. "She's dead." The airbag had deployed on impact, but she had already been twisted against the door where she'd tried to get away from Emmet. The violence of the deployment had slammed her head into the door frame hard enough to kill her.

Linton looked over at Emmet. His old friend still breathed, but was unconscious. Still, the man chuckled lightly as he slept.

The sound of laughter outside got louder.

"Lint, we gotta go!" Michelle threw her door open and crouched, shouldering the rifle.

Linton scrambled across the seat and got out beside her. The crowd was less than a hundred yards away. He reached back into the car to grab his own gear and weapons. Seeing Emmet beginning to stir, he opened the front door and yanked his friend's pistol from his holster.

"Outta time, Lint!"

He looked once more at Emmet, remembering his thoughts about whether or not his friend would be able to kill him if he went crazy. He raised the pistol in his hand, put it against Emmet's head.

"Linton! We have to go. Now!"

Unable to bring himself to pull the trigger, he turned and picked up his pack. Together, he and Michelle ran between the wrecks, heading down the freeway.

CHAPTER 72
CHARLES GRIFFE
"WHO'S FRED HARTMAN?"

Taking the announcements to the rest of the group had been a good news, bad news situation. Everyone had been saddened by the loss of Shane. But other than his girlfriend Julie, none of them had known him all that well, but he had been one of their number, and that counted for something. The news about Houston had been welcome, and if Chris hadn't prefaced the announcement with the now standard warning about laughter, it would have undoubtedly been received with smiles and whoops of joy.

Charlie had asked Tabby and Chris to give him a few minutes to let Felicia know about his bite before they told everyone else. They had agreed, and while they were talking, he pulled Felicia aside.

"What is it, Charlie?"

"It might be nothing. But I figured you should hear it from me, just in case."

Her face got serious. "You're worrying me, sweetie. What's wrong?"

"When we were up on the bridge, there was a fight. A bunch of the crazy people attacked us."

"That's when they killed Shane?"

"Yeah."

"That was so terrible. I wonder if we'll ever find out who his family was. Someone will need to let them know what happened when we get to Houston."

"Felicia? This ain't about Shane. Focus, baby."

"Sure. I'm sorry, sweetie. It's just…"

"I got bit, Felicia. One of the crazies bit me."

353

Felicia's jaw snapped shut and her brow wrinkled as she processed what he told her.

Yeah, she ain't the sharpest tool in the shed. Is she, boy?

"Does that mean you're going to get crazy, too?" Genuine fear showed in her eyes, and she unconsciously pulled a bit farther away from him.

"We don't know. Until we know more, you should probably stay close to Tabby and Chris."

"Do they know?"

"Yeah."

She was quiet for a few seconds, thinking about it. "Charlie?"

"Yeah, baby?"

"Are you gonna die?"

He pulled her close, feeling closer to her than he had in quite some time. "No, baby. I'm gonna beat this thing. Like I said, we don't even know how this stuff spreads. It probably won't have any effect."

She looked unconvinced.

He hesitated before finishing. "But if you see me start smiling or laughing, you run and tell Tabby or Chris, okay?"

Her eyes widened as she once again realized what he was telling her. "You're scaring me, Charlie."

He wanted to smile at her, convince her with his cheerfulness that everything would be all right. But he couldn't even do that. For all they knew, smiling would trigger the craziness that had taken over the ship. And if he were to be perfectly honest with himself, he didn't really feel much like smiling anyway. "Yeah, I'm scaring me, too."

* * *

Charlie awoke to the sensation of Tabby gently shaking his shoulder. He blinked, trying to force his eyes to focus. "What? What time is it?"

She kept her voice low, so as not to awaken Felicia, who slept on the floor beside him. "It's a little after one. You seen Chris?" she asked.

"I haven't seen anything but the inside of my eyelids for a while now. Why?"

"He was acting all worried earlier. I wanted to ask him what was wrong, but Celina needed some help with Merl. He's got a heart fibrillation, and he's out of his meds. I wanted to see if Chris could take some of us to the ship's infirmary."

Charlie looked down at Felicia sleeping beside him, then quietly got to his feet. "I'll help you find him."

It took them almost an hour, but they finally found him back in an office on the mess deck, cursing quietly at a computer screen. Tabby and Charlie looked at one another before Tabby interrupted Chris's tirade. "Chris?"

Chris grabbed his meat cleaver off the desk and whirled. He relaxed when he saw them and turned back to the screen. "You really shouldn't sneak up on people, what with..." he waved the cleaver absently in the air, "...all this crap going on."

"Sorry," Tabby said. "Something wrong?"

Chris's shoulders slumped. "Yeah, something's wrong." He turned back to face them. "I think we need to go back up to the bridge."

"What!" Charlie was shaking his head before Chris could say any more. "No fucking way! We barely made it out last time."

Tabby put her hand on his arm to calm him down, looking at Chris the entire time. When Charlie clamped his jaw shut, she asked Chris once more, "What's wrong?"

With a huge sigh, he pointed at the computer screen. "Fred Hartman."

Charlie and Tabby stepped closer to the monitor. "Who's Fred Hartman?" Charlie asked.

Tabby was closer to the screen, blocking his view. "Not who."

"What?"

She nodded. "Exactly."

Charlie blinked, trying to figure out where the conversation had derailed. Tabby stepped aside and pointed him to the screen. "Fred Hartman is a bridge."

Charlie peered at the screen and saw that it displayed a web page. *Fred Hartman Bridge Statistics*. With the power back online, Chris had managed to get to the internet. Displayed on the screen was a page that explained the history of how the bridge had been built. On the right hand side of the web page was a column that showed number of lanes, length of spans, and a variety of other specifics. A small paragraph was highlighted.

The Fred Hartman is a cable-stayed bridge that traverses the Houston Ship Channel as part of State Highway 99 (aka The Grand Parkway). It is 147 feet wide, 436 feet high at the apex of the pylons, with a vertical clearance of 262 feet. Clearance beneath the bridge is 178 feet.

He remembered Chris's comment about the Bahama Queen being a floating, eighteen-story luxury hotel. "Didn't you tell us the ship was about two-hundred-fifty feet tall?"

Chris nodded. "And that's why we have to get back up to the bridge. I need to reprogram our course. Otherwise," he looked at his watch, "we crash into the Hartman in about two and a half hours."

"Are you fucking kidding me?" Charlie looked at his watch.

"So what do we do, then?" Charlie was surprised to hear his own frustration echoed in Tabby's voice. She was usually the calm one of their little trio. "Are we supposed to just float around out here until we run out of food and water? Or maybe we're supposed to jump overboard and swim the last hundred miles to shore?"

"No, I'll reprogram the course to stop us in the middle of the Ship Channel, and then we can launch one of the life boats."

Charlie blinked. That actually sounded like a good idea. He hadn't even considered the life boats. Then he took the thought a little farther. "Why don't we just shut the engines back off and take one of the life boats to shore now?"

"They don't have that kind of range. They're only designed to get people off the ship and keep them in the same area for rescue. Their range is only about ten miles or so. But if we get into the Ship Channel and drop anchor, we can take one of the life boats to shore and get with the Port Authority. Let them figure out what to do with the rest of the passengers, crazy or otherwise."

Charlie nodded. "That makes sense." He wiped his hand across his face. "I'm just not wild about making another run to the bridge. We barely made it out of there alive. What if another group of crazies catch us?"

"Look, I'm open for any better ideas. You got any?"

Charlie looked to see if Tabby had anything. When she shook her head, his shoulders slumped in defeat. "All right. When?"

Chris shrugged. "It's not going to get any better if we wait. Is there anything you need to do here?"

"You mean you want to go now?"

"Unless you have something better to do."

"Hang on," Tabby said. "Who are we taking? You don't mean just the three of us, do you? There were four of us before, and we're down one person."

Chris shook his head. "Who else? There's no one else in the group who's in good enough shape for something like this. The rest of the group is either too old, or too…" Chris looked at Charlie, "delicate."

"Me? Delicate?"

"I meant Felicia."

"Hang on. That actually brings up a good point. We need to talk about Charlie, too." Tabby looked embarrassed as she turned to face him. "How are you feeling?"

"What? I'm fine. What do you…?" Then his father's voice reminded him. *She means are you fixin' to start laughing and biting on one of them.* "Oh. The bite."

"Yes. I'm sorry, Charlie, but I have to ask. Do you feel in the least bit… different?"

"Other than aching all over from being beat half to death, no. And thanks so much for the kind words of support."

"I'm sorry, but we have to think about all the possibilities. What if we hand you another knife and you decide to start using it on us?"

"Jesus H, woman. Talk about a vote of confidence." Charlie started to get angry. "Look, I'm bit. I get it. Hell, I get it a hell of a lot better than you do. But the real problem isn't mine. I feel fine, and I know it. It's you that has to decide whether or not you trust me enough to want me near you with a blade. 'Cause if you think I'm going back out there unarmed, you're the ones that're fucking crazy."

He stared at them for a moment, letting them think about that. Finally, Chris turned to Tabby. "He's right. We either take him with us or leave him here. We might need him if things get rough up there again. And we can't expect him to go with us unarmed. Bottom line, we need to trust him."

Tabby nodded, then turned to face Charlie. She drew the knife he had given her earlier and handed it back to him, hilt first. "Sorry."

He shoved the knife into his belt. "Yeah, me too."

* * *

They left after a few quick words of explanation to the group. Felicia was as clingy as ever, but Charlie didn't have time to worry about that. He, Tabby, and Chris walked back to the elevator, and Chris pulled the pass key out of his shirt pocket and slid it into the slot to call the elevator below decks again. The three of them looked at each other in silence as they waited for the doors to open. A chime announced the arrival of the elevator and the doors whisked open. Chris stepped inside and held the doors open while Tabby and Charlie both hesitated. "You guys coming?"

Charlie swallowed and stepped inside, Tabby right behind him. Charlie took a deep breath. "Yeah, let's get it over with."

Chris pressed the button for Deck Twelve and downward pressure told Charlie they were moving up. They all gripped their weapons tighter as the elevator slowed. Another chime announced their arrival, and the doors slid open into hell.

The sound of dozens of hoarse hyenas invaded the elevator as hands reached through, grabbing at the three of them. Charlie jumped back to avoid the first grasping hands, and Tabby screamed as a young boy in the tattered remains of his pajama bottoms threw himself at her. Charlie stabbed at a man who stepped into the elevator and attacked. He rammed the knife into the man's chest and kicked him back out of the elevator. He turned to pull the boy off of Tabby, and sliced the giggling boy's throat as he pushed him back out, as well. Three others rushed forward as, out of the corner of his eye, Charlie saw several hands latch onto Chris and begin pulling him out of the elevator.

"Charlie!" Chris's voice was panicked as he tried to fight off his attackers. Charlie reached toward him but another man jumped inside. Tabby stepped forward to help Charlie and the two of them quickly dispatched him. He pushed forward to where Chris now desperately held on to the doorway of the elevator as three men beat and pulled at him. His pleading eyes begged for help as his fingers began to lose their purchase on the door.

Charlie stabbed one of Chris's attackers, but another immediately took his place. Charlie looked past Chris into the corridor and saw dozens more of the crazies pushing forward. He immediately realized they didn't have a chance. He stabbed at another of the attackers, grabbing at Chris's arm, trying to pull him back into the elevator, but all he succeeded in doing was loosening the man's hold on the door. Chris screamed as one of the attackers leaned in and bit his ear.

You ain't gonna save him, boy. Best look out for yourself.

Charlie stabbed another crazy, and from the corner of his eye saw Tabby facing the other way, fighting off two others. He heaved a disheveled old woman out of his way, pushing closer to Chris. He leaned in to where Chris could hear him. "I'm sorry, man."

Chris looked confused as Charlie reached into the young man's pocket, and took his keycards. He shoved the card with the blue stripe into the slot and pressed the door close button. Chris's hands were in the way, but Charlie quickly peeled the fingers away. With a scream, Chris fell back into the horde and the doors began to slide closed.

"No!" Tabby started to move forward, but Charlie yanked her back.

"It's too late."

The doors closed on Chris's screams and Charlie pressed the button to take them back below decks.

CHAPTER 73
ERICA CHAPMAN
SOMEONE'S USING GUNS

"This is absolutely ridiculous!" Matt said. "Three hours." He looked at Erica, as if daring her to deny it. "Three freakin' hours and we're barely out of Houston. And we're *still* not on the road we need to be on!" He slowed yet again to drive past another wrecked car in the middle of the lane.

Erica winced as she noticed the body of a young woman behind the steering wheel.

"See anything?"

Matt's question startled her out of her funk and she looked up and down the frontage road that ran beside the freeway. "A few stragglers headed this way, but they're a block away."

Matt grunted and sped up a bit, leaving the chucklers behind them. Five minutes later, Matt harrumphed and slowed the SUV. "Well, there's something you don't see every day." He pulled up beside a man in a gas mask jogging in the emergency lane. As they pulled near, Matt rolled his window down. "Hey buddy, you need a ride?"

The man spun, and leapt toward the Xterra. Through the mask, Erica could see he was laughing hysterically. Matt hit the gas and they sped past the man and up the next overpass. Erica looked back at the lone chuckler as he chased after them. "I guess the mask didn't help." She continued to scan for chucklers on the feeder.

A few minutes later, Matt's cursing pulled her attention back to the scene before them. A mass of twisted vehicles completely blocked the freeway ahead. There was no way to skirt around them this time. Erica scanned the frontage road.

"You're gonna have to cut across the grass here, and get back on the feeder."

Matt looked to where she pointed. "What's the GPS say?"

She tapped the screen a few times, zooming the view out. She traced a crooked route on the screen. "Looks like another—"

The sound of gunfire interrupted her. Matt slammed on the brakes and looked around frantically. "Where's that coming from?"

"I think it's on the other side of that wreckage."

Matt rolled his window back down and stuck his head out. After a quick moment, he pulled back into the cab and nodded. "You're right." He looked at her, still not letting off the brake. "What do you think?"

Before she could answer, the ground shook, and was almost immediately followed by the sound of an explosion. Seconds later, thick, black, smoke rose into the air ahead of them. The staccato chatter of more gunfire cut through the air.

Matt looked at her. "This is your rodeo. What do you want to do?"

Erica looked back and saw the chuckler in the gas mask was getting close again. She didn't hesitate. "I haven't seen a single chuckler using anything more than a club or a torch. If someone's using guns, I think we need to see if we can help them."

He nodded. "That's what I was thinking, too." He cut the wheel and quickly pulled out across the grass and onto the feeder road, once more leaving gas mask behind. They drove toward the sounds of gunfire.

CHAPTER 74
LINTON BOWERS
CAVALRY

Linton looked behind him as he ran. He really didn't need to. The constant sound of laughter told him the mob was still behind him. But it looked like he and Michelle were at least putting some distance between them. He looked forward again to see Michelle had stopped.

"What are you doing?" he panted. "No time to stop."

She looked right, then left. Linton caught up with her and saw what had stopped her. Ahead of them was a solid wall of twisted and charred vehicles. A fuel tanker bearing the logo of a multi-national oil company lay on its side, tangled amidst several cars and trucks, apparently having wrecked into them in the night. It was just over the top of the overpass, so there was no going over the side unless they wanted to shatter their legs on the road below. And there was a gap between the northbound and southbound lanes that was simply too large for them to contemplate jumping across.

"Linton?"

"Start climbing!"

"What?"

"Climb over! I'll cover you. When you get up, you turn and cover me while I climb."

"But I—"

"There's no time. Go!"

Linton turned and hefted his rifle, sighting on the first of the crowd. *Us or them.* He began firing into the leading line as they ran toward him. They were still about two hundred yards away, and staggering as much as running, but there were so many of them that he couldn't miss. He pulled the trigger as quickly as he could sight in on a target and was through his first magazine in a matter of seconds. Hand shaking, he dropped the spent magazine in one pocket with a shaking hand. "Just like in the drills," he chided himself. He slammed another magazine into the receiver and was firing again in less than three seconds.

The report of Michelle's rifle sounded from over his head, and she shouted at him. "Come on, Lint!"

He swung his rifle over his back, letting it hang behind him as he scrambled up the hood of the first car in the pileup, making sure not to cross his wife's line of fire. He slipped for a heart-stopping second as he stepped onto the roof of the next car, then reached the tanker truck. Laying on its side, the truck's underbelly was in front of him, and there were ample handholds. He jumped from the roof of the pickup to one of the eighteen wheels and clambered up atop the overturned wreck. Once he was in place, he tapped Michelle on the shoulder. "Get down the other side and keep running. Let me know when you're down, and I'll be right behind you."

To her credit, she didn't try to argue this time. She scrambled down the other side of the wreckage and yelled. "I'm clear!"

Linton scrambled down the side of the truck, and as he hit the ground, he saw his wife standing quite some distance away digging in her pack. "What are you doing?"

She pulled out a road flare and he saw the thin stream of liquid trickling down the freeway. Fearing that she might be planning what it looked like she was planning, he looked along the stream, tracing it back to where it leaked out of the fuel truck from a hatch in the top—the top that was now on the side of the truck. "Oh shit!"

He sprinted to get as much distance between himself and the explosion in waiting. Once he drew close to Michelle, she dropped the flare into the stream of fuel and the two of them ran down the back side of the overpass. Once they reached the point where the bridge turned into embankment, they climbed over the concrete side barrier and onto the grass on the other side.

Linton ducked behind the concrete barrier beside his wife, both of them panting from the run. He peeked back over, watching as the leading edge of the mob jumped down from the tanker, a huge crowd coming into sight behind them as they scaled the side of the truck. He looked to the flaming trail as it progressed relentlessly toward its goal. It happened much slower than the movies had always shown, but as he watched, the flames licked up the side of the tanker and finally reached the hatch on the top of the truck. There was a second's pause, and Linton imagined the nearly instantaneous chain reaction that must have gone on inside the tank as the flames expanded inside it until there was no longer any room for further expansion. The pressure would likely build up within the confines of the metal cylinder until the walls of the tank were ripped apart, freeing the burning fuel in a massive fireball.

Whether the process was inevitable, or they simply got lucky, the truck went up in an explosion that he could feel from more than a football field length away. But there were still plenty of the mob that had already made it past the truck, and they were still coming after them. "Come on, babe. We gotta go."

Linton and Michelle jogged down the embankment to the level ground of the feeder road. As they hit the street, Linton looked back to find several of their pursuers stumbling over the concrete barrier, still chasing after Michelle and him with the single-mindedness of insects. He turned and fired several rounds into them then continued down the road.

The other side of the feeder hosted a neighborhood, and Linton recalled the insanity of his own subdivision yesterday. *Was it really only yesterday?* He quickly scanned the area for anyone coming out of the houses. He ran for the sidewalk.

Beside him, Michelle looked over her shoulder, slowed, and while jogging backward, opened fire as well. After three shots, she stumbled and went down with a shout. Her rifle went flying from her grasp.

"You okay?"

"Fine." She was already crawling after her weapon. Linton immediately turned, dropped to one knee and began firing again. He was momentarily surprised at how few of the crazies still pursued them. The explosion had killed or stopped most of them, and there were only ten or fifteen still coming.

How many rounds do I have? Enough to take them all before they get to us?

He heard Michelle shout at him. "Ready!"

"Take a knee and start shooting the ones on the right. I'll shoot from the left, and we'll meet in the middle."

Michelle's rifle barked beside him. Between the two of them, they took out the last of their pursuers in less than a minute. Linton turned to make sure they hadn't attracted any unwanted attention, but there was still no movement in any of the surrounding buildings. "Let's get moving before any more of them—"

"Lint?"

"What?" Michelle was looking past him. He dropped back to his knee and swung his rifle up, thinking that another crowd was coming at them. Instead, he saw a lemon-yellow SUV driving toward them. "Stay behind me, and keep your rifle ready if things go bad."

"Lint?"

"What?" He looked at her over his shoulder, determined to keep himself between the coming strangers and his wife. The look on her face told him she was irritated. "What?" he repeated.

"You're being ridiculous. I'm not helpless, and they aren't crazy. The crazy ones can't drive, remember?"

There was no chance to argue. The SUV pulled up in the street away from them, and the front doors opened. A man and a woman stepped out, weapons drawn, but pointed down and away. The man looked around at the bodies scattered in the street before turning his attention to them.

"We were going to see if you folks needed any help," he said. "But I can see you already have things under control."

The woman wasn't quite as glib. "Are you all right?" Linton could see the tension in her gun hand as she asked. He opened his mouth to answer, but Michelle beat him to the punch.

"We're tired, depressed as hell, and scared. But we're not crazy, if that's what you're asking."

The man nodded. "We can see that. Far as we can tell, chucklers can't use guns."

"Chucklers?" Linton got back to his feet.

The woman nodded. "It's what they were calling them on the news the other night."

They all stood in silence for a moment before the woman put her pistol in its holster and stepped forward, hand extended. "I'm Erica."

Michelle stepped up and shook her hand, as Matt walked around the SUV and shook with Linton. Once the greetings were done, Erica cocked her head at Michelle. "I don't suppose you guys have a cell phone I could borrow?"

CHAPTER 75
CHARLES GRIFFE
RUNNING OUT OF TIME

The loss of Chris hit the group hard, and the news that the ship was going to crash made things even worse. He turned back to the group. "Look, Chris said we only had until about four thirty, or maybe five o'clock. That just gives us…" he looked at his watch, "just about an hour to get to a lifeboat. We need to get moving if we're going to make it."

"How are we supposed to get there if those things are waiting outside the elevators?" Celina asked the question that was on everyone's mind.

"We're gonna have to go back to using the emergency stairwell."

Some of them muttered, but Charlie raised his hands. "Look, the lifeboats are on Deck Six. We're on Deck Two. That's just four flights of stairs. And we have an hour to make it. We can do it, but we have to be careful and get moving."

They muttered for a bit, but eventually acquiesced. As they gathered themselves, Charlie saw that Tabby kept watching him as if she wanted to say something. He pulled her aside. "Something wrong?"

"How'd you get his keys?"

"What?"

"In the elevator. How'd you get Chris's keycards?"

His heart leapt. Had she seen? No, she'd been busy fighting off her own attackers.

"He must have known he was done for. He slipped the key to me just before he let go of the doorway."

She kept looking at him like she didn't know whether or not to believe him, but she didn't say anything more. Still, he could see the distrust in her eyes. *She's gonna be a problem, boy. You might have to do something about her.* But Charlie pushed his father back into a quiet corner of his mind. There was no time to worry about her at the moment.

They gathered again at the door to the emergency stairwell. "Everybody ready?" Charlie scanned the faces around him. Nervous determination showed in most faces, but they all nodded. He pulled the door open and peered into the stairwell. With the power back on, there was no more of the frightening darkness he had dealt with for the first few days. He turned back to the group and put his finger to his lips, then stepped through the door and listened. Nothing.

He climbed to the first landing and turned to face the first doorway. Still nothing. He looked back to where the rest of the group nervously gripped knives. They watched him, waiting for him to give direction. Still silent, he waved them up and moved to the next floor.

They took it slowly, quietly, taking nearly ten minutes to climb two floors. Then Charlie rounded the landing to face the door to Deck Four and saw something he hadn't seen before. The top of the stairs was blocked by a door. It wasn't across the landing as they were for every other floor. This one blocked access to the landing itself.

What the fuck?

Then he saw the card slot beside the door. Pulling Chris's key from his pocket, he slid it into the slot. There was a beep followed by a click as the door unlocked, and Charlie pulled it open. The landing beyond was still empty. He held the door open and waved everyone up. As they passed him, he let the door close quietly. The sign on it read NO ENTRANCE — AUTHORIZED PERSONNEL ONLY.

He turned and found everyone waiting for him. Taking ownership of the key had evidently advanced him to de facto leader of the group. He moved back to the front of the group, squeezing Felicia's hand as he passed. Tabby waited at the head of the stairs and nodded silently at him. Her expression was still somewhat reserved, but he couldn't tell if it was distrust or the tension of the situation.

He crept around the next landing and approached Deck Five. Somewhere far above, a door banged against the metal wall and faint footsteps sounded. Charlie almost panicked and bolted through the door before him, but listening to the sound for a moment told him it was too far away for whoever it was to know he was there. He turned to the others and put a finger to his lips. Everyone froze. A few moments later, another door opened, and the sounds left the stairwell.

Charlie breathed a sigh of relief and moved forward once more. After only a few more minutes, the group stood in front of the door to Deck Six.

Charlie kept his voice to a whisper. "Everybody ready?"

Nervous nods confirmed.

"Wait here for a minute. I'll see if we're clear."

Felicia grabbed his arm, clinging desperately to it. "How long?"

"Just a few... make it five minutes. I'll be back in five minutes, all right, baby?"

She nodded, but he had to gently pry her fingers off his arm. "I'll be right back."

He pulled the door open slowly, peering through the small opening until he could see the coast was clear. As quietly as he could, he slipped through and closed the door silently behind him. Immediately across the corridor to the right was the entrance to the Stardust Theater. The doors were closed, and Charlie hoped they would stay that way. He turned right and crept to the corner of the theater. Peeking around the corner, he checked up and down the starboard corridor, for movement. When he was convinced no one was coming, he slipped quickly up the corridor toward the front exit. He heard a dull pounding coming from up the corridor. He licked his lips nervously and kept going. This close to the front of the ship, the corridor curved around so that he wasn't able to see straight out through to the jogging track, though he saw the light of the doors.

He also saw moving shadows. He pressed his back against the wall and froze, ready to run at the slightest indication that anyone was coming through those doors. After several heartbeats that pounded so hard he was convinced anyone nearby would hear them, he crept forward. As he got closer to the door, the heavy bass beat of a techno soundtrack was obvious. That was what he had heard. Swallowing hard, he inched his head out to where he could see through the door.

His attention was torn between two items of importance before him. First, he saw a huge crowd of what appeared to be several hundred cavorting crazies staggering drunkenly about in a huge, open-air fitness area. There were all sorts of weight machines, treadmills, stationary bicycles, and other fitness equipment. And of course, the jogging track ran right through the middle of it.

And all over the open deck, the crazies cavorted about, grinning, flailing about, and shoving one another as they danced to that heavy bass beat.

You ain't getting through there, boy. Not in one piece anyway.

Charlie growled and slapped his fist against his forehead. "Dammit, old man, you need to shut the fuck up and leave me alone."

As he was about to duck back out of sight, he caught sight of the second item of import. Past the horde of crazies, past the rail and the ocean beyond, he could clearly see land. The ship was headed through a break in the coastline, still under the guidance of Chris's programmed course on the bridge.

They were running out of time.

* * *

Charlie spotted movement back down the corridor as he trotted back to the stairwell. His hand went to his knife, then relaxed as he recognized Tabby. "What are you doing out here?" he hissed at her.

"Checking on you. You said five minutes. It's been almost ten."

He hadn't realized how long he'd taken. "Sorry. I ran into a problem."

"Bad?"

He shrugged. "Might be. I don't really know how it's going to affect us yet. There are hundreds of the crazies blocking our way through the forward exit."

"Crap. Now what?"

"Let's get back to the others. I have an idea."

They were back in just a moment, and Felicia moved to him and pushed her head into his chest.

Clingy little thing, ain't she?

Charlie ignored his dad.

"What's the story?" Merl asked.

"They're all over the jogging track. There's no way to get through."

Celina began her irritating prayer mumbles. "Oh, stop it, Celina," Charlie snapped. "It's just a minor hiccup. I have an idea. We're going to have to go up one more deck."

"What's up there?" Merl asked.

Charlie pulled the key to his and Felicia's cabin out of his back pocket. "My cabin."

CHAPTER 76
ROSS MAYFIELD
PROPHETIC WORDS

They had spent Thanksgiving night resting up. Alex was exhausted from his ordeal at home, both physically and emotionally. He wouldn't talk about it, and Ross figured it wouldn't do either of them any good to rehash whatever had happened, so he left it alone. Ross's own sleep schedule was still screwed up from the drugs he'd taken the day before. All in all, they decided that it made more sense to rest and plan while they had a relatively safe place like his dorm room.

So when they awoke on Friday, they spent the morning packing anything of value into a couple of gear bags. They spent the rest of the morning perusing the internet for more information. There really wasn't anything new, and the social media sites became as much a source of information as any other place. Within hours though, the sharing of knowledge devolved into frantic and repetitious of pleas for help.

Around noon, Alex stood from the desk chair beside Ross, rubbing his face. "This is getting depressing as hell."

Ross had to agree. "So how about I start making good on my promise?"

"What promise?"

"You wanted me to teach you some of the meditation techniques I use. This is liable to be the last free time we have for something like that. At least for the foreseeable future."

Alex shrugged. "Sure. Why not?" He settled onto his knees and closed his eyes.

"Sifu? What are you doing?"

Opening his eyes, Alex cocked an eyebrow at Ross. "Getting ready to meditate."

Ross squatted on his haunches beside him. "Sifu, if you want me to teach you, then you have to accept it when I tell you that you have to throw some of your traditional stuff out the window.

"You have to be able to maintain a calm state of mind no matter what's going on around you. I don't get the luxury of dropping to the floor and closing my eyes every time something distracts me."

Alex nodded. "All right. In this, you're the teacher, not me." He stood back up. "So what should I do?"

"You're familiar with the breathing techniques, and the muscle relaxation and mental state you work for when you meditate, right? Well this is very similar, except you have to teach yourself to work toward them in everyday life."

For the next half hour, he talked about breathing and how it related to muscle contraction. He had Alex walk around the apartment, tightening and relaxing his core muscles while concentrating on his breathing, paying attention to things that his body normally did automatically. Then he had him do things that were contrary to what most people viewed as normal. Things like tightening his abdominal muscles when he exhaled and then, rather than relaxing as he inhaled, he had him concentrate on tightening even more.

"And this is how you keep in the zone?"

"This is just the beginning. You also have to become aware of your involuntary muscles, and eventually learn the mental techniques to control them as well."

"Holy shit."

"It takes a while, but there are tricks that I can teach you that might help."

"How long did it take you to learn all this?"

"I'm still learning. I've been working on it for six or seven years."

Alex's shoulders slumped.

"Don't worry. It won't take you anywhere near that long. I started from scratch, piecing this all together from various disciplines. And I didn't have anyone to help me. You already know basic meditation and breathing techniques, and you understand a lot of what that does to your body. That's a huge advantage."

"So how long for me, then?"

"At a guess? Probably just a few weeks to teach you the techniques I use."

"Really?" Alex's eyebrows raised hopefully.

"How well you learn to apply them depends on you. It's like playing chess. You can learn the moves in several minutes. Mastery can take years."

He was distracted by the chiming of his phone. Alex and Ross looked at one another. Ross pulled the phone from his pocket and stared at the blinking indicator letting him know he had a new text. Oddly enough, the timestamp was a couple of hours old, and he didn't recognize the number. Chalking it up to the unreliable cell network, he took a calming breath and opened the message.

LOST PHONE. CHUCKLERS EVERYWHERE. HOUSTON UNSAFE. TRVLING W/ FRNDS. SAFE 4 NOW. CMING TO MONTGOMERY. TXT THIS # WHEN U GET THIS MSG.—ERICA

Ross struggled to maintain an even heartbeat, taking deep breaths until he could think straight again. He replied.

GOT UR MSG. NTWRK SPOTTY. WILL TXT U IN A FEW WITH PLAN.

He hesitated before finishing the message with LUV U – ROSS.

Alex looked at him. "Was it Erica?"

"Yeah."

Alex was silent for a moment, and Ross saw him struggling with his own inner demons. He knew things must have gone badly for Alex and Jeanette, and he figured she had likely turned into one of the chucklers, or Alex would have brought her with him. Ross knew it must be hard on his friend, knowing that Erica was alive and well, and he almost felt guilty. But Alex recovered quickly.

"So what's the plan?"

He hesitated. "I'm not sure."

"Well, you better make one if we're gonna go get her." He walked back toward the bedroom. "I'll do another walk through and make sure we didn't miss anything useful. You work on putting our route together."

Ross turned back to the computer, pulling up maps, plotting routes, and making contingencies for anything they could think of. Half an hour later, he had a plan. He snapped a picture of his planned route on the computer & texted it to Erica's new number. He followed that with a simple text, in case the picture didn't make it through to her. Eventually, convinced he had done all he could to put everything in motion, Ross shut the laptop down.

"Ready?" Alex's voice from behind called.

Ross turned to see him sitting on the sofa. "Ready." He disconnected his laptop and slipped it in a backpack. He grabbed the power cord and threw it in as well, then grabbed one of the duffels they had packed with as much loose cash, food, water, and drugs, as they could find. He looked up to find Alex already holding the other duffel. They looked at one another in silence for a moment, then Ross nodded at his friend. "Let's do it."

Pistol drawn, Alex led the way as they slipped through the campus. Laughter and screams still sounded from the various buildings, and more than once, Alex waved them into hiding while groups of chucklers ran past. As stealthily as they could manage, they eventually wove their way through the campus to the visitor's parking lot. Once they reached the car, Alex opened the trunk and they tossed the bags inside. Alex reached in and pulled out his *jian*. Ross held his *dao* tucked underhanded behind his left arm. He thought back to his words of just a few days before.

"...when is knowledge of swordplay ever going to be important...?" What terrifyingly prophetic words those now seemed.

Ross climbed quickly into the passenger's seat of Alex's Chevy compact. The car had definitely seen better days, and the door squeaked as Alex climbed behind the wheel.

"So where are we going?" he asked as he pulled out of the parking lot. "I know you said Texas, but Texas is a big state. And to be perfectly honest, I don't know if my car will hold up for a trip like that."

"You think it'll get us to Mobile?"

"Alabama?"

"Yeah."

"It should."

"Good. Then for now, let's just get to Mobile. If we can get to my parents' place, I think we'll be all right."

"They have a decent car there we can use?"

"Something better." Ross leaned back into the passenger's seat. "Let's get going, and I'll tell you what I have in mind."

CHAPTER 77
ERICA CHAPMAN
SOMETHING YOU DON'T SEE EVERY DAY

The farther they got from Houston proper, the less wreckage they had to contend with. Erica had sent a text to Ross from Michelle's phone, letting him know she had lost her phone and he should contact her at that number. She took over driving and let Matt relax in the passenger seat. He and the new guy, Linton, seemed to hit it off all right and the conversation flowed inevitably to discussion about the outbreak. Erica told them what she'd seen on the news, but Linton and Michelle had more in-depth information. They explained what Emmet had told them about Kampala Syndrome.

"Emmet was an officer at the Office of Naval Intelligence. He was able to get us a little bit of a jump on things so we could get word out to our group."

"Your group?" Erica asked.

Linton hesitated only a second. "We're part of a survivalist group called the Bee Hive. Emmet was a member."

Erica looked at Matt, a little at a loss for words. He just shrugged.

"Yeah, I know. You hear the word survivalist, and you think about all the crackpots on TV, right?"

Erica blushed a bit. "Sorry, but yeah. Of course, the way things look now, maybe they were the only ones who actually had it right."

There was a bit of an uncomfortable silence as they drove. Erica broke the ice again. "Sorry if it's something you don't want to talk about, but where's Emmet now?"

Linton looked away. After a moment, Michelle answered for him. "Emmet turned into one of them a little while before you found us. We had just outrun a mob, and he…"

"Started laughing?" Matt prompted.

"Yeah. Attacked our driver and wrecked the car."

"Sorry," Erica said. "The wreck killed him?"

"No," Linton finally turned back to face them. "No, it killed Lesslie, the driver. But Emmet lived. He was unconscious, still laughing inside that damned gas mask. But he was breathing."

Erica looked at Matt significantly.

Matt cleared his throat. "He was wearing a gas mask?"

"We all were until last night," Michelle answered. "I lost mine while we were trying to get away from a bunch of those... chucklers, you called them."

Matt looked at Linton. "So what happened to yours?"

Linton looked at his wife. "Sickness and health."

"What?"

Michelle finished for her husband. "Until death, do us part." She laid her head on his shoulder.

Matt fell silent at that, and Erica recalled that he had just lost his own wife. Wanting to keep him from dwelling on that, she tried to steer the conversation down another path. "So you called the survivalist folks on TV crackpots. How do you mean? I mean, I'm not trying to start an argument or anything, but how are you guys different? You carry assault rifles and gas masks. You say you have a bunker stocked full of supplies. That's pretty much what I saw on those TV shows."

"Maybe," Linton agreed. "But the truth of the matter is that those shows were never intended to show the real nature of survivalists. That would have been too boring. They wanted people who were on the fringe. It makes for better ratings."

"So what's different?"

Linton had evidently been asked this question often enough that he had a ready answer without having to think about it. "I think it's all in how you approach it. The people on the shows were planning on the end of the world. One week they're talking to someone who's planning for a nuclear war, the next week it's someone who's convinced that global warming is out of control and we're all going to drown in a giant flood.

"We got into it slowly, first planning for what would happen if I lost my job. How would we get groceries? Pay the bills? Stuff like that.

When the hurricane hit a few years back, we saw the food disappear from the grocery stores in a matter of hours. When people realized that, there were riots and murders, and we realized how crazy things could get if the system broke down for a few weeks. So we got our concealed carry permits. And we figured if we were going to carry, we should get proper training.

"Eventually, we met other people who were thinking the same way, so we started pooling resources... learning more about being self-sufficient. After a few years, we had a core group of about a dozen people, and others were asking to join up. So some of us turned it into a business. We started training other people and selling survival gear. It gave us a certain amount of freedom and let us get great discounts on our own gear."

Erica nodded. The way he explained it, it was just a logical progression. One that made perfect sense from their perspective. She said as much. "Besides, considering what we've all seen going on out there, maybe the loonies on TV weren't so crazy after all."

Linton only grunted at that.

Erica was willing to let the conversation die for a bit. Matt was lost in his own thoughts, undoubtedly thinking about whatever he had encountered in his own home with his family. She hadn't asked him about it... didn't figure it was any of her business. He would talk about it when and if he felt like it.

Linton and Michelle were evidently exhausted and fell asleep in the back seat. She thought about them; a man who was so committed to his wife that he would remove his own mask to share in whatever fate awaited her. Erica wondered if she and Ross could ever find anything close to that level of commitment.

Then she wondered again if he was even alive.

She drove in silence for a while, winding through the few wrecks without much trouble for another twenty minutes. The route Linton and Michelle had proposed seemed to have been spared most of the carnage they had seen toward Houston's inner city. But that wasn't to say there wasn't other damage. Off to the left, smoke and flames billowed from a storage tank at a small oil refinery. Erica recalled that the area south of Houston was well known for its oil processing plants and storage facilities. This was evidently one of them. A strong northern breeze blew most of the smoke away from them, but the smell still permeated the air.

The farther they drove, the less she smelled the burning oil, and the more prominent the smell of salt water became, and as she took the Highway 146 exit, the terrain changed as well. As they rounded a small copse of trees and scrub turning northward, the path suddenly opened up before them. The evening sun glistened off water to the right, and the freeway turned into a huge bridge. There were still a few wrecks, but only a few.

Seagulls spiraled about in the air above, drawing Erica's attention to the giant triangular structures that held dozens of inches-wide steel cables, suspending the bridge above the water. Her mind boggled at the engineering involved in keeping the massive ribbon of concrete and steel floating magically over the water below. To her mind, it was akin to a person lifting themselves into the air by pulling on their own shoe laces.

They reached the apex of the bridge when Matt drew her attention to the right. "Look at that."

"That" was the largest cruise ship Erica had ever seen. She looked in the mirrors out of habit, then pulled the Xterra to a stop in the middle of the road.

Stopping the vehicle woke Linton and Michelle, and as they looked around to see what had caught Erica's and Matt's attention, Linton whistled. Then he repeated the same words Matt had used as he had pulled up beside the gas-mask-clad chuckler. "Now there's something you don't see every day."

CHAPTER 78
CHARLES GRIFFE
MEET FRED HARTMAN

They made it to the cabin without incident, and everyone was visibly relieved to be back behind a locked door.

"So what's your plan?" Tabby asked. "We're on the wrong deck for the lifeboats, and..." she looked at her watch, "...we have somewhere around twenty minutes to get off the ship."

"It's worse than that."

"What?"

"From what I saw outside, we're almost in the Ship Channel. Hell, by now, we probably *are* in it."

"Seriously?"

"Yeah. We gotta get off this ship right away."

Tabby licked her lips nervously. "So what's your great idea, then?"

"Go open the balcony and look down."

Tabby just looked at him for a second, then shook her head. "You're not serious."

"Yes, I am. This cabin is directly over one of the life boats. I remember seeing it when we first got here."

She looked at the group of misfits. "You can't expect this bunch to drop over the railing like we did. They'll never make it."

"They won't have to. When I say we're right over one of the lifeboats, I mean we're *right over* one of the lifeboats. As in, about half the distance we had to climb to earlier."

He led her onto the balcony, and they leaned over the rail. She nodded. "Nice."

They went back in and called everyone together.

"We have a plan," Charlie told them. "We're going to climb over the rail on the balcony and directly onto the lifeboat below." There was immediate muttering and Charlie held up his hands. "It's only about a five-foot drop. I'll go first to help everyone else. The only thing we need to worry about is keeping quiet so we don't attract any attention from the crazies up at the front."

More muttering, and Charlie hissed at them. "Look, I get that you're scared. But our situation is really simple." He walked over to the balcony door and pulled the curtain aside. Sure enough, there was land drifting past outside. "We only have a few minutes before Chris said we were going to hit that bridge. Now, I don't know what's going to happen when we hit, but I'm not planning to wait around and find out. You want to stay and take your chances? Well, be my guest. But I'm getting the hell off of this train wreck."

With that said, he stepped onto the balcony and looked at the shoreline as the Bahama Queen slipped through the water. He moved over to the rail and looked over the side at the bright yellow top of the life boat below. It looked so close that he was tempted to simply jump over the rail, but knew that the sound of his impact might be loud enough to attract some very unwanted attention.

He turned to find Felicia beside him. "I'm scared, Charlie."

"Me, too. We just need to get off this ship and head back home." He pulled her in for a quick kiss on her forehead. "Leave this damned nightmare behind us. Right?"

She nodded.

They were interrupted as Tabby stepped onto the balcony. "You ready?"

"Yeah."

"Got your knife on you?"

Remembering the crowd of crazies at the front entrance, Charlie quickly checked to make sure the chef's knife was securely tucked into his belt. "Got it."

Some of the other members of the group stepped out with them. Tabby was in the front, and she held out a large piece of white cloth. He recognized the bed sheet and raised an eyebrow. "It'll help you set down quietly."

"Good idea," he conceded.

He took a deep breath, then, as he had twice before now, swung his leg over the balcony railing. Tabby held his left hand, helping him to balance as he took hold of one end of the sheet. "All right. Let's do this."

Tabby, Merl, Celina, Carlos, and Felicia pulled back on the sheet and he stepped back off the lip of the balcony and slid down to lightly step onto the yellow rooftop. He looked carefully up and down the jogging track, paying special attention up toward the front entrance where he had seen the crowd.

They were roughly a football field's length back from where the music still reverberated through the air, and so far, he hadn't actually seen anyone. They were evidently still concentrated around the corner, in the fitness area. But with it being an open-air gym, that could change at any moment. Seeing everything was still clear, he looked up to see Tabby, Felicia, and Merl looking over the rail at him. He nodded and gave them a thumbs up, and Merl came down next. Charlie helped the older man from below, while much of his weight was supported by the others on the sheet above. Celina came down next, easily aided by Charlie and Merl. She hugged her husband, then turned and glared at Charlie.

I don't think the old cow likes you very much, boy.

Charlie gritted his teeth, and once more looked up toward the front of the ship. Still no indication they'd been spotted. He looked back up to see the next person coming down. He whispered to Merl, "You got this? I need to figure out how to get us loose."

The old man nodded, and Charlie left him and his wife to help the others down while he went to examine the rig that secured the life boat to the ship. Once more checking up and down the jogging track, Charlie slipped off the roof of the boat and onto the catwalk that led from the front lifeboat entrance to the ship. Above the door in bold black lettering were the words 410 PERS. RESCUE VESSEL. There was some kind of assembly consisting of some large metal hooks, pins, and levers holding the life boat in place. The lever was firmly in the LOCKED position. He looked up and saw a cable suspension system that held the lifeboat up. There was a second cable on the other end of the boat. He didn't know yet how to operate the lifeboat, but he knew they weren't going anywhere as long as the thing was locked to the Bahama Queen. He eased the lever smoothly and quietly up to the UNLOCKED indicator.

Turning, he opened the door into the lifeboat, intending to cross over to the other side and examine the corresponding assembly over there. But as he entered the lifeboat, he stopped for a second at the sight before him. The interior of the thing was huge. Four entry doors across the wall facing the ship, two levels of seats, and a pilot's station raised up in the front. It reminded him more of a small ferryboat than a lifeboat. He shook off his surprise and stepped quickly across to the pilot's station.

At first glance, it looked incredibly complex. A single seat was nestled before a computer screen surrounded by all sorts of dials, indicators, and buttons with symbols on them. For a moment, he despaired ever piloting the boat. But as he looked closer, he realized it was really relatively simple. Many of the symbols were basically the same as those in his car. He was surprised to see that there were ten windshield wiper buttons, but looking around the pilot's area, he saw ten corresponding windshields. There were also buttons for a horn and various light settings. There were a few other symbols he had to think about, but understood with a moment's reflection. But the four he was especially glad to see showed a simplified boat symbol, with up or down arrows at the bow or stern, respectively. On seeing them, he knew he would be able to raise or lower the lifeboat.

There were two throttle levers and a compass, and a power button beside the computer screen. But most importantly, there was a radio transceiver mounted to the left of the seat. Charlie snatched it up and pressed the button on the side. There was no sound to indicate it was on. Scanning through the instrumentation, he saw a button with a symbol that looked somewhat like a radio antenna with waves emitting from it. He pressed that button.

Still, there was no sound.

At the top right of the console, there were two green buttons. One was labeled ENGINE, the other, ELEC. SYSTEMS. Embossed on each button was a familiar symbol; a circle, interrupted by a vertical line through the top of it. It had become the universal symbol of power in the computer age. He didn't want to start the engine yet, but thought starting the electrical systems might get the radio online. He pressed the button and was rewarded by the console flickering to life, and a slight crackle from the radio.

Charlie pressed the button on the mic, then let go. What was he going to say? He remembered what he had always seen in movies. "Mayday, mayday. This is the Bahama Queen, and we have an emergency."

He let off the button and listened. After a moment's silence, he repeated his call. "Mayday. This is the Bahama Queen. Please respond."

Still, there was nothing but static. "Is anybody listening?" After several more seconds, he tossed the mic into the seat. "Shit." The monitor flickered as the system began booting up.

Looks like you're on your own, boy.

Charlie beat his open palm against his forehead. "Fuck you, old man," he growled. "If you don't have anything constructive to offer, just shut the hell up." He took a deep breath, calming his nerves, and looked at the controls once more. All in all, they looked simple enough. "Yeah, I can run this."

He trotted back to the door opposite where he had entered. Sure enough, there was another lever release on this end. He was about to unlock this one, when he heard Felicia call his name from the roof. "Charlie? Charlie!"

What the hell is wrong with that woman? They'll hear her!

But her voice sounded panicked. He looked instinctively toward the fore of the ship, expecting to see a crowd of infected coming toward them, but didn't see any movement. "Over here!" he called quietly. He waved his hand so she could see him from the roof. In only a few seconds, Felicia and Celina both came into view. "What's wrong?" he asked them.

Grim faced, Celina simply pointed ahead of the ship.

At first he didn't see anything. Then he understood. "Oh shit." He turned back to the women above. "Is everybody down yet?"

Felicia shook her head. "Still five of us up on the balcony."

He looked back at the power lines that crossed the Ship Channel. They looked like they were probably at least a hundred feet above the water. Unfortunately, the Bahama Queen towered more than twice that height. "Tell them to jump! We're gonna hit those cables in about sixty seconds!" He turned to the release mechanism and slammed the lever up. He was careless in his haste, though, and the metal clanged loudly, echoing through the air.

Dammit, boy! You tryin' to get the attention of every damn body around here?

He froze, eyes wide, and looked up toward the bow, fearing the worst. His fears were realized as first one, then two, cackling crazies looked around the corner and began their staggering run toward the lifeboat. They were immediately followed by scores more, and soon there was a veritable wave of them running toward the lifeboat.

"Hurry up," he yelled up as loud as he could. There was no longer any need to keep quiet. "We got company!" He heard footsteps on the roof above him and glanced up to see several members of their group gaping at the rushing throng of crazies.

They ain't gonna make it. Hell boy, if you don't do something fast, you ain't gonna make it, either.

"Don't just stand there, you fucking idiots!" Charlie yelled at them. "Get everyone down from that balcony!" They scrambled back out of sight, but as Charlie looked back, he knew his father was right. They were going to be too late. The crowd was going to be on top of them in about twenty seconds. Charlie looked up at the roof where Felicia, Tabby, and the others still struggled to get down. He looked back at the river of insane, grinning faces running toward them.

Come on, boy. You know what you gotta do.

Grim-faced and resigned, Charlie stepped back inside the lifeboat. Hesitating only a second, he dogged the hatch closed, then ran across and dogged the opposite hatch. He ran to the pilot's station and climbed up to the pilot's seat. Looking out the raised windshield, he saw the power cables passing overhead. He licked his lips and examined the controls. Yanking the release lever, he felt the lifeboat lurch slightly.

"Charlie!" He turned to see Felicia at the window of the hatch. She was beating frantically on the window with her open palm.

Ignore the bitch, boy. You got more important things to worry about.

"Char…" He winced as he saw an arm grab her from behind and slam her head into the window. Fingers wrapped firmly in her hair, the arm pulled back her head again, and for a split second, he saw the dazed accusation in her eyes. Then her head flew forward once more, spraying the window with a splatter of red. Her eyes glazed and closed before her face dropped from sight.

There, you see? Nothing you coulda done, anyhow. Now, get back to work.

Another face replaced it—a face framed on one side by long hair. Charlie's blood ran cold as he saw the stringy and dirty, but undeniably purple hair. The young man stared at him, grinning insanely as he leaned into the window, stuck out his tongue, and licked a streak of blood from the glass. Then he slammed his own head into the window and giggled. "Piggy!" Another face pushed against him and he shoved back, never losing his smile as he began to repeat the squealing he had used all those days ago outside the miniature golf course. The sound sent a chill down Charlie's spine. "Squee! Squee!"

Charlie cried out as more screams and footsteps sounded from the roof, and the lifeboat began to sway slightly. He turned back to the pilot's station and skimmed through the emergency launch sequence on the bright yellow sign before him. Trying to concentrate, he worked on ignoring the screams from overhead and the squealing at the hatch. He started the sequence with shaking hands and the lifeboat began to drop as the winch activated.

Then an odd sound filled the air—the odd, metallic whine of vibrating and snapping cables—and Charlie remembered the power lines. Everything lurched slightly, and Charlie looked out the windshield as dozens of power lines dropped, leaving a trail of sparks as the live wires dragged across the ship. He saw one line drag through the crowd of crazies and several of them dropped overboard. Eyes wide, he watched as the line swung inexorably toward the lifeboat.

"Well, Dad, looks like we're well and truly fucked."

He could hear his dad's sigh. *Yep. Sure looks that way.*

As the cable struck the side of the lifeboat, Charlie gritted his teeth, expecting his muscles to lock up. Images of overcooked, charred flesh passed through his mind as he anticipated the pain to come and a slight whimper escaped his throat. Instead, he felt a slight tingle, and the hair on his arms stood up for a few seconds. Then the feeling passed, and he sat staring at the immense hull of the ship beside him as the lifeboat continued to lower toward the water.

Looking back up where the lifeboat had left the jogging track behind, he thought for a moment he saw Tabby struggling her way through a swath of crazies. But before he could be sure, the crowd swarmed past. When he blinked, whoever it was, assuming it wasn't just some trick of the light, was gone. He looked down over the end of the lifeboat's hull and saw that he was about halfway down.

The ship began to cut to the left—port, he remembered—and as it began to straighten out, he could see it in the distance: the Fred Hartman Bridge. It was huge, with giant pyramids of cables strung from hundreds of feet in the air that supported the bridge beneath through some sort of arcane magic. It would have been a fascinating sight if not for the fact that Charlie was suspended from another pair of cables, tethered to the side of the massive ship that was barreling through the water with the impossible goal of fitting its Brobdingnagian height through the Lilliputian gap beneath the bridge.

Judging from the speed and distance, Charlie estimated he had two or maybe three minutes before they found out whether the Bahama Queen or Fred Hartman would win the upcoming skirmish. He looked down toward the water. It was a tossup as to whether he would make it to the water before the collision. Licking his lips nervously, Charlie examined the controls. There was a single red button that drew his attention. The simplified boat symbol was accompanied by two downward pointing arrows. The bright yellow tag beneath it had the words EMERGENCY RELEASE on it.

You got about ninety seconds to shit or get off the pot, boy.

Charlie looked back down toward the water. It was hard to tell from his perch at the top of the lifeboat, but he estimated he was still ten or fifteen feet above the water. Would the lifeboat survive the drop?

It sure as shit won't survive crashing into the damned bridge.

His hand hovered over the button.

Do it, boy.

Still he hesitated, looking ahead at the looming bridge.

Do it!

Charlie slammed his hand down on the button, and his stomach fell away in a roller coaster drop that ended with an abrupt splash as the lifeboat dropped the final ten feet to the water.

CHAPTER 79
ERICA CHAPMAN
LOOKING UP

Erica got out of the SUV and walked to the edge of the bridge. It was a surreal moment, watching a huge luxury liner pushing through the Houston Ship Channel, standing on what would normally be a busy bridge, bustling with traffic. But there was no traffic noise. In fact, the only thing she heard as she watched the deceptively idyllic scene was the wind blowing through the cables and across the bridge, and the trilling of seagulls overhead.

Car doors closed behind her, and she was joined by Matt, Linton and Michelle. Erica spoke without turning. "I always wanted to go on a cruise. I was always too busy with school or lacrosse. I never even saw a cruise ship before now."

Matt grunted. "The way things are looking, it might be a long, long time before you ever see another one."

"That thing is huge!" Michelle said.

Erica nodded, watching as the giant vessel continued toward them. It was close enough that she could see through the glass windows on some of the decks. She looked up at the upper decks, and suddenly her heart skipped a beat.

Linton and Matt must have seen it at the same time. They began to draw back to the SUV, Linton pulling his wife by the arm. "Come on, baby. We gotta go!"

"What is it?"

Erica was already behind the wheel, pulling away even before all the doors were closed. Heart pounding, she floored the gas, weaving dangerously close to the few vehicles stalled or wrecked on the bridge.

"Are we gonna make it?" she asked Matt, who had his window down, and was craning his neck out to look up at the ship.

Crap, crap, crap! He's looking up *at the ship. Way up!* There was no way that massive structure was going to fit under the bridge.

"No."

"What!" She practically yelled it at him. "What do you mean? You mean we're not going to make it?"

"Not completely. It's gonna hit the bridge before we're off of it."

She pushed her foot to the floorboard, trying her best to shove the accelerator through floor, and the Xterra roared down the road. No one had to tell her when the ship hit. The bridge lurched beneath the tires, and Erica struggled to keep them pointed in the right direction. The sound of snapping cables giving way, sang through the air like ice cracking on a lake as she fought the steering wheel. The bridge would lurch and sway to the left, lurch again, sway to the right, back and forth, up and down and though Erica had never been in an earthquake, this was what she imagined it might be like to be caught in a big one.

But she found a kind of rhythm to it, sensing when the bridge had reached the apex of its swing, bracing for the sudden change, steering to compensate for it. In fact, she was beginning to adapt to the new method of steering so well that when the tires hit solid ground again, she nearly drove off the road, anticipating another swing. The tires bit into unmoving concrete as she was wrenching the wheel back to the left, lurching forward so suddenly that she had to jerk the wheel back on center to keep them on the road. Realizing they were past the danger, she slammed on the brakes.

Heart pounding, she took several panting breaths, staring straight ahead as the previously silent evening was filled with the groans and cracks of shattering concrete and twisting steel.

CHAPTER 80
CHARLES GRIFFE
RAINING CONCRETE AND BOUNCING WATERS

Charlie's head flew forward with the sudden reversal of inertia and he barely kept from hitting his forehead on the panel before him. Dazed, he shook his head, then looked up at the towering cruise ship sliding through the water beside him. The wake of the larger vessel rocked the lifeboat, and spun it about fifteen degrees to starboard, even as it dragged the smaller boat through the water alongside it. Looking up and to his left, Charlie saw the bow of the ship passing beneath the huge bridge.

"Oh, holy shit." He looked back down at the pilot's controls. He pressed the green power button for the engine and panicked as nothing happened. "Now what?"

He hit the button again, and still nothing happened.

A shrieking of tearing metal sounded across the water—the sound of Godzilla battling Mothra—and Charlie looked back at the ship. Its upper decks had collided with the side of the bridge, the concrete ripping through the ship. Chunks of concrete began to break off the bridge, splashing into the water around the lifeboat. Charlie pressed the button over and over, cursing at the lack of results.

Turn the key, you damned idiot!

Charlie blinked. The key had been in his periphery, just to the right of the control panel. He switched the key to the plainly labeled ON position and punched the button once more. "Yes!" This time, the engine thrummed to life, and Charlie slammed the throttle levers forward.

He looked up to where the Bahama Queen was locked in her final battle with the Fred Hartman Bridge. The deadly rain of concrete increased as Charlie watched, and increasingly larger pieces showered down. Beside him, the Bahama Queen began agitating the water. Upper decks hung under the bridge, her momentum still pushing forward. The resulting vectors of force began to raise her bow several feet higher. As a result, the stern, having nowhere else to go, began to drop lower into the water.

The lifeboat was almost directly beside the stern at that point, and the water around it began to seethe as if he were riding a toy boat in a hot tub. Green water turned brown as mud and silt from the bottom of the Ship Channel was stirred up by the huge ship's propellers. Charlie recalled Chris mentioning that the ship would only have about five feet of clearance. Judging from the amount the bow had raised, he thought it was a safe bet that the propellers in back were cutting deeply into the muck at the bottom.

Charlie cranked the wheel hard to the right, trying to get away from the raining concrete and bouncing waters, but the lifeboat seemed to have difficulty navigating in the swirling channel. "Come on, you bitch! Turn, dammit!"

A huge section of concrete splashed a few hundred yards ahead. Charlie cursed. That one had been about the size of a bus, and would have crushed the lifeboat, had it hit. Slowly, the boat began to respond, inching away from the roiling water beside the ship. And all the while, over the sound of the straining engine, the noise of battling Titans clamored.

Charlie pounded his fist on the control panel, willing the lifeboat to move faster. Finally, the engine seemed to find purchase and started moving steadily away from the ship. Within seconds, the water was smoother and progress was significant. He turned to look behind him through the rear windshield. The Bahama Queen drew farther behind him, and he watched as it began to shift its forward momentum to the side, beginning a slow list to starboard. He swallowed as he saw dozens of people falling or jumping overboard and wondered how many of them were crazy, and how many might be survivors like he and his group had been. He also wondered how many of them survived the fall into the churning water forty feet or more below.

You keep worryin' about things that ain't none of your concern, boy. Pay attention to keepin' yourself alive.

Charlie nodded. Dad was right.

Dad was always right.

Charlie steered the boat toward shore.

CHAPTER 81
ERICA CHAPMAN
IRRESISTIBLE FORCE MEETS IMMOVEABLE OBJECT

They stood beside the Xterra, looking out at the huge ship struggling to pass beneath the bridge. There was absolutely no way it was ever going to make it, but Erica wondered whether it would be the ship or the bridge that would give way first. As they watched in perverse fascination, Michelle's phone chimed. Erica looked at her as she pulled the cell out and opened the screen. She glanced at it, then handed it to Erica. "Ross."

Heart pounding again, though this time for totally different reasons, Erica struggled to keep her face straight as she read the text. Ross was alive! She read through it three times, making sure she had it memorized before she handed it back to Michelle. She wanted to smile. She wanted to laugh. Hell, she wanted to jump up and down, and sing to the skies!

Instead, she walked back to the SUV and slammed her fist into the door hard enough that the pain overrode her euphoria. Wincing, she turned to find the others looking at her warily.

Michelle raised an eyebrow. "Any particular reason you feel the need to beat on our transportation?"

Flexing her bruised hand, Erica shrugged. "Felt the need to smile, and I didn't figure that would be such a great idea."

"So you decided to take it out on a metal door?" Linton raised an eyebrow. "You got an odd way of looking at things, don't you?"

"Look, from what we've seen, if you laugh, you go crazy. I don't plan on going crazy."

"We don't know that's how it works."

"No, we don't. We don't know anything for a fact. But I'm not taking chances. Not when I've finally got proof that Ross is all right."

Linton took the phone from his wife and read the text. He whistled. "Erica? All due respect, but I think you might already *be* crazy. Houston was bad enough, but New Orleans? That's gotta be even worse."

Erica climbed back behind the wheel as Linton and Michelle got in the back. "Everyplace is bad," she continued. "It's all just a matter of degrees now."

Matt interrupted their discussion. "Guys?"

He was still standing beside the SUV, watching the cruise ship's mighty struggle. "Guys, there's a lifeboat coming this way."

Linton pulled some binoculars out of his pack and they all rejoined Matt. As Linton raised the binoculars, Erica looked at the mammoth cruise ship as its huge engines continued to propel it through the bridge. For a moment, she thought of the old koan; what happens when an irresistible force meets an immovable object? The thought of koans in general led to thoughts of Ross and she flexed her hand, once more using the pain in her knuckles to distract her from the threatening smile.

Erica sighed. "I suppose we should see if the people in the lifeboat need any help."

"They do." Linton handed the binoculars to Matt. "They've got some chucklers running around on top of the thing."

"Huh." Matt passed the binoculars to Erica.

"What?" She raised the glasses to her eyes, adjusting the focus as she spoke.

"Looks like one of 'em has purple hair."

Bringing the view into focus, she saw Matt was right. Three chucklers cavorted atop the bright yellow shell of the lifeboat, dancing and beating on the top with their hands and feet. One of them had the left side of his head cut close, but as he turned she could see the other side had long purple hair. She lowered the binoculars to find the others looking at her, apparently waiting on her to make a decision, and she wondered how she had become the leader of their little expedition. "All right," she said. "Let's go give them a hand."

They climbed back into the Xterra, and she drove east to meet the lifeboat.

CHAPTER 82
CHARLES GRIFFE
TIME TO SLICE AND DICE

The sound of running feet on the roof above and behind him told Charlie he wasn't alone, and he had little doubt that his companions were more of the crazies that had swarmed over the lifeboat. How they had managed to hang on during the wild rollercoaster ride off the ship was beyond him, but somehow at least two of them had done so.

He looked down at where his knife rested on the console, nodding to himself. Okay. They want to play? He could play.

Damn right you can, boy!

He looked ahead through the forward windshield. The little channel he headed down ended up ahead in a series of beachfront homes with private docks and boats. If he didn't slow down soon, he was going to make a mess of things. He reached for the knife and began to pull back on the throttle.

Now, that ain't playin' to win, boy. Think!

He cocked his head to the side as he thought through the ramifications of what his dad suggested. There were only seconds to make up his mind and he watched the docks ahead draw nearer. Finally nodding, he threw the throttle all the way forward and checked to make sure his seat belt was secure.

"All right, Dad. You asked for it. Hang on tight." He braced his feet and gripped the steering wheel as the lifeboat glanced off the first dock. The boat lurched to the side, righted itself, and he jerked the wheel back toward the docks. The boat leapt forward to hit the cigar boat in the next dock, bouncing upward as the lifeboat drove over the lower profile racing boat, finally coming to rest, partly on the smaller boat, and partly on the wrecked dock. The prow of the lifeboat crashed down on the next dock, and Charlie's seatbelt was tested as the vessel came to an abrupt halt.

He pulled the throttle all the way back, shut off the engine, and grabbed his knife. The deck canted at about a thirty-degree angle to port and aft, and Charlie stumbled as he unstrapped and half-ran, half-fell toward one of the portside doors that would be closest to the dock. Unlocking the latch, he threw the hatch open and stepped onto the narrow, crazily leaning deck.

Wheezing laughter warned of an attacker behind, and he spun to see the man leaping from the upper deck. Sliding to the side, Charlie shoved the knife out, impaling his attacker in mid-air. Blood ran down his arm as he deflected the dying man to the side and let him roll down the deck and under the railing. He spun, looking frantically for another attacker, even as he heard the first one splash in the water.

He knew he'd heard at least two sets of feet running overhead, but it looked like his plan might have worked. Wrecking the lifeboat into the dock had evidently thrown the other crazy overboard.

Moving carefully, he grabbed the portside rail with his left hand, keeping a tight grip on the knife in his right, and pulled himself up the deck toward the prow. He looked over the side as he went, scanning the ruins of the dock below, looking for a stable area to jump down. At first, all he saw was broken boards and lapping waves. But when he reached the front of the lifeboat and crossed to the starboard side, he finally found a relatively safe section of the dock. He jumped, landing clumsily, realizing that he'd gotten so used to the movement of the waves beneath him that dry land felt odd. He turned slowly, watching for any sign of movement, but still saw nothing.

Stepping carefully over broken or missing boards in the dock, he finally made his way to dry land. Running footsteps sounded on wooden planks behind him, alerting him that a second assailant was coming even before he heard the gasping laughter. He spun, staggering a little, still clumsy on land, and held his knife before him, ready for the charging enemy.

He gaped. The man rushing at him was huge! Charlie knew he was a large man, but this behemoth was easily a head taller and looked to weigh in a good fifty pounds heavier. Charlie swallowed nervously. Run? Fight?

I didn't raise no damn pussy, boy. Time to slice and dice.

Charlie took a deep breath and braced himself. He watched as the bigger man rumbled off the dock and onto dry land. Less than fifty feet away, and Charlie shouted at him, "Come on, you damn son of a bitch! Let's do this!"

The laughing juggernaut took two more steps and Charlie jumped as the crack of a rifle sounded from the right. He glanced that way to see movement, but didn't want to take his eyes away from his attacker for more than a split second. One distraction at a time.

Looking back toward the dock, he saw the giant drop to his knees. Blood dripped from a comically small hole in the man's chest as he tried to get back up. Another shot rang out, and he fell to his face. He twitched once before laying still. Charlie looked wildly back to his right, back to where he'd seen movement a few seconds before.

A man stepped from behind the pillars of a nearby beach house. He was joined by another man and two women, all of whom carried rifles. Charlie squeezed his knife nervously, watching for signs of laughter, but none of them appeared to be infected. They stopped a few yards away, watching him silently.

"You planning to attack us with that thing?"

Charlie looked down at his knife, then back at their rifles. "I don't think it'd do me much good, would it?"

"Not likely. Mainly wanted to make sure you weren't laughing."

They stared at each other nervously, until Charlie finally asked, "So, are you the one who shot the big guy there?"

"Yeah." The man stepped forward, hand extended. "I'm Matt." He pointed to each of the others. "That's Erica, Linton, and Michelle."

Charlie slipped the knife into his belt, then shook the Matt's hand. "Charlie. And thanks for that. I've had about as much of this shit as I can stand."

CHAPTER 83
AUGUST GRAPPIN
EASTWARD

The first impact of the lifeboat threw Gus off the upper deck and into the air. There was a thrill of terror as he flew, followed by a brief, exquisite pain when his head hit the wooden deck of the cigar boat. Then all went black.

A loud noise brought him back to consciousness, a crack like sharp thunder, followed seconds later by another. Fuzzy memory told him he once knew what that sound was, but now it was nothing more than a noise on which to focus. As he began to gather himself, he noted with passing interest that he lay in darkness, in water that smelled of gasoline and rotten fish. And the water seemed to be getting steadily deeper. He tried to get up, but found himself trapped between the deck of the boat below, and a structure of wood and Styrofoam above. There was barely enough room to crawl on his hands and knees.

He heard voices in the distance, speaking of things that didn't matter. What *was* important was the familiar tenor of one of the voices. It was the big man—the giver of pleasure and pain.

Gus scrambled to find a way out of his prison, and saw bright light streaming through the wreckage behind him. He crawled through the flotsam and water toward the light and began frantically clawing his way out. It took only a few minutes, but when he finally broke free, there was no longer anyone in sight. Waterlogged, he clambered up to the remains of the wooden dock above him and followed it up to dry land. One of his companions from the ship lay dead in the grass between the dock and a beach house, and Gus tittered as he ran past the corpse with barely a glance.

He rounded the corner of the house just as the big man got in the back of a bright yellow vehicle, closing the door behind him. Another man got in the front and they drove away even as Gus raced toward them. Chuckling through his raw throat, he came to a stop, watching as the yellow SUV carried the focus of his attention down the street, turning right when it reached the main road. Flashes of yellow through the bushes showed the direction they took as the man and his new friends left Gus behind.

There was disappointment at having missed the man again, but he was determined that this was only a temporary setback. Still laughing, he trotted up to the end of the street, turned right, and watched the rapidly disappearing speck of yellow in the distance.

He would find Big Man. He had no idea how long it would take. In truth, his concept of time had become fuzzy, so it really didn't matter. But they moved away from the setting sun and Gus was determined to follow. After all, they had to stop sometime. And wouldn't it be funny if he managed to catch up to them in the middle of the night? Wouldn't it be hilarious?

The laughing teen with purple hair began to jog eastward.

SATURDAY
NOVEMBER 26

EPILOGUE

An excerpt from Presidential Proclamation 9437

...a national emergency exists by reason of the recent pandemic of unknown origins. The illness, currently called Kampala Syndrome, is believed to be responsible for the recent rioting and communications blackout in Uganda. Recent outbreaks in major cities in the United States indicate that the illness has spread to our shores, and constitutes a continuing and immediate threat of further attacks on the United States.

Therefore, by virtue of the authority vested in me as President of these United States of America, and by the Constitution and the laws of the United States, I hereby declare that the Union is in a state of national emergency, and pursuant to the National Emergencies Act (50 U.S.C. 1601 et seq.), I intend to utilize the following statutes: sections 123, 123a, 527, 2201(c), 12006, and 12302 of title 10, United States Code, and sections 331, 359, and 367 of title 14, United States Code.

This proclamation immediately shall be published in the Federal Register or disseminated through the Emergency Federal Register, and transmitted to the Congress.

This proclamation is not intended to create any right or benefit, substantive or procedural, enforceable at law by a party against the United States, its agencies, its officers, or any person.

In Witness Whereof, I have hereunto set my hand this twenty-sixth day of November...

Here ends *Chucklers: Laughter is Contagious*, Book 1 of the Chucklers saga.

Jeff Brackett is the author of "Half Past Midnight", "The Road to Rejas", and "Streets of Payne", as well as a variety of short stories and novellas published in magazines and anthologies. After having lived almost his entire life in and around Houston, 2014 presented several life changes that brought him, his wife, and two dogs (Bella and Cricket) to Claremore, Oklahoma. There, they found a nice little house with a much larger yard, and are all adjusting to the new lifestyle quite well. Jeff has even begun learning to garden.

His writing has won Honorable Mention in the action / adventure category of the "Golden Triangle Unpublished Writer's Contest", first place in the novel category of the "Bay Area Writers League Manuscript Competition", and was a finalist in the science fiction / fantasy / horror category of the "Houston Writer's Conference" manuscript contest.

His proudest achievement, though, is in having fooled his wife into marrying him more than thirty years ago, and helping her to raise three wonderful children. He is now a grandfather twice over.

And his gardening? Well, let's just say he still has a bit to learn in that area.

You can follow Jeff's blog and sign up for notification of his latest publications at http://jlbrackett.com

CHECK OUT OTHER GREAT APOCALYPSE BOOKS

XY
by D.S. Lillico

An iron fortress protected by automated gun turrets is the only world Elsie has ever known.

When tragedy strikes, Elsie is forced to leave the sanctuary of her home and out into a brutal new world. A post-apocalyptic wasteland filled with savage mutants.

Hunted and alone Elsie stumbles into the care of a giant named Punch, but the world is now full of worse things than giants. Cannibals are starving, bandits are roaming and war is coming.

Elsie's arrival plunges the new-world further into darkness... and is there really something hidden inside of her?

SANCTUARY
by Ian Page

Deeta Nakshband, a Connecticut physician is attacked by a local surgeon while on duty in the hospital. Her friend, Janelle Jefferson, has similar experiences in Miami. Both of them become aware of an increasingly violent world as acts of isolated brutality escalate into civil unrest. They grapple with their paranoia as family members and coworkers become dangerously unpredictable. Worldwide, military units go rogue, war begins in Korea and cities implode as people slaughter each other in the streets. Martial law is declared in an attempt to maintain order. People are arrested, detainment camps are set up and interrogations end with tragic consequences as modern civilization crumbles. Deeta and Janelle band together with family friends and coworkers to save each other and find sanctuary.

SEVEREDPRESS

CHECK OUT OTHER GREAT APOCALYPSE BOOKS

THE DEAD FAMILIAR
by J.D. McKenna

In the twilight hours of a failing world, one man seeks to bring his loved ones to safety. Jack Hightower: Marine, bar-keep, and doomsday prepper. He knows of the coming calamity, and on the final night of an old world he seeks a new beginning.

This is the story of that night, the tale of how Jack and his survivor's colony in the north came to be.

DOMINION
by Doug Goodman

Dominion has been taken from man. Now, six friends must cross an apocalyptic wasteland dominated by a hell's me-nagerie of mega-fauna. Their middle-class suburban skills are no longer applicable to the world they live in. To find a safe haven in this world they will need to develop a new set of survival skills and fight the mutated denizens of the animal kingdom for every step of their terrifying journey.

CHECK OUT OTHER GREAT APOCALYPSE BOOKS

WHITE OUT
by Eric Dimbleby

An apocalyptic snowstorm sweeps the globe. Experts predict this freak storm will be "The New Ice Age." Electricity is gone, as are all forms of communication and road travel. As each member of a divided family tries to survive in their own way, they must deal with a snow-driven madness that has gripped the underlying evil in the hearts of men. In an epic struggle to get home and reunite, they will find that terror lies around every snow drift... and even in their very own backyard.

NIGHT PLAGUE
by Rowan Rook

Humankind will soon be extinct. A mysterious pandemic cut through two-thirds of the population in just four short years, and within another four, it will decimate everything – and everyone – left.

The last days are ticking by, relentless and ruthless, and the reclusive Mason Mild finds himself torn between a peaceful end and a brutal immortality. Between his hopeless, but comfortable days with his family, and something new...something violent and wild.

Have the fang marks above his heel dealt him an early demise or a second birth?

www.ingramcontent.com/pod-product-compliance
Lightning Source LLC
Chambersburg PA
CBHW030619250626
47154CB00006B/1847